With a Little More Practice

by

Paul Janson

JM Publishing

All characters, events and organizations contained in this book are fictional. Any resemblance to persons or organizations is entirely coincidental

Published by JM Publishing May 2014

Cover Design: Elm Street Design
Author Photography: Sarah McGrath

For more information contact

Paul Janson
JM Publishing
36 Elm Street
Georgetown, MA 01833

Paul_janson@AOL.com

PaulJanson.com

ISBN 13: 978-0990742418

Dedication

To Mary, my wife and inspiration.

Acknowledgement

I would like to thank so many people for their support and assistance in the preparation of this novel that space will not allow. It could not have happened without all of you to help.

Other books by Paul Janson include

Mal Practice a mystery of medicine and murder. The current offering is the sequel.

Scratch a young adult novel of magic and cats. A magical cat named Onyx saves lives by scratching people.

The Ice Cream War a mystery of hot fudge and murder. The story of two rival ice cream shops and the body in one of them.

The Child In Our Hearts. A children's picture book about adoption and based on the belief that all children begin in the heart of their parents regardless of how they come to be in a family and regardless of what kind of family they become a part of. There are several versions of this book for different families, including two mothers and two fathers, and single parents. Some are available in Spanish as well. There is also a version for Assisted Reproductive Technology births

Chapter 1

She stood among the only friends she had ever known, the only people she had ever wanted to call family. They were young women, all, and they had come here for a variety of reasons, but one of those reasons was shared by all: it was bad where they were, but not as bad as where they had come from.

They were standing outside a hotel and they were being ignored by most of the people passing. Those who did notice them pointedly looked away. But there was a man in the car parked beside them and he smiled at them. The car was an old Cadillac, probably older than she was. He got out and spoke to them, but she already knew what he wanted. He liked to hurt little girls. He had money, though, and she didn't, so she knew she had no choice. Her friends knew about him as well, and they looked on in fear and disapproval. They did not need his money that badly, but she had to get away. She knew that and he did to. If she went with him he could do whatever he wanted with her, because she could not stop him. She could not go to the police. They would not help her without finding out who she was, a runaway, and then she would be sent back to her mother—and her mother's boyfriend—and that was so much worse than whatever he had in mind.

He smiled and raised his hand. In it he held a hundred dollar bill. She looked at her friends, who stared back but did not move. Finally she walked over to him. He handed her the bill, motioning with a jerk of his head to the passenger's seat of his car. She looked back at her friends and saw genuine fear on their faces now, but she finally went around the car and got in.

Paul Janson

He got in too and handed her a hundred dollars and then shifted the car into drive, preparing to leave from the spot before this grand hotel, one of the most ostentatious in Las Vegas. He did not leave yet though. His hand slipped to her leg and then pushed up her short skirt. His hand went up her leg to where it joined her body and then he squeezed it hard, hard enough to hurt. He smiled at her as she shut her eyes and then he relaxed the grip and drove away, down the street named Las Vegas Boulevard, the Strip. Down this street in the city of dreams, the city of bad dreams, the city of nightmares.

"Call me Ishmael," Joe said softly. It was a fitting thought for the journey he was beginning, cast adrift from his home as he was. That sentence had been penned by Herman Melville years ago to begin his classic novel Moby Dick, probably at about the same time Joe's family had first moved to the hills of Eastern Kentucky. He had never considered anywhere else to be home. Now there was blood dried on the collar and sleeve of his shirt, and the man whose blood had dried there was dead.

Joe was flying in a private jet to Las Vegas and away from Kentucky, where less than a week ago he had been the defendant in a malpractice suit. The trial involved the wrongful death of a four-year-old girl, and just a few hours ago he had almost died, almost been shot to death by the man who had murdered that child three years earlier. What had happened since the trial began seemed so improbable as to be almost impossible, but here he was: a pediatrician on his way to a police-ordered "vacation" in Las Vegas, accompanied by his wife, whom he was divorcing, and with her was the woman she thought should be his new girlfriend and possibly his next wife. She was also the woman who had saved Joe's life by shooting and killing a murderer, spattering his blood on Joe's shirt. Also with them was the man his current wife thought would be a good addition to the "career part" of her life, but probably not the personal part. He was the chief of operations at the hospital in which Joe and his wife worked, the hospital where his four year old patient had been killed. These four were the only passengers.

The other three were sleeping now while Joe couldn't slow his thoughts enough to even shut his eyes. His hand touched the blood stains on his collar as the flight attendant, a pleasant young man of maybe thirty, approached and inquired softly whether Joe wished a drink or something more to eat, or perhaps something to read. Joe asked for water, thinking that would make it simple, but it didn't.

He had to choose from among four different bottled waters that were stocked, and then reply as to whether a slice of lemon should be added. He said that the first offered choice of waters would be fine, and that lemon would be nice, too. He had just cheated death for a second time in his life, and decided that this fact alone was reason enough for him to have a slice of lemon in his water. He wasn't sure why he was still alive, but God must have something really important for him the way he kept interfering with his death.

Twenty years ago he had nearly died in a mining accident. Rock had fallen from the roof of a coal mine, and he lay there with his foot caught beneath an unmovable pile of rubble. The doctor had cut his foot from him in order to save his life, and that had changed his life in ways he could never have imagined. Joe came to realize that the doctor had taken an enormous risk to come down into the mine to save him, and he was convinced that he had been saved in order that he should become a physician himself. He had done just that, and now in the religious nature of his upbringing, he wondered if there was another mission intended for him that had kept him from death.

His wife stirred now, brushing away her blond hair and opening her eyes. "Just wanted to make sure you're still alive, Joe," she smiled.

He smiled back and said, "Thank you, Carolyn."

"I was never really worried," she replied. "Natalie's a good shot. So what if the killer had you held in front of him with a gun at your neck? Easy shot for Nat'lie, even if Carl would have rather seen his assets seized or some such punishment." She nodded toward the man sleeping soundly across from her and next to Joe.

Joe wondered how Carolyn could be so sure of Natalie's shooting ability since they had met only two days ago. She had never seen Natalie shoot at all before. Such things didn't bother Carolyn. Joe, of course, had known Natalie only that long as well, and had trusted her to shoot, told her to shoot in fact. Shoot the man who had killed two people already and had a gun against Joe's neck, so there was no ground for his criticism of Carolyn.

Natalie stirred too and shook back her dark, shoulder-length hair. "You are still alive, Joe," she said.

"I'm still alive, too," said Carolyn. "But I'm not sure about Carl. He can sleep through anything. Must be the years of practice in those interminable meetings that a vice president of operations has to attend in that hospital of ours."

Natalie shivered. "I don't think anything could be worse than killing a four-year-old child. Of all the things that have happened in the last twenty-four hours, that's the one thing I can't get out of my mind. It's worse than shooting that murdering bastard in the airport all the time praying I didn't hit you by mistake, Joe; knowing they would have liked to bury us all." She shook her head.

"I was deployed to Afghanistan, for God's sake, and I never saw anything as callous as that. I'm sorry, it's just that I'm— I'm glad he's dead, that's all." She sighed and looked close to tears.

Carolyn reached over and squeezed her arm. "I would have shot him myself if you hadn't." She smiled now and added, "You'll have to teach me to shoot sometime, Natalie. Joe is a good shot, from when he was a kid growing up hunting in the mountains. But when I asked him to teach me, he just told me to go out and shoot at something, and if I did that long enough I would learn to hit it."

Joe looked out the window. It would take him a while to sort this all out. He and Carolyn were physicians in the same hospital, getting divorced because he wanted to stay in the place he had always called home and she wanted to move on. Carolyn and Carl were interviewing for positions at the Medical Center in Las Vegas tomorrow. They would have been flying to the interview alone and probably on a standard commercial carrier were it not for Joe. Linda Murphy had been killed and she was the niece of Reginald Murphy, the wealthiest man in the region they had just flown from. Her murder had almost gone unsolved, unpunished, but Joe had confronted the killer in the Lexington airport as he was trying to escape. He had produced a gun and threatened to kill Joe, and Natalie had shot him to prevent him from doing that. They still wore the clothes they had been wearing, including Joe's shirt with the bloodstains on it.

The police investigating the murder had advised them— ordered them, in fact—to be "out of sight" for a week or two for their own safety. The crime had involved locals but clearly extended into criminal organizations beyond their rural community in Appalachia. The crime involved more than murder, and probably had involved organized crime with international connections, and probably the local police as well. Until the arrests were made, the state police advised them to be out of Kentucky. So here they were, approaching Las Vegas, and Joe wished very much to put it all out of his mind. This trip was at the expense of Reginald Murphy as sort of a token of his thanks for solving the murder of his niece and avenging it.

The pleasant young man who had been serving them came over now. "We have started our descent into Las Vegas, and I must suggest that you put on your seat belts." He smiled and added, "We must follow the same regulations as the commercial airlines, you know."

Joe didn't know that, and thought that the young man was slightly amused, and perhaps even a little offended, that they did have to follow those "same regulations as the commercial airlines" had to follow. This young man worked for Reginald Murphy, who owned this airplane and the hotel that these four were heading to, and possibly one or two of the commercial airlines that must adhere to the same regulations as his private jet did. This trip was an expression of gratitude to Joe and his companions for seeing that some sort of justice was done.

The seat belts were fastened, and Joe's empty glass was cleared away. Carl's belt had remained fastened the whole trip, even as the man inside it had slept. "Let's forget what happened in Kentucky for a while and enjoy the city of Las Vegas," Joe said. The young man smiled, and the two ladies agreed.

Chapter 2

This being both the private part of the airport and Las Vegas as well, the limo came to the plane. Bags would have been placed directly into the trunk except that they had left Kentucky so hastily they had not packed any luggage. Carolyn was disappointed that the "full treatment" would not be given here, and vowed that there would be luggage to be placed in the trunk of the limo on the return trip, even if it were empty luggage. Carl was awake now, but seemed unable to understand the importance of the luggage, and Joe and Natalie preferred to ignore the whole issue.

When they arrived at the hotel, they were escorted to a private check-in area and the chauffer accompanied them. Only when they were duly placed in the care of a hotel employee did the chauffer turn to leave.

"My name is Raul Perez," the fiftyish year old Latino gentleman in the chauffer's uniform said. "If you need any transportation, please call. You're to be my sole client while you're staying here in Las Vegas, so there will be no delay in my arrival." He handed each of them cards with his name and the name of his agency, with phone numbers marked "office" and "mobile." With this accomplished he disappeared, leaving them with a smartly dressed young lady whose name, Suzanne, appeared on a badge beneath the title "Assistant Manager". Everyone was duly impressed so far.

"I have been instructed to find you accommodations in the suites on the Sky Floor. They can only be accessed by inserting your room key into the slot in the elevators marked 'Sky Rooms.' How many suites is it that you will be needing?" she asked.

They looked at each other and finally Carolyn replied, "There are four of us, so two rooms would be fine, I guess."

The assistant manager smiled and said, "I agree. Each suite has two bedrooms and a sitting area. Each of you will have a bedroom to yourself." She smiled again and added, "If that's what you wish."

Carolyn smiled and nodded, while Joe and Natalie grew slightly embarrassed. Carl seemed puzzled by the whole exchange.

"Yes," replied Carolyn, and turning toward the other three she said, "Natalie and I will take the suite nearest the elevator, and Joe and Carl will have the other." Turning back to the young lady she said, "Just two keys for each, please."

"Yes, of course. Now if you can sign here." The assistant manager smiled. "The hotel policies are listed above your signature." She didn't encourage them to read those policies, and in fact removed the form as soon as it was signed. No sense in wasting any time with that.

This accomplished, they left with their keys to go try them in the slot marked "Sky Rooms" in the elevator. As they left, Carolyn grinned and said, "I'll not have my reputation slandered by an assistant manager; a *manager* maybe, but not an assistant."

"Why wouldn't we each want our own room?" asked Carl.

"We do want our own rooms, Carl, and that's all that needs to be said about it," replied Carolyn. Natalie just smiled, and Joe shook his head.

"What I want is a hot shower and to get out of these clothes," said Natalie.

"And into what?" asked Carolyn. "We were hustled out of Kentucky without any time to pack, so we only have what we're wearing. Shopping should be the first thing on the list, but not in this place. I bet the prices are over the top, if the decor is any sample."

"Well, we have a limo at our disposal. Have you ever had a limo drop you off at the thrift shop? It might be a good story," said Joe. "On the other hand, you and Carl have to interview at the Medical Center, so maybe one upscale outfit is in order."

"Yes," said Carolyn. "I'm hoping the position here will suit me. I could be director of their Emergency Department if I like them, and they like me, so I'd better dress the part."

"Will they let us back in here if we're dressed from the thrift shop cast-offs?" asked Natalie.

"That's an interesting question," said Carl. He looked around at the people they were passing and added, "There doesn't seem to be much of a dress code here. If there is, it must relate to the amount of body covered by clothing, not the type of clothing covering it. There's definitely a trend toward minimalist attire."

Everyone giggled except Carl, who looked slightly offended by the reception his comment had received.

The rooms really were suites, with expansive views of the Las Vegas skyline and the suburbs, and then the desert beyond. The rooms were expansive as well, with two ample bedrooms and a large sitting area with couch, love seat, chairs and a table. There was a large-screen TV and a small but well-stocked bar. Carolyn and Natalie came down to Joe and Carl's room to see if theirs was the same. The ladies decided their suite was better, but for reasons that were not easily put into words. Both were adequately sumptuous, they agreed.

They were settled in quickly, with no unpacking necessary since there was no clothing to unpack. There was a bottle of champagne chilling in each room, along with a platter of snacks. The champagne was saved for later, and as Joe was pouring juice and soda for everyone, there was a knock at the door. When Carolyn answered it, a handsome young African American man in a suit entered, wearing a badge that gave his title as "Associate Manager" and his name as James.

"I am James Monroe," he said, and smiled. "No. No relation to the former president; but I am an Associate Manager, and I wanted to explain to you the arrangements that we have been asked to make on your behalf."

The four looked inquisitively at the man who was not related to a former president to find out what arrangements *had* been made for them.

He smiled and continued. "The room and of course all meals, here or in our dining facilities, have been paid for already. The pool, exercise facilities and spa, as well as any of our shows that you wish to attend are included as well. Please indulge yourselves, and charge it to your rooms for as long as you choose to stay."

He nodded toward the surprised people he was addressing. "There was some concern that you would not have brought any luggage, so I have been asked to arrange that you may purchase whatever you need in any of the establishments here in the hotel or in the attached mall. Again, simply charge it using your room key."

The surprise seemed to grow in his audience, but James Monroe was undeterred. "I am afraid that you will not be able to charge any gaming to you room, however."

"Of course not," stammered Joe.

"Yes," said James. "While that was a practice some years ago, it … well, it came to be seen in an unfavorable light by many, including those on the Gaming Commission. They're the people who are really in charge in Las Vegas, you know." He smiled at them.

It was Carl who spoke at this point. "Yes, there were some rather well-publicized incidents a few years ago. It's not surprising that the practice has been abandoned. We won't be gambling, in any event." The looks on the faces of the others said that Carl was speaking only for himself.

James continued, "Just so. You will be unusual, however, if you do not leave a little of your money here for us to spend." There were nods from the other three.

"The wise people see it as entertainment," James continued. "There are some, however, who think they can beat the house. I hope you're not numbered among those who believe that. It is an awfully big house." He motioned to the "house", the hotel that surrounded them.

"A great many people seem to have left a great deal of their money here to be spent by other people," said Joe as he looked around.

"Yes," said James. "There are a surprising number of people who believe they'll be the ones who will win. They believe that they're the lucky ones, or that they have a 'system' that will not fail. They seem to believe that they can perfect it with just a little more practice." He shook his head. "They believe that they can win it all *with a little more practice*." He smiled a very charming smile at them.

"Have a good stay," he added. "And if you need anything, please ask for me personally."

Chapter 3

Carolyn smiled after James as he left. "We'll try our very best to have a good stay, Mr. Monroe." Turning back to her companions she added, "And *that* associate manager might easily be able to slander my reputation." She looked at Natalie, who smiled but said nothing.

"Ah, but there's shopping to be done, Natalie," said Carolyn. "I can hear the most fantastic clothing calling to me all the way up here. No one will believe this if I don't have something to show for the trip."

"No one will believe you even if you *do* have something to show," said Joe. "Shall we walk or call the limo?"

"The lobby first," said Carolyn. "Is Reggie the richest man in the world? I mean, is there any chance we could spend too much of his money?"

"The rest of us would have trouble getting anywhere close," said Natalie. "But I think you might be able to, Carolyn."

"Let's try, shall we? You boys will need something too, but be warned that the girls are out to *break the Reg,* so if there's nothing left over for you two, it's your own fault."

"I'll get some underwear, at least," said Joe.

"It actually would be improbable that you could buy enough to bankrupt Reginald Murphy," said Carl.

"I happen to be somewhat familiar with his estate, and it's quite substantial. That, and of course he already owns the merchandise you're buying, so it's only possible for you to interrupt the cash flow"

"Oh, be quiet, Carl," said Carolyn. "Even if I can't, I want to try."

She slipped her hand through Carl's arm and they left the room. As they entered the elevator a moment later, Carolyn said, "Come, children. The playground is open!"

"I can't believe this is all happening," said Natalie. "Twenty-four hours ago we were sitting in a restaurant two thousand miles from this place with this man: Reginald Murphy, who none of us had ever met before. Now he's paying for us to live lavishly in Las Vegas."

"More than twenty-four hours, really," said Carl. "There's a time change, too."

"An extra hour or two will not help to make any sense of it, Carl," said Carolyn, pulling him a little closer. He didn't seem to notice.

"Perhaps something to eat," suggested Carl. "I didn't eat anything on the flight here. Did they have any food, I wonder?"

"Yes," said Carolyn. "Everyone else ate quite well."

"Perhaps a night's sleep will help," said Joe.

"Or some shopping," said Carolyn.

Natalie shrugged and then nodded. "Why is this happening?" she asked.

"Reginald Murphy is quite wealthy," said Carl. "The money we're spending will not be missed."

"But …" Natalie persisted.

"Reginald is also an enigma," said Joe. "It was his niece who was killed three years ago, and that death started the malpractice case. He said that he decided to pursue the case against me in order to force me to solve what he was convinced was a murder all along. I don't know if that's true, but that's what he said."

Joe shrugged. "Strange man, and if he weren't so strange I might think he felt guilty about putting me through it all. But I don't think Reggie feels guilt about making people do what he wishes them to do. On the other hand, I don't think he minds paying those people; rewarding them for their service to him.

"Besides that, I did point out to him that the state police felt we were in some danger because of what we had done, and that he was responsible in no small way for that jeopardy, and that it would be best for us if we couldn't be traced by our credit cards or hotel reservations. There are some police back home who might want to find us."

"But I was not of any *service to him,*" persisted Natalie.

"It was you who shot the man who killed Reggie's niece," said Carolyn. "That's worth a dress and a swimsuit, too. The pool looks inviting."

Natalie shivered slightly as they exited the elevator to face the shops and casino. "Killing someone isn't—" she began.

Carolyn stopped walking and turned to face her. She was serious now, with all frivolousness gone from her face. "You didn't kill anyone to get a swimsuit, Natalie. You killed him to—"

Natalie frowned. "I did it because I had to."

"Exactly," said Carolyn. "Just as I'm going to do what *I* have to. I have to interview tomorrow for a position at the Medical Center as a first step toward solving the national healthcare mess. I'll need something to wear, and so you, Natalie Moore, will have to make your own sacrifice and help me shop. You don't have to enjoy it, but you do have to do it. So come along to help me become presentable for tomorrow's interview."

Natalie smiled. "Will you buy what I tell you to buy?"

"No," said Carolyn. "Well, maybe."

"I won't be your friend unless you do."

"Well, maybe one thing then. You boys are on your own until supper, but be prepared to dress elegantly, or at least to accompany two elegantly dressed woman to the most expensive dining we can find in this place."

"Okay," said Joe.

Carl seemed oblivious to the conversation just finished as he looked around the casino next to them. "I wonder how these machines work?" he said.

"The slot machines?" asked Joe.

"Yes. That's what they're called, although I don't see any *slots* on them."

"There used to be slots when they used coins," said Joe. "And as to how they work: you just put money into them."

"Don't you take money out?" asked Carl.

"Not really," said Joe. "You put it in, but take out less and less until you don't have anything left to take out. It's really pretty simple."

"Hmm," said Carl. "Perhaps we should do some shopping too, Joseph. That shouldn't take too long." His gaze was still on the casino.

Chapter 4

Natalie walked along with Carolyn past the most expensive shops she had ever seen, seen up close at least. "Are we really going to be able to buy anything we want?" she asked.

"I don't know," said Carolyn.

"Maybe we should try something small first," said Natalie.

"Or maybe we should try something big. Small might get past, but if big goes through, we'll know we can buy … well, more big stuff," suggested Carolyn.

"But," said Natalie, "maybe we should get some small essentials first, in case we can't use it for big stuff. That way we won't blow it and not be able to buy anything."

"Let's settle this like reasonable, avaricious women," said Carolyn, turning and walking into the shop they had just passed.

When a saleslady approached, she pointed to a pastel flowered print dress on one of the manikins. "How much is this?"

"Only eleven hundred dollars," the saleslady replied.

Natalie gasped, but Carolyn said, "Do you have it my size?"

"Oh, I think we do. You look like a size ten maybe. Would you like to try it on?"

"No," said Carolyn. "Just charge it to my room please." She handed a somewhat astonished saleslady her room key and waited as she hurried off to charge an eleven-hundred-dollar dress.

"That should answer our question. I don't think I like the dress, though. Should I cancel the sale now and disappoint her, or return it later, do you think?"

"I kind of like it," said Natalie.

"Really?" said Carolyn as the saleslady returned.

"If you would just sign here I'll get your dress," she said, handing a slip to Carolyn.

"We have decided to try it on after all," said Carolyn, signing the slip.

"Oh, of course. Right this way."

Carolyn and Natalie were soon in a dressing room as large as many bedrooms might be. There were the usual mirrors, and seats, and hooks on the walls, but there was also a table with two chairs, fresh coffee, and dainty little pastries. They had been offered a choice of beverages, of course, including champagne, but had been too surprised to ask for anything except coffee.

"Well, try it on," said Carolyn.

"Me?" replied Natalie. "I thought this was *your* dress."

"But I don't like it and you do, so try it on. We look about the same size."

Natalie did, and then looked appraisingly in the mirrors. "It's a little tight," she said.

"It's supposed to be," replied Carolyn. "Can you breathe in it?"

"Well, yes."

"Then it's not too tight."

"But it makes my breasts look large."

"It's supposed to do that."

"But they look like they're going to fall out at any minute."

"That's the way they're supposed to look."

"But everyone will be looking at them."

"That's what they're *supposed* to be looking at," said Carolyn. "I'm sure that Joe will notice them."

"Joe?" said Natalie, turning sideways to the mirror. "Do you really think he'll notice?"

"Definitely."

"But doesn't he have this thing about fidelity?" frowned Natalie. "Will he—"

"He's not dead," said Carolyn. "He just believes that you should be married to the person you're having sex with. I think he might be the only person who still does believe that, or at least the only man. But just because you're not going to eat the apple doesn't mean that you don't notice that it looks delicious."

"Oh," said Natalie.

"And," continued Carolyn, "you have a great pair of apples, so show them off! Joe won't bite. Not yet, anyway."

"It does look nice," said Natalie, looking at herself in the mirror again.

"And you want Joe to notice you, don't you?"

"Well ..." said Natalie.

"You don't think you might want to marry him?"

"Well, I think I might. He's an awfully nice guy, but are you sure you want to—"

"No, I'm not sure I want to divorce him, but I'm sure I have to. I believe that I have to try to straighten out the mess the healthcare system is in. I want to be the surgeon general of this friggin' country, and Joe would be miserable if I dragged him away from the mountains of Eastern Kentucky. That's where *he* can make a difference."

Natalie looked unconvinced and Carolyn continued. "If I were a *man* making a sacrifice to benefit all *man*kind, everyone would think I was noble. But because I am a woman, no one seems to understand. No one thinks I'm serious. Besides, I'm not giving up my best friend. Joe is still going to be my friend, and I hope you will be too, Natalie. I'm just giving up the best sex I have ever had. But knowing how Joe feels about fidelity, you won't find that out until you marry him. He's so strange that way."

Carolyn's face took on a look of puzzlement as Natalie smiled.

"Maybe I'll keep the dress," she said. "Can I ask you something, Carolyn?"

"Yeah, sure."

"Do you have someone else you like? Someone who'll go to Washington with you? Carl maybe?"

Carolyn looked surprised. "Carl? He's nice, and probably one of the most intelligent people I know. I count it a plus to have him in operations, but there's not the least hint of physical attraction there.

"I may find someone, but right now I want to get the job. I'm not leaving Joe for someone better." She shrugged and asked, "Do you have someone else? Or did you?"

Natalie frowned. "I did, but …"

Carolyn just waited.

"Oh, hell," said Natalie. "I had a really bad tour the last time I was in Afghanistan, and my husband couldn't understand it. He's military too, but … well, he vacillated between telling me I was wrong to be upset and I should just get over it, and telling me the whole military sucked and I should just quit. He finally realized I wasn't listening to what he said about the same time I realized I didn't want to hear it anymore. I think I loved him, but—"

"Of course you loved him," said Carolyn so matter-of-factly that it left no doubt. "But you can't live on love alone. Not love in the past tense, anyway. Did he want you to join the police force?"

"Well, no," said Natalie. "That was kind of the final straw. We might have worked it out if I had just settled down and cleaned house and raised kids, but I wanted …"

"And he didn't," said Carolyn, when Natalie said nothing more. "And furthermore, it wouldn't have worked out. That's what's going on with Joe and me. Love, yes; shared beliefs, yes; but living together? It just wouldn't work. Are you still friends?"

"No," said Natalie. "By the time we realized we needed space, the love had turned to … well, to hate I guess. More for him than me. He took it personally that I didn't want to clean his house and raise his family, so he went and got himself someone who would."

"And you joined the police, where you belong," said Carolyn. "How'd that happen?"

"That was strange, too," said Natalie. "I was separated, not divorced yet, and driving the ambulance back home in Kentucky. One day I had to drive this really sick guy who was having a heart attack, and this doc was riding down with us."

"Diana Connors?" asked Carolyn.

"Yeah. Ya know her?"

"Met her a couple of times. Works in the clinic, right?"

"Yeah. But—"

"That ambulance ride is something of a legend back home," said Carolyn. "Twenty-mile drive over two-lane mountain roads in under fifteen minutes! It's legendary."

"Yeah. Scared the hell out of Doc Connors. But she had this boyfriend, I guess he was, who drove the guy's wife down. And anyway, he talked to me, and had the state police sergeant talk to me, and the two of them just badgered me until I applied. And then they both told everyone that I would be a great police officer."

"And they were right," said Carolyn immediately.

"My ex didn't think so."

"Then he was wrong." Carolyn shrugged. Her reassuring attitude drove all doubt from Natalie's mind. "Husbands should support their wives, just as wives should support their husbands. It's not one or the other, it's both."

"Yes. You're lucky it's Joe, Carolyn."

"And so are you. With a dress like that you have nothing to worry about except whether you really want him or not." Carolyn looked at her appraisingly. "Joe is pretty lucky, too."

"Yeah," laughed Natalie. "Two gorgeous women fighting over him."

"Yes," smiled Carolyn. "One divorcing him, and the other trying to keep her 'apples' from showing too much."

"Did you just make up that about apples? I've never heard them called that before."

"Yes, I did. Pretty good, don't you think?"

"Yeah, pretty good."

"You don't think Eve tempted Adam with a piece of fruit, do you?"

"I hadn't thought of that," said Natalie. "You know, Joe *is* lucky to have two gorgeous women like us notice him at all." With this Natalie looked at herself in the mirrors surrounding them and winked at Carolyn.

Chapter 5

Carolyn and Natalie were off somewhere enjoying themselves, Joe was sure. Carl had wandered into a couple of shops and looked at various clothing items with remarkable disinterest, so much disinterest that Joe decided he would be better shopping on his own.

There were several men's clothing stores to choose from, none including *boutique* in their names. That word was apparently reserved for the establishments that catered to females. Joe realized that there was a great deal of variety available, and he also soon realized that he could tell what the clothing would look like by observing the salespeople. Those with young, muscular gentlemen waiting to attend to the client's requests would sell flamboyant shirts best displayed with several buttons left open. And the accompanying pants, referred to as *slacks* he was sure, were fashionably, if uncomfortably tight, or redundantly loose and baggy. Neither appealed to him. He only had to walk through one such store to know he would not find what he liked to wear in one of these. The salespeople appeared as relieved as he was when he left.

He finally came to one that seemed more likely to match him. The manikins in the front were dressed in sport jackets or shirts with ties, and the slacks were pants of neutral colors. Testing his recently formulated theory, he glanced at the salespeople. They were dressed well, but more plainly compared to the previous establishments. They were somewhat older, and some were women. As he entered, one of these women came over to him.

"Can I help you find anything? Or would you rather look around yourself?" she asked. She had a slight accent that Joe thought might be from Kentucky, or from near that state at least. Not the hills he was from, but the flat country around Lexington and Louisville.

"Perhaps you can help me," said Joe. "I've ended up in Las Vegas without a stitch that I'm not wearing right now. I'll need more than these, I'm afraid." His own accent was usually not very evident, but now it had become clearly audible.

"That happens," she replied. There was no hint of surprise in her voice, and while Joe had feared that this confession would lead to questions, it didn't. Either it was, in fact, a common occurrence here, or this lady was not easily surprised by anything. He looked at the name tag and read "Janet."

"Well, Janet, there's another problem that I would like to clarify before I start picking out the clothing. I've been told that I may charge whatever I buy to my room, and that there's no real limit on those charges. Do you think you could verify that?" he said, handing her the plastic card that was his room key.

"We can charge things when you leave, if that would suit you."

"I would be more comfortable if you checked it before I make my purchases," Joe smiled.

Janet nodded, and departed for a few minutes. When she returned, she handed him the room key and said, "You're as good as the gold in Fort Knox, Dr. Nelson. I can pack up the whole store for you if you want."

"My stay here isn't going to be that long," he smiled. "So, now we face the more difficult task. What should you pack up for say a week, or maybe two? What would a middle-aged gentleman like myself need here?"

"Well, first," said Janet, "you must not admit to middle-age, even if it is true. Going by the standards in this town, by the way, you lack ten years."

"Perhaps I look younger than I am," smiled Joe.

"Perhaps your demographics, including your birthday, are included in the file that's opened by your room key. It's part of the security we have here so people who possess keys or cards can verify that they're the persons who are supposed to have those keys or cards.

It includes your picture, your date of birth, your social security number, along with your arrival date and, when you leave, your departure date. Soon your fingerprints as well."

Janet smiled and Joe stared. "There's very little that's secret here, Doctor," she added. "You arrived with your wife and another lady and a gentleman; the two ladies have been placed in one room, and you and the gentleman have both been in the other room. At least the keys you were issued have opened those rooms, I should say."

"I can explain the arrangement," Joe began.

"No need for that," Janet smiled. "You should have been advised of the security precautions by the person who checked you in, anyway. All the keys appear to be able to open both rooms. If you wish privacy, you should request that that be changed."

Joe continued to stare, and Janet's smile broadened slightly. "We have a fairly advanced system here. The room keys are imprinted electronically with a numbered code. When inserted into any lock, or store charge, restaurant, or whatever else, the code is transmitted to the central computer, where it is either verified for the use 'requested' or it is denied. Few hotels have a system this elaborate. One in Lexington, Kentucky does. I used to live there before I moved here."

"Oh," said Joe.

Janet smiled again. "You might want to advise your companions of this situation with the keys. Also, you should know that while the keys work in either room, only you will be able to charge anything with your key. Your picture appears every time it's used."

"How did you get my picture?"

"It was taken by a surveillance camera when you checked in," said Janet. "It's mentioned in the small, the *very* small, print in the registration form you signed. We have a great many surveillance cameras here."

"Oh," said Joe again.

"So, unless you and your companion resemble each other very closely, he will not be able to use your room key; to charge anything, at least."

"I sincerely hope that Carl and I do not resemble each other," replied Joe. "And I'm sure that Carl shares that wish."

"So, Dr. Nelson, let us attend to your wardrobe, shall we? Are you thinking of a change, or are you comfortable with who you are?"

"Well," said Joe, "I think I'm dressed fairly well, actually."

"Most men do think that," smiled Janet. "Most women would disagree, but that's not my job. Carolyn and Natalie will supply an ample critique."

"You know their … of course," said Joe. "The computer. They're shopping right now."

"Wrong, Dr. Nelson," Janet said. "They are *buying*, and so is Carl. If there's any competition, you are way behind, so let's get cracking, shall we? New look? Old look? Better look? Bold look?" She chuckled slightly at her own joke.

"I think I'll trust you and see how I do. I'm from Kentucky too, you know."

"Yes, I know," replied Janet. "Your address is in the mountains, though."

"I have no secrets," smiled Joe.

"You have a couple, which you may not wish to share, even with a fellow Kentuckian."

Joe looked at her and she continued, "About the time I was leaving Kentucky, there was a story on the news about the death of a little four-year-old girl in a hospital from up in the mountains where you live. The story was about the impending malpractice suit, and I seem to recall that the doctor's name was Joseph Nelson." She looked at him to see his reaction. He frowned a little bit but nodded, and Janet continued.

"This morning I saw a story about a shooting in the Lexington airport," said Janet. "The TV is on all the time in the lounge here. The story said that one man was dead, and that there was an *unconfirmed injury to a local doctor.*

No name given, but it was mentioned that the doctor was involved in a malpractice case that involved the death of a four-year-old girl named Linda Murphy. Reginald Murphy owns this place. Possibly just a coincidence, ya think? I follow the news from Kentucky.

"I also sell clothing, so I tend to notice clothing. Those stains on your shirt collar and sleeve? They look like they might be blood perhaps?"

"Oh," said Joe, instinctively reaching for the collar of his shirt.

"Did you get those in the lobby of the Lexington airport, Dr. Nelson?"

When Joe made no answer she said, "You also have a very slight limp. I hope you were not injured."

"What? No, I wasn't," said Joe. "Almost killed, but not injured." He raised his pant leg to display the prosthesis. "I lost the lower half in a mining accident twenty years ago. Most people don't notice."

"I'm sorry," said Janet. "About your leg, I mean, and about whatever happened in Lexington this morning."

"No need to apologize."

"That being as it may, I'm still sorry about your leg. It doesn't show much. I sell shoes sometimes too, so I notice. That's all."

"It used to be important to me," said Joe. "That it didn't show. That no one knew I was … it's not important any longer."

Janet smiled slightly; a sad sort of smile. "My husband died in a mining accident a few years ago. That's how I ended up in the retail sales business. Tough to find work if you're a middle-aged woman with no real skills or education. Lexington wasn't far enough from the mines, though. I kept running into miners in the stores. So I moved here, and then you come in. Maybe it was foolish to think I could—"

"I'm sorry," said Joe.

"Well, now we're both sorry, and that's not the Las Vegas way, so we'll have to do something about it. Let's get you the best outfit that money can buy. And I work on commission, so we'll not spare one dime doing it, okay?"

"Okay," said Joe.

# Chapter 6

Joe shopped, but quickly realized he was out of his class. Janet always chose something that even he had to admit looked better than what he had chosen, so he finally let her pick them all out. It was easier that way and further, she picked the right sizes, without failing even once, just by looking at him. The clothing was tried on only for look, not for fit. Joe wasn't sure it even needed to be tried on for look, since it always looked good, but he was enjoying talking to Janet, so why not? He didn't have anything else to do in boring old Las Vegas.

"So, how long have you been here, Janet?" he asked.

"Only a year. I sold clothes in a mall store in Lexington, and when the opportunity to come here presented itself, it seemed to solve all my problems."

"Seemed to?" asked Joe.

"The job disappeared as soon as I arrived. The job reappeared when a lady younger than I appeared." She shrugged.

"Oh," said Joe.

"Common occurrence in Vegas. It's not only Hollywood that runs on youth and beauty. Those are the currency here, too. Sexist? Yes, unapologetic in all its forms. Prostitution is legal a few miles outside this city, and while it's not legal here, it's practiced quite openly."

Joe remained silent and Janet continued. "Would you believe I landed this job on the basis if my physical attributes? Be gentle with your answer, Dr. Nelson."

"Well ..." began Joe.

"No, it was not my beauty, and I was not even asked for gratuitous sex. I looked middle-aged and motherly, they said. That was what was wanted in this shop." She smiled now. "If beauty is only skin deep, Las Vegas never gets beyond the makeup. Nothing is real here; it's all appearance."

She stood back from him now and looked. "Yes, I think you can wear that shirt. It's the cutting edge of fashion here, not to mention the West Coast. But it may be a year or two before anyone in Kentucky is wearing it. Maybe everyone there will think that Joe Nelson started the trend, do ya think?"

"No," smiled Joe. "Everyone there knows Joe Nelson too well."

"It looks good," said Janet.

"I like it. And the pants, too."

"Good enough then. Do you want to wear that, or put on your old shirt?"

"I'll wear the old one for now. I'll be going up to my room when I finish; to shower I think," he shrugged.

"Some jeans next?" asked Janet. "Will you be doing any outdoor activities? Hiking or horseback riding?"

Joe thought of his traveling companions. Carolyn? Probably not. Carl? Definitely not. Natalie? "Maybe," he said.

"Then let's move to that section."

They walked a few aisles further into the store to the back wall. There were a few jeans displayed, but most were on shelves arranged according to size and name brand. "Is there really any difference in the brands?" he asked.

"Yes and no," said Janet.

"I'll take the 'no' if those are the only two choices," he replied.

Janet smiled. "If you look closely at the stitching, the quality can be the same regardless of the price or the brand. Some more expensive items are not made as well. If you shop for what your particular physical characteristics are, they'll look good, too, even if you don't spend much money. It's impossible to get cheap prices here, but you can get less expensive prices. Of course, if you're dressing for Las Vegas, it doesn't matter how it looks as long as the printing on your butt says the right thing."

She smiled again and asked, "What should your butt say?"

"Did the pictures of Carolyn and Natalie come up when you checked my room key?"

"Yes."

"Then you know that no one will take any notice of my butt."

"They might," said Janet, looking at him. "Now that I'm picking out your clothes, anyway."

Joe became embarrassed and changed the subject immediately. "If it's not a security risk, can I ask you about those pictures?"

Janet shrugged as she went through the shelves of jeans.

"Are there surveillance cameras in here?"

"Yes," she replied.

"I've noticed the ones in the ceiling domes out in the casino, but I don't see any here."

"You haven't seen any in the casino, either," said Janet.

When Joe looked at her she said, "The domes are fake. They're put there to make people think that's where the cameras are. The real ones are very well concealed. We're being watched now, to ensure that neither of us is stealing any of this shit. Since you're not paying for it, you may as well know that as far as jeans go, the discount places have better quality and better prices. They want to keep me honest too, perhaps more so. In the casinos it's all about the staff. The dealers are watched very closely. A single slip can get you fired, and make it difficult to find any other job in this town; any job dealing at least. Everyone is watched closely in the casino; customers and staff. They trust no one."

"Yes, I know," said Joe.

"Oh."

"Yes," Joe said absently. "There was a study done to see if cardiac defibrillators handled by non-medical people could be used to save lives. It was done in Las Vegas because people are observed so closely here, they would be resuscitated immediately."

"So Las Vegas really is doing a good deed?"

"Maybe," said Joe.

"Oh?" asked Janet. "Isn't building a better cardiac defibrillator a good thing?"

"That depends," said Joe. "The study proved that it can work here where everyone is watched very closely, maybe more closely than anywhere else on Earth. That's why the study was done here in the first place.

"It might not be as successful somewhere else. Besides, the purpose of medical research today isn't necessarily to discover the next great medical advance. It's often used to facilitate the sale of the next expensive medical product."

He smiled at her and said, "Sorry. I'm a little jaded sometimes. I'll have Carolyn talk to you. She still believes in the potential of humans and their technology."

"Well," shrugged Janet. "I had hoped that at least medicine was still a noble art, and now I learn that it's the same everywhere. We all live in Vegas, I guess, just with different names for the places, that's all." She shook her head.

"Here, try these on, Joe, and pick out a couple more while I ring up the rest of this stuff," she said, handing him a stack of blue jeans.

He did, and when he came out, he went to the register where Janet was ringing up the last of his purchases. A hotel manager was leaning on the counter, saying, "You've been tied up with one customer for over two hours, just chatting with him most of the time. We expect more productivity from you, Miss Lewis."

Joe looked at the scene and said, "Thank you, Janet. You've been very helpful. I'll be sure to mention how helpful you've been when I see Reggie again. Mr. Murphy, I mean. Is he the sole owner of this complex, do you know?"

The manager blanched slightly and stood. "I'm Robert Bevins, Mr. …"

"Nelson," said Joe.

"*Dr.* Nelson," said Janet, without looking up.

"Oh, yes," said Robert. "I was just complimenting Janet here on what a fine job she's been doing. Please continue your good work, Miss Lewis, and if there's anything I can do for you, please don't hesitate to ask, Doctor."

With this, Robert Bevins turned and left.

"You've already done the best thing you could have done, Mr. Bevins," said Joe, looking after him. "Leaving."

"That's the truth," echoed Janet. "Worst prick I've ever worked for. Now, if you can just sign for this, I'll have it all sent up to your room, Dr. Nelson. It should arrive by the time you've finished your shower."

Joe signed and said, "I'll have to start calling you Miss Lewis if you don't start calling me Joe."

Janet smiled. "And which of your rooms do you want this sent to?"

"You already know which room I'm staying in." Joe smiled. "Maybe I should find the rest of my party first."

"I can tell you where they're spending their money," Janet said. "Or at least where they're spending Mr. Murphy's money."

"Yes, if it's not a problem."

"Not at all. Are you and Reginald Murphy really friends?" she asked.

"We met two days ago. A little more, maybe."

"Oh," said Janet. "The ladies look as if they're together, each buying for themselves. At least they're charging in the same shops at the same time. They're not twins, are they?"

"What?"

"One isn't using both cards do you think? *All About You* is the last shop they charged in. Go straight across the casino and they're moving down that side, so turn left and check the shops they might be in. You'll probably find them easily enough."

"And Carl?"

"He last charged about an hour and a half ago, just a few doors down. Several items, but nothing since then. He didn't go to either one of the rooms. At least his key didn't open either one."

"Maybe something to eat."

"No restaurant charges." She looked at Joe and smiled. "Maybe he's in someone else's room?"

It took a moment for Joe to realize what was being suggested, but when he did, he blushed deeply.

"Or perhaps the casino?" offered Janet.

"Maybe. Thank you very much, Miss Lewis."

"Have a good stay, *Joe*."

"Oh, excuse me. Thank you, *Janet*." He turned to leave but stopped.

"To whom would I send a letter complimenting you on your service today? Reggie might be too high up the line, and Mr. Bevins might misplace it."

"There's an associate manager named Monroe who's in charge of special guest arrangements. He'll make sure your letter is handled appropriately, and he would be the manager who is handling your stay."

"Ah," said Joe. "James Monroe, no relation to the former president. I'll drop him a note."

"Then you've met him," smiled Janet. "It's not necessary to write a letter, but it would be nice if you did."

"I have nothing else to do in this boring city, so that's what I'll do. Thank you again, Janet." And with this Joe left to search for his friends.

Chapter 7

Joe wondered about Carl as he crossed the casino. Shopping done? An hour and a half ago? That meant it was done in less than an hour. Was he in someone else's room? Not at all like Carl. But that left the casino, and that seemed unlikely, too. Should he call? They all had their cell phones, but maybe they shouldn't be using them. The people that were being arrested in Kentucky right now, the organized crime people, were people who the state police thought might want to do them harm. They might also be able to access their cell phone locations since some of them at least were police back there. He would ask Natalie. She was police back home too, and she would know how likely that was, and whether it would be a problem. Carl could take care of himself, Joe decided.

He looked around him at the casino. He was walking between the slots and the tables and noise was coming from both. The excitement of winning or losing came from both sides, and the cacophony of the machines was coming from the slots. There were no coins used anymore, except for some quarter and nickel machines that would accept these ancient relics. Everyone put bills in, and was given a credit. When they cashed out they were given a ticket. These tickets could be exchanged for cash, but usually were put into another machine. In spite of the fact that no coins were used, the machines still produced the sound of the phantom coins dropping into the pan at the bottom of each machine. People had gotten used to that, and he suspected that casinos didn't thrive on quiet and restful ambiance.

He was exiting the casino area and was facing the shops on the other side. As Janet had predicted, he was only one shop down from a boutique with a neon sign announcing the name *All About You*, although the script was so ornate that he might not have known that was the name if he had not been warned.

He drifted towards his left, looking for the next likely stop for Carolyn and Natalie. He thought Carolyn would be in charge, but wasn't sure.

Natalie was an interesting person; fascinating, he would say. He was not sure that he would end up marrying her, but he was sure that he would like to know her better. The fact that she had saved his life had made him think seriously about her, but lasting relationships were based on much more superficial things than this. Where two people wanted to live, for instance, was more important than who saved whose life.

He passed *The Game Starts Here*, which was not worth a second look, nor was *Man's Best Shoes*. Next was one titled *The Witches' Cauldron*. It seemed out of place here with its eerie display of dragons and knights, until he saw the display of lucky charms and amulets surrounded by those eager buyers wishing better luck, he supposed. Next was jewelry. If they were serious about *breaking the Reg,* they would be here.

He saw them almost at once when he stepped inside. A young saleslady, wearing more jewelry than clothing, he thought, appeared immediately, but he motioned toward Carolyn and Natalie and walked away from her. She was already looking for a replacement customer.

"How are you two doing?" he asked.

"Oh, Joe," said Carolyn. "Which do you think looks best on me? This is a little large, but I like the shape. And this one is more ornate, but it's silver."

"Silver *plate*," said Natalie. The young man standing by to help with their purchase frowned slightly at this remark.

"It's not solid gold, either," offered Carolyn.

"Well, of course not," said the salesman, frowning a little more deeply.

"Get them both," shrugged Natalie.

The frown turned into a broad smile. "They're well worth the price," the salesman said.

"They look nice," said Joe, shrugging.

This earned him a frown from the young man, but Joe smiled, saying, "The gold is understated, and could be worn to an interview without seeming out of place. The silver is more appropriate for an evening party."

"You see, Carolyn?" said Natalie. "You will need both."

She turned to the salesman and said, "She'll take both, along with the bracelets and earrings to match. Here's my room key for mine, and here is Carolyn's." She pulled it out of her purse to hand it to him.

The young man beamed. He was probably on commission, just as Janet was. Probably all the salespeople here were.

"I'm exhausted," said Carolyn.

"Don't fade on me yet," said Natalie. "We only have one pair of shoes apiece, and I want at least three-inch heels for tonight."

"You'll have to carry me back to the room," said Carolyn.

"I'll have them deliver you up there with the shoes if you want, but if you don't come with me I'll buy yours myself, just to make you look uglier than I do, so suck it up."

"Can you walk in three-inch heels, Natalie?" asked Joe.

"Not yet," she replied. "Are you all done, Joe?"

"Yes. I even got some jeans to go hiking in."

"Hiking?" asked Natalie.

"That sounds like fun," said Carolyn. "Or horseback riding, maybe."

"Well, maybe horseback riding," said Natalie. "Hiking reminds me of the time I spent in the army."

"Have you seen Carl?" asked Joe. He was having trouble figuring these two out. Natalie was the one who was supposed to like hiking.

"No," said Carolyn. "He must still be shopping."

"Hasn't bought anything in an hour and a half," said Joe with a shrug.

They both looked at him and he said, "I'll explain later. Natalie, I was wondering about our cell phones. Can anyone trace them? Someone like the people involved with Chief of Police Andy Wilson, back in Kentucky? If we use them, will they know we're here?"

Natalie frowned. "They might be able to do that even if we're not using them."

Carolyn and Joe looked quizzically at her. "Well, that's what the *cells* in *cell phones* are. When I call you, there's a computer that searches all the five- or six-mile radius cells spread across the world to find which one your phone is in. The computers are what make cell phones possible."

"Then maybe we shouldn't use them," suggested Joe.

"We don't have to use them for someone to locate us, to locate the cell we're in. If they call us, the computer will find our phone whether we answer it or not."

"What if they're turned off?" asked Carolyn.

"I don't think so," said Natalie. "I'm not sure."

"Well turn them off now, and since I have no more shopping to do, I'll find a place where I can rent some phones for us while we're here."

"Or buy them," said Natalie.

"I'll rent if I can," smiled Joe.

The salesman returned with slips to be signed and beamed at them. "If you can just sign here," he said.

"Can you have these taken to our room, please?" asked Natalie, handing the packages to him. "Where could we find a place to buy cell phones?"

"Or rent them," said Joe.

"Three doors down," he smiled. "Ask for Margery. She'll take good care of you."

"I'll get the phones and meet you in the room," said Joe. "When you're done shopping."

The ladies headed off down the row of shops, and Joe ambled a little more slowly, looking casually for the cell phone store and Margery. It wasn't three, but four doors down. Margery was there, and was pierced and tattooed, and she suggested renting cell phones. "Good deals on that," she said.

Joe couldn't believe she would get as large a commission on rentals as on purchases. She even pointed out that if the phones had any problems, it would be better if he had purchased them in his local store, from his local carrier, so renting was better here. Such honesty made Joe wish he could disregard her advice and buy them from her. He almost did when he realized that back home they would pay with their own money, and here it was Reggie who would pay. He handed her his room key and she ran it through her register.

"The new numbers are consecutive, so ya want me ta put the numbers inta the address book for ya?"

"That would be very helpful," replied Joe.

"These for the people with you?"

"Yes."

"So I'll make you the first number: Joe, on all the other phones. Who's next?"

"I'm not sure."

"Ya married ta one of these ladies?" asked Margery, looking at his wedding ring.

"Oh, yeah, of course. Carolyn should be next I guess."

"Good move, dude." Her purple fingernails moved incredibly fast over the phone's keyboard. "So who's next? Natalie or Carl?"

Joe smiled. "Natalie," he said.

"Yeah," said Margery. "She's way cuter than Carl is."

She winked at Joe and put the phones into a bag.

"So, can someone find out say … where this phone is?" he asked, holding up his old phone. "Can they track it on the *cell system,* or whatever it's called?"

"Network? Oh, yeah, sure," Margery replied. "If they can get on the computer. I can't and you can't, but *Big Brother* can. Ya know, like the police. Tell what *cell* you're in. If ya got GPS in it, like all the G3 and 4's do, they can tell what bathroom stall you're usin'." She giggled, which made her spiked red hair bounce just a little.

"If I've activated the GPS option on the phone," said Joe.

"Even if you haven't," smiled Margery. When Joe looked surprised she added, "They can turn it on from the big computer, dude. That's what they do when ya pay for it, after all."

"Yeah. I guess that's right. But if the phone's turned off it's okay, right?"

"Maybe," offered Margery with a smile, raising her pierced eyebrows. "Pull the plug is the best way."

"The plug?"

"The battery," she said, and shrugged. "Just take out the battery and the thing is like totally dead, man."

"Yeah," said Joe, signing his receipt. "I'll do that. Thanks, Margery."

"Maggie," she said. "That's a pretty cool shirt you got, dude."

"What?" asked Joe.

"The stains on the collar and sleeve. Pretty cool." She smiled and said, "I went with this guy who had a shirt, looked just like that, only the stains were real blood. He was some kinda weird old punk rocker or something. Too much for me, quiet little Maggie; but it was fun while it lasted. 'Til he got inta the drugs an' violence too much."

"Really?" said Joe, touching the collar where the stains that looked like blood were. He was a pediatrician, and he had worked in the emergency department too, so he was used to the drugs and violence that were the background of many people's lives. But he had never accepted it.

"Yeah," Maggie said. "I got this tattoo ta cover a scar where he cut me. I think he was trying to kill me."

She touched her neck and an elaborate tattoo and shrugged. "Hell, I was only sixteen an' he musta been like thirty or forty or somethin'."

Forty like Joe was himself. He could feel the pediatrician rising in him. "How old are you now?"

Maggie smiled and winked. "Twenty-two," she said, as she pushed the slip over to him. "Have ta be ta work here. You're a doctor? That's cool. That's not really blood, is it?"

"No," said Joe. "Of course not."

"Still pretty cool," said Maggie. "What kinda doctor are you?"

"Pediatrician," said Joe.

"No shit," said Maggie.

"No shit," said Joe. "I've only told one lie so far today."

Maggie smiled and asked, "What was that?"

"I'll take the batteries out," he said, picking up the bag she had placed on the counter.

Maggie smiled and looked like she could be one of his patients. "So, what was that lie you told. You really are a pediatrician, aren't you?"

"Yeah, I'm really a pediatrician," Joe said, touching the stain on his shirt collar.

"Oh my God," said Maggie. "Is that really blood?!"

Chapter 8

Joe walked out of the store and was facing the casino again. He was uncomfortable with Las Vegas, and all the underlying violence and sexuality that lay behind the glitz and masquerade he was looking at. How old was Maggie, he wondered? Was it really as bad as Janet had said it was? Was it any different anywhere else, or was Las Vegas just more honest about it?

The patrons were having fun while they lost their money. The casino employees were looking intense; for them this was serious business. The male employees wore suits, or long-sleeved shirts and ties and vests, while the women wore clothing meant to display cleavage and thighs. None were of such a physical form that made their attire anything except flattering.

The dealers were equally male and female, but while the males varied in age from young to middle-aged, the females were all young. He began to wonder if all this was just him, or was there really a sexist, violent and abusive culture underlying the beautiful city of Las Vegas. He didn't want to go up to his room and brood alone, and he did think that he ought to find Carl to assure himself that he was in fact safe. When he looked around it was not Carl he saw, but James Monroe.

"Good afternoon, Dr. Nelson. I hope you got some shopping in."

"Yes, I did," said Joe, suddenly aware that his shirt was stained and he hadn't changed it yet. James had seen him earlier. "I haven't had a chance to change yet."

"Busy place." James nodded. "I'm looking for one of your companions."

"Carolyn or Natalie?" asked Joe.

"No," said James. "Ah, here he's." Carl was waving and got up immediately. He had been sitting at one of the slot machines and cashed out when he saw them, taking a card from the machine along with the slip it produced. He walked toward them holding the slip and the card which said Player's Club on it.

"Thank you for coming," said Carl. "I have a few questions about these slot machines."

"Yes?" said James. "They're really quite simple."

"Yes. They randomly show symbols in the window, correct?"

"That's how they work," smiled James indulgently. "And the right combination of symbols produces a jackpot of varying size."

"But they're supposed to be random," persisted Carl. "Those symbols are supposed to be random, and the jackpots as well?"

"That's correct," said James, with a look that said his patience was being tried right now.

"How do you know that's true?" asked Carl.

"The manufacturers assure us that's the case, but of course, the Gaming Commission verifies that they're random as well. They're the final judge of all gambling in this city."

"What do they verify, Mr. Monroe? Do they verify that all the symbols appear randomly, or just the jackpots?"

"I am not an expert on what they verify. They do not publicize their exact method, only that the machines have the required payback, I believe. They may also verify that the machine has not been tampered with."

"But not the distribution of payoffs or the randomness of non-paying occurrences."

"I am not really that familiar with what they check, only that they do check regularly and are satisfied with what they find. They have a website if you wish to contact them directly."

"Yes. Yes. I'll do that," said Carl. "Thank you, Mr. Monroe."

"You're quite welcome, and good luck."

"Have you been playing the slot machines, Carl?" asked Joe.

"A little," said Carl. "You see, I was just watching some others, and it seemed to me that there were occurrences that were not entirely random. I'm in the process of verifying that myself."

"Do be careful," said James.

"Yes," echoed Joe. "People have lost a great deal of money doing what you're doing."

"Other people," said Carl. "I'm just investigating. Is there a bookstore where I might buy a book on this, and maybe a notebook to take down some of my observations?"

"Oh, there's one," said Carl, before either could answer. "I'll see you later, Joe."

"Here's a new cell phone I rented for you, Carl. Take the battery out of yours so it can't be traced to us."

"What?" said Carl.

"Just give me your cell phone and take this one," replied Joe. "I think the ladies will be anxious to get to supper soon."

"Yes, of course," said Carl, walking off toward the bookstore.

"I do hope—" said James.

"So do I," replied Joe. "I have a couple of questions too. Can I ask them over some coffee?"

James nodded and smiled. There was a café next to them with tables inside, and a few along the front where one could watch the shoppers walking by and the gaming beyond. They sat at one of the outside tables. The waiter appeared immediately, and obviously recognized James, who just nodded. He took an order for coffee from Joe and left without asking James what he would like, probably because he already knew.

"So, what are your questions, Dr. Nelson?" asked James. "Not about slot machines I hope. I also hope your friend has not been seduced by the allure of the *game*."

"It's not at all like Carl," said Joe. "I'll talk to him, but my question is about the age requirement for employment here."

"The age requirement? You're not thinking of applying for a job I hope."

"No, of course not. Not unless I have to work off Carl's losses at the slots. But is there an age requirement?"

"Yes there is: twenty-one. There are really only a few places here that younger people can legally be employed. The casino, and the bars and restaurants where alcohol is served cannot employ them, and the employees move their positions frequently to cover shifts. It's ... well, it's easier if they're all over twenty-one."

The waiter returned with Joe's coffee and a cappuccino for James, who looked at him and smiled. "Not doing valet today, Peter?"

"No, Mr. Monroe. Sally's sick, so I'm filling in. Shall I put this on you, Mr. Monroe?"

"No," said Joe. "Put this one on me." He handed his room key to Peter who, after a moment of puzzled hesitation, departed.

When James looked at Joe he said, "I'm not paying anyway. How closely are employees scrutinized? I mean, is it possible that people younger than twenty-one might *sneak* in?"

James frowned a little. "The scrutiny of employees is fairly comprehensive. Not impossible, but difficult. Nothing is impossible, of course."

Joe nodded silently.

"Is there a particular problem?" asked James.

"No," said Joe, realizing that to say otherwise might be trouble for Maggie.

James considered this answer for a moment, clearly not convinced. "You see, the corporation," he gestured to the building around him, "is more interested in protecting itself than protecting the underage workers. If they can prove that they were misled by the employee, they would be absolved of responsibility. That's all they really wish."

"No concern ...?" Joe let the sentence hang.

James thought for a moment. "I'm African American. My family were slaves. I have Native American blood and I'm told Latino blood, left over from when this all belonged to Mexico. My father died of tuberculosis because he was not permitted to enter a sanatorium for treatment. My mother was raped by a white man, but no charge was ever brought. She was not a member of an important race."

He mused a little now. "When I was a child, I remember reading about Billy the Kid, the famous *white* outlaw, famous and celebrated. He was said to have killed twenty-one men; but the book dismissed this, saying that eighteen were Indians, as if that made the accomplishment of no consequence."

Joe waited quietly. James was obviously not finished.

"Do you know why I was hired here, Dr. Nelson?"

"No."

"Of course you wouldn't. Because I'm *black*. That was what my race was called back when I was hired, and the staffing department thought that guests would like to have *black* people parking their cars for them. I was what Peter is now." He looked at the waiter bringing another order to a nearby table.

"I had a college degree when I was hired. When they needed to have a racially mixed staff, to prove they were not the bigots that they were and still are, I was moved about, and finally I'm here. My boss, Robert Bevins, isn't burdened with an education, so he has risen while I …" He was silent for a moment.

"I met Robert Bevins earlier today," said Joe.

"Ah," said James. "And did you notice that he's a bigot and a sexist pig?"

"I noticed he was a sexist pig," smiled Joe. "It was only a brief encounter, but the observation didn't tax my powers of deduction very much." James chuckled a little.

Joe looked across the casino and his gaze settled on one of the dealers, a blond lady, pretty, and maybe thirty or thirty five. She wore too much makeup he thought, and of course she wore the cleavage- and leg-displaying uniform all the ladies wore.

James followed his gaze. "Yes," he said. "It's probably worse for the women. At least it's worse if your boss is named Bevins. You can ask Tyla." He motioned toward the lady they were looking at. She seemed to know they were looking, and maybe that they were talking about her. She smiled at them; smiled at James, really. She had no way of knowing Joe.

"Are all the hotels as bad?"

"I don't know," smiled James. "But people come from other hotels to work here."

Joe paused for a minute and then asked, "Do you enjoy working here, Mr. Monroe?"

James considered this question and the man who was asking it before answering. "No," he said.

"And yet ...?"

"I was not aware that my enjoyment was required, or even of any concern. I was under the impression that that's why they pay me. I assure you that if they didn't pay me, I would not be here."

"I have always hoped that I would want to do my job, and that being paid would be an additional enjoyment," said Joe.

"I had that hope as well," said James. "When I was younger and more naive. Thank you for the coffee."

With this he got up and left the table. Peter returned Joe's room key and asked for a signature and then he too left, leaving a confused Joe sitting there alone. Carolyn and Natalie were enjoying spending someone else's money while Carl was wasting his own. Janet and Maggie and even James Monroe were victims of the same system. Every one of them was caught in the seductive trap of this city, and right now Joe wished he had never come here in the first place, regardless of how dangerous it might have been back in Kentucky.

Chapter 9

Joe was more than restless now and had to do something to bring reality and sanity back. First, change his bloody shirt, he decided. If he was going to forget the murders and the airport lobby in Kentucky, he had better get rid of it altogether. He walked through the casino and as he passed the table where Tyla stood he stopped, on an impulse only. She was alone; her table open, but with no players at that moment.

"James Monroe said you were one of the finest dealers around. Tyla, is it?"

"Yes, it's Tyla. I'm not sure James would know who deals well and who doesn't. This isn't part of his responsibility," she replied warily.

"He said that I should talk to you," said Joe. "What game is it that one would play at this table, and how is it played?"

"He said that?" Tyla looked even more skeptical. "The game here is blackjack, and I can show you better than tell you." She pointed to a sign that said: "Blackjack, ten dollar minimum."

Joe pulled out some money and asked, "Do I give it to you, or do I have to get chips or something first?"

"If the bills are small enough I can take them. Chances are, if you don't know at least that much, you'll not have anything I can't take."

When Joe tried to hand her a twenty dollar bill, she smiled and pointed to the table in front of her. "I can't take it directly from you. You have to put it down first. Are you counting on winning, or is this going to be a short lesson?"

"Let's see what happens," said Joe as he placed the bill on the table.

She placed four chips in front of him.

Joe looked and then asked, "If the bet is ten dollars, why are the chips five dollars? I can't bet five dollars."

"You'll see," smiled Tyla. "So, ten dollars," she said, pointing to a spot on the felt table with cards printed on it, and Joe placed two chips on it.

"Now I get a card and you get a card face down, and then one each face up. The object of the game is to get twenty-one. Do you know the value of the cards?"

"The numbers are what they are," said Joe, "and the picture cards are ten, right? And the ace is eleven or—"

"Or one, whichever you want. The dealer has to count it high if he can. If he has a low enough hand to take eleven." Joe looked puzzled, and Tyla continued. "With only two cards, the dealer has to take eleven, so a five and an ace will always be sixteen for the dealer, but you can take a hit if you want."

"But you can, too," said Joe.

"No," said Tyla. "The dealer doesn't have a choice. Sixteen or less takes a hit, and higher than sixteen stands … for the dealer. The player can choose, the dealer cannot."

"That doesn't seem fair," said Joe.

"It evens up," said Tyla. "Ties go to the dealer, but if the player gets blackjack, an ace and a black jack to make twenty-one, he gets one and a half times his bet. So look at your card. You can turn it over, and then you can raise your bet if you want. After that, you say whether you want another card. Most people do that with a signal, and the dealers want you to do it that way to avoid any confusion, so do it that way. A tap on the table means you want a card, and a wave over your cards means you don't want a card: you want to *stand* or *sit* or *stay*. They all mean the same thing."

Joe turned his card over. A ten and a king. "I could try to get an ace," he smiled. "But since I'm new at this, I guess I'll stand." He waved his hand over his cards.

Tyla turned her card over; seventeen. "Player wins," she said.

Joe reached towards his chips as he said, "Can't you take a hit?" "Don't touch your chips until I've paid," said Tyla. "And no, the dealer can't. The dealer has to do whatever the rules say. No flexibility."

"Is that fair?" asked Joe, returning his hands to the edge of the table.

"Very fair," said Tyla. "The rules for the dealer are based on the odds. This has been thoroughly studied, I assure you. If you have over sixteen, the odds are you'll win, and with less than sixteen, you'll lose.

"One more thing and you're an expert," she added. "If the player gets two identical cards, two twos, or two tens or two queens, or whatever, he can double down or split—take another card on each and play them separately. But he has to put in another ten bucks." She pointed to the sign announcing the minimum.

"So, shall we play?" she asked.

"Okay," said Joe.

They did and Joe won, up to forty; lost down to thirty; then won twice and was up to fifty. It was just him and Tyla at the table, until Robert Bevins came over.

"Only one player, Tyla. You scaring them away?"

"I'm being my usual charming self, Mr. Bevins."

"Hello, Mr. Bevins," said Joe. "We meet yet again. Tyla was just teaching me the game so as to allow me to leave some of my money with you."

"Oh, Dr. …"

"Nelson," said Joe, extending his hand.

Robert Bevins took it and said, "From the shop with Janet. Yes, you spent a lot there."

"It's a big house," said Joe. "Needs a lot of support." He cast a gaze at the vaulted ceilings above him.

"Well, enjoy," said Robert, "and keep up the good work, Tyla. See you later maybe."

"Not if it can be avoided," said Tyla softly as Robert walked away.

"I've heard he's a prick," said Joe.

Tyla's face shot up and she said, "From whom did you hear that? James?"

"No," said Joe. "So, ten is the minimum. What's the maximum?'

"I can cover up to a hundred before I call the pit boss," she smiled.

"The pit boss isn't Robert Bevins is it?"

"No."

"Then fifty," he said, placing all his chips on the square in front of him.

Tyla dealt: fifteen for Joe, fourteen for the dealer. Joe stayed, and Tyla took a card, a king, and she added fifty dollars to Joe's stack.

"Do you call the pit boss now or next hand?"

"Next hand ... if you win."

She dealt, and then she had to call the pit boss. "Betting two hundred?" asked the man.

Joe nodded. Tyla dealt; fourteen for Joe. He looked and then waved his hand, indicating no card. Both the pit boss and Tyla looked at him, but he waved again, and Tyla turned over her card to show twelve. She took a hit, another king, and Joe was now at four hundred.

Joe nodded and left the money where it was, and then the pit boss nodded and Tyla stepped aside to let him deal. There were a few people gathered in back of Joe now.

The cards went down; sixteen for Joe. He looked, and then tapped the table for a hit. There was a gasp from the crowd as a three went down: nineteen. Joe waved off another hit and the dealer showed his card; seventeen, and Joe had eight hundred dollars in front of him.

He looked and nodded again. The pit boss smiled, and the now three-deep crowd murmured a mixture of approval and amazement.

The cards went down; fourteen for Joe. He looked, and then waved off the hit. The dealer turned his cards: fourteen again, and he had to take the card Joe had refused, a jack. He smiled and made the stack in front of Joe sixteen hundred dollars as applause and a little cheer came from the crowd.

Joe pulled the chips to him and asked, "How do I get this changed back into money? Real money I mean."

"I'll color you out," said the pit boss, "and you can get them changed at any of the windows." He began making neat stacks of the chips as the crowd dissipated, one or two slapping Joe on the back as they left. When the stacks were made, they were exchanged for more colorful hundred-dollar chips.

"Can I leave a tip?" asked Joe.

"Yes," smiled the pit boss. Joe put a hundred-dollar chip in front of him and pocketed the rest. The pit boss gave him change: five-dollar chips, twenty of them. This was the correct thing to do. Never assume that the customer won't want the change. Always allow for whatever tip the customer wanted to leave. This man was a professional.

Joe made two even stacks and then pushed one toward each of them, Tyla and the pit boss. After a nod from the pit boss, Tyla placed her fifty-dollar tip to the side of the table. She had no pockets in her uniform.

After another moment, the pit boss added his stack to hers and said, "The dealer gets the tips."

She smiled and said, "Thanks."

"That was interesting, but this doesn't look much like a *pit*," said Joe to the man.

"It can be," he replied. "Particularly when people are losing."

"Oh," said Joe. "Sorry if I kept too much of your money."

Tyla was surprised at this sentiment, but the pit boss just smiled. "Those people in that crowd will be trying to duplicate your move all night long. We'll get back ten times what you're taking with you on that alone. The only way we lose is if people don't play."

He smiled more broadly and said, "That must be your lucky shirt. Those coffee stains on your shirt?"

"Yeah," said Joe. "This is the luckiest shirt I've ever owned."

The pit boss chuckled as Tyla smiled, saying, "And I thought you were just hitting on me."

Joe looked pensive and said, "I wish I'd thought of that before we started playing." Then he smiled, winked, and walked away.

Chapter 10

Joe felt as if he, too, had been seduced by this city as he entered his room. Carl was nowhere to be found, and he decided to change before looking for Carolyn and Natalie. He found his clothing in his room and looked next door to see if Carl had really done any shopping. He had, although his purchases all seemed to be the same clothes he was already wearing: dress shirts and tan slacks and one sport jacket. Joe congratulated himself on his choices. His and Janet's, that is.

He took off his shirt and pants, putting both in a drawer in the dresser. He wasn't sure, but he thought he would keep the shirt. It *was* the luckiest one he'd ever owned. Brought him fifteen hundred dollars and, oh yes; his life. He would keep it just as it was.

He showered and dressed. It had been early morning when they'd arrived, but it was now approaching supper. They had last eaten on the private jet that brought them here, except for the snack tray in the room, and suddenly he felt hungry. He couldn't call their cell phones, but decided to try their room. When he picked up the phone he noticed the message light was blinking, but he called the other suite first anyway, assuming it was a message from them.

Carolyn answered, "Hello."

"Hi," said Joe. "You ready for something to eat?"

"Oh, hi, Joe. We're dressing and showering and … well, that may take a little time. Where is Carl?"

"He's figuring out how to win at the slots," chuckled Joe.

"Carl?" said an incredulous voice.

"Carl," said Joe. "And he's taking it very seriously, too. Buying a book, and taking notes."

"Oh, that's just Carl. He knows no one ever wins at any of those games."

"Someone must win once in a while," said Joe.

"Never," replied Carolyn with certainty.

Joe shrugged, although she couldn't see it. "I have your new cell phones," he said.

"Oh, great," replied Carolyn. "I feel naked without a cell. I am naked, as a matter of fact. I'm on my way to the shower. Natalie's decent though, so drop them down here, okay?"

"Yes," said Joe and hung up, thinking of Carolyn naked. It was a pleasant thought. He remembered the message, and wondered if it had been Carolyn or Natalie. Carolyn probably would have mentioned it, if it were she. Maybe Carl? Maybe just listen to it?

When he did, the voice of James Monroe said, "My apologies for my boring tirade. To compensate for that, let me offer you a dinner at the Golden Nugget in the old town. Fremont Street is where Las Vegas was born, and where some believe it still displays its best. I believe that no one can say they have been to Las Vegas without spending an evening there. The dinner vouchers will be waiting at the front desk if you want them."

Yes, thought Joe. Maybe they did want them. He walked down the hall to the other suite and briefly thought about letting himself in with his key, but remembered that Carolyn at least was naked, and wasn't sure what she considered "decent" for Natalie. Possibly it wasn't what Natalie considered "decent." He knocked.

Natalie answered, and was decent. She was smiling and wearing a dress, the first Joe had seen her wear, and looked very decent indeed. The dress showed a lovely figure and stopped modestly above her knees to show lovely legs as well, but no shoes. Her hair was pulled back but only loosely, and there was little or no makeup.

"Here are the new cell phones," Joe said, handing them to her.

"Oh, thank you, Joe," she said. "You're so sweet." With this she stood on her tiptoes and kissed him on the cheek.

"Come in," she said, turning back into the room. "Carolyn and I are splitting the champagne, and if you don't have some, we'll both be drunk before we leave for supper."

She sat on the couch, picked up her half-full glass and crossed her beautiful legs beneath her. "I'm enjoying this a little. Not what I thought I would ever like to do, but … are you enjoying it, Joe?"

"Some," he said. "It's a strange place, if you pay attention to what's going on around you."

"That's a strange thing to say. Have some champagne." She motioned toward a half-full bottle, and Joe went over and poured a glass.

He sat opposite her and smiled at himself. "It was a strange thing to say."

"You don't have to be that agreeable," she said, taking a sip of the champagne.

Carolyn came out of her room at this point, wet and wrapped in a towel. "I didn't know you were here, Joe. Just came out to get my champagne."

She smiled and added, "You're dressed up tonight, Joseph. Did you do that yourself?"

"Janet helped me pick out the clothes."

"Janet?" said Carolyn.

"The clerk in the clothing store," Joe replied with a shrug.

"Oh," said Carolyn. She picked up a glass of champagne, which caused her towel to slip, showing a little more of her breasts. She didn't seem to notice, but Natalie did, and looked to see if Joe had, too.

"I'll be dressed in a minute, and then we can do the hair and makeup. You'll have to be in charge of that, Natalie," said Carolyn. "I've never been good with either." With this she disappeared back into her room.

"I've never been good with it either, but maybe together, Carolyn," said Natalie to the closed door.

She turned again to Joe and said, "She's beautiful, so that will help."

"Yes," said Joe absently. When he came back to himself he added, "And you are too, so that will help."

"Thank you," said Natalie, raising her glass. "I wasn't really fishing for a compliment, but thank you."

After a moment she asked, "Do you love her, Joe?"

Joe should have been surprised by the question, but somehow he wasn't. "Yes," he said. "I'll probably always love her, even if I'm not married to her. Love her as a friend, I mean."

"More than a friend, maybe?" said Natalie. "Carolyn thinks you should be divorced. What do you think, Joe?"

"I think that Carolyn thinks we should be divorced. More than that doesn't matter."

"Yes it does," said Natalie.

"Not really," smiled Joe. "I cannot force her to stay in a marriage. Someone else maybe, but certainly not Carolyn. I don't think I would want to try, even if I could. In fact, I think that I think she's right."

"You sound pretty certain, that you think you think that," smiled Natalie. Her face became serious and she looked away. "It's an important question for me right now, Joe."

"It's important for me, too," he said. "I think there are important things we can do with our lives. We can join the army and defend our country." He nodded toward Natalie, who had done that. "We can practice pediatrics in an underserved area in eastern Kentucky. Or we can become surgeon general and help set the country on the right track with its healthcare program. Carolyn will be very good at that last one, and not so good at the first one."

Natalie chuckled a little. "She might become a general of the army if she tried that. Joint chiefs or something. But couldn't you … you know …?"

"Prolong the relationship and learn to hate it? Me stifling in Washington or Carolyn running back to Kentucky for a weekend every few months? How long would it take before we hated the marriage and hated each other? I would rather love my former wife than hate her." He shrugged now. "And then there's Natalie. She's lovely, and I would like to know her better; maybe know her a lot better."

"And I would like to know Joe better than I do. What I have seen so far has impressed me."

"Not as impressive as what I've seen of Natalie."

"The airport? It was you who told me to take that chance. To try to shoot around you to stop the bastard who killed little Linda."

"And it was you who did it."

"If you and Carolyn decide to get divorced ..." began Natalie.

"Pretty much decided," finished Joe. "And if we decide to get divorced, will Natalie be interested in Joe?"

"Natalie is already interested in Joe. Natalie just doesn't want to steal her friend Carolyn's husband, if there's any possibility that her marriage might continue. And furthermore, Natalie doesn't want to get involved—you can read *married* for *get involved*—if that means she will have to share Joe with her friend Carolyn." Natalie frowned and looked at her champagne glass. "Does any of that make sense?"

"Yes," said Joe. "If it gets that far, Joe will be a friend to Carolyn and married to Natalie, because you know how he feels about fidelity."

"I find that endearing, Joe. Refreshingly endearing these days. And Natalie can wait, but if Joe and Natalie are married, she will be more demanding."

"If Natalie decides to marry Joe, I don't think that will be a problem."

"What will not be a problem?" asked Carolyn, walking in from her room. She wore a dress of flowered prints contesting well with her blond hair and showing her very favorably.

Natalie blushed slightly, but Joe said, "The makeup and hair. Your cell phones are here, and all our numbers are in the address book. Don't forget to pull the plugs on your old cells."

"Pull the plug?" asked Natalie.

"Take out the battery," smiled Joe. "That's what Maggie said."

"Maggie?" asked Carolyn.

"Shall I wait for you here, or downstairs? Will this be a few minutes or a few hours?"

"Minutes," said Carolyn. When Natalie looked at her she added, "Sixty or seventy or possibly eighty minutes. Men are all alike. They expect you to be beautiful, but don't see why you have to take any time to do it."

Natalie looked at Joe. "They're not all alike."

"No," said Carolyn. "Some are worse than others."

"Doesn't that mean that some are better than others?" asked Natalie.

"No," replied Carolyn, and she kissed Joe on his cheek. "Wait downstairs, Joe."

She looked at him and added, "Wipe that lipstick off before we go out. And the lipstick better be Natalie's, not Janet's or Maggie's."

She turned and winked at Natalie as she said, "Come on, girl. Let's get started. Could take a while for you to make me beautiful."

"See you in a few, Joe," said Natalie, kissing him on his cheek as she passed. "Better wipe all those off."

 *Chapter 11*

Joe smiled. Maybe this evening would be good after all; two lovely ladies … and Carl, if he could find him and pry him away from the slot machines. If he couldn't, he would just have to escort two ladies himself to Fremont Street. He remembered as he exited the elevator that he hadn't mentioned Fremont Street to Carolyn or Natalie, and that he hadn't changed his chips into cash. He decided to pick up the vouchers anyway, and convince them they wanted to go when they came downstairs. They would be hungry by then, and more likely to want to go anywhere to eat.

First he changed his winnings to cash, and then went looking for the vouchers. When he asked at the front desk, he also asked for the limo to be called. The young man who produced the vouchers smiled and said, "You're a bit overdressed for Fremont Street, sir."

Joe looked at his sport jacket, dress shirt and tie and asked, "Really?"

The young man shrugged. "A little bit. You may find the tie will not be necessary."

"It will be for the ladies I'm accompanying, and they're more important to please than Fremont Street."

The young man's smile broadened and he said, "That's always true. The company is always more important, even here in Las Vegas. When shall I ask that the limousine be here?"

"Half an hour maybe," said Joe.

"It will be waiting out front. Have a good time tonight. After this place, Fremont is my favorite."

Joe smiled and left to see if he could find Carl. He called the phone and was surprised when Carl answered immediately. "Are you ready for dinner?"

"Oh, yes," said Carl.

"Where are you?"

"At the slots," said Carl. It didn't sound to Joe as if Carl was paying full attention to him.

"Have you changed? The ladies and I have."

"Yes. I scooted up a few minutes ago. I'll wait here until you're ready."

"Where are you, Carl?"

"Oh, I'm … there's a neon sign that says something about wheels and twenty-five cents," replied Carl.

"I see it," said Joe. "Wait there for me."

He closed the phone and walked toward the sign. Carl was sitting at a slot, his book open and his notebook in his hand. "Hi, Joe. This is fascinating!"

"Are you winning or losing?"

"Losing, of course. But I think I'm learning how these things work. It's not all that it appears to be."

"Like I said, Carl: you just put your money in and forget about it. The house always wins if you play." Joe thought of the pit boss and his comment from earlier that evening. *The house only loses when the people don't play.*

"How much have you lost?"

"Well," said Carl, "my ATM card limits me to a five hundred dollar withdrawal a day, so that's all I have to lose. Just about done now, so I'll have to wait until tomorrow. Where are the girls?"

"Soon," said Joe. "You've lost five hundred dollars, Carl?"

"No. I had about two hundred in cash with me, so that's seven hundred. I wouldn't be nearly as far along with this project as I am now, if I hadn't had that extra two hundred." Carl had not stopped playing since Joe arrived.

"I thought you said you changed your clothes, Carl?"

"I did."

"You look the same. Your clothes, I mean."

"Of course," said Carl, looking at Joe for the first time since he arrived at the slot machine. "I bought the same clothes as I always wear. I think I look rather good that way."

"All men think that," said Joe, echoing Janet's comment.

There was noise around them, but a familiar voice rose above the noise now. "I told you I didn't want to see you here until you pay, Harry."

It was Robert Bevins, and he was talking to a bearded and poorly dressed man of about forty, or maybe older. It was hard to tell.

The man seemed to know Robert. "I got to get a little more …"

"No," replied Robert Bevins.

"I got money …" he tried again.

"You don't need to get anything, not here and not now. Move it!" replied Robert.

Harry looked as if he were about to speak, but Robert cut him off. "Move it, Harry."

Harry moved toward the door, and the small crowd gathered didn't seem upset, much less were they inclined to defend Harry in this conflict. When Robert turned away he saw Joe, and his frown immediately turned into a smile. He nodded, and went back towards the gaming tables.

"That man was interesting," said Carl.

"Robert Bevins, the manager?" asked Joe.

"Is that his name? No, I meant the other one. Harry, did he call him?"

"You know him?"

"Not really, but he was playing a lot this afternoon and we chatted. He seems to think there's a system here as well. I'm not sure he's going about investigating properly though."

"Not like you are," said Joe.

"No, definitely not. He lost considerably more than I, I think."

There was another voice raised above the din of the gambling. This time a young man was standing in front of one of the slots yelling, cursing and kicking the machine.

It was required where Joe worked for all personnel to be trained in "Non-Violent Intervention." Joe had taken those classes, but his instructors could have learned from the security in this hotel in Las Vegas.

Within seconds this man was surrounded by three security officers and two hotel management personnel. Every limb was firmly held and he was being told to calm down and allow himself to be escorted, or the police would be called. So efficiently had this been done that it would have been impossible for him to injure himself or anyone else.

"This fuckin' machine ..." he began, but was cut short as James Monroe took charge.

"Please control yourself, and allow us to help you get to an exit, sir. If you do not allow that to happen, I'll call the police, and they may not deal with you as gently as we're prepared to do. How much have you lost, sir?"

"My whole fuckin' paycheck!"

"Here is fifty dollars, sir," said James, handing him the bills. "I'm keeping your Players Club card, and I must warn you that you're not to return here in the future." The man was already being carried as much as he was walking toward the exit.

"I'm sorry, man."

"So am I," said James. "Did you park your car with the valets?"

"Yeah."

"The ticket please," said James, as they went through the exit door. "I'll wait with you to ensure that you're safely in your car. Perhaps you could wait with us, Nathan," he added to the largest of the security officers.

Joe was fascinated. Yes, his hospital could learn a great deal from the Las Vegas non-violent intervention. Enough force, quickly applied, had avoided any possibility of injury to anyone. And now when the situation was defused, the force was dissipating by design, not by the random drifting away of bored security officers as was so often the case in his ER. Joe found that he was drawn outside to see the conclusion.

As he did, the security officers and the managers were reentering, with the exception of Nathan and James, who was speaking to the valet captain. There were several people waiting for their turn to have their cars retrieved, but this man had his car almost immediately. No time offered during which the situation might escalate. James opened the door for him while Nathan stood close by.

"Go home, sir. Calm down, get some sleep, and go to work in the morning," he said, as he shut the door.

"Sorry," said the man.

"Yes," replied James. "I know you are." Courteous, respectful even; but to the point. No condescending lecture, but no hint of negotiation, either. An acknowledgement that perhaps this man had a reason for his angry outburst, but reason or no, that outburst would not be tolerated.

James walked back into the hotel followed by Nathan, and either didn't notice Joe or decided not to speak to him. The whole episode had taken less than two or three minutes. The man was on his way, perhaps home, and when James opened the door, the sound from the casino said that it was back to normal as well.

Chapter 12

Joe found himself comparing these two episodes, as closely timed as they were. James had efficiently handled what appeared to be a potentially dangerous situation, all the while looking very professional and even appropriately sympathetic. His boss, Robert Bevins, had appeared belligerent, and even unnecessarily aggressive. There had been no obvious reason why he should have dealt with Harry as he did, while James Monroe had appeared appropriately restrained.

Joe looked up to see that Robert had been less successful as well. Harry was standing next to a beat-up old Cadillac, talking to a group of young women at the end of the hotel drive. They were probably young women, but their clothing made them appear younger; teenage, or maybe even younger than that. It took a moment for Joe to realize what was going on, but soon one of the women put out her hand and received something from Harry, after which she walked around to the passenger's side of his car and got in. Harry got into the driver's side of the Cadillac and they drove off. He could see some looks of apprehension on those remaining at the end of the drive

He was staring so intently at the scene that he didn't even notice as Maggie, from the cell phone shop, walked out of the hotel and started down to where the group was clustered. She seemed to know the group, and when she arrived, she began speaking at once. After a minute she also seemed to be angry, although Joe could hear none of what she was saying. Her gestures were angry, and she pointed frequently at them and then toward where Harry had been, and to the spot from which he and his companion for the evening had just departed.

Joe could feel his pediatric anger rising as well, and started walking over to the scene.

As he approached he could hear Maggie saying, "Why'd ya let her go with him? Katie should know better, and so should you!"

"She needs the money, Maggie. She got ta get—" began one of the others.

"Percy woulda …" began Maggie, but stopped speaking as soon as she saw Joe.

"Are you all right, Maggie?" he asked.

Maggie was surprised, surprised into speechlessness.

Joe frowned and continued. "What just happened here?"

No one answered.

"How old are you? How old are you really, Maggie?"

"I'm … old enough." There was both fear and defiance in her voice.

"And the rest of you? Was Harry picking up a sexual companion just now? Are any of you old enough to be—?" His cell phone rang just then, but he ignored it.

"We are—" began one of the others, shaking her pink hair. She was stopped by the looks cast by her friends.

"This isn't any business of yours, Doctor," said Maggie.

"It is," said Joe. "The abuse of women is everyone's business, and the abuse of children *is my business*. It a national dis—"

"What do you know about abuse, asshole?" said the pink hair. "You men all abuse everyone ya touch!"

"Yeah," added another. She smiled and struck a seductive pose. "You lookin' for some tonight?"

Joe would not be backed down though. Not by someone young enough to be one of his patients. "No," he said. "And you don't need to sell it to me or to anyone else. There are agencies—"

"That will send me back ta my lovin' home!?" said the pink hair. "Where my stepfather can fuck me up some more? I'd be better off with Harry. At least Katie gets paid for it." She nodded toward the drive down which Harry and the Caddie and their friend, Katie, had recently disappeared.

"You don't have to do this," persisted Joe. "There are other ways. I can find out what's available here, and maybe help you get in touch with someone who can help. If you're being abused in your home, you'll not have to return there."

"What are you talkin', asshole?" sneered the pink hair.

Maggie looked embarrassed now and said, "He's a pediatrician, for Christ's sake, Angie."

"Oh," said the pink-haired Angie, as if this changed everything. "Sorry, I didn't know that."

Joe began to speak again, but was interrupted.

"Joe!" yelled Carolyn, standing at the entrance to the hotel. "What the hell are you doing!?"

Several heads in the crowd outside turned as Carolyn and Natalie were starting to walk towards them, followed by Carl and then by James Monroe. Even on his dark skin Joe could see a blush of embarrassment mixed with anger.

Carolyn reached them first. "What are you doing, Joe?" She was calmer, but no less accusative.

Joe blushed, too. "I was just trying to—"

He was interrupted by James. "We do not allow this sort of activity on hotel premises. Neither the propositioning nor the solicitation." He looked squarely and accusingly at Joe.

"We ain't on—" began one of the women.

"You are," said James, pointing to the gate inside which they all stood, "on hotel property."

Angie looked first at James and then at Joe. "He wasn't doin' nothin.' Not pickin' up, I mean. Just trying to help, that's all. Tryin' to … he's a pediatrician, for God's sakes." Her gaze finally came to rest on Carolyn and she spoke directly to her. "He wasn't doin' any sol … solic …"

"Soliciting," offered Carolyn, her face softening as she spoke.

"Yeah," said Angie. "I mean, no. He wasn't doin' that at all. Honest."

Carolyn's face showed reprimand and a little hint of amusement as she turned to Joe again. "You can't do this sort of thing, Joe. People don't understand that you're just trying to save everyone on Earth, all at the same time."

James looked slightly confused. He was clearly one of those who didn't understand Joe. "You cannot do this on hotel property, Dr. Nelson." He pointed again to the gate. "Whatever it was you were doing. The appearance is …"

He shook his head and turned again to face the group of young women. "Are you finished for the day, Maggie, or are you on your break?"

"I'm done for the day, Mr. Monroe."

"I would not want Mr. Bevins to see you then," James said, as he turned and walked back to the entrance, still shaking his head.

Chapter 13

"What *were* you trying to do, Joe?" asked Natalie.

"These ladies are … well, I think they're underage, and I was trying to find out how old they really are, that's all. So maybe I could get them some help."

"Well, did you ask them how old they are, Joe?" said Natalie. "Politely and with concern in your voice, I mean?"

Joe shrugged, and Natalie reached into her purse, pulling out her badge. "Police, girls. Let's see some ID. Off hotel property," she added, pointing toward the sidewalk.

They moved the few steps to the other side of the gate as Natalie flashed her badge at them quickly. She was replacing it in her purse when Angie said, "Hey! That's not a Vegas badge. Not Nevada, either."

"No," replied Natalie calmly. "But I can get someone who has one of those to come and show it to you if you don't want to prove to me that you're not the girls I'm looking for from back where my shield is good. We can do it nicely, or I can get backup. That's up to you." She nodded at them as they began rummaging through their purses and pockets.

The first to show her ID pulled it out of her cleavage and handed it to Natalie. Natalie looked at it and then at the young woman. "Nineteen, Teresa?" she said. "Pretty good. It looks like it could be you, too."

She handed the ID back to Teresa and said, "Don't keep it there. Likely to fall out when you're working. If you're afraid your purse will get snatched, put a hole in the ID and pin it to your clothes somewhere. Somewhere that isn't going to get used too much when you're working.

"Your pimp should have told you that," she added.

"I didn't tell Percy," Teresa replied.

"He should have asked," scowled Natalie.

"He did, but I was embarrassed."

"Don't be embarrassed about this stuff. It'll get you hurt."

Natalie scanned through the rest with an occasional comment. "First one over twenty-one," she said to one, who blushed and looked several years younger than her stated age when she did.

Maggie produced two IDs. "So, are you nineteen or twenty-two?" asked Natalie. "They both have your picture on them, but different social security numbers."

"I'm really nineteen, but I need the other one to work here." Maggie looked a little fearful as she added, "If I can't work here, I gotta go back on the street, so please don't—"

"Who the hell would I tell, anyway?" smirked Natalie. "I'm a friend a' Joe's, so that pretty much blows my credibility ta pieces."

Carl cleared his throat and spoke for the first time. "You'll lose all of your social security contributions if they're credited to the wrong number."

"Well … but I have ta …" began Maggie.

Carl frowned. "We could probably file a petition to combine the numbers. You would have to say it was a mistake, of course, but … yes, we could do that."

"Maybe when you're twenty-one, Carl could help you with that," offered Carolyn, with a hint of sarcasm in her voice. "We might be working here if the Medical Center hasn't heard that *I'm* a friend of Joe's, too."

"Yes, of course. When you're twenty-one," said Carl. "We might need letters from your employers."

Angie showed her ID last, and looked nervous when she did.

"Who the hell is Sally Smart?" Natalie asked Angie. "She doesn't look a thing like you. Can you really use this? With a name like Sally Smart? It sounds like something off a cartoon show. That's not your real name, is it?"

"It was the only one I could afford," Angie said.

"I'll get Percy to get ya a new one, Angie," said Maggie.

"Do that," said Natalie, handing the ID back to her. "Can you really use that, Angie? Like, can you get a drink with that ID?"

"Sure. No one around here cares." Angie shrugged.

"Okay, I'm satisfied. What about you, Joe?" Natalie asked, smiling at him.

"Joe is satisfied too," said Carolyn.

Natalie looked at all of them and said, "You girls take care of yourselves or I'll sic Joe on you. You don't know what embarrassment is until he gets onto you. And don't give this little country girl any lip next time, y'all hear?"

She winked at them and smiled as she turned to leave. "I have to sit down somewhere. These shoes are killing me."

They started walking up the drive to the hotel as Maggie handed her keys to Angie and said, "Get my car, will ya? You know where I park. I wanta talk to 'em a minute."

Joe looked back as the others walked away, all of them wearing higher heels than either of his companions wore, but showed no difficulty walking in them at all. He looked over at Natalie now as she wobbled, struggling to walk up the slight incline to the hotel entrance.

By the time they had reached the entrance, Natalie had reached her limit. She pulled the three-inch heels off her feet and held them over the trash container. "Damn it, I can't wear these a minute longer. We'll have to go back to the room and get something less like medieval torture."

Maggie had caught up by now, in spite of her shoes. "I just wanted to say, like thanks, and all that." She was looking at all of them, but seemed to be talking to Joe.

"You're, like, really sweet. All of you are, I mean," she added.

Carolyn blushed slightly, but not as much as Joe. Natalie looked at her feet out of embarrassment, but Maggie seemed to think it was because she had no shoes on them.

"Somethin' wrong with your feet, Ms. Moore?" Maggie asked.

Natalie looked up with a startled expression.

"Your name is on the computer," said Joe, answering her unasked question. "It comes up whenever any of us charge anything. We should probably ask that they change that." He shrugged.

"Oh," said Natalie. "It's just these damned shoes." She motioned toward the trash container beside her with the offending shoes.

"You're not throwin' 'em away, are you?" asked Maggie.

"May as well for all the good they are to me," replied Natalie, chuckling a little. "Ya want 'em?"

"What size?" asked Maggie, turning serious in response to Natalie's joke.

Natalie turned serious too, in time to say, "Seven and a half. You really want them? They're difficult to walk in, ya know?"

Maggie ignored the last comment. "They'd fit me, if you're really throwin' 'em out, I mean. I can't afford ta buy 'em from ya though." She shrugged.

"I wouldn't ask anyone to pay for them," replied Natalie. "Are you sure you can walk in them?"

"Oh, yeah," replied Maggie. "They're easy. Ya know what ya should buy is ones like these."

She bent her leg backwards, pulling off one of her shoes with what were easily three-inch heels. "Ya see, they look real narrow from the side, but they really have, like, more than an inch of heel on the back." She turned the shoe to show that the heel was narrow sideways, but wide where it would rest on the floor. There was a piece connecting the heel to the shoe about midway down, for support, Joe supposed, or maybe as decoration, or maybe both. He also noticed that Maggie had no difficulty maintaining her balance on one three-plus-inch heel and only the toes of her other foot on the ground.

"Here, try 'em on if ya want. I'm a seven and a half too, or maybe eight."

Natalie hesitated, but then took the shoe and tried it, balancing herself by holding onto Joe. "Yeah, it is better," she said.

"Then let's swap," said Maggie, taking off her other shoe and replacing it with one of Natalie's.

"An' men don't usually notice the shoes when they look at girls from behind," added Maggie reassuringly.

"Men don't usually notice the shoes when they look at girls from the front, either," said Carolyn.

"Or the side, or any which way," added Natalie.

Maggie shrugged, and nodded in agreement.

"So, what do we wear them for?" asked Carolyn.

"They make your legs look sexier," replied Maggie in a very matter-of-fact tone.

"So, I just wanted to say, like, thanks," she said, as she stood on her tiptoes, which added less than an inch to her height, to place a kiss on Joe's cheek. She then did the same to Carl before he had a chance to react.

"So Natalie gets new shoes, and Joe and Carl get kissed, and I get what?" asked Carolyn.

"Oh, sorry," said Maggie, and hugged Carolyn, looking for all the world like a little girl hugging her favorite aunt. "Thank you, too, Mrs. Nelson. Oh, I forget, you're a doctor too. Sorry, Dr. Nelson."

With this she smiled and walked down the hotel drive without any difficulty, to where an old and dented car waited, with Angie driving, and three others in the back seat.

Chapter 14

"That was interesting," said Carl, rubbing his recently kissed cheek.

"Wipe off that lipstick," said Carolyn. "Both of you."

"Yes, that was interesting," smiled Natalie. "And *Mama got her new shoes*. Isn't that what they say when they're playing craps? *Mama needs new shoes*?"

"Or *Baby needs new shoes*, either one," said Carl. "I'm not sure why. The explanation for much of the slang is lacking in the book I have."

"Let's get something to eat," said Carolyn. "Did you make us reservations, gentlemen? And are you and Natalie going to embarrass us this whole trip?"

"I did," said Joe, motioning to the limo parked at the entrance. "I made plans for this evening, and I, at least, probably will. Keep embarrassing you, Carolyn, that is. It's not that I want to, it's just what I do best."

Raul Perez was opening the door for them, and Joe motioned for them to get in.

"What?" asked Natalie.

"I'll explain," said Joe, turning to Raul. "Fremont Street, please, the Golden Nugget."

"Yes, sir," he replied, closing the rear door and walking briskly to the driver's door.

"Where are we going?" asked Natalie.

"And who is paying?" asked Carolyn. "Not Reggie, if it's not here, and I have no cash."

"James Monroe gave us some vouchers," said Joe. "I want to be away from this place tonight."

"James gave them to us? Before he saw you talking to … well, before the episode *on hotel property,* I'm sure," said Carolyn. "Or did *he* want to get *you* off hotel property tonight?"

"What did happen back there, Joe?" asked Natalie.

"Robert Bevins threw this guy, Harry I think his name is, out of the casino for no apparent reason. Then James escorted a belligerent man out after he swore and kicked a slot machine. James was so much more professional, I went out to see him finish, and get some pointers on the correct way to conduct a non-violent intervention."

Joe shook his head. "He did it well, but while I was out there, I saw Harry picking up one of the young ladies, Katie, I think, and … well, I got upset and went to talk to them. To see if—

"Who is this Robert Bevins?" asked Carolyn. "Didn't James tell Maggie he didn't want Mr. Bevins to see her?"

"He's one of the managers. A notch above James on the management chart, and a sexist pig and a bigot," Joe said.

"Oh," said Carolyn. "Is that on his badge, above his name? 'Sexist Pig and Bigot'? I wonder what that job application has for questions."

"I met him," said Joe. "He doesn't need it to be on his badge. It's obvious even to me."

"But what happened with Harry and Katie to get you so upset?" asked Natalie.

"He gave her something, money or drugs or something, and she left with him. It just bothered me, that's all."

"They know what they're doing," offered Natalie.

"Joe doesn't always need a good reason to get upset," said Carolyn.

Joe flushed a little. "They're children. None of them is old enough to be doing what they're doing. They're being ignored by the authorities and exploited by their clients. This is pedophilia, for God's sake. Child abuse! Right out on the street, and all anyone cares about is that it shouldn't happen *on hotel property!*"

"They weren't underage, were they?" asked Carl. "I mean, the IDs were …" He stopped speaking as his face became pensive and then filled with revelation. "Do you think some of them had false IDs?"

"I think most of them did," said Carolyn.

"Maggie was the only one that I'm sure was real," said Natalie. "But what can we do?"

"We can stop pretending," Joe said. "Stop pretending it isn't there. Stop pretending it isn't happening. Stop pretending we can't do anything."

"But what can we—" began Natalie.

"I can go to my interview tomorrow," said Carolyn.

"I've been meaning to discuss that a little with you, Carolyn," Carl said "Have you researched the position?"

"Well, a little. Before things went all to hell back in Kentucky. Have you? You didn't even know you were going to interview until yesterday."

"And today you spent studying slot machines," said Joe.

"I did make a few inquiries," said Carl. "I'll have to admit the slot machine problem was much more intriguing."

"Perhaps you can earn enough there so neither you nor Carolyn will need a job," suggested Natalie.

"I think that might be a possibility," said Carl, "but not a certainty yet. In any event, the calls I made yielded the following information: The CEO of Emergency Services is a woman named Mellissa Burke. A 'bitch on wheels', one of my contacts said. She did fire him, though, so that may have colored his opinion, although several others had similar assessments of her. It was also suggested that she doesn't value the opinions of her subordinates in the hiring process, so it will be she and she alone whom you must impress, Carolyn. We'll likely interview with some others, but that will be our opportunity to interview them. Ms. Burke will be interviewing us."

"Okay," Carolyn said. "I got that. What about you, Carl? You'll have to impress her as well."

"Not to the extent that you will." Carl shrugged.

"Oh?" said Joe. More a question than a comment.

"Yes," said Carl. "You see, I'm making a simple transition, while Carolyn is attempting a leap."

"A leap?" asked Joe.

"Well, yes. I'm the chief of operations in my current hospital. It's what would be considered a second-tier facility: level two trauma, basic referral center, and all those things; and I'm applying for a midlevel position in the operations department at a larger, tertiary center: a very logical progression. I have risen as far as I can where I am, and now I'm making what's really a lateral transition to a lower position in a larger facility that will allow either advancement within that facility, or gain added experience to move to another facility.

"Carolyn, on the other hand, is an associate director in her current position, attempting to move both *up* to director *and* to a larger facility. More challenging, that's all."

"You're discouraging me before I even start, Carl," said Carolyn.

"She's a very good physician," offered Joe.

"Oh, I didn't mean to suggest otherwise. Excellent performance and superb references, I'm sure. I hope you didn't get our CEO to write one for you, Carolyn. I hadn't thought of that."

"No," said Carolyn. "He and I didn't get along even before all hell broke loose back in Kentucky. Is it really going to be—"

"No, of course not," reassured Carl. "You must simply be prepared. People like Mellissa Burke generally have substantial egos. It will be necessary to bear that in mind. She'll be hiring as much to advance her position as to benefit the Medical Center, so take some time to point out how having you as Medical Director of Emergency Services will benefit her."

"Benefit her?" asked Carolyn.

"Yes," said Carl. "Point out that you've run a smooth department, free of complications. How you built a new ED while seamlessly maintaining the services provided. How you're able to function well with only minimal guidance from your CEO. Given the turmoil in the hospital right now, that will be obvious. And try not to say what plans you have to improve things. Ms. Burke is likely to interpret such comments as criticism of her personally."

"What about the murder?" asked Natalie. "Ms. Burke will have heard all about that. Won't that scare her away from hiring either of you?"

"Not necessarily." Carl shrugged. "The full extent of the story is unlikely to be available, and what's on the news mentions no names."

He nodded toward Joe and added, "The mention of an injured physician states repeatedly that *HE* was a pediatrician. If the opportunity arises—and if I were you, I would try to make the opportunity arise—you can point out that your application to the Medical Center here was submitted months ago, and you might want to hint that your uneasiness with the hospital administration contributed to your decision to apply. To move away from your current position, that is. If you're pressured by Ms. Burke for details, simply say that the police have requested that you not discuss the situation. Several people that I spoke to asked, and that's what I told them. The fact that they all did ask indicates that the full extent of the story isn't yet available, officially or otherwise."

Carolyn gave a huge sigh and asked, "Have you written any notes for me, Carl? Any suggested comments or questions?"

"Only a few. I didn't have much time. I'll give them to you to read tonight."

Natalie and Joe looked at him in surprise, but Carolyn seemed nonplussed. "I figured you would," she said. "What are you and Joe going to do tomorrow, Natalie, while I'm being impaled by Mellissa Burke?"

Natalie looked at Joe, slipping her hand through his arm and leaning her head on his shoulder. "Maybe we'll see if we can save some victims of child abuse in Las Vegas. What do you think of that, Joe?"

"What?" said Joe, sitting up straight.

"Natalie!?" said Carolyn, causing her to sit up as well, releasing Joe's arm.

"What?" she said.

"Stop doing that," replied Carolyn. "It just encourages him. We'll be chasing after wayward girls all over this friggin' city if he has his way. Until we all get arrested, that is. Two consenting adults ought to be able to occupy their time far less productively than doing insane things like that."

"Maybe, maybe not," said Natalie, as the limo pulled up to the Golden Nugget Casino.

Chapter 15

Raul was out opening the door to let them exit the limo. This was Las Vegas, so a limousine dropping people at a casino attracted no attention at all.

"I'll have to park beyond the traffic, but can pick you up within ten or fifteen minutes at any point along the street," he said, as they exited the back seat. "You may leave any valuables you do not wish to carry with you in the limousine. They will be safe here."

"I don't think I'll need my notebook," said Carl, depositing it and his book in the back seat of the limo.

"Will we need our purses?" asked Carolyn. "Will anyone card me, I hope?"

Raul smiled. "It's always a good idea for the younger ladies to have an ID on them."

Carolyn and Natalie both smiled at this.

"Won't you need to eat or something, Raul?" asked Joe.

"I'll eat now so as not to interfere with you. Do you still have my card?"

All four nodded and he continued, "Just call when you're ready then."

"No gambling?" asked Joe.

He smiled and said, "I'm a chauffeur, but I'm not stupid."

"No, of course not," Joe said, looking at the card. "Raul Perez, is that right?"

Raul nodded.

"Thank you, Raul. It will probably be a few hours before we need you, so eat as slowly as you wish. Do you have any suggestions as to what we should see while we're here?"

"It's all entertaining, sir. The Golden Nugget is famous. The Pioneer used to be here," he said, motioning toward the iconic forty-foot-tall cowboy with his mechanical arm rhythmically pointing its thumb toward the souvenir shop beneath. "That's Vegas Vic, famous in his own right, but the street is the most entertaining. Gamble a little, dine a little, but save some time to just wander outside a little, too."

"Thank you, Raul," said Joe, handing him forty dollars. "And dine on us tonight."

"Thank you, sir," Raul replied, pocketing the money and returning to the limo.

The scene around them was the atmosphere, the flavor, the substance of Las Vegas. There was something happening everywhere, and all at the same time. At least three street bands were playing, one dressed like the Fab Four, the Beatles, but sounding only faintly like them as they attempted to cover that iconic quartet's hits. They had a stage above the milling crowd, so they probably had some official status. Several single musicians or groups of two or three vied, usually unsuccessfully, for attention at street level, with hats or cups in front for 'donations'." Further down the street, another stage offered a female singer with a backup band. She had a crowd in front swaying to her music, which the people at this end of the street couldn't hear at all.

Overhead there was a metal canopy running the length of the street. A light show was just beginning with its own musical accompaniment, and this put all the others into its acoustic shadow. Lights and images appeared and then moved along the canopy to make room for the next images. The Fab Four finished their number and waited patiently to begin again. There was no use in competing.

Along the sides of the street were shops advertising gambling, souvenirs and strip clubs. There were usually scantily clad women standing at the entrances, inviting people in. Among all this was the crowd. Teenagers and twenty-year-olds dressed in jeans and tees and all other assorted clothing.

Nothing seemed unusual because as soon as something did, a more outlandish costume appeared. There were older people, too; some equally flamboyantly dressed, some bikers, and some that were clearly tourists. Some of these had sport jackets, and one or two had ties. A few also had name tags, probably from some convention they were attending and which they had forgotten to remove. It didn't matter, because it was all so crazy, nothing was crazy. If the casino at the hotel had been boisterous, Fremont Street was bedlam.

There were women along the sidewalk who were clearly assessing the passing men with a professional eye. Occasionally a gentleman would stop to "assess" the product being offered as well, and often it appeared that an acceptable bargain was reached, as evidenced by the fact that they departed together.

There was one lady who, on close inspection, appeared to be older by a decade or more than Joe or any of his companions, but who was dressed in a white showgirl's outfit, complete with feathered hat. She smiled brightly and offered to pose with anyone for tips. Her small purse had *TIPS* in large black letters printed on it, in case there was any question as to how she should be compensated for posing. The poser or a friend used their own camera for the picture, of course.

"Let's get something to eat," said Carolyn finally.

They entered the Golden Nugget, which had two restaurants open at this time of night. They were obliged to walk through the casino to arrive at either, as was the common practice in Las Vegas. Eating was optional, gambling was encouraged. Carl watched the slot machines closely as they passed, and the rest looked only casually. When they arrived, Joe showed their vouchers, and they were seated immediately.

"Say hello to Jimmy for me," said the hostess taking the vouchers, "and to Michelle, too. His wife, I mean."

They said they would, but Joe had to ask the server what the hostess' name was. Pauline, he was told.

The food was good, although somewhat short of excellent. It would not have been worth a trip here, but the outside show clearly would be.

"I would really like to compare the slots here to those at the hotel casino," said Carl. "Do any of you have some cash you can loan me?"

The ladies shook their heads, but Joe smiled. "I can loan you a little if, and only if, you tell me what it is you're looking at."

"Well, it's really quite simple," said Carl. "As I walked about in the casino, I noticed that there seemed to be non-random events. I'm verifying that."

"Non-random events?" asked Carolyn.

"Yes."

"What sort of non-random events, Carl?" asked Joe.

"Oh," said Carl. "Not the payout. That would be obvious to everyone. The non-paying events occur on what I'm calling the 'tease-line' as opposed to the 'pay-line.' The line above or below the line that pays is the tease-line; teasing you to play again. What I noticed is that the maximum jackpot occurs there relatively frequently, but of course doesn't pay. It's not on the pay-line."

"But if it's not on the pay-line, what difference does it make if it occurs relatively frequently?" asked Natalie.

"If there's a non-random event at the tease-line, there has to be a non-random event at the pay-line."

"I'm not sure," pondered Joe.

"Either the machines are random or they're not. If the events at the tease-line are not random, then the events *everywhere* are not random. If they're not random, then they're systematically determined, and therefore predictable. They must be." Carl nodded to himself, as if what he had said was the most logical thing that could be.

"And you think you can …?" said Joe.

"I'll simply study the events to determine the possible patterns, and then verify the patterns, and then … well, then I'll be able to predict the outcome on the slot machines."

"You think you'll be able to predict the outcome of a spin on the slots?" asked Carolyn. "That's impossible."

"I don't have to predict the outcome of *every* spin," said Carl. "I simply have to improve my percentage."

"What do you think you'll predict then?" asked Joe.

"The slots usually pay between 95% and 99% return, depending upon the machine. If I'm playing a machine that pays 99%, all I have to do is improve those odds by 2% and I'll win more than I lose. It's as simple as that."

"It's as *crazy* as that," said Joe. "Don't you think that if that were true, someone else would have figured it out long ago?"

"Not necessarily. I'm more logical than most people are, and most people are trying to figure a systematic occurrence prediction based on the pay-line like that gentleman Harry at the hotel casino. That's foolish. I'm figuring it on the tease-line."

Joe shook his head, and Natalie giggled. Carolyn sighed and said, "And I'll be interviewing for medical director of emergency services with you tomorrow, Carl. Do I stand any chance at all?"

Natalie giggled again. "I think Carl stands a better chance of winning at the slots."

"It's all very logical," replied Carl.

"Well," said Joe, "a deal's a deal, even in Las Vegas." He pulled out his blackjack winnings and began counting.

"Three hundred seventy-five each," he said, handing that amount to each of the other three and then pocketing the rest.

"Where did you get that?" inquired Natalie.

"Tyla gave it to me," Joe replied.

"Who the hell is Tyla?" asked Carolyn. "What were you doing today? You were hanging out with Janet, then Tyla, and then Maggie and her friends. If I were married to you I'd be pissed as hell."

"You are married to him," smiled Natalie.

"Not really," frowned Carolyn. "Well, maybe I am. A little, anyway. So, who is Tyla, Joe, and what did you do to make her give you all that money?"

Joe smiled and shrugged. "I showed her my cards … at her blackjack table. Now *that's* an interesting game. She thought I was hitting on her, though."

"And *were* you hitting on her?" asked Carolyn.

"I had already finished playing before I thought of doing that."

"You have to have a little trust, Carolyn," said Natalie.

"Or we could just cut his balls off," Carolyn replied.

"Sorry. I was thinking I might be using those someday," said Natalie. "Let's see what Fremont Street is up to, shall we?"

Chapter 16

Carl decided to see what the slots at the Golden Nugget were up to instead, but he pointed out that the world's largest gold nugget was on display at this hotel. They went past it in the lobby on their way to the street; the "Hand of Faith" a sign proclaimed, found in Australia and now displayed here at the Golden Nugget since 1981. At 875 troy ounces it was currently worth one million five hundred thousand dollars … approximately.

Out on the street, another light show was just ending on the canopy above them, and the bands were beginning to play again, but not the same ones as before. The Fab Four had been superseded by five gentlemen playing horns and keyboards with an elaborate percussionist in back. Jazz it would be called, Joe supposed, but no one in the French Quarter of New Orleans would have either recognized it as such or have been much impressed. At the other end of the street was something that resembled disco music, what could be heard of it, with three ladies dancing in front of two singers and a backup band. A dozen people in all. There were several uniformed police officers standing about, more enjoying the scene than supervising it. They didn't interfere with anything while Joe and the ladies were walking around.

At the corner were a fire truck and an ambulance, and Carolyn being Carolyn, she stopped to chat with the young uniformed men and women standing in front.

"Yeah, usually not much happens, but often enough to make it better to have us here rather than call us in when it does," offered one of the paramedics. "Traffic can be heavy sometimes."

"Good idea," Carolyn replied.

Natalie talked to one of the police officers. "We try not to interfere with anyone's fun if we can avoid it. As long as no one gets hurt," he smiled.

"Yeah," said Natalie. She looked over at a group of young people passing a joint around, and the officer just shrugged.

"Probably just tobacco." He smiled again and winked at her.

"Probably," said Natalie, and smiled back.

They drifted back down the street, talking about whether they should go into any of the stores or casinos. They all said they probably should, but somehow the vibrating excitement on the street kept them outside.

About halfway back to the Golden Nugget, Joe stopped and looked at a group of young women with an African American man standing in front of them. He was talking, it was clear, although he couldn't be heard from the distance that separated them. He was gesturing and pointing. The young women were the same group that had been at the hotel.

Carolyn slipped her hand through Joe's arm and said, "Let's go. This is getting boring." But as they turned, one of the girls called to them.

"Hey, Doc, you havin' a good time?"

It sounded innocent, and was probably just a greeting, but Joe turned back, glaring. "They shouldn't be …" he murmured.

"Yeah!" Carolyn yelled back. "Let's go," she said to Joe quietly.

The man had turned now, too. He wasn't tall or muscular, but he was dressed for this street named Fremont. Black leather pants fitting tightly with a red patterned shirt, and a black vest. He wore sunglasses beneath bushy hair which looked like it couldn't possibly be real.

"Hey, man, you lookin' for somethin'?" he yelled.

Joe's anger was apparent, and Carolyn pulled him, saying, "Let's just—"

"Ya lookin' fer somethin'?" the man asked again, as Joe shook his arm free and began walking the two dozen or so feet that separated them.

"Joe, don't!" said Carolyn, but by now Joe was standing only a few feet away from the man who had just yelled at him.

"Are you their pimp?" he asked. "Percy, is it?"

The man eyed Joe up and down a few times before saying, "Yeah. That's me."

"Well, Percy, I just want to take this opportunity to thank you for fulfilling all my expectations. I always thought pimps were the scum of the Earth and now … well, now I know that you are."

Percy looked at Joe with a puzzled expression. He had clearly not understood all of what had just been said, but the realization seemed to come quickly that he had not received a compliment.

"Ooo, smart-mouth man. Schoolin' behind that asshole. Oh, sorry, that's yer face, not your ass? Couldn't tell the difference." Percy grinned and glanced behind him, to see if everyone appreciated his wit. When he saw their silent stares he seemed to grow angry.

"Ya want somethin'? 'Cause if ya don't, take it back home."

Joe glared back for a moment and then turned to leave. A small crowd had gathered and a few chuckles passed through it. Two police officers stood about twenty feet away, but made no move to interfere.

"Come on, Joe," said Carolyn again. "Not worth—"

"That's right, Mama!" yelled Percy. "You take your little boy home now. Past his bedtime for sure."

Joe stopped momentarily, and Percy reached out and nudged him. It wasn't much of a push, but Joe slipped and went down on one knee. Percy stood over him, looking down. "Sorry, little man. Did I push too hard?"

When Joe started to stand, Percy nudged him again, but Joe kept coming up. Percy couldn't see his face, couldn't see the anger in it, but Carolyn and Natalie could.

"Joe!" yelled Natalie.

At the same time Carolyn yelled, "No! Joe! No!"

Joe continued up, swinging one leg above him as Percy reached to push him again. Joe spun quickly, but Percy saw the kick coming and started to duck, leaning forward. He would have missed another man's shoe by this maneuver, taking a glancing blow from the slower-moving and softer calf, but not from Joe. What hit his head was the hard, plastic-covered metal of the prosthetic leg, and it sent Percy sprawling to the ground.

Joe stood over him, his face a mixture of retreating anger and advancing embarrassment.

"Oh, shit, Joe," said Carolyn. "Now see what you've done?"

"Yeah," said Natalie. "That was cool."

"Natalie!" said Carolyn.

"What!?" said Natalie.

The police had finally been galvanized into motion, one on his radio as they advanced through the crowd. Percy lay on the pavement, shaking his head, his sunglasses half a dozen feet away and his hair only a little closer.

"Hey, Percy," said one of the cops. "Where'd ya get that rat?"

Percy reached with both hands to his bare head, with only a few wisps of hair on it, as a few chuckles started through the crowd. Most were still silently looking at the two men.

"Ya want to go ta the Medical Center an' see if they can sew that back on, Percy?" the cop asked

"What the …?" said Percy, as he rolled onto his back and looked at Joe.

The cop looked at Joe too, and grew suddenly very serious. "Maybe you had better go to the Medical Center, sir."

"What?" said Joe.

Percy was staring up at him now. "Shit, man. That's gotta hurt!"

"What?" said Joe again, as gasps spread through the crowd and several people turned away.

Joe just looked around until Carolyn said calmly, "It's your leg, Joe. Look at your leg."

Joe looked down and said, "Oh. It's okay. Really."

"Don't look okay," said Percy. It didn't look okay, of course. Joe's foot was pointing to the side, almost backwards. There were more gasps from the gathering crowd as they followed Joe's gaze.

"Maybe you should lie down, sir," said the cop

"No. It's okay," said Joe as he reached down, turning his foot to face forward with both hands and then stamping it on the ground several times.

"That's better," he said.

There were gasps, a few screams, and at least one person was vomiting into a trash can.

"Holy shit," said Percy.

"It's a prosthesis," said Joe, pulling up his pant leg.

"Holy shit," said Percy again. He looked up, and then quickly scrambled across the pavement to retrieve his wig and sunglasses.

"Sorry," said Joe. "I just kinda lost it."

"Lost your leg, too," said Percy, standing and adjusting his hair. "How the fuck that happen? Street fightin'?"

"Mining accident," Joe replied.

"No shit," said Percy.

"You two okay?" asked the paramedics, just arriving at the scene.

"You boys gotta run a little faster," said Percy. "Ya missed the whole damned thing."

"I'm fine," said Joe.

"Yeah, me too," said Percy. "Show's over folks, but come on back tomorrow night!" he yelled to the crowd.

"Sorry," said Joe again.

"Holy shit," Percy replied, shaking his head. "Mining accident, ya say? Holy fuckin' shit. Well, let's get goin', ladies, an' see what else we can find tonight. Not goin' ta match this though. No way."

The ladies started off, following Percy, a couple waving at Carolyn and Natalie. Maggie, wearing Natalie's shoes, smiled and waved, and then left the group to join another gathering that were drinking beer and saluting Joe with their paper bag-covered cans. There were a few people still staring, and Joe's embarrassment grew a little as the three walked away.

"You're going to keep embarrassing me, aren't you, Joe, even if Natalie refuses to help you embarrass me," said Carolyn.

"I'll try not to," said Joe.

"Liar," replied Carolyn.

Chapter 17

They found Carl easily enough. There was a small, curious group around him, and he seemed to be giving a little lecture. He was also writing on several small napkins arrayed in front of him. They were the kind put under the free drinks that the casino provided to players, but Carl had no drink in front of him, just the napkins.

"You see," he said. "There's another jackpot just below the pay-line. Third one on this machine, and not one on the pay-line. Statistically, that's very unlikely."

There were a couple of casino managers standing menacingly nearby, probably watching to see if Carl was doing anything that should cause them to ask him to leave the casino. Carolyn preempted them.

"We're ready to leave, Carl," she said.

"Oh," said Carl, standing. "So am I. I put your money to good use, Joe."

"Do you have any left?" asked Joe.

"Well, not that much, but I have a great deal of data. I'm not sure, but I think the slots here are similar to the ones at the hotel. There might be subtle differences that I don't have enough information to demonstrate yet, but … well, tomorrow after the interview maybe."

"Ah ha," said Natalie. "So it's a city-wide conspiracy, is it? Or maybe it's larger than just Las Vegas. Shouldn't you check out all the gaming spots to see if it's worldwide?"

Carl looked as if he were considering this seriously. "Let me verify my finding here first, and then … yes, there's enough to investigate in Las Vegas. Did you have a good evening?"

"Yes," replied Natalie. "We saw the world's largest gold nugget, chatted with some local police and EMS people, oh, and Joe got into a street brawl. That was interesting."

"Yes, that does sound interesting," replied Carl absently. "Have you called for the limousine yet?"

"I'll do that now," said Joe, "since it looks like the opportunity for street brawls are limited in here."

"I'm sure you could get one started," said Carolyn, "but let's not try to do everything all in one night."

They didn't try to do everything in one night, and soon they were in the back of the limo riding peacefully away from the excitement.

"Do you think I should have gotten a manicure for the interview tomorrow, Natalie?" asked Carolyn.

"Your nails look okay," Natalie said, looking at them. "Too late now anyway."

"You don't think I could get an early morning appointment?" said Carolyn. "We're not due at the Medical Center until ten."

"Well, maybe," said Natalie.

Joe looked over at Carl, who seemed to be intently examining his collection of napkins. He shrugged and tapped on the dark glass that separated Raul from them. A few seconds later it rolled down as they began driving up the entrance ramp to the expressway.

"Yes, sir?"

"Do you think you could drive us down the main street instead of the expressway, Raul?" asked Joe.

"Of course," said Raul, as he began a complicated set of turns that brought them back to where they had started their trip home. "There's an intercom that you can use."

"Oh," said Joe. "I think I would prefer to see you when I talk to you if that's okay."

"Of course."

They were riding by the ambulance and fire truck with their personnel standing in front, along with the two police officers that had been on the scene with Joe and Percy. As they looked up at the limo, several waved, but Raul made no response.

They couldn't see inside the rear, but Raul was clearly visible. Maybe they knew the limo but not the driver, thought Joe. The police and the limo drivers probably knew each other in this town, and maybe Raul didn't acknowledge them for another reason.

"Did you eat well, Raul?" Joe asked, as they started down the main street.

"Yes," replied Raul. Joe noticed a canvas sack on the front seat next to him folded neatly, and supposed that he had probably eaten well, but not on Joe's money.

"How long have you lived in Las Vegas, if I may ask?"

"Three years," said Raul. "Before that I lived in San Diego." He looked in the rear view mirror at Joe and added, "I was born there. I'm retired now."

"Oh," said Joe. "Is this what's called The Strip?"

"We'll be on it soon. Right now it's just Las Vegas Boulevard. That little chapel we're passing," Raul added. "Elvis Presley and Ann Margaret were married there."

"Really," said Joe, looking as they passed a small chapel in a quaint country setting surrounded by the gaudiness of this city.

"No," said Raul. "They were never married, but in the movie *Viva Las Vegas*, the marriage scene was shot there," he chuckled.

They were slowing as the traffic began to impede their progress. "This will take longer, but the scenery is better," said Raul.

"No hurry," replied Joe. "You're retired, but still driving?"

"Yes," answered Raul. "The money comes in handy, and it keeps the boredom in check."

"Bored in Las Vegas?" smiled Joe.

"It's not always what it appears to be."

"No, I guess not," sighed Joe, as they crept down The Strip past opulence and imitation. Rome and Paris, Egypt and New York. All here in one place.

"Do you enjoy it here?' asked Joe.

"Yes, I think I do. There are parts I don't like, but there were parts of beautiful San Diego I didn't like, either."

"Yes," said Joe. "I find there are many parts of Las Vegas that I don't like."

"Oh?" Raul was silent for a few minutes.

"There were some young ladies on Fremont Street," Joe finally said. "They were—"

"Practicing *the oldest profession,* as my mother used to say?" asked Raul.

Joe smiled. "My mother said the same thing. Your mother from Kentucky, too?"

Raul chuckled. "Tijuana. Is that near Kentucky?"

Joe chuckled too. "Maybe spiritually, ya think?"

Raul nodded and after another minute Joe sighed. "They're just children."

"True," said Raul.

"So what's …?"

Raul sighed too. "Many people come to Las Vegas. It's one of the fastest-growing cities in the United States, they say. They come for many reasons, and unfortunately some come with little idea of what they're coming to, and with even less preparation."

"But …?" began Joe again, only to stop again without a finishing thought.

"Sex," said Raul, "is the second industry of this city." When Joe said nothing, he continued.

"Outside this city there are legal houses with sultry names: *cherry* and *hill; ranch* or *farm.* Any newspaper will give a dozen ads complete with pictures. They're fairly well supervised by the state to ensure that *the state* doesn't get a reputation that it would not want to have. All the ladies are of age, all supervised as to their health, no pedophilia. Those young ladies who come here below that age must find other opportunities, and that can be difficult for someone with few skills. There are few jobs available to underage workers. Most hotels, casinos, even stores, sell alcohol, and therefore they must be old enough to handle alcohol. The sex trade is often …" He shook his head.

"So they're thrown out onto the street at the mercy of …" Again the thought was too much for Joe to finish.

"It's sometimes like that, but more often they're working for a gentleman who will offer them some protection. That's the usual practice."

"A pimp?" asked Joe. "Who will abuse them as well?"

"Some do, but some take an interest in their employees. Many treat them better than they were treated in the homes they ran away from in the first place."

"You seem to know …" Joe stopped when he realized what he was suggesting.

Raul just smiled. "The seat on which you sit right now has been used for more than sitting. Limos are popular places to enjoy Las Vegas in. It's part of the city's attractions."

When Joe said nothing, Raul continued. "There's a sign that you can put on your doorknob in the hotel where you're staying if you do not want to be disturbed. It says: *Do Not Disturb For Intimacy.* If you're living in a city where the selling of sex is a normal function, it's not a question of whether it's appropriate, but rather, how it should be done. How it can be done safely for both the client and the provider."

"Do your clients pick up children?" asked Joe.

Raul might have been offended, but didn't seem to be. "My agency has a policy that prohibits that. I'm instructed to prevent that from happening in my vehicle." He smiled and added, "It's also suggested that I be very certain they *are* children before I prevent it. Many of the ladies dress to look younger than they are, and most have IDs to 'prove' it, even if they are underage. Some gentlemen prefer that."

Joe looked back at his companions, who didn't seem at all concerned about the fate of children in Las Vegas right now. Carolyn and Natalie were still discussing nails, and Carl was engrossed with his array of napkins.

He looked back at Raul, who smiled faintly. "People come to Las Vegas to leave their boring and frustrating lives behind them and to find excitement. That's true for those who come here to live, as well as those who come to visit. The visitors are usually happier if they do not look too closely at the city."

"True," said Joe. "Why did you come here, Raul?"

"Oh, to leave a boring life behind and find excitement. This is pretty exciting tonight, driving down The Strip in a limo, isn't it?"

Joe chuckled. "Yeah, I guess. What was the boring life you left in San Diego, if I may ask?"

"Police," said Raul. "I was a homicide detective, and before that I was on a SWAT team."

"Oh," said Joe. He looked back at his companions to see them all looking at Raul now. They had been listening after all, just not interfering with the conversation.

"We have arrived at your hotel, sir," said Raul.

Chapter 18

They had arrived, and before any had managed to move toward the door, Raul was standing next to the door opening it for them. He had moved very quickly. *Probably his SWAT training,* Joe thought with a chuckle.

Carolyn and Natalie parted from Joe and Carl to see if it was possible to make an early appointment at the salon this late at night. When they arrived in their suite, Carl immediately pulled out the notebook he had been carrying and sat at the desk.

"I didn't want to transpose these in the limo and possibly lose some of the data." He began the process now, and it looked as if it was going to be a lengthy task. Joe thought of checking in with Carolyn and Natalie, but decided they had their own mission tonight. He was suddenly very fatigued, and his bed looked very inviting. He also realized he had purchased no pajamas and would have to sleep in his underwear. The last thought that came to him before sleep arrived was to wonder if any of the others had thought to buy pajamas.

Joe was awakened by his cell phone. He had been afraid he would not hear it so he had put it on vibrate and placed it in a wine glass next to his bed the night before. He had read about this once, but this was the first time he had tried it. The noise was enough to wake him instantly.

"Hello, Joe," said Natalie. "Carolyn and I are down at the salon getting beautiful. Want to meet us for breakfast? We'll be in the coffee shop within the next twenty-four hours or so."

He did want to meet them for breakfast, and was dressed in jeans and a casual shirt in a few minutes. He would shower and shave later, he decided. Carl was nowhere to be found, so he headed for the coffee shop that Natalie had said she and Carolyn would in *"within the next twenty-four hours."*

When he arrived he found not only Carolyn and Natalie waiting, but Carl and Raul as well. "We twisted Raul's arm to get him to share coffee with the common tourists," said a coifed and manicured Carolyn.

"We won," added an equally well-appointed Natalie, dressed as if she were interviewing, too.

Raul just sipped his coffee and smiled. "I put up a good fight, but I was woefully outmatched."

"Now, Carolyn," said Carl. "As I was saying, this will be principally an opportunity to gather information. Ask about budgets and expected renovations, and those sorts of things. I have bought you a notebook to write them down in." He handed her a small notebook and a pen.

"I have a pen," said Carolyn. "Is this necessary? To write down the figures, I mean."

"Use my pen," said Carl. "It's an expensive one and that will impress Ms. Burke. And yes, it's important to get the numbers *and* to write them down. That way they will know you have a record of their verbal commitment, in case they intend to change them. They may mention compensation, and you may write those down too, but don't pay too much attention to those figures. They will likely lowball your salary, and we can negotiate that later if you decide you wish to accept the position."

"Yes," said Carolyn, looking a bit intimidated.

"Now, they're going to discuss the ED as well. Volume, demographics, percentage of free care provided. All those sorts of things. I'll be getting all those numbers as well."

"So I don't need to write those down," said Carolyn.

"On the contrary. Write those down scrupulously. First of all, it will demonstrate that you're serious, and we can also compare your numbers with mine, as well as verify them on the computer. In case they're misleading you."

"Why would they mislead me?" asked Carolyn.

"Why wouldn't they?" asked Carl. He shrugged as if this answered the question completely. "Finally, they may offer you a contract today. Perhaps they'll even pressure you to commit yourself. I would strongly advise that you not make any commitment."

"Even if it's a very good offer?" asked Carolyn.

"*Especially* if it's a good offer. They'll be there tomorrow, just as they are today. Used car salesmen do not pressure their customers into signing today because they're afraid those customers will think about it and decide the vehicle is worth more and offer to pay more for the car tomorrow. These people will offer you a contract only if they think that you might change your mind if you think about it. So … think about it. We can negotiate better that way."

"Okay," said Carolyn as the server approached their table. More coffee was poured, and Joe ordered his breakfast.

"I'm impressed, Carl," said Joe as the server departed.

"With what?" asked Carl.

Joe was silent and Natalie said, "I'm thinking of going with them to the interview, Joe. If that's okay with you."

"Oh, I guess I can find something to do until you all get back. What are you planning to do at the interview?"

"Just look around and talk to Raul, maybe." Natalie nodded toward him. "Compare police stories from Kentucky and San Diego. Don't worry, I'm not planning to get a job in Las Vegas or San Diego. Just talk a little shop. If that's okay with you, Joe."

"Yeah, sure," said Joe, trying to conceal his disappointment. "I have to buy some pajamas anyway."

"So do Natalie and I," said Carolyn. "Be a sweetie and pick up a couple pair for each of us, will you, Joe?"

"Joe picking out our lingerie? Is that safe?" asked Natalie.

"No. But it will be interesting and possibly embarrassing for Joe. Even us up after last night."

The server returned with the order. Joe took a drink of his coffee and began to eat his breakfast. "Of course I'll be glad to buy you some lingerie. It will be an excellent excuse to meet some of the salesladies in the intimate apparel shops. Do you need PJs, Carl?"

"I got three pair yesterday. That should be sufficient."

"All three are beige, aren't they," stated Joe.

"Yes. How did you know?"

"Lucky guess." Joe smiled. "And can I pick up anything for you, Raul?"

"My wife purchases all my lingerie, thank you," he replied, raising his coffee cup to take a sip.

 *Chapter 19*

Joe found himself alone, his three companions off to interview, although he couldn't quite see what Natalie was doing, going along. He tried not to get depressed or paranoid, but in truth he had been looking forward to having some time with her. Maybe later; pajamas now.

He went down to the shop he had been in yesterday, hoping that Janet would be there, and she was. She was finishing with another client, but Joe said he would wait, and looked around casually while he did. He saw some things that he liked, but somehow felt he ought to get Janet's opinion.

"Ah, what can I help you with today, Joe?" she said when she came over after completing her other client's order.

"Pajamas," he replied.

"Should have asked about that." Janet shrugged and smiled.

"As should I. So, this one should be easy. Just standard PJs."

"No red satin or velour? No, I think I agree. A man who needs to sleep in satin generally ought to sleep alone," smiled Janet. "Assorted colors, or all the same?"

"All the …" began Joe but stopped, remembering his comment to Carl. "No, three different colors and well, patterns or … I don't know, they're just pajamas."

"Yes, that's what they are," said Janet, smiling. "Send them to your room?"

"Yes," said Joe, realizing that if he was this embarrassed buying plain PJs for himself, he might never be able to even talk to a saleswoman in the lingerie store. "You don't carry lady's …?"

"No," Janet replied, shaking her head. "Unless you think they would like to sleep in men's pajamas. Is that a possibility?"

"I don't think so. They might sleep in them, but I would never live it down if that's what I bought for them."

"Well, is this a gift of passion and seduction, or function?"

Joe could feel himself blush. "Just functional things to sleep in. For both ladies," he added, as if this would make it clear that seduction wasn't his motive. He blushed again when he realized that buying for two ladies might mean he was planning a seduction of two ladies.

Janet smiled. "Are you sure they didn't buy some yesterday? As I recall they were doing quite a lot of shopping."

"They said they had not, and asked me to pick up some for them, but …"

"Would you like me to see if I can help?"

"Well, yes. But I'm not sure you can."

"Let's look," replied Janet. "May I have your room key?"

He handed it to her and she swiped it through. "I'll charge your stuff first."

She did and then said, "They seem to be buying relatively practical clothing, but nothing that looks like it might be sleepwear. I would guess they'll want the same practical things to sleep in, do you think?"

"Well, I only know about my wife, but yes, I think so."

"Maybe something practical and one … well, what you men call frilly. Not too risqué, but enough to make a woman feel she's attractive, and that you appreciate that she's attractive."

"Maybe," said Joe, blushing again.

"Here, look at these. They're from our lingerie shop: *Something Less.*" It had taken her only a minute to pick out three outfits apiece; two that resembled men's, with shirt and pants, but satin and with embroidery, and then one lacey and revealing, one in red and another in black.

"Well!" said Joe approvingly.

"I thought you'd like them. I would advise you to have them all sent to the room, and let the ladies decide which they want. That okay?"

"Yes," said a relieved Joe. "Simpler than I thought. Can you look at all the merchandise on the computer?"

"It's on the computer so people can browse or shop online, from their rooms, or even from home. Sizing is a problem, but not for this kind of thing. I know the sizes the ladies are buying, and the clothes are exchangeable in any event. Anything else I can help you with?" she asked.

"No. That has finished all my responsibilities for the day. Maybe I'll try to find something fun to do."

"Where are the rest of your friends?"

"They're off interviewing or something, so I'm on my own."

"Then have a good time, and … don't shave to do it."

"What?" responded Joe, rubbing his stubbled face.

"Doesn't look too bad, and men these days always enjoy *not* shaving."

"Sometimes *not* doing something is what gives us the most fun," Joe replied, smiling. "Thank you, Janet. For the advice and the help with the shopping, too."

He walked around the casino, and quickly realized that he was still dressed better than most, and that his beard was less than most. If he wasn't shaving, then what should he do? It was early, and the casino wasn't yet busy. Slots were occupied only sparsely, and the tables were mostly empty, those that were open at all. Maybe he could learn to play craps, dice. It looked complicated and very "interactive," and the only tables that were open had other players at them. Not now, he decided. Just then he saw Tyla standing alone at her open blackjack table.

"Good morning," he said as he sat across from her.

"I guess," replied Tyla. "Going to try to beat your own record from yesterday? Go for a new personal best?"

"I might," he said, placing a hundred dollars on the table.

Tyla began moving the stacks of five-dollar chips toward him, saying, "Not as confident as yesterday, though. Yesterday you only needed twenty."

The pit boss walked by in back of Tyla now and stopped. "Back to show us all how it's done?" He smiled.

"Did you get it all back last night? My winnings, I mean."

"Every penny and then some," he said as he moved on. "I'll be here if ya need me again, Tyla. If he decides to try to break the house again."

"So," said Tyla. "All hundred on the first hand, or do you want to start slowly."

"Ten is fine with me."

Joe won, and Tyla commented that he should have bet the whole hundred. He lost the next couple of hands, but they had started chatting.

"Have you worked here long?" Joe asked.

"A year or so. I've been divorced about two years. Needed the income."

"Good place to work?"

"No, but the pay is good. The boss, Bevins I mean, is hard to take. Hard to ignore, too."

"Hard to ignore?"

"I'm expected to provide … well, sex for him, if I want to keep my job."

Joe's face must have shown something close to shock at this revelation. The casualness of this admission, in spite of the nature of it, surprised him completely."

"Not as bad, as …" began Tyla.

"No … I mean yes, it is. Is it really …?"

"Yes and no. When I get enough time to get a good reference I'm outa here. Kiss the asshole goodbye instead of just kissing his ass."

"How long will that be?"

"Not as long as this game, if you're just going to sit there without anteing up."

"Oh," said Joe, placing ten dollars on the square in front of him.

"I can't talk to you if you're not playing, after all. So, is this going to be my life story or yours? Most people just play, but the ones who want to talk usually talk about themselves."

"Not much about me worth talking about, so it's up to you," he said. Joe lost again. He wasn't paying much attention to the game right now, but he put up another two chips.

"Not much about me, either. Divorced card dealer in Las Vegas. Pretty common."

"Why … well, that's probably personal," said Joe.

"Are you really interested, or is this just … are you hitting on me *again*?" She smiled to make it clear this was a joke.

"I never stopped. Hitting on you, I mean."

"Well, this part is personal and some major ashes in my life, so don't ask if you don't want to hear."

Joe lost again and put up two more chips by way of an answer.

"I don't know what there is about you that makes me want to tell you this, but—"

"I'm a pediatrician?" offered Joe.

"Do I look like a kid or something?"

"I'm pretty sure you used to be one."

Tyla smiled, a rather sad smile. "I used to be a virgin, too. And I used to have a kid, but neither is true anymore."

Joe was silent.

"And there's the bastard that took my kid from me." She nodded behind Joe and he turned to see Harry entering the casino.

"His name is Harry?" asked Joe.

"You know him? Not a friend of yours, I hope?"

"No," said Joe. "Not at all."

"Yeah, that's Harry, small-time when he's not less than small-time, but he started my daughter on the drugs. He likes them young."

"I saw him picking up an underaged … well, she *looked* underage …"

"If Harry picked her up she probably was. My daughter was only fourteen. I told him I would cut his balls off of he ever touched her, but Harry is small-time in everything he does. Game a little, drug a little and … well, little kids.

I don't think my daughter ever … anyway, he got her started on the drugs and I couldn't stop it, and … well, six months later she died of an overdose. I went over the deep end, and my husband couldn't deal with his daughter's death and me at the same time, so now I deal here and have to deal with Bevins in order to keep dealing here, and … hell, I didn't mean to tell you all this, but I swear that if I ever get a chance I'll kill that bastard." She was beginning to cry now, as she looked at Harry sitting in front of one of the slot machines.

Tyla shook her head and turned to the pit boss standing behind her. "I need a break," she said.

"Sure," he replied. No further questions asked.

Tyla had no sleeves on her *uniform,* but raised her arms above her head and showed both sides of her hands in the tradition of dealers as they left their tables. Some unseen camera was watching her, Joe was sure.

"So, do you want to play some more, sir?" asked the pit boss. "You have fifty left."

Joe shoved all his chips onto the square in front of him and turned to look at Harry, who was oblivious to all that had been said about him just now. His attention was pulled back to his game by the pit boss asking, "Do you want a hit?"

"No," said Joe, without looking.

"Player has only nine. Four and a five. You can take anything in my deck."

"No," repeated Joe, and turned to face him. After a moment he came back to himself and waved his hand over his cards.

The pit boss shrugged and said, "Dealer has twelve and," he turned a card from the deck, "a queen. Player wins." He smiled.

As he moved the piles of chips to where Joe's were sitting, Robert Bevins walked by, heading for Harry.

"Tips go to the dealer, right?" asked Joe.

"Yes," said the pit boss.

Joe shoved all his chips toward him and said, "Tell Tyla I'm sorry, will you?"

"Sure," he replied.

Chapter 20

Robert Bevins was saying something to Harry, but Joe couldn't hear them. He was suddenly disgusted by the whole thing; Harry and Bevins—all of them. He wanted to be outside, but as he walked toward the exit, so did Harry and Robert Bevins. By the time he was through the door they were walking down the drive.

"Can I get your car, sir?" said a voice from behind him. Joe turned to see that he was standing in the valet parking area, the only one standing there right now, facing a familiar face that he couldn't place. It was the kind of situation where one sees someone familiar in an unexpected situation and can't recall where the previous encounter was, or who the person is.

"Do you have a ticket, sir?" the young man asked again.

Joe shook his head and then said, "Peter, isn't it? You were working in that café yesterday. Covering for …"

"Sally," said Peter. "Yeah, you were with Mr. Monroe, *no relation to presidents past or present*, right? Ya need your car?"

"No," said Joe. "I actually don't have a car. Sorry."

A car did drive up just then, with a woman in the driver's seat. "Where is the self-parking?" she asked.

"The valet parking is free," Peter replied.

"Including your tip?" she asked.

"No," said Peter. "Self-parking is right around the corner. Follow the signs. Ya can't miss it."

She drove away, and Peter turned back to face Joe. He followed Joe's gaze to Harry and Robert Bevins. Robert was showing a piece of paper to Harry, and Harry was looking very upset.

"Looks like Harry's in trouble," said Peter.

"Yes," said Joe. "I wonder why?"

"Harry plays here a lot lately," said Peter. "He has some money. Might be Bevins extended him a line, and he's behind on the payback. That would be pretty stupid, but Robert Bevins is no Rhodes Scholar."

"A line?" said Joe.

"A line of credit," replied Peter. "The casinos used to do that a lot, years ago, but not much anymore. Harry wouldn't have been a good risk anytime. Small-time hustler and big-time loser."

The lady from the car that had just driven to self-parking walked by pulling her two suitcases, and Peter moved quickly to open the door for her. "You find the self-parking all right?" he asked.

"Yes, and sorry about the tip." She smiled as she entered the hotel lobby.

Joe looked after her as she entered and thought that not everyone was wealthy in Las Vegas, or at least not everyone threw their money around liberally. Peter was talking to another man who had exited the hotel as the lady had entered, and they were looking after her as they did. They seemed to know each other.

Robert was walking up the drive and went back into the casino as Harry walked away quickly. Nothing more to see outside and the temperature was beginning to get oppressive, even in the dry Nevada weather. Joe went back inside as he heard Peter saying, "I'll get a tip outa her before she leaves. Bet ya twenty I do, Sarge."

They gamble on everything here, Joe thought.

Inside, the casino was beginning to buzz, but Joe wasn't interested. Maybe coffee and a snack. Not coffee; he usually didn't drink coffee after his morning cup, but would switch to hot chocolate. A few days ago when he had first met Natalie it had been over coffee and hot chocolate, and Natalie had said she was embarrassed to be sitting with a pediatrician who was drinking hot chocolate. He hoped he had impressed her more since then, but he had tried not to drink hot chocolate in her presence after that.

Natalie wasn't here right now so there would be no harm done, he decided as he took a seat in the same café he had been at yesterday with James Monroe. The young lady who waited on him wore a name tag proclaiming "SALLY."

"What can I get for you, sir?" she asked.

"Hot chocolate, please. Large. Are you feeling better, Sally? Peter said you were sick yesterday."

Sally was a little startled, but recovered quickly. "Oh, yeah. He covered for me." She seemed a little embarrassed, and Joe wondered if she had been sick or just needed a "mental health" day off, as he used to say.

"What's a good snack today?" he asked.

"Do you like sweet rolls?"

"Not really."

"Good," said Sally. "They're not at their best here. The raspberry tart is one of my favorites."

"One of those then, and hot chocolate," said Joe.

"Ya want ta try the mocha chocolate? It's really good."

Joe wasn't sure he wouldn't rather have had plain hot chocolate, but consented to try the mocha. When Sally left, he felt as if he had been forced to give up hot chocolate for Sally, just as he had for Natalie. Next time he was going to insist on hot chocolate and nothing else.

This time, however, he drank mocha and ate raspberry tart and had to admit that at least the tart tasted good. He told Sally both were excellent, and she seemed very pleased. He paid in cash, too, ten dollars for a six-dollar charge, and that pleased her even more. He didn't want Reggie paying for his snack right now. He was about to leave the café when his cell phone rang.

"Hello,"

"Hi, Joe," said Natalie. "You upstairs, or the casino, or someplace else?"

"In a café beside the casino," said Joe.

"I'm coming into the casino now, which side should I … oh I see you." She waved and closed her phone as Joe waved back.

When she reached him, she smiled and said, "Are you leaving or coming?"

"I was leaving, but if you want to sit I can have something to drink."

"I would like something, if that's okay."

"Yeah, yeah sure," he replied. They sat at the same table he had just stood from, as the busboy cleared it.

"May I get you …" began Sally as she came over to them. "Oh, you're back already?"

"I brought reinforcements," Joe replied, nodding toward Natalie.

"Oh, sure. What can I get ya this time?"

Joe looked at Natalie and said, "The raspberry tart is good."

"Yeah, okay," said Natalie, "and coffee for me. Hot chocolate for Joe, right?"

"Ya don't want another mocha, sir?" asked Sally.

"He likes plain hot chocolate," explained Natalie with a shrug. "That was one of the first things I liked about you, Joe. That first night I met you and we shared coffee and hot chocolate." She smiled at him, and he couldn't tell whether she was serious or kidding. It had only been four days ago, and he remembered her saying she was annoyed at him for drinking hot chocolate instead of coffee.

"Okay," responded Sally. It clearly didn't matter to her at all what he drank. "You want something to eat, sir? Another raspberry tart, maybe?"

"No, the hot chocolate will be fine," said Joe.

"Sure," said Sally, as she left to get the order.

"How old do you think she is?" asked Joe.

"I don't know, but I have a question for you too, Joe. What do you think of Raul Perez?"

"What?" said Joe.

"You think he's real, or fake, or both?" asked Natalie.

"Raul? The chauffer?" asked Joe. "I hadn't thought about it. He's …"

"Yes?" Natalie said. "What is he? I wasn't sure either, that's why I wanted to go this morning and *talk shop* with him. After we got done talking and after I got done nosing around the ED, and after I realized that Carolyn and Carl were probably going to be treated to lunch and I wasn't, I decided to let you buy me lunch. That, and see what you thought of Raul *the chauffeur* Perez."

The coffee and hot chocolate and raspberry tart arrived to break into the conversation and to give Joe a chance to think.

"So?" said Natalie as she sipped her black coffee. "What do you think?"

"It's rather strange, I guess," Joe said. "A homicide officer and former SWAT team member, driving a limo. Do you think he was telling us the truth?"

"That was actually my first thought," said Natalie. "That he was just full of it; but I think he's telling it straight. He talks like he's a cop."

"So, what's he doing driving a limo? Could he really just be retired and leaving the stress of his job behind, ya think?"

"Well," said Natalie, taking a bite of raspberry tart. "This is good. I might say yes to your question, except that he talks like a cop who is *still* a cop, not a retired cop."

"You can tell the difference?"

"Yeah, sometimes. The retired guys usually talk about the *war stories*, the exciting stuff or crazy stuff, or the disgusting, frustrating stuff; but Raul talked about procedures and crime demographics and … well, stuff that guys still doing the job worry about."

"Maybe," said Joe.

"Another thing," continued Natalie. "We walked around the ED, and he seemed to know where things were and where the trauma stuff got brought in and things like that. Things a *chauffeur* wouldn't know, but a cop would. I was asking about that guy Percy, too, and that was strange."

"Percy?" asked Joe.

"The guy you mixed it up with last night on Fremont Street. What he was about and all that."

"He's a pimp," said Joe.

"There are different kinds, Joe. Like Raul said, some of them really do look after the girls. Sounds like Percy may be one of those. One of the security guards even said that when one of Percy's girls got brought in they would call him, and he would come down to make sure they were all right and everything."

Joe just nodded.

"Strange thing was that they were willing to talk to me at all. Here I was, this tourist walking around with this chauffeur, with no official anything, and these guys were telling me all about the place. They all seemed to know Raul, but he seemed to be trying not to know them; not to appear to know them, anyway. Really strange, I thought."

Joe thought and then replied, "That happened last night, too. We drove by the fire truck and ambulance and they waved at him, but he didn't wave back. No acknowledgement at all. That's strange."

Natalie frowned. "He's still a cop. Not retired, but still doing it either for the cops, or on his own, maybe."

"On his own?"

"Yeah, I think Raul is either still a cop, or he's more likely in the private cop sector now. But he's still doing the cop scene, not the chauffeur scene."

"Yes," said Joe finally. "That makes sense. But if he's still a cop, what's he doing driving a limo?"

"Driving a limo *for us*," corrected Natalie. "Driving us, who recently were exposing an organized crime connection in Kentucky. We were advised to leave Kentucky because the state police, or at least Captain Hank Morgan, thought some of those people, yet to be apprehended, might be a threat to us. And now a cop who is pretending to be retired is driving us around."

"It's strange, isn't it?" said Joe. "I wonder who picked Raul Perez to be our driver."

"I don't think we can just ask him and expect an answer."

Joe thought for a moment before saying, "Maybe we ought to take taxis if we need to leave the hotel from now on."

"Good idea. The food here is pretty good anyway; at least the raspberry tarts are."

# Chapter 21

"So, you left Carolyn and Carl at the Medical Center with Raul? Should we warn them, or am I becoming paranoid?"

"You're being safe … and paranoid," responded Natalie with a smile. "Take a good stiff drink of that hot chocolate and call them. Paranoia isn't always a bad thing."

"I thought you didn't like me to drink hot chocolate."

"That was when I first met you, and someone had just shot at you and someone was about to be murdered, and I wasn't sure that a hot chocolate-drinking pediatrician was going to be any help at all. But that was when I thought you were just a hot chocolate-drinking pediatrician. Now I know that you're a pediatrician who isn't afraid of anything, not even drinking hot chocolate in public. None of that mocha shit for you, Joe. Hot chocolate, straight up.

"Now call Carolyn and Carl, and figure out how to get them to take a taxi back here. You're better at that than I am. And when you finish, call Raul and tell him he has the rest of our stay off." She smiled at him and looked like she might lean over and kiss his check. The look passed, but the smile remained.

Joe did take a drink of hot chocolate and then opened his phone. "No sense in calling Carl. He'll do whatever Carolyn says to do."

He dialed and when she answered he said, "How's it going?"

"Damned Carl," said Carolyn.

"What?" said Joe.

"They did offer me a contract on the spot, and promises and money, and I would have taken it if Carl hadn't told me not to. What are you up to?"

"Natalie and I were thinking of driving out into the desert a little, just to look around. Do you think you and Carl can catch a cab back to the hotel so we can ask Raul to drive us?"

"Yeah, sure. We're here for another hour or so at least."

"We'll be back when you are, and I'll make a reservation here for supper. Give everyone a chance to relax a little; how's that?"

"Sounds great. I never realized how stressful this whole thing has been."

"What whole thing? The interview?"

"And the shooting at the airport and running out of Kentucky and street fighting in Las Vegas. Take your pick. Quiet will suit me fine tonight. Quiet and a little elegance. You think you can arrange that?"

"I'll try my best," Joe said, and closed his phone.

"So that part is good," said Natalie. "But I'm not sure I like the part about driving out into the desert with Raul."

"Here, have a taste of hot chocolate. It will clear your mind. We don't have to do anything except call Raul to have him come here to pick us up, and then cancel. Oh, and make reservations at the best restaurant in this place for tonight. By the time it all gets sorted out, no one will care whether we drive in the desert, walk in the sun, or lie through our teeth."

"I'll make the reservations if you want, and you can dance around Raul, okay?"

"Sure," said Joe.

He dialed and talked while Natalie dialed and talked, and when they were finished, Sally was asking them if they wanted anything else.

"Yes," said Joe. "Coffee, hot chocolate and two raspberry tarts, please." Sally smiled and left them.

"Raul will be here in thirty minutes, so I'll either call or meet him out front and tell him we've changed our minds. If you're with me, I'll suggest that we decided on something else to occupy our time, and if you're not, I'll say that you're ill or something."

Natalie smiled. "I can either be an accomplice to your lie or surrender my reputation. In Las Vegas neither is of much value. Honesty or virtue, I mean."

Joe's face took on a somewhat puzzled expression. "The choice isn't an obvious one, dearest Natalie. Your virtue is worth preserving, but your reputation may be beyond recall. Did I tell you that I think you look incredibly beautiful today? I do, and I'm sure Raul has noted this as well. He may have even imagined that you made yourself beautiful to impress him, since it was he with whom you spent the morning. Men can sometimes be egotistical like that. He probably cannot imagine any man resisting your charms and therefore he will assume … well, you know what it is he will assume.

"As for your honesty: if you allow me to mislead Raul, you'll be an accomplice in any event, whether you utter a word yourself or not. No, I'm afraid your honesty has already been compromised, and your reputation as well. At least your virtue is intact."

Natalie looked puzzled herself now. "You really think I look beautiful, Joe? It's been a long time since I've felt beautiful, and even longer since anyone else thought so. I think I'm going to go up to the room and bask in that feeling, and take hot bath and then take a nap. Alone, I'm afraid.

"But you said something else, didn't you? About honesty or virtue or something like that. I'm afraid I didn't pay any attention after the part where you said you think I'm beautiful. Was any of it important?" She smiled a mischievous smile and winked at him.

"Not a word of it was in the least important," said Joe. "Go and bask until supper. You did make reservations, I assume."

"For seven o'clock. I bet you didn't buy me any pajamas, did you?"

"You lose," smiled Joe.

"Flannel, I bet."

"You lose again. Now go and bask while I spend my pitifully small remnant of honesty upon useless lies."

"You're sweet, Joe," she said, and did kiss his cheek this time before she left him alone.

# Chapter 22

Joe was alone, but much happier. He still had nothing to do, so he decided to meet Raul in front of the hotel rather than call him to cancel. He wondered about Raul and whether Natalie was right, or whether they were both just paranoid from all they had been through in recent days. It did seem strange that a SWAT team member should be driving an ordinary limo. Even if Natalie had been mistaken about what Raul had said to her, that part still seemed strange. Meeting Raul might give him a chance to look at him with this in mind and draw his own conclusion, but he really didn't want to think Natalie was mistaken, and they really didn't need to use the limo, so why be bothered by it at all?

At the appointed time, Joe went outside to find Raul Perez and the limo waiting. "I'm sorry, Raul," he said simply. "There has been a change in plans and we'll not need you this afternoon. I talked to Carolyn and she said they have gotten a cab back here and we have reservations to eat at the hotel tonight, so you can have the entire evening off." There was no sense in developing an elaborate lie when a lesser one would do. The plans had not *changed*; they had just never required Raul at all.

Raul smiled and nodded, and Joe smiled in return. He had been a pleasant man last night and one that Joe had enjoyed talking to, but now Joe felt uncomfortable and he wasn't sure why. Was there a change in Raul, or had Natalie's suggestions brought about a change in Joe? Maybe it was just the fact that he was lying to Raul that made Joe feel this way.

Finally Raul said, "Well, if that's the case, I'll be leaving."

Joe turned as someone called, "Hey, man!"

Raul turned back to see Percy walking up the drive, still dressed as he had been the night before; same black leather, red shirt, sunglasses and outlandish wig.

"Hey, you! Yeah, I'm talkin' ta you, dude," he said as he walked straight toward them.

He was facing Joe now and said, "I gotta talk ta ya, man. What's your name, anyway?"

"Joe."

"Yeah, that was what the girls called ya last night," said Percy. "I gotta talk ta ya, Joe."

Raul was standing close at hand now, and Joe was looking intently at Percy. "So, talk."

"Not here, man. Someplace private," Percy said, eyeing Raul.

"How about Fremont Street?" suggested Joe.

"Fremont Street? Shit, man, don't you have a room here or something?"

"Not my room, Percy. You want me to buy you a cup of coffee?"

"Here?" asked Percy, looking at Raul again.

"I'm not going anywhere else, Percy."

Percy shook his head. "What's da matter with you, man? Just wanta talk is all. Yeah, sure, coffee or something. Let's go."

He started walking into the hotel and Joe started to follow. "I think I'll be okay, Raul. Thanks."

Raul shrugged and departed, and Joe followed Percy into the casino. He had expected Percy's entrance to cause a stir, but it was hardly noticed. As Joe looked around, he saw that the crowd was now up to full strength, and while Percy might be more outlandishly dressed than most, he wasn't going to win the gold medal for dress today. He might not even get the bronze. He looked at Joe, who motioned back toward the same café he had been at all afternoon. They sat, and of course their server was Sally.

"Didn't you just leave here?" she asked, looking at Joe.

"Yeah, but I just can't seem ta stay away."

"So, what can I get for ya this time?" asked Sally, looking first at Joe and then at Percy. If she thought Percy was unusual, she didn't show it.

"The raspberry tarts are good," said Joe.

"Yeah, okay," said Percy. "An' I'll have a hot chocolate."

"The mocha was pretty good too," said Joe.

"Nah. Just plain hot chocolate, Sally," said Percy, looking around.

"Then just plain hot chocolate for me, too," said Joe.

Sally left and Percy said, "He's a cop, ain't he? That chauffeur. You sure it's okay ta talk here, Joe?"

"It's the only place we're going to talk, Percy, so it has to be okay."

Percy shook his head and wig in disgust. "You're some kinda weird, man. Look, I got a problem and I need your help."

"Okay," said Joe.

"Katie got picked up by a fella named Harry last night an' she ain't checked in since then. I told her not ta mess with him. Bad guy. Hurts the girls sometimes." Percy shook his head again. "I told 'im not ta mess with my girls, but—"

"Yeah, I saw him pick her up," said Joe. "That's how I met your *young women,* and how I met you," said Joe.

If Percy was aware of the accusation in Joe's voice he didn't react to it. "Yeah. What Maggie said. Said there was a cop with ya, too."

"Natalie," said Joe. "What is it you want my help with?"

"Katie's missin' an' I need ta find her," said Percy, as if he was stating the obvious.

"It's been less than twenty-four hours," said Joe.

"They's supposta check in," said Percy. "Katie knows that. There are guys that abuse girls out there."

"Maybe her cell phone died, or maybe Harry paid for some overtime," suggested Joe.

"She knows ta check in. She's got two phones, anyways."

"Two phones?" asked Joe.

"Sure," said Percy. "I get all of 'em one regular one that's got all the fancy stuff that the kids like these days, an' then I get 'em one a' the *mama* phones too. An' I pay for both ta make sure they're working. Get 'em on a family plan, so's they ain't that expensive. These girls can't remember ta pay rent or phone bills or nothin'."

"*Mama* phones?" asked Joe.

"Yeah," said Percy. "One a' those phones that the mamas give their little kids wid the GPS stuff built in. So's they can track where their kids are. Can't be turned off or nothin'. Mama thinks she can track 'em on the computer, like that works."

"Like what works?" asked Joe.

"Can't track da kid, just the phone. Little Johnny leaves da phone wid little Billy and he just tells Ma, Johnny's in da bathroom or somethin' Then he calls little Johnny an' tells him ta call Ma. Don't work for shit 'less the kid wants it to. My girls want it to work in case they gets in trouble. I can tell where they are an' be there like the fuckin' cavalry. Got my laptop in the car." He smiled with obvious pride.

"So Katie has a phone that will tell you where she is; go find her."

"Phone's off, man. Wouldn't need no help if it was simple."

"I thought you said the phone couldn't be turned off."

"Can't be. Someone pulled the plug, or smashed it."

"Took out the battery?" asked Joe. "Why would Katie do that?"

"Katie wouldn't. She's in trouble," said Percy. "Girl's get abused, ya know. Men take advantage of 'em."

"Yeah," said Joe, staring at Percy.

"What?"

"Well, you're a pimp, Percy," said Joe

"What's that supposed ta mean?"

"Pimps abuse women, Percy, don't they?"

"Some do. An' cops abuse women. An' lawyers, an' doctors, too. What da ya know about bein' a pimp, man?"

"Well …" began Joe, and stopped. He really didn't know anything about being a pimp.

"I take good care a' my girls. I got doctors who treat 'em if they need it. I don't allow no drugs. Make sure they use condoms, an' if they get inta somethin' they want out of, they can split an' I'll take care of it. Hell, I send more a' 'em back home than I keep here, but most of 'em don't have no place ta go back to. That, or the place they got ta go back to is worse than bein' here."

"But you're selling them for sex, Percy."

"*They're* sellin'," corrected Percy. "I don't tell any of 'em ta go out there, but there ain't much else for 'em if they don't. Can't get a job without reportin' themselves ta the cops an' getting' thrown in jail or sent back ta where they were. Back ta what they run away from in the first place. If they have ta work the street, at least I help keep 'em safe for a while, 'til they can get some ID, an' get a real job."

Their hot chocolate and tart arrived and Percy looked at Sally. "Ain't that right, Sally?'

"What?" she asked.

"We got ya this job here, didn't we?"

"Well, yeah," she replied. "Couldn't spend the rest a' my life out there, could I?"

"No way," said Percy. "Not a smart girl like you."

"Saved my life, Percy," said Sally, bending over to kiss his cheek.

"Ah, yer goin' ta embarrass the ol' man, Sal."

"You deserve it," replied Sally, and left to wait on the next table.

Chapter 23

"Okay," said Joe. "So you're a *good* pimp, and Katie should have checked in and … well, what do you want me to do, cruise the strip looking for her?"

"Got da other girls doin' that. She ain't on the street anyways or she woulda got to me by now. Girl's in trouble, man."

"So what can I do?"

"Not you, dude. That cop with you."

"Raul?"

"No, man. That girl what was with ya last night."

"Natalie?" said Joe.

"Yeah, that's her name."

"Okay," replied Joe. "What can she do?"

"She can get some a' the local cops ta go out lookin' fer Katie, can't she? Maggie said she was checkin' out fer runaways or somethin' and said she could get the local guys to back her up. So maybe she could …?" Percy stopped as the expression on Joe's face turned to bewilderment.

"She's a cop, right?" asked Percy.

"Yeah," said Joe. "But …"

Percy frowned for a moment and then looked at Joe. "But she ain't lookin' for nothin' here 'cept a vacation, right? Just hastlin' the girls last night. Is that it?"

"Yeah," said Joe. "That's about it."

"Shit," said Percy.

"So we gotta go for Plan B," said Joe.

"That don't work real well, Joe. The mornin' after pill? My girls are all on the *day before pills* or da injection or somethin'; an' condoms too, a' course."

"No," said Joe, shaking his head. "Not contraception. I mean we need a second plan to get the police to start looking for Katie. Do you really have all your girls … I mean *young women,* out looking for her?"

"Well, yeah, a' course."

"How long can you have them do that? Without working, I mean. Don't you need their income?"

Percy shrugged. "I got maybe three weeks or a month saved up. Girls can draw on that so's they don't need ta work for a while. 'Til we find Katie."

Joe looked puzzled and asked, "You have three or four weeks' worth of money saved?"

"Well, more'n that, man. But I'd have ta tap in on the bond funds ta get any more."

"The bond funds?"

"Yeah," said Percy. "Munis mostly, and some triple A commerce paper. We don't have much equities right now, with the economy an' all dat, an' I'd like ta hold onta da gold for a li'l longer."

"The gold?" asked Joe, looking at the chain around Percy's neck.

"Ah, man. Not this. It's as fake as it can be. Even you gotta be able ta see that. It's just fa' street show. I got gold bullion in the bank vault, but I think it's got a little more ta rise 'fore the bubble bursts." Percy nodded.

"The bubble?"

"Yeah. Ya don't think this is goin' on forever, do ya? It's like the real estate bubble. Got outa that one just in time, I did." Percy whistled and shook his head as Joe wondered if his financial planner had any of his retirement money invested in gold.

"Look," said Joe. "You're right. You're not likely to see Katie on the street if she hasn't contacted you. Get your *women* to start looking for Harry, too, if you think Harry is the one that grabbed her. He was here earlier, but not with Katie. Not that I saw, anyway. Robert Bevins threw him out again.

"Do you know where Harry lives? If Katie is with him, she's likely there, don't you think?"

"That's true," nodded Percy. "I can find out where he's livin.'"

Joe nodded too. "Now, as for the police, I think the best approach might be to get them to look for one of my patients. I'll talk to Natalie to see what the best line is, but I can tell them that I saw her, recognized her, and they need to find her."

"They'd do that, man," chuckled Percy. "Drop everything and scour da fuckin' city for you."

"If I tell them she's sick and needs treatment and has run away … or something like that, that'll convince them. Natalie is police, and she can tell us what will get their attention."

"But Katie ain't your patient an' she ain't sick. Ya think they'll buy any story you lay on 'em without checking it?"

"You know Vegas maybe, but where I come from I can get a dozen people to lie for me with one phone call. More if they knew it was lying to the government. We used to call them *revenuers* back when I was a kid and people were making moonshine, and folks back up in the mountains still call them that. Not much trust of the authorities there, even now. All we have to do is figure out what the best story is. Let me call Natalie and see if she can come down."

As Joe reached for his phone, it rang for him instead.

# Chapter 24

"Hey, Joe," said Carolyn's voice when he answered. "Where are you and Natalie?"

"I'm in a little café beside the casino with—"

"Carl and I are just coming in. Oh, I see you." She closed the phone and waved and Joe waved back, trying desperately to think of any explanation that might work. Carolyn was standing beside the table before he had even a glimmer of an idea of what that explanation might be.

"Joe?" she said, looking not at him, but at Percy.

"You know Percy, don't you, Carolyn? We met last night."

"That's not what I would have called our encounter last night, but I do remember you, Percy," replied Carolyn. "I hope you haven't come over here to even up some macho score with Joe or something."

"With Joe? What you talkin', babe?" said Percy as he got up and indicted she should sit in the empty chair between him and Joe. Both remained standing.

"Yeah, with Joe, the guy who knocked you on your ass last night and will do it again if needs be," said Carolyn. "And don't call me *babe*."

"Ah, sugar. I don't mean no harm. Joe an' me are real tight, ya know?" Percy reached over and slapped Joe on the shoulder.

"How tight are you, Joe? Have you two been drinking?" asked Carolyn.

"Drinkin'? What ya talkin', ba— I mean, miss?"

Carolyn stared and Percy looked puzzled, until finally Joe said, "When da white folks get ta'gether an' talk, Percy, bein' *tight* means bein' *drunk*. Whole different world. Whole different language."

"No shit," said Percy, shaking his head.

"And this would be Carl, Percy, whom you have not met yet, but whom I know you'll like," continued Joe.

Carl looked apprehensive, but finally extended his hand. "Pleased to meet you, Percy."

"Percy was just expressing some concern about the *gold bubble*, Carl," added Joe.

"Precious metals, really," corrected Carl. "I'd be careful, Percy."

"Oh, I am, Carl. I think I can hold on for a li'l while longer, maybe."

"Possibly, but watch closely. Caution is necessary in these times," Carl said.

"I's slippin' a little out already, but don't know where ta move it, Carl," said Percy. "Whatcha doing with yours?"

"Oh, bonds of course. Munis, and triple A commercial paper, too. They're pretty secure, don't you think, Percy?"

"Short-term, yeah. No equities, though."

"Equities are very risky right now," agreed Carl, "and of course, you must stay short-term in the bond market as you suggest. Interest rates cannot possibly—"

"Stop it!" said Carolyn. "Stop it right now, both of you. I am not going to stand here while you two act as if you're *normal people*, so just stop it right now!"

"I hear that, mama," Percy replied.

Carl could only stammer.

"Perhaps you had better sit, Carolyn. People are beginning to watch us closely," Joe intervened.

"Where the hell is Natalie, Joe?"

"Upstairs, either in a hot bath or napping in her bed," replied Joe. "I need to talk to her though, so let me call."

"Not as much as *I* need to talk to her," said Carolyn, opening her phone.

Carolyn dialed, sat, and a moment later said, "Natalie. Where are you?"

"What?"

"Red what? In bed wearing …?" She looked at the three men, now seated and staring at her. "Can you come down here to that café by the casino?"

"Yeah, sure. You can have the red one. What color is the … black? But I don't think I'll look good … what? Lace and …? Did you buy these, Natalie? Joe bought them!?"

Carolyn fixed an accusing glare at Joe and said, "Can you come down here, Natalie? Now?"

"Tell her to change first," suggested Joe.

"Or maybe not," said Percy. "I'm guessin' that red an' black, with lace and in bed are … well, what did ya buy 'em, Joe? An' one for each a' 'em, ya say?"

"Tell her to change first," repeated Joe.

Carolyn closed her phone and said, "She will be down here in five minutes."

"Okay," said Percy. "You two is both doctors, right?"

"Is this a trap or something?" asked Carolyn. "Yes, we're both physicians."

"I got a'other problem ya might be able ta help me wid."

"We should wait for Natalie to discuss that," said Joe.

"No, no. I got this other problem. It's my hair," said Percy.

"Bad hair," said Carolyn.

"Not this hair," said Percy. "This hair!" he said, as he pulled off his wig to reveal a scalp, scaling and red, with a few wisps of hair on it. "Docs don't seem ta know what this is."

Carolyn's face showed first surprise, and then interest. "Turn toward Joe, Percy. Inflamed and scaling edges with central clearing and hypopigmentation. What do you think, Joe?"

"Could be fungal?" replied Joe.

"Yeah, what I was thinking too. How long have you had this, Percy?"

"Little bit for a while, but bad fo' just a year maybe," said Percy.

"When did you start wearing the wig?" asked Joe.

"When it started gettin' bad." Percy shrugged.

"Before or after it started getting bad?" asked Carolyn.

"Maybe before it got real bad," said Percy.

"Must sweat under that wig," said Joe. "That might make it worse."

"Sure might," said Carolyn, as Sally came over to their table.

"Um, hi folks, an' you too, Percy. Can I get you somethin'?" Sally asked.

"Coffee," said Carl, with more than a trace of embarrassment. "Large, please."

"Yes, thank you," said Carolyn, with no hint of embarrassment at all. "Coffee will be fine for me, too. And do you think you can get me a clean plastic baggie and a sharp knife? Maybe a steak knife or something? I have to cut Percy's throat."

She grinned and then said, "I'm just joking!"

"Cut my ... she is jokin', right, Joe?" asked Percy.

"With Carolyn, it's hard to tell," replied Joe.

"I just need to take a sample. Don't be such a wuss, Percy," Carolyn chided.

"We could just recommend something," offered Joe. "I can't prescribe here in Nevada."

"Better to get a sample for micro," replied Carolyn.

"Sample a' what?" asked Percy.

"Just a little scraping of your skin," said Carolyn. "It won't hurt. Stop being a baby."

"Thought ya said we weren't callin' each other *babe* or nothin'." Percy frowned.

"Well," said Carolyn, "we'll only use that term if someone acts like a baby. How's that? Or a *babe*."

"Well, you's a babe, honey." Percy smiled. "No doubt on that."

"Takin' a big chance sassin' a woman with a knife, Percy. Might carve my initials on your head."

"Okay. Okay," said Percy. Sally arrived with the coffee and a small plastic baggie with a sealable top and a steak knife. She said nothing, but stayed by the table. Carolyn took the knife by the blade and scraped a small amount of the scaling skin into the baggie and then sealed it.

"There," said Carolyn. "That wasn't so bad. Want Mama should kiss it an' make it all better?"

"Yeah," smiled Percy. "That'd be real nice, if'n Joe don't mind, I mean. Don't got nothin' red or black or lacey ta give ya, though."

"Put your friggin' wig back on, Percy, before we get thrown out of the hotel," said Carolyn, placing the knife back on Sally's tray. "Thank you, and make sure they wash that well."

Sally left, tossing the knife into the trashcan on her way to the kitchen, and Percy replaced his wig as he had been told to do and said, "She's a pretty good surgeon, Joe."

"Not really surgery," Joe replied.

Percy shrugged. "So, can you write down some medicine fo' me, Joe?"

"I can't really prescribe anything here in Nevada," Joe replied. "Where are you going to take that sample, Carolyn?"

"I'll take it to the Medical Center tomorrow. I'll make up some bull about wanting to see how the lab works or something." She shrugged.

Percy shook his head and said, "An' I thought you was such a nice lady, sugar."

"Wrong, Percy," said Carolyn.

"So jus' write it down an' I'll get it, okay, Joe?" said Percy, turning back to Joe.

"I don't even have a prescription blank," said Joe.

"Just write it on a napkin," Percy said, handing Joe a pen. "I'll get somebody to get it fo' me."

"That's an expensive pen, Percy," said Carolyn. "Carl got me one like that to impress the people at the Medical Center when we interviewed."

"This is a knock off," replied Percy. "Pretty good one, but only three bucks, Carl. Hope ya didn't pay no more'n that." Percy chuckled as Carl cleared his throat.

"So you's going to work at the Medical Center, that right? Maggie said somethin' 'bout that," said Percy. "That where ya was showing off your pen?"

"Well, yes," said Carolyn.

Carl cleared his throat again and looked intently at Percy. "What do you know about the Medical Center, Percy?"

Percy just shrugged, and the others stared at Carl.

"I saw a lot of money being spent," continued Carl. "Offices well appointed, as was the lobby. The ED itself was less tidy. I wasn't able to assess their bottom line. That was too well buried for me to easily find on a brief visit. But the amount being spent was more than the revenue I would think was possible."

"Lots a' fundraising?" guessed Percy.

"Well, many hospitals rely on donations these days," said Carolyn.

"How much did you donate, Percy?" asked Carl casually.

There were stares directed at Carl and then at Percy as he answered, "Only ten grand this year."

"Ten thousand?!" said Carolyn.

"I thought so," said Carl. "Your name and your picture were on one of the plaques." He turned to Carolyn and continued. "I'm sure you noticed that there were plaques in several of the ED rooms thanking people for their donations, with their names and a small picture of some of them. I'd not seen that before. Must be an aggressive marketing department."

Carl turned back toward Percy and said, "Percival Prince. I remember the name."

"Don't say that, man," hissed Percy.

"Say what?" asked Carl.

"Percival Prince. What kinda name is that? Told my Ma not ta marry 'im."

"You father?" asked Carl. "How old were you when she married him? If you were old enough, you needn't keep his name, if you'd rather not."

"No, man. They'd been married for ten years when I was born, but I told her not ta marry 'im. She didn't listen though, an' then on top a' that she named me *Percival*!"

"You told your mother not to marry your father ten years before you were born?" asked Joe.

"Well, yeah," said Percy. "You're a pediatric … *ist*, so you know kids talk ta their folks for years before they're born."

"Yeah, Joe. You must know that," said Carolyn with a smirk.

"I thought the evidence was still theoretical," said Joe.

"They got my picture, too? An' *Percival Prince* written on it?"

"It wasn't a bad likeness," offered Carl.

"Shit," said Percy.

"Shit," echoed Natalie, as she walked over to their table.

Chapter 25

"Well, this was worth interrupting a good nap," said Natalie, looking around, but settling her gaze on Percy.

Percy rose immediately and offered her his seat. "Please," he said, motioning to her. "I'll get a'other chair." He approached the table next to them and took one of the vacant chairs after asking permission from the couple sitting there. They didn't look like they would have refused him, even if they were going to need the chair; probably not even if one of them was sitting in it.

As Percy sat, he said to Joe, "I think she'd look good in red, Joe. 'Course, I think Carolyn'd look good in black, too."

"What did you say?!" asked an angry Natalie.

"Do you really think so, Percy?" asked Carolyn.

"Carolyn!" said Natalie.

"What?"

"Don't encourage him!"

"He's a pimp, Natalie. He's a professional. His opinion is important, and valuable, too," Carolyn replied. "You really think I'd look good in black, Percy?"

"Well, mama," said Percy. "Ya got da bod' for it. You too, Nat'lie."

"Carolyn, stop this right now," said Natalie.

"Oh, Percy knows we're just joking," said Carolyn.

"I ain't jokin'," said Percy, but was silenced by the look on Natalie's face.

"So what the hell is going on here?" asked Natalie.

"Well, all I know so far is that Percy has what looks like a fungal infection of his scalp, but I think there was something else they want to talk about too," said Carolyn. "Oh, and Percy talked to his mother for ten years before he was born, but she still married his father anyway, but … well, I guess I'm not supposed to tell you that."

"I hate to ask this, Joe, but are you the only responsible person here, or are you the person who is responsible for all this?" asked Natalie.

"Both," said Joe. He held up a hand as Percy began to speak. "Let me, please. I think I mentioned that one of Percy's young ladies had left the hotel with a man named Harry last night."

"Pick'd up a client," corrected Percy. "Told her ta be careful a' him. Told 'em all. Told Harry, too. He messed with one a' my girls once, but only once."

"That would be the same gentleman who was trying to analyze the slot machines?" said Carl.

"That sounds like Harry, 'cept for the part 'bout bein' a *gentleman*," said Percy.

"Anyway," Joe continued, "Katie has not checked in with Percy, and he's worried."

"But," began Natalie, "I mean, do they have to check in with their pimp by bedtime or something? Maybe she's … well, earning a little extra. What's the big deal?"

"She supposed ta," said Percy as Sally came to the table … yet again.

"Okay, folks, more coffee or hot chocolate, and something for you?" she asked, looking at Natalie. "We're all out of the raspberry tarts."

"Yeah," said Joe. "Same all around and coffee for you, Natalie?"

"Yeah, okay, although I'm not sure we'll be here that long."

"Sally," said Joe. "You know Percy, right?"

Sally nodded tentatively and Joe continued.

"Katie left here last night with a guy named Harry, and hasn't contacted Percy since then. Would you be worried about that?"

"Katie?" said Sally. "She didn't call ya, or nothin', Percy?"

"Not a word. Nobody's seen 'er neither," replied Percy

"She's supposed ta check in," said Sally. "That's the rule, ain't it? Everyone's supposed ta check in every day. She's got ta be in trouble if she didn't."

"Wha'da ya mean *the rule*?" asked Natalie, mimicking Sally's slang.

"That's the rule when ya work for Percy. Check in every day no matter what," said Sally. "Percy's more like a mother hen than a pimp," she added.

"Stop with dis *mother hen* shit," said Percy. "It's da way a pimp is suppose ta act. Keep da girl's … an' *the women* safe." He smiled at Joe and added, "Sally here's from out in da sticks like you, Joe."

"And she just insulted a bunch of *mother hens*," smirked Natalie, but Percy seemed to miss this subtle accusation.

"Harry's a bad actor," said Joe. "If Percy's women report in every day and Katie hasn't, then maybe he should be worried."

"Yeah," said Sally.

Percy looked at her. "Katie got any family, Sally? Never said nothin' ta me."

"Not ta me, either," said Sally. "Maybe ta Angie. They were pretty tight." Percy looked first at Carolyn and then at Joe, but let his smiling face say what his words didn't.

Sally looked around and said, "I better get your coffee an' stuff."

"So, what can we do to help?" asked Carolyn as Sally walked away.

"Oh for the love of Jesus," said Natalie. "I can't believe you of all people, Carolyn, are talking like this is serious."

"It's just that … well, what if she's really in trouble?"

"Okay. Okay," said Natalie. "So what *can* we do?"

"I don't think we can go to the police tonight. Percy is going to check out Harry and look for Katie," said Joe. "But in the morning, we need to get the police to look for Katie too."

"And how do we do that in this city of a couple thousand underage runaways turning tricks on the street? The cops aren't going to start looking for someone just because Percy is worried," smirked Natalie.

Joe frowned. "I thought we could lie to them … a little."

"Oh?" said Natalie. "That's a great idea, because the truth sure ain't gonna cut it."

"Well," began Joe, "That's where you can help, Natalie. I thought that if I went to the police and told them I saw one of my patients here outside the hotel, and that she has some disease that needs treatment, and that she has run away and—"

"And when they stop laughing, what are you going to do for an encore?" said Natalie.

Joe was undaunted. "I think it could work. I can get Rose back in my office to get me a good match for Katie, and I'll call someone back home who will pretend to be her mother or father or something to confirm what I tell the cops. They'll have to have a good description of her, but Percy can help with that, or maybe one of his girls."

"*Women*, ya mean. Better ta have a picture, ya think?" asked Percy.

"Well, yeah, of course," said Natalie. "Ya got a family photo on ya?"

"Nah," said Percy. "Just single shots, front an' side. Got 'em on all *the women*. They're on my laptop in my car. What would I be doin' with family photos, anyway?"

"You have pictures of all your girls?" asked Natalie. "What do you need pictures for if they work the street? The Johns can see what they're buying."

"'Course they can," said Percy. "But I need 'em in case I need ta find 'em. 'Sides, everybody knows I got pictures, so they don't mess with me or mine. They know I look after my *young women,* an' they knows I'll come lookin' for 'em, too."

Natalie looked at Percy with a little respect now. "So, we can get a picture if we hook your laptop to a printer maybe?"

"Gotta printer in my car, too. Color, Wi-Fi an' all," responded Percy. "I can send da picture ta your office if ya think that'd work better, Joe."

"Yeah," said Natalie. "That'd be cool, Percy."

"I'll call Rose in the morning and set up a cover story back there," said Joe. "All we have to do is figure out what story will galvanize the local cops into action. That's the part I need your help with, Natalie."

Natalie was deep in thought. "We'll think of something before morning. With the local constabulary in disarray back home, the local cops here will have a hard time finding any reason not to believe you, Joe."

"Forget da constabularies, what 'bout da local cops back home?" asked Percy.

"They're in disarray too," said Carolyn. "Joe arranged to have the chief of police investigated before we left."

"No shit!" said Percy.

Chapter 26

"Okay," said Joe. "We're all set. Percy will get people looking for Harry as well as Katie. Be sure to call me if she surfaces before morning." Percy nodded, pointing at Joe's phone.

"Get all the numbers off it," said Joe, handing it to him. "Natalie and I will visit the police after I get the story lined up back home. Going to them now would be a waste of time."

"And I'll have Raul drive me over to the Medical Center to see if I can get Percy's skin examined," said Carolyn. "And while I'm there, I'll casually ask how they track cases like Katie, if she came in and wasn't identified and was too sick to be able to contact anyone. I'll say I want to see how a recent case was handled. Ask if anyone like that came in so I can see if it might be Katie."

Natalie cleared her throat and Carolyn asked, "Am I *not* going to get the skin examined?"

"Maybe *not* use Raul to get there," said Natalie.

"Okay," said Carolyn. "Why would that be?"

"Raul?" said Percy. "That cop in da chauffeur suit?"

"*Retired* cop," said Carolyn.

"Maybe," said Natalie.

"Maybe not," said Percy. "Looks an' acts like he's still on da job."

"You think …?" said Carolyn.

"He's more than a chauffeur," said Natalie, nodding toward Percy. "I'm not sure how much more he is, but …"

There was silence for a moment until Joe spoke. "We were in trouble with the local cops back home, and we left there because there was concern we might be in danger. Now Raul shows up looking like a chauffeur, but acting like a cop and … well, I think we might want to take taxis for a while until we're sure."

"Okay," said Carolyn. "I guess I've got enough for a few taxis."

"I can get ya a few bills, mama." said Percy, pulling out a roll of cash.

"Shit, Percy," said Natalie. "Is the business that good here? I mean, is that more than one night?"

"I pulled out some for da girls," he said. "They ain't going ta be working 'til we find Katie."

"I've got enough for now, thanks," said Carolyn. "I'll let ya know when I run short."

"You do that, mama. You's working on my dime 'til we find Katie." He dropped forty dollars on the table and put the barely diminished roll away.

"We can …" began Joe, but Percy just shook his head. "My dime."

They were silent until Carl cleared his throat again. "You know, Harry has been here the last two days. Since it appears I'll not be occupied tomorrow, maybe I should situate myself near the entrance and watch for him?"

"Good idea, Carl," said Percy.

Carl nodded. "And what should I do if he does come in?"

"Ya watch him, an' call me," said Percy. "I'll get someone on 'im if he leaves, an' when I gets to him I'll ask him 'bout Katie. An' I'll get some answers."

"We'll have the police—" began Joe.

"*I'll* get da answers," said Percy. He handed Joe his phone and said, "I got all da numbers an' I put mine on this, too. Call me. Okay?"

Percy got up and left as Carolyn looked at Joe. "I'm a little nervous about this, Joe. How about you?"

Joe just shrugged.

"I mean, I'm not sure …" Carolyn let the sentence hang there, but Joe still said nothing.

"I don't want to be hunting down this guy Harry so Percy can beat the shit out of him. Percy wasn't exactly a friend of ours last night. Maybe he's hunting down this Katie to beat on her, too. Who says he's a *nice pimp* besides him?"

Natalie frowned. "The guys at the ED said he was a *nice pimp*, but they also said he would protect his girls. I got the idea that meant he wouldn't mind beating the shit out of someone who hurt one of his girls."

"I don't know," said Joe, "but I think—"

"Percy isn't just a pimp," said Carl. "He's a pimp, but he's intelligent, too. He knows you're not going to believe him, and he knows better how to find someone in Las Vegas than you do, so I see no reason he should come to you at all if he wished to deceive you on this. Why get you involved when it's unlikely you'll be able to help, and very possibly you'll interfere?"

"He's right," said Natalie. "Why come to you unless—"

"Unless," said Joe, "Unless we don't have a clue what's really going on."

"Now you're becoming paranoid, Joe," said Natalie. "You saw Katie get picked up by Harry last night and you were upset by it. And Percy's girls are upset by it, too. It was you who walked over to Percy on Fremont Street, and you who insulted him and then flattened him. He comes here and talks to you, and … and why the hell am I trying to convince you to do something that's stupid in the first place? We can't do anything, even if it's all true!"

"Don't let your idealism run away with you, Natalie. Joe will take care of that," said Carolyn.

Sally approached their table now. "Ya think ya can help Katie?" she asked.

"I don't …" began Joe. "Is Katie really in trouble, Sally?"

"Well, yeah. I mean, it's fuckin' dangerous out there on the street. I got beat up once and robbed. Maggie got me hooked up with Percy an' he took care of it though. Got my money back, too."

"How …?" asked Joe. "Doesn't matter, does it? Is Katie really in trouble, and can we really help?"

"Well, yeah," said Sally again. "Cops'll listen to you. You're a doctor, aren't ya?"

"Cops don't always listen to doctors," said Carolyn.

"But we got to find Katie. I called Maggie, and she's like frantic. Maggie knows what Harry is. She was … ya got to help!"

"What's Harry?" asked Joe. "Was he the one who hurt you, Sally?"

"Nay. I don't like him. He's like so weird an' well, he likes little kids. I mean like, *real* little kids. Katie looks like she's twelve or something."

"How old is she?" asked Joe.

"Sixteen, but almost seventeen I think. I'm not sure."

"Shit," said Joe.

"Ya gotta help," said Sally.

"Yeah, I have to," said Joe.

"*We* have to," said Natalie. "But I'm not going to enjoy this. So, what can we do?"

"There's nothing we can do tonight," said Joe. "Not unless Percy finds Harry, or the police come over to ask us if we have anyone they should be looking for since they have nothing else to do. I have to get the story set in Kentucky first and that will have to wait until morning."

"We do still have reservations for supper." Natalie frowned. "Not all that festive, but we have them, and we have to eat, and there's nothing we can do until tomorrow anyway."

Chapter 27

They discussed some more, and finally went to "the best restaurant in the place" and were served a fine meal with a fine bottle of wine. Joe reiterated all the reasons they should *not* become involved in this, and everyone listened quietly. Carolyn knew what would happen, of course, knowing Joe as she did. But Carl, and even Natalie, were soon convinced that he would *have to* try to help Katie, so unconvincing were his reasons not to do that. They let him ramble until he finally sighed and said, "So, what can we do?"

"Enjoy our last meal before we make fools of ourselves, or maybe even get arrested for committing a felony," said Carolyn. "Is lying still a felony? It's done so commonly now it should be a misdemeanor, don't you think?"

"It's still a felony when you do it to the police," said Natalie.

"So …" began Carolyn, "we're pretty sure Joe is going to commit a felony sometime tomorrow, and probably the rest of us will be accomplices, more or less, so … what shall we do with our last hours of freedom? You know, to avoid having people at this restaurant testify in court that we were a glum and suspicious group the night before the crime. It would be better to be gay and carefree, don't you think?"

"Have a little more wine, and then find out where the swingers go at night in this shabby town. Do you dance, Carolyn?" asked Natalie.

"No," said Carolyn, shaking her head. "Not at all. But I do make a fool of myself on dance floors sometimes. Does that count?"

"Close enough, girlfriend," said Natalie. "I'll give you a run for it in the *making a fool of yourself* competition. You boys want to be in this game?"

"Of course," smiled Joe.

"I was hoping to—" began Carl.

"Dance the night away," said Carolyn. "I know, Carl, but you should get some sleep tonight to be bright enough to return to the slots tomorrow and watch for what's his name, the villain."

"Harry?" said Carl.

"That's the one. So, it's settled. Finish your wine, pay the tab, and get ready to dance until … well, hell, maybe as late as ten o'clock!" said Natalie.

Carolyn turned her glass up to the ceiling, draining it into her mouth. "Done," she said.

The others followed her lead. Joe signed the bill, and soon they found where the swingers were that evening. A band was playing fifties and sixties rock and roll, pretty good covers of the originals, and soon they were joining the crowd on the crowded dance floor. There were a good number of middle-aged persons not afraid to join the *make a fool of yourself* competition that night.

Natalie and Carolyn were not anywhere close to the worst, and even Carl managed to avoid total embarrassment, in part because the dance floor was too crowded for anyone to really stand out. Joe was actually pretty good, and even knew some of the ancient dances that had been all the rage in the fifties. He really looked good doing *the stroll*.

Natalie wanted to comment about this, but feared it would embarrass him with his prosthetic leg. Her dilemma evaporated when Carolyn asked, "Do you think I could dance as well as you if I had my leg cut off, Joe?"

"No." He smiled.

"Then I won't do it. But I'll dance with you if you promise not to embarrass me."

"I'll make no such promise tonight, Carolyn."

"Where have all the gentlemen gone?" asked Carolyn.

"'Where Have All the Cowboys Gone,' you mean?" said Natalie.

It wasn't embarrassing, but it soon wore them out. By mutual agreement, they gave the night back to the young, and to the middle-aged trying to be young, and headed for bed to sleep soundly until morning.

The morning came to Joe with the sound of Natalie's voice on his cell phone. "You awake, Joe? Hope I didn't disturb you."

"No," his sleepy voice replied. "I had to wake up to answer the phone anyway."

"What?" said Natalie.

"Just an old joke," said Joe. "What time is it?"

"Time for the police to have some visitors. We need to lay out our plan. Do you want to come down here, or shall I come to your room, or shall we meet in some neutral breakfast place?"

"I can come down there. I don't want to disturb Carl. Is Carolyn awake?"

"Carl called already and is checking out the casino for any signs of Harry, and will wait there for the slots to open," said Natalie.

"The slots are always open," said Joe.

"It's a joke, sleepyhead. Come down and I'll order some coffee and breakfast from room service."

Joe dressed, well this time, since Natalie thought they would be going to see, and be seen by the police. He had shaved for dinner last night, but shaved again. The shower had grab bars, which he preferred, although he had learned to shower balanced on one leg.

He arrived as the room service waiter was leaving a cart with three full breakfasts upon it: scrambled eggs, sausage and bacon, fried potatoes, pastries and two pots of coffee. It looked as if Natalie intended to do some serious work this morning.

"I didn't know what you wanted so I got all three the same. That way you wouldn't be jealous," said Carolyn. "Have some coffee."

Joe poured himself a cup and took a plate with eggs and potatoes. Carolyn was dressed neatly, but much less formally than she had been yesterday. "I thought I would call and tell them I'd like to come over and look around a little more. Maybe meet again with the CEO or something if they pressure me, but show up early and get done what I'm really there to do."

"You think you can?"

"Of course I can. You just make sure you and Natalie do your part."

"Are you sure we should get into this?"

"No, of course we shouldn't. We're going to though, so do it right, okay? Any more questions?"

Joe might have thought of some, but Natalie came out of her bedroom and said, "All right, Joe. Eat quick, and let's get this thing going."

"Okay, what do we do after I eat quickly?"

"We take our story to the police," said Natalie. "You tell them you saw your patient here. You were sure it was she, and called her family because you couldn't believe it, as sick as she was. They were frantic because she had run away, scared of the treatment or some other line, I don't know, but she's missing. Have you checked at your office to make sure Percy faxed the pictures?"

"Well, not yet."

"Gotta do that," said Natalie. "As soon as we decide who she is."

"And what she has," said Joe. He sipped his coffee, while the breakfast was untouched.

"I was thinking AIDS would be a good disease," suggested Carolyn through a mouthful of egg. "And maybe lymphoma. One of the ones the AIDS patients get."

"That would make finding her important, and leaving her out on the street turning tricks dangerous," added Natalie. They had obviously discussed this before Joe arrived.

"That might work," said Joe. He didn't want to label the suggestion brilliant, partly because he needed to think about it, and partly to avoid inflating the other egos present in the room.

"Can you really get a cover back home for that?" asked Natalie. She, at least, seemed to think the idea had been accepted completely, and Carolyn's ego seldom needed further inflation.

"Yes, I think I can," said Joe.

He looked at his watch; almost ten. That would be eight back home. Rose might be in the office. He dialed the number and she answered immediately.

"Hello, Rose."

"Dr. Nelson," she replied. "How are you? There's a rumor you were injured."

"No, no," said Joe. "But I do need your help."

"Well, things are a little crazy here, but what can I do for you?"

"Crazy?" asked Joe

"Well, yeah. The hospital is in turmoil. Someone is shot dead while trying to kill one of the physicians, the someone who a few years ago killed the niece of the wealthiest man in these parts. Then that physician and his wife, also a staff physician, along with the director of operations at the hospital and a police sergeant, leave town headed for Las Vegas, I'm told. Everyone seems to think I'll know all the details."

"They know we went to Las Vegas?"

"That's just a rumor," said Rose.

"Do they know what hotel we're staying in?" asked Joe, with more than a hint of sarcasm in his voice.

"Well," said Rose, "You left in Reginald Murphy's private jet, they say, and the smart money is also saying he owns a hotel and casino in Las Vegas. Is that true, Joe?"

"Shit," said Joe.

"I'm sorry, I didn't catch that, Dr. Nelson." The sarcasm virtually dripped out of Joe's phone.

So much for traveling anonymously. Everyone obviously knew where they were. "Did you get a fax, Rose?"

"Yes," she answered. "A picture is all. No explanation."

"Well, here is the explanation. I saw this young woman here in Las Vegas and she's in trouble. I need to convince the police to look for her and get her out of trouble, so I thought that if I told them she had, say, AIDS, for instance, and was being treated for lymphoma, that might get them to move a little more aggressively."

"But she's not one of our patients," said Rose. "Is that a problem for you, too, or is it just me that worries about those things?"

"I thought I could … well, lie a little," said Joe.

"Oh," said Rose. "Am I to be part of the lie? Is this another poor little waif in need of rescuing, Joe?"

"Well, yes."

"This kind of thing is going to get you in trouble someday. So what's the plan, anyway?"

"Well," said Joe, his embarrassment increasing, "I thought maybe Laura Perkins wouldn't mind saying she has a sister: Katie Perkins."

"Laura might do that for you, Joe. You helped her take care of her mother for years before she died."

"And her mother had AIDS," said Joe. "So that works, too. Her mother is dead, so she won't be able to talk to the police."

"Yeah, and knowing Laura's mother, Laura could have several siblings out there," added Rose. "Birth records can be confusing here."

"All you have to do is send the pictures when they call, and tell them she's one of our patients, but you can't release any information. *Contact Dr. Nelson.*" Joe smiled at Natalie and Carolyn and added, "The diagnosis of AIDS will make the confidentiality believable and defensible, and I'll be here to give any information the police request."

"And when we get caught, it will allow me to say that this was all your idea and I knew nothing about it," added Rose.

"And I'll swear that that's the case," said Joe.

"Good," replied Rose. "Because I'll be swearing too, and probably using words you have never heard before. Do you need Laura's phone number?"

"Yes, that would be helpful," said Joe.

"Get something to write with then. I got a call from a Captain Hank Morgan from the state police asking that I call him if I heard anything. I think he meant about the murder, but I'll call him about this, too. Tell him *you* said *you* saw one of our patients in Las Vegas and all that. The local cops are all suspended, so the state guys are in charge here. If Las Vegas calls they'll probably get referred to him. You ready for that number?"

Joe was, took the number, and thanked Rose before hanging up.

He smiled at his companions and said, "Let me call Laura Perkins and see if she'll tell the cops her sister is missing."

"Will she do that?" asked Natalie. "How old is she?"

"Twenty," said Joe. "I think she will if she knows it will help someone. She's almost as idealistic as I am. She's even a vegan. Doesn't want to hurt anything."

Joe called and Laura answered, asked how he was and why he had called. When Joe explained, she said she would help if it was important. Joe said it was, and that it would help a child in a lot of trouble. That was enough to convince Laura Perkins she should help.

"That went fairly well," said Natalie.

"Yes," said Carolyn. "You always impress me when you lie, Joe. Probably because you so seldom do it. But when you do, you do it well."

 *Chapter 28*

Carolyn departed for the Medical Center in the taxi directly ahead of the cab carrying Natalie and Joe toward police headquarters. Joe called while they wound their way through gathering traffic. The dismissive tone of the man on the phone continued when they arrived and were greeted by the sergeant on the desk. *Not really an emergency. Maybe they could leave a number.* Natalie bristled both in her appearance and in her responses, while Joe maintained a quiet but forceful insistence. It soon became a contest between Joe and the sergeant. Natalie was impressed with Joe's assertiveness and correspondingly became quiet, letting him convince their antagonist. *Life or death* and *possible spread of HIV infection* were phrases that slipped into his language, and finally the sergeant came to the tacit conclusion that she would rather have someone else handle these two. The someone else was a Lieutenant O'Connor. As they walked into his office, they saw a sign stating that security cameras were in use in this section of the building. *The same as in the casinos*, thought Joe. He was sure the idea had started there and had been borrowed by the police.

Lieutenant O'Connor was a man of maybe fifty or so; white shirt and dark tie, and bald except for short-cut hair along the sides and back. If he had been younger he probably would have shaved his scalp clean, as was the fashion with the younger generation; but he still maintained the little hair he had. He wasn't antagonistic, just bored, as he ushered them into his cubicle.

"Dr. Nelson, is it? What is it I can do for you?" he asked.

"Thank you for taking the time to see us, Lieutenant. This is Natalie Moore," Joe said, motioning toward Natalie. "We're visiting Las Vegas with my wife and another friend. My wife is interviewing for a position at the Medical Center right now, but that's not important, of course.

"What's important is that I saw one of my patients on the street here. It surprised me because she's quite ill and is undergoing treatment for cancer."

"Oh," said Lieutenant O'Connor.

"Yes," said Joe in his most earnest voice. "I was quite surprised, and couldn't believe what I saw at first. I couldn't talk to her. She disappeared before I could, but I did have an opportunity to talk to some of her friends. They said her name was Katie, although she's using a different last name, not Perkins, which is her real name." Joe nodded vigorously.

"Where was this … er … encounter?"

Natalie looked at Joe, but he spoke at once. "Fremont Street. I think she may have been … well … picking up a sexual partner. For money, I mean." Joe managed to blush deeply, and Natalie almost laughed out loud.

"Then I saw the same group of young ladies, but not little Katie, outside my hotel. That's where I spoke to them." Joe nodded again and continued. "I called her family back in Kentucky, of course, and she's been missing for several days. Really very upsetting. Very."

"I see," said Lieutenant O'Connor. "We'll have to see what can be done." His enthusiasm was very noticeable by its complete absence.

Joe cleared his throat and said, "I can talk to your superior." The Lieutenant's head shot up, but Joe ignored it. "If you think that would be helpful, I mean."

"Well no, I don't think that will be necessary."

"But helpful, perhaps," offered Joe. "I wouldn't mind at all."

Joe waited while the lieutenant looked uneasy. "I'll have my office send her picture here if you want," Joe said. "I have pictures of all my AIDS patients. To screen and follow them for the development of Kaposi's Sarcoma, of course. She already has the lymphoma, and is in the middle of treatment for that. Very dangerous to interrupt that treatment, but I'm sure you know that."

Lieutenant O'Connor nodded. "Well, yes."

"I would be very upset were she to be endangered by an interruption of her treatment, especially when we know she's here. There's also the likelihood that she's spreading the HIV virus as well. Many government agencies take that seriously back in Kentucky. Is that much of a problem here, Lieutenant?"

"Well, yes."

"Of course it would be," said Joe. "What with those intrusive news mongers all around these days. Very distressing when they get hold of some story like this one. Never even consider the circumstances … well, never mind that. I suppose I shouldn't really have revealed so much of her medical history to you, should I? Please don't repeat any of that, if you wouldn't mind. I can have the pictures sent, or you can contact my office directly. That might be better, to ensure they're transmitted properly. And here is the number where you can reach little Katie's sister, Laura. Half-sister, really. Her mother is dead, but I'm not permitted to discuss that."

"We'll look into this, I assure you, Dr. Nelson. I'll contact her family and the local police right now to get the necessary background information. See if they have anything helpful."

"Yes. Very good. You will of course have to contact the state police, not the local police, given the circumstances back home, I mean," said Joe.

"The circumstances?"

"Well, I'm sure you've heard," said Joe. "Big scandal right now. I've been instructed not to say anything, but …" Joe looked around at the cubicle walls and leaned in with the look of a conspirator upon his face. "A major scandal. Three years ago a four-year-old patient was killed in the hospital, and then just a few days ago, the murderer was shot to death while trying to escape. The whole thing involved several local people and – " Joe looked around again before continuing. "Possibly an international criminal organization and even the local police!" Joe shook his head in the best display of disgust and dismay Natalie had seen in a long time. Lieutenant O'Connor was on the hook.

"No kidding!" he said.

"No kidding at all." Joe shook his head again.

They gave phone numbers and office numbers. Lieutenant O'Connor asked for Joe's medical license, to copy it, something he should have done earlier, of course. He looked as if he thought he should be asking for something from Natalie as well, but couldn't think of anything. Joe kept up a remarkable stream of conversation, none of which contained anything of substance, but prevented the lieutenant from concentrating on questioning them.

They finally left, and as they walked down the hall, Natalie smiled at Joe and leaned her head towards his shoulder. "You were very—" she began, but Joe immediately straightened as she did, causing her to straighten as well. No head touched anyone's shoulder.

"So you suppose they have cameras in the hallways?" Joe asked quietly and without looking at her.

"Oh," said Natalie. "They might, I guess. Better not to—"

Again Joe cut her short. "You know," he said, stopping and turning towards her, causing her to stop and turn back toward him a step later. "This is a very dangerous situation for little Katie, with her AIDS and everything. There's that newspaper back home that loves to run scandals like this, too. I'm glad we came to the authorities here, so at least we'll not be held responsible." He was speaking loudly now, loud enough to be heard by passersby, several of which were looking at him.

"I'm glad Lieutenant O'Connor is going to take this seriously," he added. Natalie again began to speak, but Joe started walking, and she had to turn quickly to catch up to him. She did, just as he exited the building and hailed a cab.

They were seated in the taxi before Joe said anything. "I interrupted you back in the police station."

"Oh," said Natalie. "I was just going to say that you were very impressive the way you manipulated Lieutenant O'Connor. I didn't realize that you hadn't finished manipulating him yet."

"I thought you were going to do something else," he said, as he reached over and pulled her a little closer to him, leaning his head toward hers.

"I was going to do that," she confessed.

"I thought so," he said, as she turned towards him to place a light kiss on his cheek.

"You're an interesting man, Joe Nelson. Not yet fascinating, but getting close. Carolyn's right, though; you do lie very well. Did you ever lie to Carolyn?"

"Never, and I'll never lie to you," said Joe, kissing her forehead. "But I'm glad you didn't kiss me in the police station with the cameras rolling. Especially after I told the lieutenant my wife was here with us."

"Oops," said Natalie. "Sorry."

"We're not in the police station now," said Joe, and kissed her forehead again.

 *Chapter 29*

They arrived at the hotel and saw Carl at once. He was sitting in front of a slot machine, making his bets and writing the results in his notebook. As they approached he looked up and said, "Oh, hello. I didn't notice you come in."

"Did you notice Harry?" asked Joe.

"I didn't see him, either. I mean, he's not here, is he?"

"I haven't seen him," said Joe. "But I wasn't here watching for him."

"Well no, but I was," said Carl. He looked at his notebook and at the slot machine and then at Joe and Natalie. "I didn't notice you, Natalie."

"That's me. Miss Un-noticeable."

"Were you successful at the police department, Natalie?" asked Carl.

"Joe was. I think the police will be looking for Katie with at least a little enthusiasm. How is your research going, Carl?"

"Slow, but interesting. These machines definitely do seem to have a pattern inherent in their workings. Carolyn called to say she will be back here shortly, and she's hungry. She said she didn't eat anything for breakfast."

"*Anything* has several definitions, I guess," said Natalie.

"Only two," corrected Joe. "Carolyn's, and the one the rest of us use. Matters not one bit, the difference. She'll be hungry, and that's all that matters. I'm going to look around until she gets here. Just to see if Carl missed anything."

"Shall I stay here and help Carl look for things?" asked Natalie.

"Probably not a bad idea."

"Yes," said Carl. "I have a little theory developed and you may be able to verify it. Here, sit at this machine and just play for a little while, and let me see if the results are as I predicted."

Natalie sat reluctantly and then looked at Joe, who just shrugged. "Good luck," he said.

"It's not a matter of luck, Joe," Carl responded.

"Yes, it is. At least it is for Natalie." Joe smiled as Natalie frowned.

Joe walked around the casino but found no sign of Harry. He passed through the blackjack tables and saw no sign of Tyla, either. On an impulse he went to the café he had spent so much time in yesterday, but found Peter serving, not Sally. No one from yesterday was here today. It was as if maybe yesterday hadn't really happened after all.

He sat, and Peter approached almost immediately. "What can I get you, sir?"

"Is Sally ill again, or is this your assignment today, Peter?"

"Oh, hey, it's you, right? Mr. Monroe's friend. Nay, she … well, she just said she had to be out. No reason." He shrugged as if this was reason enough.

"Hot choc … no, make that coffee," said Joe. "Black."

He didn't drink coffee black, but Natalie did. He turned to face the entrance as Peter walked away. He was watching for Harry, he thought, but was really waiting to see if anyone from yesterday would arrive to reassure him that in fact what he had just done at the police station was the right thing to have done. Reassure him that a young woman was in danger, and that he was obliged to help, morally obliged to help. He didn't know what he expected to happen that would clear away his doubts.

Nothing at all did happen though. Neither Harry, nor Percy arrived, but his coffee did, and soon he was drinking bitter liquid and wondering how anyone could possibly enjoy drinking it. His depression only deepened when his phone rang and Carolyn's voice asked him where the hell he was.

He thought of giving a flippant answer but wasn't even up to that much effort. "In the café we were in yesterday. Where are you, and where are we going to eat lunch?"

"I don't care, but I'm famished. I'm gathering up Carl and Natalie now and … isn't there a pub-type place we can get into quickly, before I devour someone at random?" Carolyn seemed to be stressed today, possibly for the same reason Joe was stressed.

He paid his bill and met them: Carolyn sulking, and Carl and Natalie subdued. They found the pub, were seated, and had ordered before any conversation passed between them.

"So, how did you two do?" asked Carolyn, looking at Natalie and then Joe.

Joe frowned. "We talked to a Lieutenant O'Connor, who will probably look into Katie's situation. How was your day?"

"I don't know. I got the skin scrapings processed, talked again to CEO Burke, pleasantly enough, but no extra time spent and … well, I looked around the ED."

"Oh," said Joe.

"Yes," said Carolyn. "*Oh* is a good word. Yes, they do have unidentified people come in, and yes, many of them are young women, but no, there were not any in the past few days."

"Oh," said Joe again.

"Stop saying that, Joe. Do you want me to tell you why I'm feeling shitty right now or don't you? You don't have to listen."

"I think I want to," said Joe. Their food arrived at that point, interrupting them long enough for everyone to think and relax. The service was fast here, maybe to get people back to the casino quickly.

Carolyn took a bite of her sandwich and grimaced. "I'm sorry. I get this way whenever I'm feeling stressed. I eat like a pig and growl at everyone, particularly the ones I like most, because they're the only ones who will put up with me. Do you really think they'll look for Katie?"

"The police? Yes, I think so," said Joe.

Natalie smiled. "Joe was pretty convincing, and you're entitled to be grouchy. I'll give it right back to you if that will make you feel better. Sometimes a good fight is what you need."

"I'll take it out on this unimportant sandwich." Carolyn smiled, taking another bite.

Paul Janson

"Care to talk about it?" asked Joe.

"Yeah," said Carolyn. "Too much mayo and not enough cheese. Or did you mean why I feel shitty?"

"Can't do anything about the sandwich," said Joe. "Already half-eaten. Why are you feeling shitty?"

"The world isn't fair."

"Been that way for a while."

"And I'm just learning that? Why didn't you tell me, Joe?"

"I didn't want to make you feel shitty. Is there something particularly unfair today?"

"I don't know," said Carolyn. "Yes, I do. A young woman, as you insist we refer to what everyone else calls 'girls,' is in trouble, and we're helpless. I talked to the people at the ED and they were ... well, uninterested. 'Lots of that around here;' 'What can you do?' they said, and what can *we* do? No one cares what happens to Katie or any of the others. It's a sorry time when the pimps like Percy are the only ones who care what happens.

"Then I looked around at the department. It's okay, but not the same amount of attention or money as the CEO's office. Do you know they have a concierge service at that place? A representative comes down from administration whenever a VIP, read *heavy donor*, comes in to make sure they get their pillow fluffed and coffee for their family. No difference in the care, they say, but ...well, how can there *not* be a difference in the care?"

"Concierge service?" asked Natalie.

"Yeah," said Carolyn. "I guess no one wants the supporters of the hospital to have to suffer the care that ordinary people get."

"Hmm," said Joe.

"I would have expected you to be more incensed, Joe," said Carolyn.

"My sandwich is actually pretty good," he smiled. "Cheese and mayo in adequate quantities and of acceptable quality. As for the hospital, that's how medicine is these days."

"True," sighed Carolyn. "I put a bug in their ears about Katie, but who knows what will happen. Did you really convince the police she's in trouble?"

"I don't know, but I may have scared them into covering their ass a little. There's a newspaper back home that would love to write about a poor little girl mistreated in Las Vegas because the police didn't look for her, even after her doctor told them she was sick. At least that's what I led them to believe. I hope I don't have to produce the name of that newspaper."

"You're such a good liar, Joe," said Carolyn. "So, you think they're going to move on this?"

"Well," said Joe, "Why don't I call and see if they already have?"

He pulled out his cell phone and was talking to Rose in his office a moment later. "Did they request the photos?" he asked, after the greetings were exchanged.

"Yes, they certainly did," Rose replied. "Sounded like a very urgent requesting, too. Asked about the local police and verified the family contact numbers. You'll be so proud of me, Joe, you'll beg me to accept a raise."

"Of course I will. What will make me be that proud?"

"Well, first I pulled Laura Perkins' file and ran through our contact numbers, for her mother, I mean. The most recent one we have was not in service when I called it, so that's the one I gave to the officer when he asked. She's dead, anyway. I also gave him Laura's number, too. Next I called Captain Hank Morgan of the state police to tell him that you were afraid one of our patients might be in Las Vegas; cousin or half-sister to Laura Perkins, but not from around here.

"He said some fairly strong words about how you shouldn't be drawing attention to yourself out there, but at least he has a heads-up."

"What did he say?" asked Joe.

"Do want to hear it with the expletive deleted?"

"Yeah, I guess."

"In that case, he didn't say anything at all," replied Rose.

"When Las Vegas called, I sent the pictures, told him I couldn't give any information, and asked him to contact you. He'll be calling Laura after her mother's phone doesn't go anywhere, and then call the police, which will send him to Captain Morgan, either of the state police or in the local bar. But they're going to be looking for this young waif, I think."

"Hank Morgan is a good Baptist. He doesn't drink," said Joe.

"He will after today," Rose deadpanned.

"Maybe," said Joe. "But you get your raise."

"Of course," replied Rose. "Call Laura and see how she did."

"Good idea. Thanks, Rose." He hung up and dialed again.

He said hello when Laura answered, "Whuz-up?" she replied.

"Did you get a call from the police in Las Vegas?" asked Joe.

"Oh, yeah, they called."

"And did they ask you about your sister, Katie?"

"Well, yeah of course. My half-sister, ya mean."

"What did they ask?"

"Oh, you know: Was she missing? Was she sick? Where was my ma? That sort of stuff."

"And you told them …"

"What you said to say. Yeah, she's missing. Yeah, she's sick. I told 'em she would die if they didn't find her. Is that okay, Dr. Nelson?"

"Yeah," said Joe. After a pause he added, "I didn't mean to make you lie to them, Laura."

"What?"

"I didn't mean to make you lie to the police, Laura."

"Well I had to, didn't I? I mean like, she's in trouble, right? Katie is. When someone is in trouble, ya have ta help or you're like … not a person anymore."

"You're right, of course," said Joe.

"I mean, the cops should be grateful we're helping 'em make sure they do their job, shouldn't they? They might not even know they should be looking for her if we didn't lie to 'em."

"No, they probably wouldn't be looking for her if we didn't lie to them."

"So it's good we lied to 'em," said Laura. There was no doubt in her voice. "I gotta go ta work now. Hurry home, Dr. Nelson." With this she hung up, and Joe felt relief spread over him. Sometimes the simple explanations are the best ones.

 *Chapter 30*

They ate, and soon Carl was explaining his theory of slots in Vegas.

"It did seem to work a little bit," said Natalie.

"What?" said Carolyn and Joe at the same instant.

Natalie seemed to have heard only Carolyn, however, and directed her response accordingly. "Well, the visible, but non-paying lines, do seem to show jackpots pretty frequently, Carolyn. What did you call them, Carl?"

"The tease-lines," he answered.

"That's not possible," responded Carolyn.

"Not *random*, you mean," said Carl.

"No," said Carolyn. "Not *possible*, is what I meant, and that's still what I mean."

"I'll explain it to you," was all Carl said to this challenge. "Unless you would like to see it now?"

"Not now," said Carolyn. "And probably not later, either. What are you going to do this afternoon, Natalie?"

"Oh, I don't know. Nothing special."

"Good! That's just what I'm doing, so we may as well do it together, ya think?"

"Yeah, sure."

They finished their sandwiches and parted company. Joe wandered about, feeling uncomfortable and wanting to know what if anything was going to come of this. He seemed to have disrupted everyone's life for no good reason, except that someone would be looking for Katie … he hoped. Laura had no doubt that lying was a good thing, and Joe felt as if he was contributing to her corruption by asking her to lie. Natalie was caught up in the lie to the police as well, and if any of this came to light, they might all be in serious trouble; *very* serious trouble. Lieutenant O'Conner would not be pleased if he found out what they had done, even if Laura felt it was a good thing to do and that the lieutenant should be grateful.

Carolyn was trying to interview for a job she wanted, and therefore that Joe wanted her to have, but now her mind was darkened by the fact that Katie was just another wayward on the streets of Las Vegas, and no one was prepared to do anything to help her, except Joe and his friends, and her pimp. So now Carolyn was upset and possibly jeopardizing her chances at obtaining that job, for no good reason at all.

Percy was out looking for Katie and Harry, and maybe with violence on his mind. Sally was out "sick" … maybe. Missing, anyway, and Joe was beginning to wonder if he wasn't the fool here to have jumped into this without checking a little on Percy, and Sally, and Maggie.

Maggie? he thought. *Maybe she was here today!* When he went to the phone shop he was told it was her day off.

He thought of calling Percy, or even Lieutenant O'Conner, but little time had passed. Not enough to have allowed anything significant to have happened. Certainly not for the police, and probably not with Percy, either. Besides, Percy would have called him if anything had happened, wouldn't he? *Maybe,* he thought. *Maybe not.*

His phone rang to save him further torment.

"Hello."

"Hey, man. Percy."

"Oh, yeah," said Joe. "I was thinking about you."

"Good thoughts I is hopin.' Look, Joe. I got a address for that dude, Harry. Guy moves around like he's got da bill collectors on his ass, but I got my contacts."

"So what now? Is he home? Maybe call the cops, ya think?" Joe asked. That was what he hoped Percy would do. Make it all simple with one stroke.

"Might," said Percy. "Drove by da place an' no sign o' nothing. No car outside, an' no garage, neither. Place is a real dump. Bad neighborhood. No sign a' Harry or no one else. Don't think I should just break in, an' da doors is locked anyways.

"All da windows, too. Place don't look like it'd even have locks. Couldn't see much inside, but looked like a dump inside too, man. Real shit hole."

"You tried the windows?"

"'Course, man. I think they's nailed shut."

"Nailed shut?"

"Yeah. Lot's a' folks do that in dis kinda neighborhood. Can't just break a window an' unlock it."

"Can't you … I mean, someone else, not you, Percy, just break the window and climb through?"

"Things is different back home, ain't they, Joe? Windows on this place are all bars an' shit like that, but a couple jus' got da wire glass in 'em. If I could get the window ta open I could get in those, but … well, I think they's nailed shut."

"Yeah, things are different back home," sighed Joe. "Most people don't even lock their doors."

"No shit?"

"No shit." Joe smiled. "Small community, and everyone knows everyone. So if ya break in, someone will know who you are, and then the guy you broke into will get his friends and they will get their guns and … well, not many break-ins back home, even with the unlocked doors."

"No shit," said Percy again. Joe didn't answer.

"So maybe da cops will have ta get in, 'less you got another idea."

Joe didn't. "Natalie and I went over to the police station this morning and talked to a Lieutenant O'Conner. Maybe you should ask for him, ya think?"

"Bald guy, right?" said Percy. "Can't do no *anonymous tip* here."

"Anonymous tip?"

"Yeah," said Percy. "This one's got to be out in da open, otherwise they's not goin' ta do shit. Girls like Katie don't count fo' much 'round here. Woman like Katie I mean, Joe."

Joe smiled. "*Woman* like Katie gotta have a pimp like you, Percy. You need me to do anything?"

"Don't think so, but I'll call ya if I need ya."

With this they hung up, and Joe's anxiety about the probability that nothing would happen was replaced by anxiety about the probability that too much would happen and too quickly. He hadn't thought to ask Percy what exactly he was going to tell the bald Lieutenant O'Connor to make him break into Harry's last known address, but then again he wasn't sure he wanted to know. That would just make him an accomplice to another felony, and he was doing all right with the felonies all by himself right now.

Chapter 31

The afternoon dwindled, with boredom mixing into the anxiety. It seemed to be true for everyone, not just Joe. He had called Carolyn and Natalie to update the situation and the responses had been subdued, evidence that the anxiety was appreciated by them as it had been by him. Finally he got a call from Natalie saying she was hungry, and could they meet some place for an early supper? Joe decided they could. The pub would get their business again it seemed, as no one was up to choosing anything different.

"So, Percy found Harry?" asked Carl as he leafed through his notebook.

"Yes," said Joe. "Found his house. That's what he said, anyway," he added, and then wondered why he had added that. Was he really considering the possibility that Percy had not found Harry, but was … well, lying about this? "Found his address, anyway."

"And is going to go to the police, right?" asked Natalie.

"What he said," Joe replied, his apprehension rising.

"Hope he's telling it straight," said Natalie, putting her anxiety, and Joe's, into words.

Carolyn nodded silently.

They ordered food with obvious disinterest to the point that no one even commented upon the meal delivered. Even the server became quiet when his efforts at light banter were met with silence. He probably thought they were losers in the casino, Joe mused. They were declining his offer of dessert when Joe's phone rang.

Although not his usual habit, Joe looked for a caller ID, and shrugged. "Blocked," he said before answering.

"Hello."

Joe listened while the others watched him, first in curiosity and then with concern, as his face showed increasing anxiety bordering on alarm.

When he hung up he looked at them and said, "Lieutenant O'Conner wants to speak with me."

"Why?" asked Natalie.

"He didn't say, but did say it was important, and implied that it wasn't exactly a request." Joe frowned.

"Really?" said Carolyn.

"Really," Joe said. "He's sending a cruiser to pick me up. I think that means it's important. Perhaps I should call Percy and see—"

Joe was opening his phone when Natalie placed her hand on it. "Perhaps not," she said. "Better not to talk to him. If he knows what's going on, you want to be able to say you haven't spoken to him about it. And if he doesn't know what's going on … well, then there's no reason to talk to him. The police will know who you called on your cell; if they want to know, that is."

"Maybe I should take him off my speed dial?" asked Joe.

"They can probably find out he was on it from the memory in the damned thing, and taking it off will make you look … well, make you look like you're hiding something, which of course you are, but you don't need to tell them that. Don't erase anyone, and don't call anyone. That's my advice."

"Sounds like good advice," said Carolyn. "When will that cruiser be here to pick us up?"

"I don't think it will be here to pick all of us up," said Joe.

"Well it *will* pick up all of us!" said Carolyn. "I'm not going to sit here while all the excitement is going on at police headquarters and worry about you two. Who will post bail for you, or smuggle in a saw to cut the bars off your cell window?"

"Not you, I hope," said Carl.

"Who else?" smirked Carolyn. "You, Carl?"

"I'll be talking to a good lawyer, Carolyn. One your brother or perhaps Reggie recommends. Your brother is an attorney, and surely will be able to recommend someone here."

"I'll have Douglas on a plane out here in the morning if it comes to that," replied Carolyn.

"Well, the police will be here any minute, so let's pay the bill and see who gets to ride to police headquarters at the expense of the City of Las Vegas," said Joe, handing his room key to the server. Despite the threat of serious trouble, he was relieved to have things moving at last.

When they exited the hotel, the police were waiting. Lieutenant O'Conner was standing by the exit and a non-descript black automobile was parked at the end of the drive, with a uniformed officer behind the wheel. Discreet, but fooling no one that bothered to look. Most didn't bother, however.

"Dr. Nelson?" asked the Lieutenant. He appeared as disinterested as he had been earlier that day. "I'm here to give you a ride to headquarters."

He seemed to be ignoring the others, but Carolyn wasn't to be ignored. "I'm Dr. Nelson's wife, so I assume you'll be giving me a ride as well." When this caused a surprised expression to spread across the Lieutenant's face, Carolyn continued, "And of course you'll want to take Natalie and her friend Carl as well. I think we can all fit if one of us sits in front with you two. I'm the smallest, so let that one be me." She opened the door and slid quickly to the middle of the front seat although she was not obviously smaller than Natalie.

After a brief pause, Joe opened the back door and motioned toward Carl. "And Natalie should sit between us in the back, don't you think, Carl?"

Carl looked as if he didn't know what to think, but got in and slid over, followed by Natalie and then Joe, leaving Lieutenant O'Conner the only one standing outside the car. This lasted only another few seconds until he shrugged and sat next to Carolyn, after which the uniformed officer shrugged and they departed for police headquarters.

When they arrived about thirty minutes later, Lieutenant O'Conner was also the first to exit the vehicle. Carolyn had kept a steady stream of conversation going the whole way without a pause for anyone to comment, and it was clear that the lieutenant was regretting "giving" her a ride to headquarters.

"Please come with me," he said from the sidewalk outside the front entrance. As they exited the car, the lieutenant thanked "Johnson," the smiling driver, as he drove away. Joe had no doubt that once out of their view, Johnson's smile would turn to outright laughter, and that Lieutenant O'Conner would hear about this trip for some time to come.

Inside the building they proceeded past the desk sergeant with only a nod, and no response to her quizzical look. Joe thought they would be placed in separate offices, but they were all escorted to the same cubicle where earlier that day he and Natalie had been interviewed by the same lieutenant. He left them alone briefly while he went in search of additional chairs. When Carolyn began to speak, Natalie interrupted her to ask if she thought there were cameras in this office as well as the main building. Carolyn was silent after that until Lieutenant O'Conner returned with two more chairs and another officer, clearly his superior, and clearly not at all friendly. He had not yet met Carolyn, but it was obvious that she wasn't going to dominate this conversation.

"Dr. Nelson," said Lieutenant O'Conner. "This is Captain Mitchell, and … perhaps I'll let you introduce your associates." *Associates* seemed like an unusual word to be used in this context, Joe thought. This promised to be an interesting interview.

"My wife, Carolyn Prentiss," said Joe, indicating her, "and our friends Natalie Moore and Carl—"

"Yes," interrupted Captain Mitchell. "I know who you are." Turning to face Lieutenant O'Conner he added, "I thought it was just Dr. Nelson that you were picking up?"

Lieutenant O'Conner smiled and shrugged. "I thought perhaps you might want to talk to all of them, and … well, they were willing to come along. Just in case you found that you did wish to speak with them as well, I thought it best to bring them."

"I would have thought we would question these people separately. Something about standard procedure I seem to recall, Frank."

Frank O'Conner nodded and smiled slightly again. "Yes, of course. Whom would you like to start with, Captain?"

"Well the doctor, of course."

"I'm a doctor too," smiled Carolyn. "Which *doctor* did you wish to start with?"

The smile on Frank O'Conner's face didn't diminish at all, and Natalie began to smile a little as well. "Are we being charged with anything, Captain Mitchell? I mean, is our cooperation being required, or requested?"

As the captain turned to face her, Carl spoke. "More to the point, should we be talking at all, or should we be requesting that an attorney be summoned?"

"What the hell? No, you're not being charged and yes, you can call any lawyer you fu— any attorney you wish. I have nothing to do this evening, so call every attorney in this city if you want. But when they're all here I'll still have some questions for you to answer."

Joe smiled slightly at this exchange. "And we'll have answers to your questions, I hope. I don't feel the need to inconvenience any lawyers this evening. Shall we divide ourselves into individual groups, Captain?"

Captain Mitchell glared at him. "Let's assume you're honest, although I have doubts on that. We can start with the whole group and move along a little faster, maybe. But if I find that you were not honest earlier today; if I find any hint that you have been *dis*honest, I'll be very upset and you'll be very sorry, Doctor Nelson."

"Let us hope that you don't find anything," said Carl.

Chapter 32

They smiled at the captain as he glared back at them. Joe glanced about the cubicle as much to ease the confrontation as to see anything, but what he saw raised his apprehension a notch. Outside this cubicle, but within another down the hall, he saw the unmistakable, outlandish wig of Percival Prince though the intervening glass.

He returned his gaze to the captain as he began to speak. "So, you saw one of your patients here in Las Vegas, is that right, Doctor? A patient named Katie Perkins?"

"Yes," replied Joe. "I thought I did. I couldn't speak to—"

"You thought you did, but now you're not sure, is that correct, Doctor?"

"I thought I did and I talked to her friends who told me—"

"That she was your patient?"

"No," said Joe. "They told me her name was Katie, but her last name was—"

"Yes, Doctor. What was her last name?"

"I … I don't recall. I'm not sure they told me her last name. I asked them if it was Perkins and they said—"

"But even though she wasn't Katie Perkins, you came to Lieutenant O'Conner to ask that the police look for her?"

"I thought she might be using a different—"

"But you thought she was your patient?"

"Yes. I thought she was." There was growing anxiety in Joe's companions, but he was trying to remain cool in this. He knew, of course, that the entire story had been fabricated, and wanted both to assert that he had acted honestly and at the same time give himself an adequate exit strategy. An opening to have made a mistake in his identification.

"I didn't see her very closely, of course, but I think it was—" he began.

"And were her friends the only people you asked about her, Doctor?"

"Well …"

"Yes?"

Joe blushed an embarrassed frown and said, "There was a gentleman, a pimp I think you would call him, that I approached."

"Percy?"

There were surprised looks around the cubicle now, but Joe frowned a little more and said, "Yes. I tried to talk to him on Fremont Street. You remember, Carolyn." He looked at her. "But it ended unpleasantly. A slight scuffle. Then he came to me at the hotel." *Say enough to explain what the Captain already knows*, thought Joe.

"Is that what you recall, Mrs. Nelson?" asked Captain Mitchell.

"Yes," smirked Carolyn. "Joe is always embarrassing me like that, I'm afraid."

The captain considered this for a moment. "We have talked to Percy," he finally said. When this drew no response he added, "We have found Katie, whose last name isn't Perkins, as well. Would you wish to see her, Doctor?"

Joe looked up in surprise. "Oh yes, I would. Very much!"

Captain Mitchell rose and turned toward the door. "Perhaps the rest of you would not mind waiting here for a few minutes." This wasn't a question.

Joe went out and proceeded down the hall with Captain Mitchell, leaving his friends and Lieutenant O'Conner in the cubicle. Joe was careful to act interested, but not anxious, as he mentally formulated his surprised reaction when he was confronted with a young lady that he would say wasn't his patient after all. He was also careful not to look in the direction where he knew Percy and his wig were located.

They were at the elevators now and the captain pressed the button. When they entered the elevator, they headed down to the basement, and Joe began to wonder if this meant that Katie was in a cell of some sort or….

He had no way of knowing what was really about to confront him, until they exited the elevator into the basement.

They entered into a chilled hall with bright lights and stainless steel tables under them, visible through glass panels. Steel partitions beneath them extended from the floor halfway up the dividing wall, with the glass panel completing the barrier to the ceiling. On the far wall were lines of drawers with labels on them. The sign above the doorway that admitted them into this area announced unnecessarily that this was the city morgue.

Captain Mitchell had not said a word since they'd left the office upstairs and said nothing now. He walked through a doorway in the partition, over to one of the drawers and pulled it open

"Is this your patient, Doctor?" he asked.

He pulled back the sheet covering the body to display the face and torso of what had been Katie. It was bruised and swollen, and Joe would not have recognized it from the single distant view he'd had that night in the hotel drive; but that wasn't what he saw now. He saw a young woman, maybe a child, who had been brutally beaten and killed. Later he would think that he had been right to have taken Percy's request seriously, but now he was revolted by what he saw, and wished he had never gotten involved in this at all.

The captain spoke, bringing Joe back to the present. He had probably done this to take advantage of his shock and the consequent lowering of Joe's defenses. "Is this Katie Perkins, Doctor?"

Joe looked for a moment at the body before him and then at the captain beside him. "No," he said. "I don't think it is."

"Is it the person you saw on the street?"

"Yes, I think … I can't be sure. I wasn't that close and she has been … yes, I think it is."

"You were mistaken then? That she was your patient, I mean?"

"Yes," said Joe. He was beginning to recover now, and looked at the body before him. "I think … may I touch her?"

Captain Mitchell frowned and looked at the bruised face, but finally said, "You may if you want to."

Joe reached not for the face but for the arm closest to him. Picking it up he flexed the fingers before replacing it gently to the steel slab on which it had lain. "How long has she been dead?" he asked.

The captain looked a little surprised as Joe looked up and added, "She has some dependent livido, not much, but some," he said, pointing to where a small amount of purplish discoloration could be seen along her back, "but no rigor mortis. She's been dead a day and a half or maybe more, hasn't she?"

The captain studied Joe for a moment.

"She was dead when you started looking for her, wasn't she?" Joe asked.

Captain Mitchell cleared his throat. "I'll be asking you your whereabouts for the time of her death, Doctor," he said. "I would rather not tell you the time of death until you tell me your whereabouts, if you understand me."

Joe looked puzzled, as if he had not heard what had just been said. "Two days, more or less. Probably the very night I saw her. Is that correct, Captain?"

"And how do you know this, Doctor?"

Joe was thinking fast now. "All the joints are loose, and that takes at least 36 hours. The rigidity, rigor mortis, begins in the small joints and spreads to the larger, and then retreats the same way; small joints first. There's not much livido, though. Not much blood pooled in the lower body, and that happens within hours of death. That would be unusual if she had been dead and lying on her back for two days. How did she die, Captain?"

Captain Mitchell nodded toward Katie's head.

"Not much injury, really," said Joe. "Some bruising, but … was that really how she died? It doesn't appear as if the brain has been examined. Was a postmortem CT scan done?"

The captain studied Joe for a few moments before pulling back the sheet to expose the entire body. On the upper legs, just below the groin, were two deep wounds with blood vessels visible within them.

"She exsanguinated?" asked Joe.

"Is that what you think, Doctor?"

Joe looked puzzled for several seconds. "It would explain the lack of significant dependent livido. Not enough blood left in her body to pool after she died; but why? Was someone trying to … he must have known these wounds would kill her, but if he intended to kill her, why this way?"

"*He*, Doctor? Why do you say *he*?"

It was Joe's turn to study the captain. Finally he smiled ever so slightly and said, "It's usually men who do this sort of thing to women and children, Captain. I'm a pediatrician, and I see altogether too much of this. And it's almost always a man who is responsible. But you know that as well as I do, don't you?"

"Yes. I know a great deal about this sort of thing. I'll need to know where you have been for the past two days, Doctor. You seem very interested in the death of this girl whom you have now decided wasn't your patient after all."

"I'm a pediatrician, Captain, and while this *young woman* wasn't my patient, *she* was my responsibility. All children are, and I'll find out who did this, and I'll make sure he's punished."

Captain Mitchell smiled and said, "I intend to find him too, and I hope you're not involved in this, Doctor, because *I'm* going to see that whoever was involved in this is punished."

Joe reached down and pulled the sheet over what had been Katie and shut the drawer in which her body lay. "And I hope you're not responsible for any of this either, Captain." Joe cast a wry smile at a surprised Captain Mitchell.

"What?" he said.

"I hope there wasn't something that could have been done, and should have been done, that could have prevented this," replied Joe.

Chapter 33

They had left the morgue and were waiting for the elevator before either spoke again.

"I don't believe you're telling me all that you know, Doctor Nelson. I'm beginning to believe that you really were motivated by concern for that girl, but I don't think it was because you thought she was a patient of yours."

Joe smiled at him and said, "I was concerned about her and wanted you to be concerned about her too."

"So you fabricated this story to get our cooperation, Doctor? Is that it?"

Joe considered this as the elevator doors opened. He thought about Percy, who had made him concerned, and whom this police officer had already talked to. He didn't know what Percy had said, but Joe knew that the less *he* said, the less likelihood their accounts would conflict with one another. "She was in trouble, and the police should have been looking for her. I didn't know she was already dead."

Captain Mitchell looked thoughtful as they walked into the elevator and the doors closed in back of them. "I don't think you did know she was dead, but I'm going to make sure. Many people take the death of another runaway as part of the background noise of Las Vegas. *I* do not. If we begin to accept this as something that we *should just accept*, soon we'll not care *when* it happens or even *if* it happens or *how often* or *to whom*. We won't care about anything. Do you have children, Doctor Nelson? Children of your own, I mean."

"No," said Joe. "Do you?"

"Yes." The captain smiled. "This girl, Katie, had parents too. I don't know why she ended up here. I don't know if her parents loved her, or whether she loved them. I don't even know if they care that she's dead now, but she had parents. I'm going to make sure she's not just another statistic in this city. You can help, maybe, but you had better not screw with me, Doctor, or I'll bury you."

Joe looked around the elevator as it began to ascend, first at the walls and floor, and then at the ceiling. No obvious monitoring devices were visible, but holes and screens were where those devises might easily be concealed. "Are there video recordings in this elevator, Captain?"

Captain Mitchell smiled. "Yes," he said. "Do you want to talk to an attorney about police harassment, Doctor?"

"If I see any, I'll talk to someone about it. I just want to make sure that what I say is recorded so there's no misunderstanding here. We both want the same thing. Katie was killed, brutally, and we both want to see that crime punished. If you want to waste your time chasing me that's your choice, but I'm going after this guy. I'll tell you what I find, and if you ask me, I'll tell you what I'm thinking. When we have finished with that, you can slam me for whatever crimes you think I committed, but unless you arrest me right now I'm going to do everything I can to see Katie's killer brought to justice. Katie deserves that. It's about justice, not revenge."

The doors opened and they walked out and turned down the corridor toward the cubicle where the rest were waiting. As they did, Captain Mitchell frowned and then smiled as he said, "Louie, I think this is the beginning of a beautiful friendship."

Joe chuckled a little. "*Casablanca*?" he said.

"Yup, Doc. And I'm Bogie."

"Then I'll be Claude Rains," replied Joe. "Let's *round up the usual suspects*."

This is how they joined the others to their considerable and unconcealed surprise.

Carolyn was the first to speak. "Did you see Katie?" she asked.

Joe's face lost all trace of a smile as he cleared his throat. "Yes, I did."

He looked about, trying to find a way to say what he had seen, but the expression on his face said what he couldn't find the words to express. Smiles disappeared from their faces, replaced by dismay. Carolyn opened her mouth, but couldn't speak.

Finally Natalie asked what the others could only wonder. "Is she dead?"

Captain Mitchell should probably not have been surprised, but he was. Anger spread in him as he looked first at Natalie, then Joe, and then at Lieutenant O'Conner. "Did you—"

"No, Captain. I just asked the standard question as we had discussed. I told them nothing about—"

Natalie interrupted. "He just asked the usual question, but … well, I'm a cop back home, and I know what the questions really mean." She shrugged as the captain transferred his angry gaze from the lieutenant to her.

"He asked how long we'd known Katie, when we'd last seen her, where was that, what was she wearing. Those are questions cops ask when … well, when someone is missing, or dead. Katie isn't missing anymore, is she? She's dead."

"Yes," said Joe.

Natalie shut her eyes and bent her head toward the floor as first Carolyn and then Carl gasped. "Shit," said Natalie.

Captain Mitchell shook his head in disgust. "We have not contacted her *mother and sister* back in Kentucky. A good thing, since she was neither *daughter nor sister*, apparently."

He looked at Joe now and added, "That having been established, this no longer concerns any of you. I expect that you'll act accordingly."

Joe frowned, but said nothing.

"Do I have reason to expect that any of you will act in any other way?" He spoke as if he was addressing the whole room, but he was looking intently at Joe.

"Every reason to think I won't *act accordingly*," Joe said.

"Joe," said Carolyn. "There's no reason ... there's nothing we can do. She wasn't your ... She wasn't who you thought she was, so ..." Her voice trailed off as she realized the futility of what she was saying. "Oh shit, Joe. You can be so ... just lock him up now, Captain. That's the only way ... No wait; that was only a joke. Please don't lock him up. We'll do that for you. Honest. I was just joking."

"I'm not laughing, Mrs. Nelson," said Captain Mitchell.

Carolyn looked exasperated and shook her head. "Sorry," she said. "And it's Dr. Prentiss."

"Maybe in your hospital it's *doctor*, but we're not in a hospital here."

"Sorry," said a chastised Carolyn. This captain was one of a very small number of people that Joe had ever seen successfully chastise his wife, Carolyn.

 *Chapter 34*

Captain Mitchell glared about him, finally settling on Lieutenant O'Conner. The lieutenant seemed remarkably unperturbed, perhaps because this wasn't unusual behavior for his captain.

"Is Percy still here?" the captain asked.

"I … I think he may be," responded the lieutenant.

"Well, go get him then."

"Get him, sir?"

"Get him, O'Conner, and bring him here."

"Bring him here, sir?"

"Yes, bring him here, and stop repeating everything I say."

"But …?" began Lieutenant O'Conner, appearing very perturbed now.

"Look, O'Conner. I want this guy. I want the guy that did this to that girl, and I want him to hang. I want him to hang now. I want him so bad I can taste it."

"But," began Lieutenant O'Conner again, "the procedure is—"

He didn't get to finish his objection. "Screw the procedure! If we wait to do this by the book this guy is going to be dead and buried ten years before we get anywhere close to him. And he'll be dead from natural causes, O'Conner, but you won't, because I'll have killed you. Get Percy, bring him here, and do it now!"

The lieutenant stared at his superior as Natalie smiled. "I heard that," she said. They were in a cubicle, not an interrogation room, so several people outside the cubicle had heard it as well. A few were staring, while most were studiously concentrating on something else; anything else. All were undoubtedly listening.

The captain was calm now, but no less force was present in his voice. "I want this guy. Get Percy please, Lieutenant O'Conner."

The lieutenant left the cubicle and an uneasy quiet settled within. He returned with Percy a moment later, and the tension shifted accordingly.

"So, Percy," said the captain. "Wha'da you know?"

Percy looked around him and finally settled his gaze on Captain Mitchell. "Serious shit, I'm guessin'. Wha'da you know, Captain?"

"I'm told, that you told someone, to go look at a rundown shack down the western end of this great city."

"That I did, Captain."

"And then they told someone to go out there, and then they told me to go out there. Do you know what we found, Percy? And did you know what we would find before we went out there?"

Percy considered this a moment. "Don't know what ya found, so's I don't know if I knew ya'd find it. Wha'dya find, Captain?"

"You got a girl named Katie working the street for you, Percy?"

"'*Workin' da street*'? I know a young lady named Katie, but I'm not sure what ya mean by '*workin' da street,*' Captain."

Captain Mitchell frowned and shook his head. "Bullshit, Percy. You knew Katie, and she was one of your girls, and we found her at the address you told us to go to, with that bullshit story you fed us, and when we got there we found Katie dead."

Percy stared at him with surprise and shock that couldn't possibly have been anything except the real thing. "Shit," was all he could manage to say.

"Yeah, shit's right," replied the captain.

"How'd she ... who?"

"I was hoping you could help with those answers, Percy, seeing as you sent us out there," replied Captain Mitchell.

"Yeah, well ..."

"Why did you think we should look for Katie there, Percy? Did it have anything to do with the girl named Katie that Dr. Nelson sent us looking for? You told us there was a girl, named Katie, missing, and you thought she might be in trouble, and you thought she might be at that shack you sent us to. Is this all one great big coincidence? Do I have *stupid* written on my forehead, Percy?"

"No, Captain," said Percy. "Look, I don't know nothin' 'cept what I was told. Wasn't there at all, or it wouldn't ever have happened. Katie got into a car wid this dude named Harry. Montanez is the name he's been usin' lately, but not likely his real name, I'm thinkin.' Anyways, she drives off wid 'im and no one sees her again. That shack I told ya ta check out. He's been livin' there lately, so—"

"An' the doc here? How's he fit in?"

Before Joe could answer, Percy looked over at him and winked. "Does I know you, man?"

"Yes," said Joe. "And Captain Mitchell knows we know each other, too."

"Oh, yeah," said Percy. "Fremont Street. Couple nights ago, right?"

Joe nodded.

"And maybe at the hotel yesterday, too," said the captain.

"Yeah," said Percy. "Forgot 'bout that."

Captain Mitchell shook his head again.

Joe smiled a slight smile. "When I saw Katie getting into Harry's car, I was upset. When I saw the rest of the young women who had been with her on Fremont Street that evening, I went over to talk to them … and to Percy. To see if I could … well, that's not important. But Percy remembered me, and when Katie didn't show up in the morning, he came to see if I could help."

Captain Mitchell smiled broadly. "Because he knew she was one of your patients from back in Kentucky, right?"

"Yeah, that's it. Figured he could help. That's all." Percy smiled.

"Because he thought I could help," said Joe. "So I tried to do that, because I was concerned, and I wanted to do whatever I could do."

Captain Mitchell frowned and looked first at Percy, and then at Joe.

Joe frowned too. "So, what you want to know right now, Captain, is whether Percy and I had anything to do with Katie's murder. Is that a good place to start?"

Captain Mitchell nodded slowly. "Where were each of you two nights ago, say six o'clock to ten or eleven or so in the evening?"

Percy stared, and Joe blinked a few times. "Two days ago? Percy and I were … we were on Fremont Street," he said. "Together on Fremont Street."

"For the whole four or five hours?"

"No. But probably right in the middle of those five hours," replied Joe. "Neither one of us could have done … it would not have been possible to kill Katie the way she was killed, and to have been on Fremont Street when we were there. Not if the time was between six and ten or eleven."

Percy looked at the floor. "Kill'd her the way … wha' way was she killed, Joe?" he said, looking up.

Before Joe could respond, Captain Mitchell interrupted. "Providing some entertainment on Fremont, I understand."

"What?" asked Percy.

"Couple of officers on patrol down there remember you, Percy, mixing it up with a guy that they thought looked like the good doctor here. They remember the show you two put on. Especially the thing with your leg, Doctor. Oh, and your hair, too, Percy. Can I see the leg?"

Joe reached down instinctively to pull his pant leg up. He stopped for a moment and smiled at Captain Mitchell. "This will be my alibi, won't it?"

He pulled the pant leg up to display the full prosthesis and its attachment to his leg below his knee. He then knocked on it to give the sound of heavy plastic as the captain nodded.

"You knew Percy and I had alibis all along, didn't you?" asked Joe. "Your men were not going to forget that incident, what with my leg and Percy's hair."

"I's workin' on da hair, Cap'n," apologized Percy, as he pulled his wig off. "See, I think it's growin' in a little, Doc." He was looking at Carolyn, not at Joe.

Lieutenant O'Conner ran his hand across his bald dome as he looked closely at Percy's head.

"Oh, for God's sakes, put that back on, Percy," said Carolyn. "And stop calling me Doc. No one calls me *doctor* around here." Her glare went first toward Percy and then toward Captain Mitchell, who did blush just a little in response

Chapter 35

"I was afraid she's dead," said Percy, as he adjusted his wig. "That bastard, Harry."

"That who you think it was?" asked Captain Mitchell.

"Well, Cap'n—" began Percy uneasily.

"So seriously, gentlemen," interrupted Carolyn. "Why is it *Captain Mitchell* and *Doctor Nelson*, and *Lieutenant O'Conner*, and … well, Percy doesn't count, but I'm still called *Mrs. Nelson*?"

"Whatcha' mean, Percy don't count, mama?"

"I mean …" said Carolyn. "Oh, you know what I mean. And stop calling me *mama*. At least not in public. Call me Carolyn, for God's sakes."

Percy smiled. "Okay, *Carolyn fa' God's sakes.* What should I call ya in private?"

Percy chuckled, and even Carolyn smiled a little at this. "You'll never need to know, Percy."

Captain Mitchell frowned, but it was Natalie who spoke. "We're losing focus here, people. Katie's murderer is getting cold on the trail."

"It's the *trail* that's getting cold," corrected Carl.

"Whatever," said Natalie. "A murderer is getting away."

"Yes," said the captain. "So why do you think the man we're looking for is this guy, Harry?"

Percy shrugged. "Man picks up a young woman who turns up dead in his last known address, and that very night for kickers. Got to be top o' the list, Cap'n, don'cha think?"

Captain Mitchell frowned at this.

"Least be top a' the list a' people ta talk to, don'cha think, Cap'n?"

Captain Mitchell's frown deepened.

Joe looked at them both. "Little too pat, Captain? Is that what you think?"

The captain nodded slowly. "What sort of guy is this Harry … what did you say Frank?" He looked at Lieutenant O'Conner, who seemed surprised to be taken out of the audience so abruptly.

"Well," he said. "Not much, Mitch."

"You got his sheet?"

"Well, yes. Nothing major though. Picked up for drugs a couple of times, but no jail time and then for … well, soliciting an undercover officer once, but again plea bargained his way out of jail time."

"Assault?" asked Joe.

Captain Mitchell looked at Joe as Lieutenant O'Conner stared at him. "Well, yes, there was one, but dropped for lack of … well, an accuser. The young lady changed her mind."

"Did she say why?" asked Joe. He was looking at Percy when he said this, and Percy was looking away.

"No," said the lieutenant, as puzzlement crossed his face. "She actually came to court and then told the judge she had changed her mind about pursuing the case. Rather strange."

Joe frowned a moment before saying, "So she changed her mind, but didn't say why? Was it Maggie, or one of the others?"

Percy practically fell from his surprise, while Captain Mitchell stared and Lieutenant O'Conner stammered. "I'm not … I can't say who … I …"

"You need to be quiet," offered Captain Mitchell.

"Yes," said Joe. "Quiet would be best." The smile on his face said he, for one, needed no further answer to this question, at least.

"Well, what else can you offer, Doct—I mean *Mister* Nelson?"

"I wonder," said Joe, "about girls who accuse their clients of assault and then drop the charges."

Joe looked pensive as the captain said, "Not that uncommon, Doc—Mister Nelson."

"Not uncommon that they accuse someone and then come all the way back into court to tell the judge they have changed their mind? I would have thought that would be at least a little unusual."

Captain Mitchell said nothing, but annoyance showed on his face.

"What I was wondering about was why a man like Harry would … well, do a thing like this. He did have an assault charge, but even so, this seems … seems so much more than that. Not entirely in character."

The captain shrugged, albeit grudgingly. "Yes. A little unusual for a small-time hoodlum to start … to do what was done two nights ago."

"The man who did this had some medical knowledge, too. Perhaps that was why you wanted to make sure I wasn't a suspect. Is that correct, Captain?" said Joe.

Captain Mitchell's annoyance didn't diminish.

"Was Harry a violent client, Percy?" asked Joe.

"What?" said Percy. "Oh, well yeah. I mean, that's why … I mean, I told the young ladies not ta mess with him on that account."

"But murder?" asked Joe. "You surprised at that, Percy?"

"Well yeah, a little."

"Okay, enough of this," said Captain Mitchell. "I'm going to pick up this Harry Montanez, and I'll check out the other possibilities too, okay, Doctor Nelson?"

"That sounds like good police procedure, Captain," replied Joe.

"I'll start by talking to Percival Prince here to see if he has anything more to tell me. Like who this Katie really was, and where we might reach her real parents."

"Got a number for her dad," said Percy.

"Give it to me in my office. Come on." Captain Mitchell got up and left the cubicle, followed by Percy. He turned back from the hall to say, "And Frank, you talk to the good doctor and see if he has anything more to add, and try to convince him we can do this one on our own, okay? Maybe you can talk to both doctors."

Chapter 36

Percy left with the captain, and Lieutenant O'Conner turned a smiling face toward Joe. "Perhaps your friends won't mind waiting in the lobby for a few minutes while we talk, Dr. Nelson?"

"Captain Mitchell said you should interview both *doctors*," said Carolyn. "To make sure neither of us had anything more to *add*."

"Yes, you're right," answered a smiling Lieutenant O'Conner. "Do you have anything more to add, Doctor Prentiss?"

"Well, no," said Carolyn.

"Consider yourself interviewed, Doctor. Your husband will join you in the lobby in just a few minutes." Lieutenant O'Conner smiled and waited until the other three departed; grudgingly departed on Carolyn's part.

When they were alone, he turned to Joe and asked, "And do you have anything more to add, Dr. Nelson?"

"I don't think so," replied Joe. "I do think Harry whatever his last name is, should be the prime suspect, as they say on TV, but …"

"Yes?"

"Was this standard procedure today? I mean, was this the way you usually conduct interviews?"

Lieutenant O'Conner considered this a moment before answering. "Yes and no."

"If those are the only two choices, I'll take *no*. What did happen here?"

This time Lieutenant O'Conner was quiet for some time before answering. "Captain Mitchell is an exceedingly competent police officer, but … well, he's also a human being and he's … well, sometimes he … well … what do you think of him, Doctor?"

"He seemed almost manic today, and then slid into ... is he bipolar?"

"Well ... yes." The Lieutenant shrugged. "It's just that ... well, sometimes he adjusts his own medication."

"Oh," said Joe. "He shouldn't do that."

"No, of course not, but ... he's an excellent police officer. Sometimes he thinks he needs a little more ... well, more energy, and the medication makes him less energetic. I shouldn't be telling you this, but it will help you to understand what's happening and ... well *you're a doctor*. The captain will provide the energy, and someone else will need to provide the guidance. May I count on your help with that?"

"Weren't you supposed to convince me not to interfere in this case anymore, Lieutenant?"

"Oh, I'm sorry, I forgot that part. Please don't interfere in this case anymore, Dr. Nelson, and please remember that I advised you not to interfere with the case anymore. If you choose to ignore my advice, which I suspect you will, watch Captain Mitchell, and try to keep him pointed in the right direction.

"Right now I'm going to find out if Percy really does have a phone number for that girl's family and make sure that I make the call to them, not Captain Mitchell. You may take your friends back to the hotel, and remember what I told you. Oh, and also remember that I told you not to leave town until we tell you that you may."

With this, Frank O'Conner left the cubicle, leaving Joe standing there alone. He didn't escort him to the lobby, nor even tell him that he should go there. Joe was in the middle of the police station with no one to watch him save those cameras that he had been assured were everywhere. Was anyone watching them? He had no idea, but he couldn't think of what else to do, so he went to the lobby where his friends were waiting. They exited the station, hailed a cab, and were soon on their way back to their hotel, as the shock and bewilderment of what had happened began to wash over them.

"She was murdered?" said Natalie when they were seated in the cab. Carolyn was again in the front seat, next to the cab driver this time, but the back seat was organized much as it was on the trip over: Natalie in the middle, with Carl and Joe on either side.

The cab driver had looked over at Carolyn when Natalie spoke, and this caused all conversation to cease for the rest of the trip. They couldn't talk without including Carolyn, obviously, even though there was a plastic barrier between the front and back seats with its sliding panel. They couldn't talk about anything except Katie's death, and they couldn't talk about that in front of the cabbie.

When they arrived back at the hotel, Joe paid the cabbie and they entered to find themselves facing Percival Prince standing impatiently in the lobby.

"Where you guys been?" he asked.

"How'd you get here before us?" asked Joe.

"Never drive anywhere on the strip in dis town. Take the back ways," replied Percy. "Look, people, we gots ta talk. Now!"

"Yeah," said Joe. "Can I buy you a cup of hot chocolate, Percy?"

"Yeah, yeah sure. Anywheres." With this he turned to walk toward the café that had been their meeting place so often over the past twenty-four hours.

They sat and a server arrived, not Sally, nor Peter, but another young man. He didn't seem to recognize any of them, but equally he didn't seem to be upset by Percy or any of the rest, for that matter. He simply took their orders and went to get them as servers all over this city and in many other cities were probably doing at that very moment.

When he had gone, Percy said, "I saw her. I was da only one could ID her."

Joe nodded, while the others looked at a distressed Percy.

"I gots ta do somethin' 'bout it," he said.

"Let the police—" began Natalie.

"If they can, an' if they do, that'll be fine," interrupted Percy. "But if they don't, or if they won't, I will."

"Percy," said Carolyn.

"She was one o' my gi— one o' my *young women*. I gotta make this right. I owe it. 'Sides, if'n I don't square this off, the bastards out there will think they can do da same to all my *young women*. Ta all da *young women* in Vegas. You saw her, Joe. She was beat up bad."

"Be careful, Percy," said Carolyn.

"Thanks, ma—I mean, Carolyn."

They were quiet for a minute as the server brought their coffee and hot chocolate. As he departed, Joe asked, "You think it was Harry?"

"Gotta be. Picked her up. Found her at his place. Guy has been known ta hurt gi— ta hurt women."

"To *kill* women?" asked Joe.

"Well, no," admitted Percy. "Not that I ever heard."

"But you would know if girls were showing up beaten and dead before this, wouldn't you Percy?" asked Natalie. "Even if they weren't yours?"

"They's *young women*," said Percy, smiling at Joe. "Yeah, I would hear, an' pretty quick, too."

"But he did hurt Maggie, didn't he?" asked Joe.

"How'd ya know that?"

"She said she got in trouble once, and Angie got you involved and you straightened everything out. I was just guessing it was Harry. What happened, and why did she drop the charges?"

Percy shrugged. "She couldn't go to court without provin' who she was. That'd be trouble for 'er, so I told 'er ta let me handle it."

"And ...?" asked Joe.

"I talked ta Harry."

"And what did you say?"

"Shit, Joe. Ya want my life or something? I told Maggie to come ta court, just to put a little scare inta Harry, an' then drop the charge. Then I told Harry he was messin' with me an' he had lots a' secrets, 'bout drugs an' shit like that. If'n he ever … well, da cops would find out what he was hidin' if he did anything again. 'E didn't, neither."

"'Til two nights ago," said Natalie.

"Was he the one who cut Maggie's neck?" Joe asked.

"Naw. That happened before she started workin' with me. Boyfriend or something. Harry … it was just some bruises an' shit."

"Where are the rest of your *young women* now?" asked Carolyn.

"I took 'em ta a motel outside da strip for a while. They don't want ta work now, an' I don't want 'em to. Not 'til Harry's in jail or … not 'til he's not around no more. 'Sides, I don't want da police onto 'em."

"But they could have information that would help the police, Percy. Like where Katie's family is or something," said Natalie.

"If'n they need ta talk to 'em, I'll see they do," replied Percy. "Already gave Katie's father's number ta Lieutenant Baldy, an' her ma's too, but that ain't going nowhere. Not her ma's, I mean."

"Angie had numbers for Katie?" asked Joe.

Percy blushed. "I had 'em. Look, I said I didn't have 'em cause Katie asked me not to tell no one I had 'em. Figured if'n I said I had 'em in front a' Sally or Maggie, it'd get back ta Katie an' … well, I lied, okay?"

"Okay," said Joe, but Percy wasn't finished yet.

"Look, Katie's situation was da worst one I ever seen. Her ma had custody in the divorce an' her dad couldn't do nothin'. He's a nice enough guy. Talked ta 'im a few times an' he wanted Katie ta come live with him, but she couldn't, ya see."

"She couldn't?" asked Carolyn.

Percy shook his head. "She went ta stay with her dad once, an' … well, her ma found out an' made her come back, an' her ma's got a boyfriend what likes Katie, like, he *really* likes Katie, likes ta screw Katie, I mean, an' her ma thinks Katie should be nice ta her boyfriend so's he'll be nice ta her an' … anyways, her ma's got lawyers an' detectives an' all that shit, an' Katie couldn't go near her dad without her ma findin' out. Afraid ta even call 'er dad. Thought they could trace her that way. Didn't want no one ta know for fear they'd tell the cops who she was or where her dad was an' … well, I'd call every so often an' she'd talk ta him, but … not too often." He just shrugged, and everyone else was silent.

"Her mother …?" asked Carolyn.

"Yeah," sighed Percy. "She's a weasel all right. Lives over in Nebraska some place, an' she's got the law on 'er side over there. Ya know she even gets child support?"

"Child support?" asked Carolyn. "Katie's not even living with her, is she?"

"Aw, she lied 'er ass off." Percy shrugged. "Told da court Katie was away a lot, but was home some, an' she paid her support even when she was away. Guess no one checked real close, even when Katie's dad said she weren't nowhere near her ma's place 'cause a' da boyfriend. Court said her dad was da liar. Threatened 'im with liable, or something. He didn't have no lawyer so he jus' shut up an' paid after that. Even sent money ta Katie, well, ta me ta give ta Katie, fa' like her birthday an' stuff like that. Nice guy, but like they say: *Nice guys finish last.*"

"Did he know …?" asked Carolyn.

"Yeah," said Percy. "Ya mean how she earned a livin'? She told 'im an' it upset 'im. That's why she had me talk ta 'im. Told 'im I'd get her a real job when she could, but nothin' she could do 'til then. Nothin' that wouldn't get 'er sent back ta 'er ma an' da boyfriend. We agreed it sucked, but nothin' else ta do."

"That's appalling," said Carl quietly. The tone was subdued, but the force in it was sufficient to make everyone turn to look. "Do you have a name and address by any chance? I have some friends in Nebraska."

"Fer 'er dad?" asked Percy.

"No," said Carl. "For her mother, I meant. I have some friends and … well, if you wouldn't mind giving me her name and address … well, I'll ask my friends."

It wasn't at all clear what Carl meant or what he was going to ask his friends, but Percy nodded. "Yeah, sure," he said.

"So will she be notified? And Katie's father as well?" asked Natalie.

"Already called 'er dad. He'll be here in da mornin.' He can do the real ID. 'Er ma? Leave that one ta Cap'n Mitch an' Baldy." Percy smiled at this last comment. "Dat Cap'n Mitch is one weird dude all right."

"Bipolar," said Joe absently.

"Really?" asked Carolyn. "How do you know that?"

Joe smiled. "Lieutenant *Baldy* told me. So, what do we do now, Percy?'

"Sit as still as you can, chief. We wait an' see what happens. My guess is dat Harry will surface pretty quick. 'E don't got many friends, an' 'e got even less money. Cap'n Mitch wants ta get 'im, so chances are we don't need ta do nothin'."

"That's a good idea, don't you think so, Joe?" asked Carolyn.

"Do you think the police will talk to Robert Bevins, the associate manager here?" Joe asked.

"Why would they?" asked Natalie.

"Well, he seemed to know Harry. May have even extended him some credit. I saw him showing some papers to Harry and he seemed upset. Bevins might know where Harry is, if he owes money."

"Not sure they'll bother," said Natalie.

"Maybe I will then," said Joe.

"Oh shit, Joe" said Carolyn. "Just when I stop worrying about Percy, you decide to start acting stupid."

"I'm just going to talk to him," protested Joe.

"Well, make sure that's all you do," said Natalie.

Joe smiled and nodded as everyone else shook their heads.

Chapter 37

With this Percy rose to leave. "You keep a close eye on Joe, ya hear me, Carolyn? An' be careful ya'self." He smiled and left as he got a faint smile in return.

"So, this is just great," said Carolyn, shaking her head. "We're involved in a murder, involved in it by lying to the police, and the police are currently made up of a bipolar captain and a lieutenant who seems more a part of the audience than an actor in the drama. The other principle player is Percival Prince, who seems intent upon providing the comic relief for this dreary tragedy. And then there's Joe, who seems equally intent upon ignoring the script completely and taking over the role of the investigator. This show is definitely not going to get picked up by Hollywood, people."

"And there's still poor little Katie," sighed Natalie. "Is anyone really going to find out who killed her?"

"The police may," said Carl absently. "But there are other crimes that must be addressed too, crimes that the police have yet to become aware of."

"There are lots of crimes," sighed Carolyn.

"Yes," nodded Carl. "I think I'll be going." Without further comment he rose and headed in the direction of the casino, disappearing into the crowd. It was almost ten o'clock, and peak time for casino activity.

Natalie looked at her remaining companions. "It is late, I guess." The noise coming from the casino said clearly that there were many who would disagree with her on this. "I'm going to bed, I think. Please don't get into any trouble while I'm asleep, Joe. Or you either, Carolyn."

"I'll be right up," replied Carolyn. "I just want to emphasize your just-given advice, in case Joe didn't understand your subtlety. You made it sound as if it were a request, not a demand. I prefer to include threats of serious injury, myself. Much more effective."

"You have known him longer than I, but perhaps you don't know him any better. I'm not sure threats of injury or even death would dissuade him." She bent and kissed Joe's cheek, and then squeezed Carolyn's shoulder before turning to leave.

"She's right, of course," said Carolyn. "I'll be angry if you continue to interfere with the investigation of Katie's death, but I'll not be surprised. Do you like Natalie, Joe?"

Joe looked up with a start. "Oh, I guess … she's a very nice … I mean, I think she's …"

"We'll be divorced soon, Joe, and I think you'll be happier married, and married to Natalie, than you will be if you stay single." Carolyn nodded in the self-assured way that Joe had come to expect of her. They had been married for ten years, happily so, and good friends even now. Joe knew their divorce had nothing to do with how well they got along, but rather with Carolyn's insistence that she had to pursue her career, her *calling*, she sometimes said, and that Joe would be miserable living her life. Yes, she thought she still loved him, she had said, but for Carolyn there were things equally important in life. She was also sure that even if she could be happy as a single career woman, Joe would only be happy as a married man … married to Natalie, she had decided. Simple enough. Carolyn usually didn't bother much with subtleties of any sort.

"I like Natalie, but …"

"Yes?" said Carolyn.

"We'll see what happens," said Joe. "Natalie and I will see what happens."

"I already know what will happen if you and Natalie don't screw it up," replied Carolyn. "So don't screw it up, or I'll cut your balls off. If Natalie doesn't get them, no one will."

"Okay. I think I understand that."

"Good. Now as for this thing with Katie. Why don't we give the police a chance first, and not interfere until they ask us to? Can we agree on that, too?"

Joe smiled. "Yes, we can. I will not do anything until the police have had their chance, but then I'm going to have to help them, even if they don't ask."

Carolyn looked skeptical. "Really?"

"Yes," replied Joe. "Specifically, I will not talk to Robert Bevins until the police have had a chance to do so."

Carolyn's look of skepticism grew as Joe stood. "I think I'll go to bed now, and I will not speak to Robert tonight, just to prove I'm sincere."

He started to walk away, but turned back to smile at Carolyn. "If, however, by morning the police have not spoken to Robert Bevins, I will."

He walked away as Carolyn called after him, "Oh, shit, Joe, don't you ever listen to …?"

She had spoken very loudly, almost shouting, but no one seemed to notice above the noise from the casino. The only one who did seem to notice her was their server, standing next to her now. "Will you be paying then?" he asked, producing the check for her.

"Shit," she said, as she pulled out her room key and handed it to him. He took it without any further notice.

Chapter 38

The morning came, and even though Joe had given the police until eight o'clock, they had not interviewed Robert Bevins. At least they had not told Joe that they had interviewed him. The police had not told Joe *not* to interview Robert himself, either; only Carolyn had told him that. So now he stood in the outer office, waiting to begin the interview. The office was very well appointed, but he expected nothing less. There was an oriental rug over a dark hardwood floor. Tasteful art hung on the walls, and it looked to be original art, not copies or prints. A massive grandfather clock stood against one wall with a large pendulum slowly swinging in back of three ornate brass weights.

A well-dressed, attractive lady of maybe fifty or fifty-five sat behind a large mahogany desk and informed Joe that Mr. Bevins would be there "in just a few minutes," and would be pleased to see him then. She had called him on his cell phone, she said, when Joe "dropped by" to ask when it would be convenient to see him. Joe had "dropped by" specifically to pressure the interview to be scheduled as quickly as possible, and his ploy had been successful.

When Robert Bevins arrived, he greeted Joe and then his "Administrative Assistant, Beverly," as the plaque on the large mahogany desk identified the lady sitting behind it. There was no last name given. Robert then asked if Joe would kindly come into his office. If this wasn't a convenient time for him, he showed no sign that that might be the case.

Inside was an even larger mahogany desk, with the appropriate ink blotter on its top, complete with the necessary pens in their holders. Joe wondered if they were ever used. There was a small stack of what looked to be mail on one side, and half a dozen folders on the other.

None of these were given any attention by Robert as he sat behind the desk and motioned towards the two chairs in front of it, indicating that Joe could take either seat he wished.

"I'm sorry I'm a little late this morning. I had a date last night. What can I do for you, Doctor?" he asked.

Joe had thought about this, and had decided to take a cue from Captain Mitchell and surprise Robert Bevins with a direct question in order to see the response and un-nerve him a little. It had not worked all that well for the captain when used on him in the morgue, but Joe had thought it might work if the subject were feeling guilty.

"I saw you talking to a man named Harry the other day," said Joe. "I was wondering if you can tell me about him."

Robert smiled. "I know a great deal about Harry, but I'm not sure you would be interested in all that I know. There's also Harry's privacy to be considered."

Not too much anxiety evident, but Joe had prepared for this. Prepared for the question as to why he wanted to know about Harry, too. It had worked on the police, and it might work on an associate manager. "I saw him with a young lady who I thought might be a patient of mine. From back in Kentucky. She's quite ill, and may have run away from her home and … well, I was hoping to ask Harry if he knew where she might be found."

Robert frowned as he considered this question. "I really shouldn't be telling you this. You should be talking to the police. But I don't think Harry will be able to help you, Doctor. Harry is a rather troubled man."

"Oh?" Joe replied, and waited to see if any further response was forthcoming.

Robert Bevins sighed and continued. "I knew Harry in the army, Doctor. We were in the medical corps together. I didn't like what I saw, but was able to come back and pick up my life. Harry was never able to do that. The death and the damage was too much for him."

"That's true for many people, I guess," sighed Joe. Natalie crossed his mind. She was one who had seen, but returned to pick up her life in spite of it all.

Robert chuckled now. "I did quite well picking up that life again." He waved his hand around him and continued, "Nice office, ya think, Doc? I dress well, and drive an expensive car. I have the best." He pulled his cell phone out of his belt holder. "This is the best there is. Not even available 'til a couple of weeks ago, but I got one."

Joe smiled. The cell phone was the mark of status and success, the mark of *cool*. "Yes," he said.

"Ladies are impressed with all this shit." Robert smiled and winked. "Anyway, I can't say that I know where Harry is living now. He doesn't always live where his address is, if ya know what I mean. He has some pretty nasty creditors after him sometimes. If I were to look for him, I'd look over in the old abandoned warehouses west of town. He's been known to live there for months at a time. Mostly I just wait for him to show up here."

"You threw him out a few days ago."

"Harry doesn't need to be gambling here, or anywhere." Robert shrugged.

Joe nodded. "I saw you showing something to Harry outside the hotel, the day before yesterday, I think it was. Does he have a line of credit here?"

Robert shook his head. "We don't do that anymore. I have loaned him some money from time to time. An old friend in trouble sort of loan, but I realized that I was giving him money to pay for his food or clothes or rent and he was gambling it away." He seemed a little nervous now. *Had he extended credit even though he denied it?* Joe wondered.

"He thought he could beat the slots," suggested Joe. When Robert looked surprised he added, "That's what I heard, anyway."

"Oh, yeah … maybe, but I don't … I mean, someone said he had, and he did have some money last time I saw … but no one can really beat the slots, can they?" Robert was smiling now, but this suggestion had clearly taken him off guard. "Anyway, like I said. I can't say I know where you can find Harry, Doc."

Robert Bevins rose and began walking toward the door. "I can say that I have a busy morning, so if you won't mind …" He motioned toward the door and Joe rose.

"I guess you saw a lot in the army. Did you and Harry do any surgery or anything? I mean, did you at least get to save a few lives?"

"Not really," said Robert.

"No severed arteries in legs that you had to clamp, or apply pressure dressings to even?" Specific questions Joe knew, but he wanted to know what Harry and Robert knew about arteries in legs.

Robert shrugged. "We saw it, knew how to do it, but usually there was someone else to take care of those things. Lots of severed arteries in arms and legs. Body armor protected the trunk and head usually, but not the limbs. Particularly the legs. Roadside bombs." He shrugged again.

They were in the outer office now and for Robert, the interview was clearly over. He turned to his administrative assistant and said, "Send some flowers to Tyla, will you, Beverly? Thank her for a great evening."

He winked at Joe and went back into his office, shutting the door behind him. He had spoken loudly enough for Joe to hear. Probably his way of bragging, but Joe wasn't impressed.

He smiled wanly, but Beverly didn't notice, so he too left the outer office, walking slowly toward the casino. As he looked around he saw Tyla at her table, but she was busy with several players. He walked toward the café, trying to decide whether it would be coffee or hot chocolate.

Chapter 39

He sat, and settled on coffee by the time the server arrived. "Nothing to eat, thank you." It had been doubly disappointing this morning. He had gotten no closer to finding Harry. He had learned that he had been in the service, traumatized by what he saw, and therefore, by the medical standard, might be inclined to abuse people. He had also been told that Harry saw plenty of severed arteries, particularly in legs, and therefore ... well, he maybe knew how to produce those wounds as well. Harry had moved up in the suspect list to eclipse all other candidates, it seemed.

Joe sipped his coffee and began to wonder if there were any other suspects at all. Percy had an alibi, and besides, Joe couldn't see him doing this kind of thing. The young women trusted him, too, and they would have known, wouldn't they? A random act of violence? Committed by someone who just happened to use Harry's place for the crime? Yeah, sure, that was really likely; NOT. Joe didn't quite like Harry as the sole suspect, but that was the way it was beginning to look. There really weren't any others.

Still, Harry had been violent, but he had not killed before; or maybe he had. Maybe he had been clever enough to conceal those earlier crimes. But that left the question: Why had he not concealed this one? He picked up the victim in clear view of everyone, and took her to his place, and then left the body there? No, Harry didn't do anything to conceal this crime, not even the simplest of things like dump the body somewhere else. So maybe he hadn't done this before. Maybe he panicked, or maybe Percy had found him too quickly to allow him to cover it up? It was an unsatisfying conclusion, but maybe Harry was the only suspect because he was the one who had done it. That must sometimes be the case, Joe thought.

He might have continued to think if he had not been interrupted by Natalie. She sat across from him and smiled charmingly. "So, what did Robert Bevins say?"

Joe smiled. No secrets today. "Where's Carolyn?"

"The spa. In a few minutes she will be anyway. I might join her. So, what did Robert Bevins have to say?"

"Nothing," said Joe. "Well, he said he didn't know where Harry might be. No, he hadn't extended him any credit through the casino, just a few personal loans. He knew him in the army. The medics, he said. He thought Harry was traumatized by the experience, and implied that he knew how to inflict wounds that could kill. The kind of wounds that killed Katie."

"Army," said Natalie. "Like me."

"I don't think you're like either Robert or Harry."

"Same army."

"Different person. You wouldn't kill Katie, and I don't like Robert." Joe shrugged. "You're different."

"I killed a man in the airport."

"You saved my life in the airport by killing a murderer. You're not Harry, and you're not Robert. It looks like Harry probably killed Katie for ... well, no good reason, and Robert uses every woman he can and then brags about it. He was out last might with Tyla, and told his secretary to send her flowers just so I could hear him and be impressed with him."

"At least he sent her flowers," murmured Natalie.

"She can't stand him. Only reason she has anything to do with him is to keep her job, and the only reason he goes out with her is to screw her. That's what she says, anyway."

"She told you that, Joe?" asked Natalie.

"Well, yeah," said Joe. He began to wonder if he had decided Tyla was telling the truth and Robert was ... well ... that Robert was a bastard just because Tyla said he was. But Janet had said as much, of course, and so had James Monroe.

"Yes," he said again. "She did, and other people have confirmed that impression of Robert. He's a bastard."

"Okay, Joe, if you say so. So, what are you going to do with the rest of the day?"

"Sit around and drink coffee, and wait for this to all be over so I can go back to Kentucky. Maybe I can get someone to sue me again. That was interesting."

Natalie smiled. "You got to meet me the last time you got sued."

Joe chuckled and she added, "You're adorable, but switch to hot chocolate, will you? It suits you better."

With this she rose, kissed Joe's cheek and said, "I'm going to the damned spa. Lunch maybe?"

"Yeah, that would be nice."

She walked away and Joe was alone, but only briefly. Percy was at his table less than fifteen minutes later.

"You go anywheres else, Joe, or is dis where you is staying? Don't they got a room for ya?"

"How's your morning been, Percy?"

"Pretty sucky is how." When Joe said nothing, Percy continued. "Katie's dad got in yesterday, like four or five in da afternoon. Drove here. I got him into a motel an' we went down ta da station. He was tore up bad after he saw 'er. Cursin' at the cops, cursin' at the world, but mostly cursin' Harry. Cap'n Mitch kept askin' about Harry. Like, did he know 'im? Had Katie ever talk'd 'bout 'im? Ol' Mitch, he's decided who did it, an' now Katie's dad thinks so, too, I guess. Chuck, 'is name is, an' he's a nice guy, like I said, but … well, dis ain't easy."

"Where is he now?" asked Joe.

"Took 'im ta the motel … next ta a bar, an' I doubts he's seen da outside a' da motel yet. Poor bastard. Good thing he can't find Harry, I'd say."

"Yeah," said Joe. "Anyone found Harry yet? The cops, I mean."

"Don't think so. Ol' Cap'n Mitch woulda said, I think."

"What about her mother?"

"Don't know fa' sure, but Mitch said Chuck'd be da only one ID-in' Katie, so I think they probably reached 'er an' she told 'em ta screw. Figuratively, I mean."

Joe looked over at Percy. After a moment Percy added, "That means she wasn't proposing any sexual activity, just that she didn't care what happened to her daughter."

"Yeah, that's what I thought it meant," said Joe, hiding a smile.

"So, whatcha goin' ta do with the rest a' the mornin', Joe?"

"Sit right here, Percy. Everyone seems to be coming to me. Wave at Carl, Percy, he's waving at us."

Carl was waving, but Joe was wrong. It wasn't Joe he was waving at, or even both of them. Percy was the object of his attention at this moment. "Percival, do you happen to have that name and address for me?" said Carl as he sat.

"Oh yeah, sure," replied Percy, pulling an index card from his shirt pocket. "This'll be 'er name, an' I think she's used these two names from time ta time too. Boyfriend's name here, an' he might have some other ones too, but I don't know nothing 'bout that. This here's da address they's usin'." He turned the card over and continued. "This here'll be da lawyer they got, and they's used a couple different detectives. Names is here, numbers an' addresses an' all that shit. That be any help ta ya, Carl, my man?"

"I think it may be. I'll look into this—once I finish with the slots, that is."

Joe looked at his friend and asked, "Do you really think someone can beat the slots, Carl?"

"I'm reasonably certain that it can be done."

"Harry thought that too," offered Percy. "Maybe he did beat 'em, ya think? Had some money lately, I heard."

"Humph," was all Carl responded. "What are you doing with the afternoon, Joe?"

"It's not afternoon yet. The morning is still to be spent, and then Natalie has promised me lunch. Care to join?"

"Perhaps." Carl rose, looking first at the card Percy had provided, and then placing it in his pocket. He then nodded and headed for the casino.

"And what about you, Percy? What are you planning for the morning?"

"I's checking up on da gi— da *young ladies*, I mean. Ya wants ta come along?"

"You think …?"

"Sure! Wouldn't ha' asked if'n I didn't think so. Let's go." Percy threw a twenty dollar bill on the table and headed for the door, with Joe close behind.

Chapter 40

Outside, it was Peter doing the valet job today, and Joe for some reason was glad to see a familiar face. Peter didn't bother to speak, but waved at Percy and ran for the parking lot to return a minute later with an old but stately classic Cadillac.

"Is this your car?" asked Joe.

"If'n Peter will let me have it, it will be." A smiling Percy handing a twenty to the equally smiling valet.

"You take care, Mr. Prince," said Peter.

"You too," said Percy as he got in, buckled his seat belt and pulled away, with Joe seated next to him.

"Had ta have these seat belts put in special," said Percy. "Da shoulder kind, I mean. This baby's too old for 'em ta come standard."

They drove for half an hour while Percy chattered and Joe listened. He didn't listen so closely that he couldn't wonder about this man beside him. An enigma to be sure, but probably not a murderer. Not Katie's murderer anyway, and probably not an abuser of children.

They arrived at a motel in due time, off the strip, and clean-appearing, from the outside at least. Percy stopped first at the office, just to check, he said. He asked how everything was, and addressed the clerk by name. He asked if anyone had been asking about the young ladies, and particularly if any police had inquired. The man at the desk winked and said no, and added that they didn't usually answer police questions, but that no one had been by.

When they left the office, Percy walked down the row to the fourth room from the end and knocked a little tattoo on the door. He didn't wait for an answer, but proceeded to the next door and repeated the same complicated knock, and then on to the next, and then the last.

By this time, two young ladies were outside the door he had knocked on first, and a smiling Percy was asking how they were. He went into each room, scanned the scene, looked under a bed here and in a few drawers there. "No booze in here, is there?' he asked.

"Course not," said Angie.

"Better not," said Percy. "Y'all eatin' okay? Not goin' out durin' da day, are ya?"

"Nope," said someone behind Angie. Joe looked over and recognized Maggie from the phone shop at the hotel. She apparently recognized him, too.

"Hi, Dr. Nelson," she said. "How are you doin'?"

"I'm okay," Joe replied. "How are you doing?"

"Bored," said Maggie, "but safe." She glared at a couple of new arrivals from the room next door, and Joe sensed that not everyone had been satisfied staying in their rooms.

"Is Katie really dead?" someone asked. "We saw it on the news last night."

"Yes," said Percy.

"Did … was it Harry?" asked Maggie. "The news didn't say. Just gave Katie's name and said that police were investigating."

"Looks ta be," said Percy.

Angie shook her head. "Ya called her dad, didn't ya, Percy?'

"Yeah, sure. He got in this mornin.' Real torn up he was. He's stayin' over a couple blocks. Didn't think it was good ta have you in da same motel."

"Yeah," said Angie. "What about her ma?"

"Cops called her. Don't know as she'll be comin' though."

"Probably not," said Angie.

"Thought she might get onta me." Percy shrugged. "Blame me for corruptin' 'er daughter or something."

207

Angie scrunched her face, making her look two or three years younger than her mid-teen age. "Wouldn't worry much about that, Percy. No money in it for her, so she'll not likely be here at all."

Wisdom comes early here, thought Joe.

They chatted some more. All of them were in one room now, with Maggie it came to eight. With two beds to a room, they each had their own bed and a roommate.

"I might go back ta work tomorrow," said Maggie.

"Stay put a while longer, okay?" said Percy.

"Well, okay."

"When do we go back to work?" asked someone.

"When it's safe," was all Percy said.

"Can we rent another movie tonight, Percy?" was the next question.

"No horror stuff or y'all never get ta sleep, an' NO porn, ya hear?"

"Why would we rent porn?" asked another.

"Y'all got enough money?" he asked.

"Yeah," said Maggie. "'Til tomorrow."

"I'll prob'ly check on ya tonight, anyways," said Percy. "Try ta eat some salads an' veggies, too. I got ya a microwave. All pizza ain't healthy. An' make your beds, fa' God's sakes."

There were a couple of groans, which Percy ignored. "I'll pick up da laundry tomorrow, an' remember: no one goes out in da daylight, an' no one goes out alone."

"Okay," came the response, with no hint of dissention. There was real fear on the faces around them.

Percy turned and left, walking to the office again. "Hey, Dexter. Looks okay, but if'n there's any trouble ya got my number. Trouble *wid* da girls, or trouble *for* da girls." Percy slid a hundred dollar bill toward Dexter and added, "Y'all keep a close eye on 'em, Dexter, okay?"

Dexter pocketed the bill and smiled. "Sure will, Mr. Prince."

When they were in the Caddie again, Joe asked, "Do you have enough money to be throwing it around like that, Percy?"

"Ya mean Dexter? Don't get service if ya don't pay for it. 'Sides, gold was up dis mornin'. I's sorry 'bout dat thing wid da *girls* back there, Joe. I know der *young ladies*, but Dexter don't know no better."

Joe smiled and nodded. He didn't really want to chat right now, so he asked Percy about the foreign currency exchange and listened absently on the ride back. Percy was still talking half an hour later when they arrived at the hotel.

He dropped Joe off in front, waved to Peter, and said he had to check on Chuck, and then had some business to do. Robert Bevins was coming out at the same moment to enter his car. Peter opened the door for him, an expensive European model whose logo Joe didn't recognize, but nonetheless knew it was a very expensive logo based on the car to which it was attached. Joe looked after Percy and thought he would rather have that car than Robert's more expensive and prestigious one.

Robert waved briefly toward Joe, and looked after Percy before getting into his own vehicle. There didn't seem to be any envy on his face. Peter shut the door for him without waiting for a tip, but it didn't appear that Robert was intending to give him one. Perhaps there was a rule about tips between employees. Joe didn't know, of course, but wondered a little as Robert pulled out after Percy, turning to follow him down the strip.

Joe called Natalie and was told they both would be down for lunch in fifteen minutes. Carl declined to join them, so they met at the sushi bar and chatted while eating things that Carl would not like to eat.

Carolyn said she had called the Medical Center, and Percy's culture was fungal, and oh yes, they were interviewing another candidate today, but it was hinted that he wasn't in the running. Carolyn said she wondered if she had been told this to put a little pressure on her and was flattered, but still ambivalent. She also announced that the spa had been great but that she was going to the exercise room after lunch.

Joe nodded, and said he might join her. Natalie groaned and said that if everyone else was going, she would, too.

They did, and even Natalie had to admit that the exercise had made her feel better. All four ordered room service for supper, and talked about watching a movie together. Joe had related the events at the motel where Percy had the young ladies hidden, and they all thought the movie lecture was the most amusing part of the tale. They then decided to watch a movie themselves. There was argument about what to watch, however, and finally Carl mentioned that there were six TVs in their combined suites: one in each sitting room, and one in each of the four bedrooms.

It wasn't clear, as was often the case with Carl, whether he thought they should get two more people to use the other sets, or watch six shows, wandering from one to the other. The threat of watching alone was enough to inspire compromise, however, and the "chick flick" won first viewing. Carl watched with disinterest, but Joe thought it was entertaining. The compromise involved next watching the adventure-comedy that the men had voted for, and apart from the fact that Carolyn and Natalie kept saying that it was extremely silly, they all enjoyed it right up to the extremely silly ending. It was late, and they were spiritually in bed by the time it ended in any event, and almost as soon as it was finished, they were physically in bed and asleep as well.

As Joe drifted off, he wondered if he should try to pursue this anymore in the morning. Maybe he should talk to the young ladies a little by way of counseling them, or maybe try to see if he could help Katie's father, Chuck, make sense of it all. His last thought was that he should just settle for solving the country's economic situation, since that was a much simpler problem than any of these others would be.

Chapter 41

Sleep was obtained and morning came, but true rest was denied. Too much was bothering the weary minds of the sleepers.

Natalie and Carolyn came knocking on the gentlemen's door at eight that morning. When answered by a sleepy Joe, they entered to find Carl awake and dressed, poring over his papers.

"I'm tired," announced Carolyn. "It's lonely down there. Why don't you guys come down and sleep with us?"

She looked from a puzzled Carl to an alarmed Joe. "Oh, hell, I didn't mean that. I have almost convinced Natalie to share a bed with me, and you and Carl could … well, at least we would all be in the same room! If you don't want to do that, can we at least vote on when we're going home?"

"I'm ready now," said Natalie.

"Well …" began Carl.

"It may not be safe," said Joe. "And Lieutenant Baldy told us to stay around until he said we could leave."

"I'm not sure I care," said Carolyn. "We could call the police back home and find out at least."

"We could," said Joe.

"Except that you want to stay so you can see that justice is done, right, Joe?" said Carolyn. "Well, I'll give you twenty-four hours and then I'll … well, then I'll probably give you twenty-four more. But there will be a limit to it, I promise you that. What about breakfast? I only want coffee. Everyone keeps pushing food at me around here. I must have gained a hundred pounds."

"We can grab some coffee downstairs," suggested Natalie. "I'm running out of clean clothes. Do we shop or launder?"

"I don't think I can face shopping," said Carolyn, as Joe stared in disbelief. "Does the hotel have a laundry service, I wonder?"

"Yes," said Carl. "Twenty-four hour turnaround if you get it out by seven in the morning." He looked at his watch and added, "Too late today."

"Shit," said Carolyn.

"You know," said Joe, "Percy said something about picking up laundry for his tribe yesterday. Maybe he could throw ours in with theirs, ya think?"

"With Percy's?" asked Natalie.

"With the ladies'," corrected Joe. "He probably has some laundry service that washes their stuff."

Carolyn looked at Natalie, who just shrugged. "Okay with me. I really don't want to go shopping anymore, and wearing the same outfits for the next two weeks—"

"It's not going to be two weeks," interrupted Carolyn. "Call Percy, Joe."

"You have his number too," Joe replied.

"Just call him, or we start washing our clothes in your shower."

Joe opened his phone and hit the numbers that would connect him to Percival Prince.

"Hey, Joe. What's happenin'?" Percy said, loud enough for everyone to hear.

"Hey, Percy," replied Joe. "Did I hear you say you were picking up the young ladies' laundry yesterday?"

The answer was more subdued this time, but Joe nodded his head to show the answer had been affirmative. "Could you throw some of our stuff into the bags?" he asked.

Another answer was given, but heard only by Joe. "Sure, about thirty minutes. You're taking it to a laundry service or something, right? I mean, when will it be back?"

"Oh," said Joe, and then to everyone, "He's taking the clothes to a Laundromat and washing them himself. He wants to know if you want to go along."

Natalie looked as if she was considering the offer, but Carolyn said at once, "Sure, we'll go along. How many tourists get to see a Laundromat in Las Vegas?"

"Okay," said Natalie. "All of us? Is there room in Percy's car?"

"I have something I must attend to," said Carl, "but I would appreciate giving you some laundry if you wouldn't mind."

"And I—" began Joe.

"Good," interrupted Carolyn. "Then it's just the girls and Percy. Gather up your laundry, gentlemen."

The gentlemen needed no further encouragement, and within fifteen minutes they were headed to the lobby with sacks of clothing, essentially all that they were not wearing or that didn't need dry cleaning. Percy was waiting for them outside, chatting with Peter and leaning on his Caddie. He wasn't really supposed to be "parked" where he was, in front of the hotel, but the admiring crowd around the car was sufficient to keep hotel security from asking him to move, which would have disappointed that crowd of hotel guests. More expensive, but less impressive vehicles were required to leave after their business was completed.

"Hey, folks," said Percy. "I don't know as we can all fit in here." He motioned toward the Caddie as he said this.

"Is this your car?!" asked an incredulous Natalie.

"Sure 'nough," smiled Percy. "Got it just for you an' Carolyn. Remember I said that when I bought it, Peter?"

"I remember when you bought it," said Peter. "I don't remember that you mentioned anyone's name."

"Sure I did," said Percy, undaunted by the facts.

"It's just us girls and you, Percy. Laundry in the trunk, I guess?" asked Carolyn.

"Trunk's full," said Percy. "Three in the front leaves plenty a' room for da laundry in da backseat." There were already several bags there.

Natalie wasn't distracted by the mundane seating arrangement. "This is like, so awesome, Percy. And a rag top, too! Can we put the top down?"

"Little cool this early in the mornin', but what da hell, sure. Give a hand, Peter."

Peter did lend a hand as he shook his head. "I remember the day you bought this, Percy. Parked right here where it is now." A couple of security officers came over, not to move them along, but to help with the top. It was manual, not automatic, of course, on this classic car.

"You bought it here, Percy? Right in front here?" asked Natalie.

"Sure did," said Percy. He glanced at Peter as he continued, "An' with you two in mind."

"There was this guy," said Peter. "Sellin' this car to get money for a poker game. What'd you pay Percy? Five grand?"

"Six," corrected Percy. It was his turn to shake his head. "That guy rode into Vegas in dis car and rode out again in a hundred an' fifty thousand dollar ..." He paused just long enough for the crowd to gasp and hush again. He was speaking loudly enough for them all to hear.

"Rode outa here in a hundred an' fifty thousand dollar Greyhound bus, he did!" Percy beamed and the crowd roared with laughter, hooting and then applauding.

"So, who gets ta ride next ta Percy?" he asked, looking at Natalie and Carolyn.

Carolyn smiled and said, "Your choice, Natalie."

"Shit," said Natalie. "I want the window, you can have Percy."

Carolyn shrugged. "That's just the way I wanted it."

"Outdone by a window," said a smiling Percy. "Always knew I was a pane. Get it: a window pane?"

There were more groans than chuckles from the crowd this time.

"Well, let's go, ladies," said Percy, opening the door for them. Carolyn entered first, and Natalie sat next to the window. She immediately rolled it down.

"It's cold out, Natalie," said Carolyn. "How far is the Laundromat?"

"We don't have to go straight to the Laundromat, do we?" asked Natalie.

"Oh, we can cruise a little if'n ya want," said Percy. "An' I'll keep you warm, Carolyn. That is, if it's okay with Joe."

"You be careful, Percy," said Joe. "Might be more than even you can handle. Just bring my laundry back, will you?" He placed the bags containing the clothing in the back seat on top of the others and waved them away.

As they drove down the drive the crowd disappeared, mostly into the casino, to see if they could win more than a Greyhound bus ticket. Joe couldn't help but remember being told that the only way the casino lost was if they didn't play. It wasn't going to lose today.

Chapter 42

Carl mumbled something, and disappeared immediately. He didn't go to the slots, but headed back toward the offices, or maybe an ATM. Joe hoped he wasn't spending all his money investigating the possibility of beating the slots. This thought caused him to wonder if Harry had really figured out a system. People had mentioned he had money all of a sudden, so maybe he had. What did that mean? Joe couldn't think that it meant anything, except that if Harry was guilty, or even if he weren't, with money he could be gone to almost anywhere by now. Maybe Captain Mitch and Lieutenant Baldy wouldn't find him.

What Joe wanted to do was find out whatever he could about this crime. About Harry, about Las Vegas, and about what the media was saying. He stopped by a magazine shop, bought a copy of every newspaper they had, and then went back up to his room. With the TV on to the local cable news channel, he pored over the papers to extract any bits of information they contained. Only small bits were there now, since the crime had only been reported yesterday, but much speculation. The brutality was hinted at, possible serial killings mentioned, and historical references made to past crimes, but little real information. The victim's name had been given, but no other details. There was no speculation as to motive or her occupation. The TV had more recent, but no more detailed news on the event. This "breaking story" still had to share the spotlight with other "breaking stories."

• • •

Meanwhile, Percy was driving slowly down the strip, while Natalie smiled and occasionally waved at admiring passersby. Carolyn shivered a little. Later she would have to admit she enjoyed the drive, but now she mentioned only the uncomfortable cold. The day had not yet had time to warm as it would in another hour or so. It took only a short time before Natalie suggested they head for the Laundromat, and Percy agreed.

Percy cruised around a bit until a spot opened in front. When he got out he said, "If ya want ta get started, I'll be right in. I gotta set da alarm first."

"The top's down, Percy. You need help with that?" asked Natalie.

"Oh, no," he said. "Da alarm's only for da trunk." He went to the back of the Caddie while the women began carrying in sacks of laundry. It was clearly going to take several trips.

Percy pulled a remote device from his jacket pocket and pressed a button, which caused the trunk to pop open. He then quickly reached in and pressed some buttons on a box inside. After taking out a bag he reversed the process, put away the remote, and began carrying in sacks of laundry.

It was a large Laundromat, with thirty or more washers and as many dryers lining the walls. In the middle were tables to fold clothes on and chairs were spread around wherever there was room, or wherever they had been left. There were some people there reading or talking while their clothes were being washed. Two young men were at the back with a large boom box, playing loudly enough to be heard outside and clearly annoying everyone inside

Percy nodded to an elderly lady in a small office at the front as he entered. "Mornin', Millie," he said. "Who're da assholes?" He nodded toward the two with the boom box. They appeared to be in their mid-twenties, a few days' growth of beard showing, and dressed in ripped jeans and T-shirts with flames surrounding guitar players on them.

217

"Just your standard assholes," replied Millie. "Want ta talk to them about the music, Percy? They don't pay no mind to an old lady."

"Ya got a' old lady here too?" said Percy, winking and smiling. He got a smile in return.

He turned and surveyed the two and then spoke above the noise. "Hey!" he yelled. Everyone turned to look at him. "I gots ta get something from da car. Why don't you two start da washing. Ya know how ta do it, right?" He placed the bag he had taken out of the trunk on the table and showed Carolyn and Natalie a bottle of detergent and one of softener, as well as dryer sheets and a bag of quarters.

The boom box boys had turned a defiant stance when Percy had first yelled, probably thinking he was addressing them. But now they were watching the ladies as they began to sort the laundry. Percy took his time at the trunk of his Caddie and when he returned, the two were asking if Carolyn or Natalie needed any help.

Percy smiled and said, "Hey, guys. These babes don't need no help. Laundry's girls' work anyways."

The two seemed to be considering this statement and whether they needed to consider Percy an obstacle to their obvious plans for the *babes*.

"Got something you'll like better, anyways," said Percy, still smiling. "Down here." He motioned toward the back, and pulled an envelope from the inside pocket of his jacket.

The two looked at each other, and then all three walked to the back. Whatever was going on transformed these two into Percy's best friends. He showed them the contents of the envelope, and their enthusiasm couldn't be contained.

As all three walked back, Percy was saying, "Now look, boys. Got ta have cash fo' these babies and soon. We'll watch your wash an' put it inta da dryer for ya, but be back wid da cash 'fore we leave."

"We don't have quarters for the dryers. Just leave it out an' we'll be back. Thirty minutes, no more," said the shorter of the two. He had been doing most of the talking, and now neither one was paying any attention to Natalie or Carolyn.

"I gotcha quarters," said Percy. "Be back with da cash if ya want 'em." He tapped the envelope before putting it back in his jacket. "Leave dat boom box too, man. I'll keep an eye on it."

"Great," he said, and ran out the door as Percy turned the music off. They stopped outside, talked a few seconds, and headed off in opposite directions.

"What was that about, Percy? Making a sale?" asked Natalie.

"Sorta," he replied.

"I thought your young ladies weren't working?"

Percy started to answer but was interrupted by a new arrival on the scene.

"Oh, hello, Percy," said a thin young man in a button-down shirt with several pens in its pocket. He was wearing glasses, and he could easily have posed for a "Nerd of the Month" poster.

"Oh, hey, John," replied Percy.

"I haven't seen Angie around for a couple of days," John said, looking anxiously at Carolyn and then Natalie.

"She's away on a li'l vacation. I'll tell her you's askin'. You're 'er favorite, ya know."

John couldn't conceal his pleasure at this last remark, until he looked again at Carolyn and blushed so deeply he had to turn away. "Yeah, yeah. Thanks."

"Hey, John," said Percy. "Got a question. What's a thing like dis here boom box worth ya suppose?"

John had recovered somewhat as he looked at the box. He turned it over and read the labels, and opened various compartments before answering. "Speakers are good. Maybe a hundred used. Eighty anyway, at the pawn shop."

"What I thought, thanks. I'll let Angie know you's asking," said Percy.

John walked away to begin his laundry, and the three began to sort theirs. Percy asked if they should keep it separate and Carolyn said she *wished*, but they didn't need to. Apart from the fashion gap, there was a size gap that separated Percy's young ladies from Carolyn and Natalie. Natalie looked as if she wanted to ask Percy about the transaction he had initiated earlier, but didn't find a way. Percy transferred the boys' clothing to dryers and put in the quarters necessary, more dryers than were needed for the number of garments. "Quicker," was the only explanation he offered.

In another few minutes the owners of the clothes returned, and the shorter of the two approached Percy warily. "Look, Percy," he said. "We couldn't get it all."

Percy frowned, and the short guy continued quickly. "Fourteen hundred! Almost. Seven hundred a piece. We can owe ya the rest."

Percy frowned. "Don't work dat way."

"We tapped everybody we could."

"These babies is worth eight hundred. You check dat out?"

"Yeah, yeah, they're worth more than …" began the other, before stopping as he realized what he was saying.

"Look," began the shorter man again. "I get paid on Friday. I can—" He was silenced by Percy's shaking head.

"No credit transaction, boys," said Percy. He was silent for a few moments, and the boys looked on pitifully. Carolyn looked disgusted at what appeared to be a sale of sex, and Natalie just looked confused. Millie, in her office, was smirking in amusement, and John was ignoring the whole thing.

Finally Percy frowned and pointed to the boom box. "What 'bout this?"

"Yeah," said the taller man. "I paid more'n three hundred for it."

"Used now though," said Percy.

The elation turned to disappointment again until Percy shook his head and said, "Your clothes is done I think. I'll take that box an' what ya got for cash, okay?"

"Yeah, yeah, sure," said the taller man.

Percy pulled the envelope out of his pocket and slid out what looked like two tickets. "Best seats in da house."

The clothes were gathered, tickets given and the money tucked in Percy's pocket. "You boys have a real good time," Percy said as they ran from the Laundromat.

"What was …?" asked Natalie.

Percy shrugged. "Da tickets? Some bitch what sings with 'er cloths on, an' then sings with 'er cloths off, an' da guys an' da girls think she's da only show in dis world. Sold out all three a' 'er shows in two hours, but ol' Percy was first in line. Paid three hundred apiece, plus a hundred ta be first in line, an' those is the last two I got ta sell."

"How many did you get?" asked Natalie.

"A dozen," answered Percy with a shrug.

"Eight hundred dollars a seat? Does she sing that well?" asked Carolyn.

"They's playin' her most recent when we came in," smiled Percy. "Want I should play it again fo' ya?"

"That's okay," said Carolyn quickly.

Percy nodded. "Hey, John. Ya think ya can take care a' this for me?" He pointed to the boom box.

"Sure. A hundred dollars, maybe a little more if you can wait."

"Sure," said Percy. "CD in there too, but ya can keep that."

"My ma doesn't allow me to play that kind of music," admitted John.

"Nah, course not," said Percy. "Jus' give da money ta Angie, okay?"

Chapter 43

Carolyn shook her head. "You *do* know what I thought you were selling, Percy, don't you?"

"What?" said Percy.

Carolyn just frowned while Natalie chuckled.

"What ya thinking, Carolyn?" asked Percy again with genuine bewilderment.

"Well, you're a pimp, aren't you? Or are you a scalper of concert tickets who pimps on the side?"

"What ya sayin'?" asked Percy. "I is shocked ya'd think I would … Carolyn, you should be ashamed thinkin' somethin' like that. In a Laundromat?"

"Oh, Percy, just stop it right now," replied Carolyn.

"Da *young ladies* do da sellin.' They's better at it. This ain't no mail order catalogue business."

Natalie smiled and asked, "Can I ask you something, Percy?"

"Sure, Nat'lie."

"Why do you do this? I mean, you just turned more than eight hundred while you were doing your laundry. You don't need to pimp, so why do you recruit girls to—"

"Ain't like that for me, Nat'lie," said Percy, turning serious. "Der are some guys out there, some pimps, that recruit girls an' … well, I'm sure ya know da story, but that ain't me."

"Well then, what are you?" asked Natalie.

"Look. Da girls, they mostly come ta me from da street. Already turnin' tricks by the time I see 'em. My ladies get respect out there, an' some come 'cause they want ta get that, or some get in trouble an' I gets asked ta get 'em out. Lots a' different ways.

If they can go home, an' they wants ta, I send 'em. If they can get real jobs, I can sometimes help with that. But if they can't do either one, well, I help 'em survive. They got ta follow da rules is all, an' I look after 'em."

"The rules?" asked Natalie.

"Well, yeah," replied Percy. "Look, most a' da women on da street gets inta trouble 'cause they drink too much or drug too much, an' I don't 'llow neither one. They drug an' they's out. They got ta use condoms an' be on some birth control, too. Case da condom breaks or something. I got this doc what checks 'em, an' if they need treatment, they gets it. All cash, 'cause he lost 'is license or something, but he's good, an' no one gets reported ta da authorities or any other trouble like that."

"You pay cash for their health care?" asked Natalie.

"Only way."

"How'd he lose his license?" asked Carolyn.

"Sellin' 'scriptions, I think. Met 'im at a AA meetin'."

"An AA meeting?"

"Yeah." Percy shrugged. "Don't drink or drug myself, course. Seen too much ta mess with that. But a couple a' da young women had problems so's I took 'em ta meetin's for a while."

"Are they sober now?" asked Natalie.

"One," said Percy. "Other's dead. Only way it ends. You gets clean an' sober, ya gets thrown in jail, o' ya die."

"So he was at an AA meeting? This doctor, I mean?" asked Carolyn.

"NA," said Percy. "Narc Anon. He's good though, an' I go with da ladies when they see 'im. Keep an eye on things. An' he don't give 'em any drugs, just medicine. I get filled what he says, and only what he says. Ladies know better than to take anything I don't get for 'em. I got 'em all in apartments over da other side a' town, so they can hang out together an' they're safe, too.

"I got this lady what shows 'em how ta do der hair an' nails an' all that shit. 'Other one ta help 'em with clothes, but they help each other a lot. Gots ta learn ta talk right, too."

Natalie and Carolyn just stared at him. "Not from me, course. They can get classes at da community college for that."

"I hope so," said Natalie, but Percy seemed to miss the criticism directed at his speech.

"You pay for them to go to college, Percy?" asked Carolyn.

"They pays for college themselves," corrected Percy. "Course, I gets 'em da resident's discount, even if they ain't residents, but they pays. Nothin' for 'em ta do during da day anyways."

"They pay for college?" asked Natalie. "Do they make that much money?"

"If ya don't drink an' ya don't drug, you'd have money for college too, Nat'lie."

"Is presentation that important in this business?" asked Carolyn.

"Not so much now, but when they go for real jobs, makes all da difference. Don't think that hotel you's stayin' at woulda touched Maggie or Sally without it. Most a' 'em don't even know how ta handle money, so at first they give me what they make an' I pay da bills, an' stuff. Give 'em an allowance."

"And rent?" asked Carolyn.

"Well yeah, but that's different."

"Different?"

"Well, ya see, I own da buildin'. They got ta pay rent, but … well … when they start managin' their own, they gots ta pay rent themselves. A lot a' 'em stay even after they get real jobs. For lots a' 'em this is da only family they knows."

"But, Percy. They're children. They're underage. This is statutory rape!" said Carolyn.

Percy sighed and his eyes narrowed. "Look, Carolyn. I don't know how old they really is, only what they tells me. I help get 'em IDs so's they don't get picked up by da cops. All I know is that they need someone ta look after 'em. If they want ta leave da street, I help with what I can, but they got no place ta go an', Carolyn, if someone don't look after 'em, they's got no chance at all. They'll end up like Katie did. What I is doin' ain't legal, but it ain't wrong, neither. We's all doin' da best we can."

"Maybe you're right," sighed Carolyn.

"Do you screen their 'dates' too?" asked Natalie.

"Sometimes," answered Percy. "I is there if they needs anything. They all got a phone ta call if they don't like what da guy's asking for. I can be there in five minutes. Most a' the guys is like John. He's smart. Writes those apps fo' cell phones. Makes good money, but still lives in 'is ma's garage. He don't want a girlfriend, but … well, Angie is what he wants."

"Is he really her favorite?" asked Natalie.

"Prob'ly don't even know 'is name," sighed Percy.

"Who teaches them … well … the trade? You, Percy?" asked Natalie.

"Ah, man. You two is really abusin' me somethin' terrible today," said Percy. "First: they already know before they gets here. Boyfriends or mother's boyfriends. Half a' 'em been assaulted by someone, cops, o' teachers; it all sucks. Better to have da other girls tell 'em anyways. An' I never do nothin' with any a' 'em. This is business, Nat'lie. An' I is not some degenerate. I is like der father, for Crissakes."

"No, of course you wouldn't," said Natalie. "Not with a car like yours."

"Ya really like it, Nat'lie?"

"Got a boyfriend who has one just like that." Natalie smiled.

"Really?" asked Carolyn.

"Yup, an' his name is Percy."

Percy and Carolyn both smiled and Natalie nodded and added, "I'm going to marry Joe, but Percy is going to be my boyfriend. That way you can keep Joe as a boyfriend, Carolyn, but just remember: no sex with boyfriends."

Percy was mystified. "What're you talking, Nat'lie?"

She might have answered, but Dexter, from the motel, came in before she could. "Percy! Where the hell's your phone?! I been callin' for an hour 'til one a' the girls told me ya might be here."

Percy pulled out his cell phone. "Shit," he said. "Didn't get home last night ta charge it. What's up, an' who's watchin' da motel?"

"I had ta have a couple a' your girls watch the office," said Dexter. "Look, Percy. Maggie an' Angie got this call from someone. Katie's dad, they said, an' they said they had ta go over ta see what was goin' on, 'cause he sounded like he was—"

Percy cut him off. "Where'd they go?"

"I don't know. Said it was some motel where he was stayin'. I called the cab, or they woulda walked. Curtis Street it was."

"Shit," said Percy. "Look, Dexter. You get back ta da motel. Girls in da rooms, an' don't let any more a' 'em leave."

"I tried ta stop 'em—"

"I knows," said Percy. "I got ta go over there. You two ladies better get gone now. Take a cab, okay? An' Millie, can ya take out da wash an' save it?"

"Sure," said Millie.

"If Millie is doing the wash, we'll go with you, Percy," said Carolyn.

"Might be—" began Percy.

"And the only way we'll find out what it might be is to go with you, so come on for Christ's sake," said Natalie. "I'm a cop, and Carolyn's a doctor. Who knows which one you'll need the most?"

"Shit. You two is going ta be da cause a' my death," said Percy. "Get back ta da motel, Dexter, an' Millie, I'll be by for da wash later. Let's go."

Chapter 44

Percy drove as quickly as he thought he could without asking to get pulled over by the police. They were only two miles from the motel he had put Chuck in, and they were there in five minutes. He parked in front of the door he said Chuck had been in last night and cautioned both ladies to: "Act natural and walk slow."

He knocked casually on the door and it was answered immediately by a frantic-looking Maggie. "Percy! How'd you …? I think he's dead."

"You okay Maggie? Where's Angie?" Percy said.

"I'm okay, but Katie's father is … he might be dead. He's bleedin', an' we can't get him to wake up," said Angie.

Carolyn pushed her way into the room. "If he's bleeding, he's still alive. Call 9-1-1."

Percy was beside her, looking at a middle-aged man lying on the bed which was soaked with blood still oozing from both his wrists. "Give a minute 'fore you call, Nat'lie. Give me your phone, Angie. You still got your other one, right?"

"Yeah," said Angie, handing him her phone.

He handed her his keys. "Don't touch nothin'. Where'd ya touch stuff already?"

"Just the bed and the door. We didn't know what ta do, Percy. He called Angie an'—"

"Later," said Percy calmly. "Take da Caddie an' drive slow, okay? Go out by da upper end a' da lot, not past da office. Park da Caddie in back when ya get back ta your place an' give da keys ta Dexter. Then get ta your room an' stay put, okay?"

They nodded and Percy said, "Now get goin'."

Percy had his handkerchief out as they left, wiping the bed and door knobs. "He's still alive, right?" he asked Carolyn.

"He is," she replied. "We need the paramedics, Percy. And here, put some pressure on this wound while I get the other side."

"Yeah. He's been here a while, ya think, Natalie? Blood on da rug is dryin' already." He was looking at the rug beside the bed. Chuck was barely breathing now, but a trickle of blood was dropping from his wrist.

"Bottle there, Nat'lie," Percy said. "Vodka maybe?"

Natalie moved to look and Percy said, "Don't touch it."

Natalie looked up and smiled. "Vodka."

"His pulse is really weak, Percy," said Carolyn.

"No suicide note that ya see, Natalie? What 'e cut hisself with?"

"I don't see anything. Maybe in the bed covering. No note, either," she replied. "Empty bottle a' vodka, slashed wrists, but no note. Suicide, ya think?"

"He was drinkin' whiskey at da bar last night. Better call 9-1-1," said Percy. "An' you ladies better leave now."

"In a pig's ass, Percy," said Carolyn. "If he dies before they get here, what are you going to do? I'm the doctor here, ya know."

"Okay, okay," said Percy. "If ya put it that way. Never did like pork too much."

"And if she stays, I stay," said Natalie. "Shall I call now, Percy?"

"Yeah, an' maybe let Carolyn talk ta 'im so's they know what ta expect. Use your phone, okay? That way Angie don't get involved. I'll call the office an' let 'em know, an' I guess Cap'n Mitch better get a call, too."

Percy used his handkerchief to pick up the bedside phone. "Blood here on da phone, too," he said, and punched the "O" on the dial.

It was only a minute before things started happening. The motel manager beat the paramedics by seconds. He had only had time for one question, something to do with "*holy fuckin' shit,*" but no one bothered to answer him.

Two paramedics arrived, and the younger one began to more or less push everyone, including Carolyn, to the sides of the room. The second was maybe five years older, and more directed in his approach.

"Are you the doctor I spoke to?" he asked. "Dr. Prentiss, is it?"

"Yes," said Carolyn.

He knelt beside Chuck and began putting an intravenous line into his arm. "Gloves in that box," he said, nodding toward a box of blue gloves. "You might want to put them on."

"Thanks," said Carolyn, pulling out a pair.

"Saw you at the ED the other day. Interviewing, someone said." The line flashed blood, and he removed the tourniquet and squeezed the bag to increase the flow. "Any blood pressure?" he asked his partner.

"Sixty palp," came the response.

"Maybe another line and pressure dressings." He turned toward Carolyn and said, "Yeah. I thought I saw you there." The smile on his face said he had not only seen her, but noticed her.

"So, what happened here?" he asked.

"Got a call from … well, I guess it was from him. Percy knew he was here. When we got here this is what we found."

"Cut himself, ya think?"

"Looks like," said Carolyn. "He's the father of that girl they found dead yesterday."

"The one on the news this morning?" He turned to his partner and said, "Almost a liter in. Get another blood pressure en route. Let's go. Want ta ride along, Doc?"

Carolyn did, and they were gone. Natalie flashed her badge to the motel manager quickly and said, "Seal this room. No one gets in. This is an official crime scene as of now."

Turning to Percy she asked, "Wait for the cops or catch a cab?"

"They'll find us," said Percy. "Let's walk ta da corner and grab a cab."

"Back to your motel or to the Medical Center?"

"Laundry first," said Percy.

"Laundry?" asked Natalie.

"I wanta wash up an' change clothes, an' so do you. Not in da ladies rooms at da motel, neither. Laundromat first."

Chapter 45

Millie had not only taken their clothes out, but sorted them, folded them, and had them all back in their bags, one short of a dozen. Percy thanked her, and asked where he could wash up. Millie motioned toward the back, and Percy took some of Joe's clean clothes and disappeared. When Percy came back he looked even more outlandish; wig, sunglasses and boots, with a light blue button-down shirt and tan slacks.

Natalie started to giggle and Millie to laugh out loud as Percy said, "Don't neither a' ya say a word."

Natalie took her turn washing and changing, but of course looked her usual self when she exited, having put on her own clothing. Natalie was surprised but disappointed that Millie had not mixed any of her or Carolyn's clothes in with Percy's more fashionable tribe. Percy gave both used outfits to Millie, along with forty dollars, and asked her to wash and throw away their clothing. Millie said she would if Percy was sure that's what he wanted. He was sure.

When Natalie asked if maybe they should have thrown them away themselves to make sure, Percy just said, "Oughta be washed first. Millie'll prob'ly throw 'em out, an' if she don't, I can say I just couldn't wear 'em after being in a room with Chuck. That way no one sees us throwing 'em out, an' wonders why. Better that way."

They took a cab to the motel, dropped off the young ladies' laundry, calmed them all down, mostly by saying that Chuck would be all right, and then they picked up Percy's Caddie, putting the rest of the laundry in the back seat. Natalie called Joe, but Carolyn had already called him and he was taking a cab to the Medical Center. They all met there, and Captain Mitchell and Lieutenant *Baldy* O'Conner were waiting in the lobby. These two didn't look pleased.

"So, what the hell happened, and why were you there at all?" asked the captain of no one and everyone.

"Well, Cap'n," said Percy. "Me an' da ladies here, was washin' our clothes an' I got word that Chuck here was … well, don't know what he was. So we went over an' found him bleedin' an' near dead. Weren't for Doc Carolyn, he prob'ly would be dead."

"Washing your clothes? The three of you? Together?" asked Captain Mitchell.

Percy just nodded as Natalie and Carolyn smiled.

"And how did you find out Charles was bleeding nearly to death, and how did you know where he would be, and why on *Earth* do you think I'm going to believe anything you say?"

"I was with 'im last night," said Percy. "'E didn't know where ta stay so I took him over ta where we found him. He was drinkin' whiskey an' I figured he'd be better if I put 'im to bed. So that's what I did."

"And you knew he was slashing his wrists how?"

"'E called me," said Percy, holding up the cell phone Angie had given him earlier. There would be a call from Chuck on it, and it was registered to Percy, of course. "Couldn't understand 'im, but den I 'membered 'e was in that motel so's we all went over. Took Carolyn in case 'e was sick, which 'e was, and Natalie came along 'cause she likes ridin' in da Caddie."

The Captain grabbed Percy's phone and they glared at each other until Natalie asked, "Is he going to be all right?"

Captain Mitchell didn't answer her question, but instead said, "Percy, you come with me. I'll talk to the rest of you later."

As they walked away, he said, "You wear the craziest clothes, Percy."

"Ya don't like this, Cap'n? Joe picked 'em out."

With Percy and the captain gone, it was just Lieutenant O'Conner with Joe, Carolyn and Natalie.

Natalie asked again, "He's going to be all right, isn't he?"

"Yes," said Carolyn.

"I think so," added the lieutenant. "You weren't there, were you Dr. Nelson; but you two were?" he said to Carolyn and Natalie.

"Yes," said Natalie.

"He was quite distraught over the death of his daughter, I imagine. Drinking at a bar Percy said, and then some more, later, in his room. A bottle of vodka and a pizza box in the room, the officers there said. What do you think of that?"

"Sounds like a suicide attempt to me," said Carolyn.

"Did you find a knife or anything?" asked Natalie.

"Oh, yes," said the lieutenant. "A knife rolled up in the bed covers. It must have been terribly upsetting for him to have his daughter die that way. I can only imagine how he must have felt."

"These things never end," said Joe. "There's no end to the misery, I mean."

"No," said Lieutenant O'Conner.

"Are we free to go?" asked Natalie.

"What?" said the lieutenant. "Oh, yes, yes, of course. We'll contact you for statements sometime tomorrow, I imagine."

They departed to find a cab, but met the paramedic that had "noticed" Carolyn earlier as he was exiting the hospital.

"Oh hey, Doc, how's that guy doin'?"

"I think he's going to do all right." Carolyn smiled.

"Suicide?" He shrugged. "Can't blame him, with his kid dyin' like that. We saved another life," he added sarcastically. "He was worse than most a' 'em. Most suicides are just mad at their boyfriend and acting out. Take a few pills to get some attention. This one; maybe you really did save him."

"Maybe," said Carolyn. "Mostly what I did was to call you."

He smiled and shrugged.

"So, where is the best place to get a cab?" Carolyn asked.

"Around by the ED," he said. "Where ya goin'?"

"Our hotel." Carolyn smiled again, a little more friendly than it needed to be.

The smile worked well. "I got room for three in my car, if ya want me ta drop ya?"

"Sure," said Carolyn, without bothering to consult the others.

In another few minutes they were in a modest sedan, not one of the flashy cars the medical shows had their paramedics driving, riding toward their hotel. Carolyn had gotten the front seat again and smiled at her driver. "So, you like it here … what was your name again?"

"James," he said. "Jimmy to most. Yeah, it's okay."

"I'm Carolyn. It's not great?" she persisted. It became apparent to the back seat passengers that this wasn't just a convenient way to get back to the hotel.

"I've worked a few places outside the city." He shrugged. "This is a little more exciting, but … well, I expected the pay to be better, too."

"And it's not?"

"Not better enough. Longer commute and, well … I could work a twenty-four-hour shift out in the 'burbs and be practically guaranteed eight hours sleep during the shift. At the Medical Center you pull twelve hours, and there's no possibility of any down time. You're lucky if you get to leave at the end of it. Burn-out city."

"Yeah," said Carolyn. "That happens a lot. What about the ED? Good care? Support for you guys in the field?"

He shrugged again. "Depends on who's on. Some are good. No real consistency, though. Maybe a new director will change that." He smiled and winked at Carolyn.

"If I get the job, I'll tell 'em you recruited me."

"Well, I'll be glad to see you come, but if you think I'll get a bonus for recruiting, forget it." They both chuckled at this, but the conversation lapsed into silence after that.

Joe looked about and finally asked, "What about the police here? They good to you guys?"

"This is my husband, Joe," said Carolyn. "He's a pediatrician, and therefore he's suspicious and obnoxious, but otherwise a nice guy."

"Hey, Joe," said Jimmy. "Welcome ta the club. Cops is cops, I guess. Same everywhere. We're on the same team, but they don't always remember that."

"Same back home," replied Joe. "I wasn't at the motel where you picked up the suicide, but the police were grilling, not thanking, Carolyn."

"Well … can I ask who the police in question were?"

"A captain named Mitchell," said Joe.

"Aw, yes. Captain Mitchell. He's a weird one all right. Speakin' a' weird, was that Percy Prince you were with, Doc?"

"Yes," said Carolyn. "He was particularly weird today. Were those your clothes he was wearing, Joe?"

Jimmy cast a surprised glance toward Carolyn, who smiled back.

"I did pick them out, although not exactly for him," said Joe. "The captain seems particularly weird, too. Is it just me, or are the police behaving strangely?"

"Well, Jimmy," said Natalie, "since you and I seem to be the only ones who are polite here and introduce people to each other, I'm Natalie, and I'm also police, back home. At least I was when I left. *Weird* would be a word I would use, too. Captain Mitchell seems to think everyone is out to interfere with him and his investigation, which seems to me to be pretty straightforward, by the way. And then there's Lieutenant O'Conner, who seems to think he should tell everyone what's on his mind, some of which is official police business only. These two are like the yin and yang of law enforcement."

Jimmy smiled into the rear view mirror. It was a charming smile. "You're also the scholar here, I guess. Yin and yang, you say? I would think Don Quixote and Sancho Panza would be more accurate. If you think he was grilling your wife, Joe, I'll bet Percy is really getting the treatment."

"I think he'll give as good as he gets," said Carolyn.

"What do you think of Percy?" asked Natalie.

"Interesting guy," said Jimmy. "As pimps go, he's a gentleman."

When no one replied, Jimmy continued. "If one of his girls gets into trouble, he's there to look after 'em. They don't get into trouble very often, though. They're clean, and always dressed pretty well, and … I think he really cares about them. If someone hurts one of his, he can get pretty angry, and I wouldn't want to be the guy that did it to them. Otherwise, he's a gentleman. He looks after his own.

"He even made a donation to the friggin' ED building fund. How many pimps do that? I think the hospital only accepted it on the condition that he promised not to attend the dedication ceremony. Guy's a little strange."

"I'm not sure I agree," said Carolyn. "Percy is *way* beyond a little strange."

Jimmy pulled up the drive to their hotel at that point. "Well, if you're going to talk like that, you can just get out right here." He smiled as he stopped and got out to open doors for them, beating Peter by milliseconds.

"Door-to-door service is a paramedic's specialty. Hope you get the job, Doc," he added. "If ya need a ride anywhere, give me a call."

Chapter 46

Joe half-expected to see Percy waiting for them in the lobby, but there were no familiar faces. It was well past lunch now, and the adrenaline was melting into hunger. Joe called Carl, who said he had not noticed the time, but was a little hungry and would love to join them.

There was only one luncheon shop they had not yet tried, and so that was the obvious choice. It was an Italian restaurant, with a lunch and dinner menu. It was mid-afternoon, so either one was available, and because it was late and lunch had not been eaten, they ordered dinner. When they had ordered, the conversation turned to the day's events. "What did happen?" asked Joe.

"Craziest laundry I ever did," said Natalie. "I'm comfortable in dirty clothes 'til I get back home."

"Riding in the Caddie was fun," said Carolyn.

"I thought you said it was cold?" responded Natalie.

"It was," said Carolyn. "But it was fun, too. There we were, doing laundry, scalping a couple concert tickets, and discussing the finer points of setting up a pimping operation, when Percy lets his phone battery go dead and the motel guy comes looking for him to tell him that Maggie and Angie had run off to find Katie's father."

"Percy let his cell phone battery go dead?" asked Carl. "Very much unlike him."

"Didn't go home last night or something," said Carolyn. "Anyway, we go over to the place Percy left Chuck last night, Katie's father, that is, and found him bleeding to death after apparently slashing his wrists. He'll be okay, Carl. I know you're concerned. Thanks to a cute guy named Paramedic Jimmy."

"And a cute lady named Carolyn, too," added Natalie.

"A little, maybe," allowed Carolyn. "Poor Chuck. I guess he got drunk and decided to kill himself, and came pretty close to succeeding."

"Slashed both wrists?" asked Joe.

"Yeah. Pretty serious about it. Deep wounds. Lots a' blood."

"Strange," said Joe.

"Okay, Joe. I'm thinking that you're thinking it's strange for a different reason than I'm thinking that it's strange. What's your reason?" asked Natalie.

"Well," said Joe. "He slashed one wrist deeply, and then manages to hold the knife in that hand and slash the other one deeply, too? Must have that *high tolerance to pain* people talk about. Then, according to the lieutenant, he wraps the knife in the bed cover to … why? To hide it? Hide it from whom?"

"He'd been drinking. That dulls the pain," said Carolyn.

"Maybe," answered Joe.

"What is it with you, Joe? You just don't want to let this be simple, do you?" said Carolyn.

"It isn't simple," said Joe. "Chuck's daughter is murdered. Percy says he's angry, swearing at cops, the world, but mostly at Harry, because he thinks Harry did it, and then he … kills himself? Does that make sense?"

"Losing a daughter the way Chuck did can take away all the sense there is in the world," replied Carolyn.

They were silent as the weight of this sank in. Finally it was Natalie who spoke. "Do you really think Jimmy is cute, Carolyn?"

"What?"

"I was thinking James Monroe is cuter than Jimmy. What do you think?" Natalie nodded toward James Monroe as he walked toward their table. He might have appeared cute at times, but right now he appeared annoyed.

"May I speak with you, Dr. Nelson?" he said when he had reached their table.

"Oh, yes," said Joe. "Of course."

"Perhaps we should have our conversation with everyone present so that there's no misunderstanding, if that's agreeable."

"Well, yes, I guess," stammered Joe. "Is there a problem?"

There was a server at James' side now, anxious to help. "Perhaps another chair, and then we'll need a few minutes during which we should not be disturbed," James instructed.

The chair appeared at once, and the server disappeared. James sat and said, "Dr. Nelson. I received a call a short time ago from the police. A Captain Mitchell seemed upset because of your recent activity."

"I ... ah ... I'm not sure ..." Joe got no further, not that he had anything he really could say in response to this.

"Doctor. We discourage the visitors to Las Vegas from personally investigating crimes, particularly when the police have specifically asked them to refrain from such investigative activities."

"I have simply been asking—" began Joe again.

"You asked questions of a manager here at the hotel, Robert Bevins, did you not?"

"Well yes, but you see, the police—"

"Are capable of investigating the crimes committed in this city," interrupted James. "It seems that your questions were regarding the death of a young lady, a prostitute, it appears, and when Mr. Bevins realized this, that is, when her death was announced on the news, he of course called the police himself."

"The questions I was asking were intended to—"

"The police are the professionals here," said James.

There was a tense silence as James stared and Joe became embarrassed and angry. The anger was winning when Carolyn spoke.

"You know I don't think he's that cute, Natalie."

"What?" said James.

"Oh, I was just wondering if it would make any difference if the victim, that would be Katie, in case you have forgotten, had not been a prostitute. You know, if she had been, say ... a guest here?"

"I don't think—"

"That's a problem, Mr. Monroe. When people don't think, just act. Follow orders. Just following orders."

James sighed a long sigh before responding. "I'm not sure you understand, Mrs. Nelson."

"That's Doctor Prentiss, if you wouldn't mind. And perhaps I do understand. Perhaps that's the problem; I do understand."

James began to experience a slight degree of embarrassment himself now. "I'm in a difficult position."

Carolyn looked ready to speak, but was silenced by James' raised hand. "Las Vegas survives on gambling, and gambling survives on the reputation of the hotels where the gambling takes place. A scandal here, a displeased police department, an investigation of any sort would be very costly. Costly to the business of this hotel. I would suggest that you bear that in mind, along with the fact that you're staying here at the expense of the owner. As a gift on his part."

"We can leave," said Carl.

"What?' said Natalie and Carolyn at the same time.

Carl considered his reply. "I have been looking into the situation that made it necessary for Katie, Kathryn Noyes, to come here. That was her given name. Did you know that, Mr. Monroe?"

"No, I didn't," said James.

"No, of course not," said Carl. "Not important, is it? We have been given an excellent welcome here, and I would not wish that Mr. Reginald Murphy should come to regret in any way his generosity toward us, however much he felt we deserved his gratitude. I would hope that we'll not do anything that would embarrass him or this hotel, but a young lady was murdered, sir, murdered brutally. She did nothing to deserve that, nothing at all. *She's* the victim here; the victim of her poverty, of the legal system, of abuse by her family, and now the victim of the prejudice of our society; of *your* society, Mr. Monroe. She was a prostitute, and therefore her death should not be allowed to disrupt the business of this city, much less of this hotel.

"We do not need to continue to accept Mr. Murphy's gratitude, and do not wish to accept it if it will upset him, or you, Mr. Monroe. We especially do not wish to continue to accept it if by doing so we'll be obliged to ignore a crime against a young lady such as Katie Noyes. I offer my apologies, Mr. Monroe; to you, to the hotel, and of course, to Mr. Murphy. It was my fault entirely. I mistook you for your better."

Having finished, Carl was sitting calmly at the table, and he was the only one who appeared at all relaxed. He took his napkin from his lap and placed it beside his plate, which, although no one else noticed, was proper etiquette, a signal that at least for Carl the meal was finished, even though they had yet to be served. The others at the table were too amazed to appreciate such subtlety.

James was the first to recover. "Thank you, Carl," he said. "I was in need of guidance, although I was unaware of that need. Please accept *my* apology and *my* gratitude.

"*We* are in a difficult situation. Robert Bevins has, for some reason, decided that he doesn't like you, and therefore he's likely to attempt to discredit you, with the police and with Reginald Murphy. I'll attempt to prevent him from doing that, but I have limited power here. Not nearly as much as Mr. Bevins possesses. Be aware of this, and be appropriately careful."

"Of course," said Joe.

"And please continue to stay here in this hotel, and please ask me if you feel I can be of any assistance."

James rose now and spoke briefly with the server who was at his side before he was fully standing. He turned back to them and said, "I have taken the liberty of changing your order slightly. The salmon sucks tonight, but the lobster pie is apparently quite good. You're doing a good thing, Joseph, but a dangerous thing. Be sure you keep your ass covered."

He started to walk away but turned back. "Thank you especially, Carl."

Chapter 47

"You were astonishing, Carl," said Natalie.

"What?" said Carl.

"That speech of yours," said Natalie. "Astonishing."

"Just the truth," replied Carl. "What you thought as well, I'm sure. Someone just needed to say it, that's all. James is a good man. He only needed to be reminded of what's important. To have said less would have been wholly inadequate."

They started with a chuckle, but all were soon laughing, Carl excepted. Their meal arrived almost immediately, and that put an end to the laughter, in any event. Joe thought that someone who had ordered lobster pie was still waiting for it, having unknowingly lost it to this table. They continued to congratulate Carl, but when this seemed to be more embarrassing to him than flattering, Carolyn was congratulated, too. She had challenged the *establishment* first, after all. They then managed to find reasons to congratulate Natalie and finally Joe, who had been the cause of their "difficult situation" to begin with. When they went to pay, there was a discussion as to whether they should use their room key, Reggie's generosity, but found that the meal had already been paid for; before it was even served.

They walked brightly from the restaurant. The release of the tension that had been building had done wonders.

"So, back to the slots, Carl?" asked Joe.

"No, I have some data I must put in place. I'm going to the room."

"And what about you, Joe? Are you looking for trouble, or are you going to keep your ass covered for at least a little while?" asked Carolyn.

"I can't even imagine what trouble I could get into this evening," said Joe.

"True," said Natalie. "Although it's still early. It all seems pretty straightforward. Harry had to be the one who killed Katie. Chuck tried to kill himself. He'll get some counseling. The police will probably find Harry any moment and it will all come together, don't you think?"

"Probably," said Joe, but as he said this, he looked to see Percy walking towards them. He didn't appear to be walking brightly at all.

"Well, folks," he said. "Looks like da cops found Harry."

"Really?" said Natalie. "I told you they would find him."

"Did ya say they would find him dead, Nat'lie?"

"Dead!" said Natalie. "What do you mean, dead?"

"Ya know what dead means. Like, not livin'. That's what Harry is."

Carl frowned a little. "The police didn't kill him, did they?"

"Shit, I didn't think of that," said Joe.

"I did," said Natalie. "That Captain Mitchell is getting way too intense about this."

"But would he …?" asked Carolyn.

"There are always opportunities to use more, or to use less force. An officer can … well, sometimes people get injured during an arrest and there isn't always a need to … hell, you know what I mean. Police are human, too," said Natalie.

"Weren't like that I don't think," said Percy. "Think they found 'im dead."

"Found him?" asked Joe. "Dead? How?"

"Don't know, but I think it mighta been dead as in killed," said Percy. "Cap'n Mitch, he's askin' questions, sorta like he's not real serious, maybe. Just askin' what I was doin' at Chuck's motel. How'd I know 'im, an' how much Chuck had been drinkin'. Shit like that. Then he asks me why'd I think he tried ta kill hisself, like havin' your little girl dead the way Katie was ain't enough."

Percy shrugged. "It was like he didn't really care. Like he already knew all he needed ta know, maybe? I don't really know, but Baldy was just standin' there an' watchin', an' then this cop comes in an' says somethin' ta da Capt'n an' he gets real quiet. Cop, he don't know what ta do, so he says somethin' ta Baldy an' he gets all excited. He starts askin' ol' Mitch what ta do, but Mitch, he don't say nothin'.

"Finally Baldy says, 'Harry's dead, Mitch. Murdered. We got ta go see …' Well, that musta made me da most surprised man in Vegas 'cause I just says … well, don't matter what, but Baldy realizes I is still there an' tells me I can leave an' he'll be in touch later. So I starts ta leave, but Baldy is still talkin' to Mitch, an' says 'You check out Harry. I got ta talk to that doc.' I think he means you, an' I'm guessin' he'll be here soon, an' I'm also thinkin' I shouldn't be here when he gets here."

"Well, you'd better not be here pretty quickly, Percy, because I think Baldy and Mitch just walked in," said Carolyn. They looked at the entrance and saw the two officers coming in and looking around.

Lieutenant O'Conner pulled out what looked like a cell phone as Percy said, "Looks like I better melt inta the crowd."

"Like that's possible," said Natalie. "With that wig you stand out in any crowd."

"Ya think?" said Percy.

"Yeah," replied Carolyn. "Take that thing off, Percy."

"What? They'll still see me," said Percy.

"Just take it off. They might see you, but they won't recognize you."

"But …" began Percy, as Carolyn reached over and took the wig from his scalp.

"Der still goin' ta recognize me!" protested Percy.

"No, they won't. Take a look at yourself. You're still dressed in Joe's clothes. You look like a nerd," said Carolyn.

"Or, like a pediatrician," said Natalie, nodding toward Joe.

"Same thing," replied Carolyn.

"There isn't enough hair …" began Natalie.

"No problem," replied Carolyn. She turned toward a group of twenty-something-year-olds walking past and smiled, glancing at the hat on one of their heads.

"Ya know, I'm a fanatic fan of … Boston. Can I buy that hat?"

The astounded man stared a moment, then took off the baseball cap to look at it. "What?" he said.

"I'll give you fifty bucks for the hat," said Carolyn.

"Well … yeah, sure!"

Carolyn snatched the cap and placed it on Percy's head. "Perfect," she said. "Now melt in, okay? Pay the man, Joe." When this was met with stares she added, "My husband, Joe. He's a big fan too. Get going, Percy."

Percy melted, and Joe paid as his phone rang. "Hello."

"Oh, hello Lieutenant O'Conner. What can I …?"

Carolyn turned back to the men from whom she had bought the baseball cap. "Now don't you gamble all that away. Buy another one of those hats and button up your shirt. You look like a slob." The boy began to button up his shirt as his friends began to laugh. A stern look from Carolyn silenced them.

She turned to the loudest of his companions and said, "What are you laughing at? You know, a few days' growth of whiskers will work okay, but you need to wash your hair. You're never going to score with the babes if you don't."

He reached for his hair as the two women with them began to giggle.

"Oh, and throw this away, please," she said, handing him Percy's wig.

They walked away stifling laughter.

"It's not that dirty," he said.

"Yes, it is," said the woman beside him.

Joe had been talking the whole time and now said, "I'm right here by the café. I think I see you." He waved, and the two police officers began to walk toward them.

When they reached them, Captain Mitchell appeared subdued and remained silent.

Lieutenant O'Conner looked at him before saying, "Doctor Nelson. I'm glad to be able to tell you that we have found Harry, but unfortunately, he was dead when we found him. Sadly, I mean. That he's dead."

"Oh," said Joe.

"Yes," continued the lieutenant immediately. "He was … well, it appeared that he was killed."

"Murdered," said Captain Mitchell. "I'm responsible. My fault. I wasn't … I went home last night. Spent the whole night uselessly watching TV." He seemed genuinely distraught.

"Yes," said the lieutenant quickly. "I mean no, it wasn't your fault. You have …"

He turned back to Joe and said, "The captain is …" He shook his head. "Anyone could have …"

"Yes, of course," said Joe, with growing bafflement.

"You see, he died between eight and ten or eleven."

"Killed," said the captain. "Murdered, while I was home al—"

The lieutenant interrupted quickly. "You have an alibi I'm sure, Doctor."

"I was watching TV as well last night. All of us were," said Joe, looking not at the lieutenant but at his captain.

"Yes, yes. It was a somewhat strange killing, but that's not important to you. You really have no reason to pursue this anymore, now that your patient's murderer is dead as well," said Lieutenant O'Conner, even though he knew Katie was in fact not Joe's patient.

The captain looked up. "Killed the same way as the girl was. Arteries slashed."

Again the lieutenant spoke quickly. "Yes, that's what we were told, but the security guard that found him at the warehouse didn't realize he was dead and called an ambulance. They transported him to the hospital and … well, it's a mess right now. In any event, we have a suspect."

Joe looked around at his friend's astonished faces. "Who?"

"I'm afraid it's the girl's father."

The astonishment was complete.

"Thank you for ensuring that his motel room was kept as undisturbed as it was," said Lieutenant O'Conner. "We should really be getting on with sweeping things up now. I just wanted to tell you that the case is pretty well closed. No need for you to worry about it any further."

With this he started to leave, but when Captain Mitchell failed to follow, he turned back and said, "We should be going now, Captain Mitchell." This was enough to nudge him into motion, and the two of them walked away.

 *Chapter 48*

"Well, that was the most bizarre display of police procedure I think I've ever seen," said Carolyn.

"Yes," said Joe.

"He did seem intent upon telling us every detail," offered Carl.

"Not every detail," said Natalie. "Just enough of the details to make it clear that we didn't need to look into this any further. He said *that* several times."

"And why?" said Joe. "Do you think that he's afraid that someone besides Chuck is a suspect? Captain Mitchell was acting really strange."

"You think …?" began Natalie, but stopped as the weight of a thought reached her.

"That a police captain could find and kill a man? Mitchell was incredibly intense about this," said Joe. "He really wanted to get Harry. Maybe he did, do you think?"

"I don't know," said Natalie, shaking her head. "He was at home alone watching TV he said."

"And Lieutenant O'Conner was really trying not to let us hear that part," said Joe. "I don't know, but I think the lieutenant thinks his captain might be a murderer."

"And what does Joe think?" asked Carolyn. "And is Joe going to be satisfied with what the lieutenant said? Is the sun going to rise tomorrow?"

"I'm not sure about the sun rising," said Natalie, "but I'm sure that Joe isn't going to leave this alone."

"It's just that …" began Joe.

"It's unsatisfying," Carolyn said, completing the thought. "Particularly with Katie's father as the suspect. The only suspect, it seems."

Percy walked over at that point. "Okay if'n I lose this hat, Carolyn?"

"I think it's cute, Percy," said Carolyn. "Not a sports fan?"

Percy took the Boston Red Sox off his head and looked at it. "What'd Mitch an' Baldy have ta say?"

Natalie reached over, taking the cap and placing it back on his head. "It looks better than your hair does, Percy. They seem to think that Chuck might have killed Harry is what they said. We're not even sure why they said that, and why they said it to us."

"Chuck?" asked Percy.

"You were with him last night, Percy. Could he have killed Harry, say, between six and ten or so?" asked Joe.

"Well …" began Percy. "Look, I weren't with him *all* night, but he was pretty drunk when I left. Don't see how—"

"Or he was *acting* pretty drunk," said Joe. "So, you weren't with him at six?"

"Six you say?" said Percy. "Yeah, but I left 'im at seven or so."

"Seven?" said Joe.

"Look," said Percy. "I gots to check this out. I'll call ya, okay?"

"Sure," said Joe. "Your phone working now?"

"Yeah, yeah. Later, man." And he was walking away.

Natalie looked at Joe and said, "Lieutenant O'Conner said eight and ten, Joe. Were you trying to trap Percy?"

"Natalie," Joe replied. "Someone killed Harry. Maybe they killed him the same way Katie was killed. That's what the police said. A lot of people wanted to see Harry dead, but how many knew how Katie was killed? I did, and Percy saw her, too. The police, and Katie's father."

"That's the short list," said Carolyn. "Of course, we only know what O'Conner and his captain told us. If you're going to look into this, the first thing to look into is how Harry died. He was taken to the hospital, the good lieutenant said, so maybe I can call Jimmy, the friendly paramedic, and find out what he looked like.

"Something like that's bound to spread quickly, even here in the urban and jaded city of Las Vegas."

"Okay," said Joe slowly. "I think I'll talk to Raul Perez."

"Raul?" said Natalie.

"He's the odd man out here," said Joe. "An obvious player, but not in the game, and no part to play … yet, that is. I wonder if he has more to do with this than I think he does. At the very least he might know something about the workings of the police force here."

"Okay," said Natalie. "You want your own police force to come along?"

"Yes." Joe smiled. "That might be a good idea. Carl, you want to …?"

"I have another mission right now. All the people who might have wanted to kill Harry are not yet accounted for."

"Oh?" said Carolyn.

"Yes," Carl said. "I want to make sure Katie's mother has not come out here too. She wasn't at her home."

"How do you know that?" asked Joe.

"Friends," said Carl, as he walked away.

"He's a strange one, too," said Natalie. "Always a surprise."

"Yes," said Carolyn. "I'm off to see if Jimmy can tell me what's going on. You two see if Raul knows anything. First one who scores, call."

"Are you intending to score with Jimmy?" smiled Natalie.

"I might," smiled Carolyn. "Except that I'm still married, aren't I? We should do something about that, Joe." She turned and walked away.

Joe smiled after her and nodded. He opened his phone and made his call. "Raul will meet us outside," he said when he had finished.

As Joe and Natalie walked across the casino, he saw Tyla alone at her blackjack table. Her makeup was a little heavy today, he thought, and one of her eyes looked like it was turning black and blue. He remembered her saying that she would kill Harry if she ever got the chance. Could she have known how Katie died? Did he know the truth about how Harry died, or was Lieutenant O'Conner misleading them? He was sure Carolyn would find out, but maybe a stop now would eliminate one suspect.

"Hi," he said as he stopped at the table. "Tyla, this is Natalie, one of the people traveling with me."

Natalie held out her hand, but Tyla just smiled and said, "Not allowed to touch anyone in this job. Sorry."

"Oh, of course," said Natalie, withdrawing her hand.

Tyla smiled and shook her head. "Did I see the police talking to you?" She spread her hands across the table and added, "Bevins is around, so we have to act as if we're going to play."

Joe nodded. "Yeah, police." He took twenty dollars out and placed it on the table.

Tyla picked it up and replaced it with four, five-dollar chips. Joe put two on his spot, and Tyla began to deal. "About Harry?"

"Yes," said Joe.

"Dealer has ten showing and Joe has sixteen. Is he dead?" she asked.

"Yes," stammered a surprised Joe. He looked down and tapped his cards.

"You sure you want a hit?" asked Tyla.

Robert Bevins was in back of Joe, smiling. "He said he did."

Tyla dealt a card and smiled, shaking her head. "Twenty-six." She reached over and pulled in the chips.

"Too bad, Doctor," said Bevins. "Just came over to thank Tyla for a great time last night." He winked at her and whispered to both Natalie and Joe, not too softly, "We started at six and didn't quit 'til dawn."

He turned toward Joe now and said, "Hope I didn't cause any trouble for you, but what with Harry killing whores around here, I had to go to the cops. Had to tell 'em you been asking questions, too." He looked neither sorry, nor apologetic.

Joe's phone rang, and he was glad to be able to ignore Robert Bevins in order to answer it. It was Carolyn, and she was excited and speaking loudly enough to be heard by everyone, even above the casino noise. "Jimmy said Harry's body is still in the ED. He's picking me up to drive me over there now. Call you later, Joe." Joe began to answer, but she had already hung up.

"Maybe your luck is running out, Doc." Robert slapped Joe on the back and smiled first at Natalie and then at Tyla. "Thanks again, babe. Six 'til dawn. It was great." He sauntered away like he was the hottest stud in Vegas.

Joe put the other two chips down and Tyla dealt. "Asshole," she said. "Sixteen again, Joe. You want a hit this time?"

"No," said Joe, waving over his cards.

"Dealer has …" Tyla turned over her cards, "…seventeen. Sorry, Joe. Bad luck all around."

"You spent the evening with Bevins? Did he …?" asked Joe.

"Hit me?" Tyla finished, touching her eye. "Of course not. I just ran into something. I wouldn't want to get my boss in trouble."

"Of course not," said Joe. "Sorry. I don't even have a tip today." He held out his empty hand.

"That's okay," said Tyla. "I have a tip for you: Stay away from Robert Bevins. Oh, and quit while you're ahead."

"Good advice," Joe replied. "You knew Harry was dead?"

"Rumors fly fast," Tyla said. "Killed was what I heard. Same way as the girl was killed I heard. What he deserved. At least that's one piece of good news. Your friend on the phone said she's going over to see Harry?"

"Yeah," said Joe, and walked away without another word.

Natalie smiled faintly. "Nice to meet you, Tyla," she said,

Chapter 49

"So, Tyla knew about Harry?" asked Natalie as they walked outside. "Was she a suspect? And why didn't she kill that Bevins character? And don't take a hit when you have sixteen and the dealer has ten showing."

"Yeah, yeah, I know. Tyla told me she would kill Harry if she ever got a chance, and I thought that maybe she got a chance." Joe shrugged. "That's all."

"But how could she have known how Katie was killed? I mean, if Harry was killed the same way, how could she have known? Besides, she has an alibi. A majorly unsavory one, but it sounds pretty solid. Robert 'the asshole' Bevins made sure of that."

Joe shrugged. "The friggin' police are like a sieve in this town. Everyone knows everything. Tyla could have known how Katie was killed. Anyone could probably have found out."

"That's true," said Raul, walking up behind them.

"What's true?" asked Joe.

"That the rumors are very prevalent right now. They have a tendency to be prevalent in Las Vegas, but this case seems to be remarkable even for here. What is it you wished of me today?"

"I need to talk to you, Raul. We can ride around, or we can walk around or we can sit around and drink coffee. Your choice."

Raul considered this for a few seconds and finally said, "Sitting and coffee sound like the best choice to me." With this said, he walked over to the valet and said his limo would be parked where it was for about thirty minutes, and then went into the hotel followed by Natalie and Joe. The valet captain didn't seem at all upset by the limo being parked where it was.

They sat at the same café they had been at all week, and the server was at their table before any conversation began. Coffee and hot chocolate were ordered and served almost immediately.

"So," said Raul. "What is it you would like to talk about?"

"Police," Joe said. "Are you police, Raul?"

"I was," Raul replied.

"And now?" asked Natalie. "You talk like you're still in the game. Are you?"

Raul smiled at her. "You talk as if you're still in the game too. Are you?"

"I am," Natalie said. "Back home I am, but not here. Are you in the game here, Raul?"

"I'm not part of the police department here," he replied, "and I'm grateful of that fact, given their recent performance. I'm retired from the police department in San Diego, to answer your next question, Miss Moore."

"Not part of any police department, but still in the game," said Natalie. "That would mean …?"

"I do occasionally work for private parties. Right now I'm driving a limo." He smiled an extremely pleasant smile. He was clearly enjoying this repartee.

"And right now I think you're working for a private party, Raul," said Joe. "My question is: whom are you working for?"

"It would be more grammatically correct to say *who* are you working for, Dr. Nelson," answered Raul. "I'm sure that you realize I would not be at liberty to discuss my employer, if I had one apart from the company for *whom*, the correct use of the objective form, I'm driving a limousine right now."

Joe smiled. He was enjoying this himself. "Thank you for that information, Raul. About the grammar, I mean. At first I suspected that you might be employed by people back in Kentucky, *who* might wish to harm us. I now think that's not the case, but rather, that you're working for our host here, Reginald Murphy."

When Raul opened his mouth, Joe raised his hand. "I do not, of course, expect you to either confirm or deny my suspicion. It's just information for you, so that you will know what I am thinking. Now that we have settled that issue, what the hell is going on in the Las Vegas police department?"

"Ah," said Raul. "At last a simple question to answer. I have no friggin' idea."

When neither Natalie nor Joe took up the conversation, he continued. "There was a young lady, a prostitute by all accounts, killed a few nights ago. Everyone already knows that, knows her name and who she worked for, and knows who killed her. There's no information that isn't common knowledge, and the police seem to be making no effort to keep anything from the public forum."

"Who does everyone *know* killed her?" asked Joe.

Raul frowned at this question. "Everyone *knows* it was Harry Melendez, or Montanez, or whatever he's calling himself right now. He picked her up right in front of this hotel and she was found dead at his most recent address. Is there any reason to think anyone else might be responsible?"

"Joe is the only one who thinks there is," said Natalie.

"It's just too pat," said Joe with a shrug.

"Sometimes it's *too pat* because they're guilty," Raul replied. "Now I understand that Harry is dead. Found in an abandoned warehouse, and my sources say his death was remarkably like that of his victim. People are already beginning to speculate that this was a crime of vengeance. Is that what you have heard?"

"More or less," said Natalie.

"Who would know how to find Harry?" asked Joe.

"Almost anyone from this town," said Raul. "He was a recognized character among a town full of characters. He lived running ahead of creditors, and his favorite hiding place was where he was found dead. He had a rental, but he hid in the abandoned warehouses. Everyone knew that."

"Everyone from around here," corrected Joe. "But a man that had arrived less than twenty-four hours ago would not know where Harry was hiding."

"Katie's father, for instance," said Natalie.

"The young girl's father?" Raul asked. "Not unless someone told him, or helped him. Many people are not at all sorry that Harry is dead."

"Including some police officers," Natalie replied.

"I'm afraid that's true," said Raul. "I would like to believe that the police would not brutally kill a man, particularly a man who would almost certainly be found guilty of a heinous crime and sentenced accordingly. The criminal justice system would have been vindicated for once."

"But it is possible?" asked Joe.

"I would like to think not," said Raul.

Chapter 50

"If there's nothing further," said Raul, rising.

"No," Joe said. "Thank you."

"I must move my limo." Raul smiled. "But allow me to pay this time." He placed twenty dollars on the table and left.

"So was Raul a suspect, or just a source?" asked Natalie.

Joe frowned. "I hadn't even considered that he might be a suspect."

"Then don't start now. The question we need to concentrate on is: who else could have killed Harry? Or maybe we need to go at it the other way. Could Chuck have killed Harry? Was he too drunk to have done it? And if he wasn't, did he know where Harry was hiding, being a newcomer to Vegas?"

Joe frowned again. "His only contact here was Percy and his young ladies. I've wanted to talk to them anyway, to make sure they're all right, so maybe we should take a trip out there while Carolyn is busy at the hospital ED."

"Might as well, although we're going to be interviewing people after the police have told us to butt the hell out of this."

"True," said Joe. "Better take a cab, not Raul and the limo. Make it at least a little difficult for the police to track us down."

"Okay, boss," said Natalie. "Maybe it was one of them, or all of them that killed Harry, ya think? They have more reason than all the rest put together."

"I don't want to think about that," said Joe. They were soon in a cab headed toward the address they both remembered from earlier, and both were silent until they were underway.

"Do you want to call Percy?" asked Natalie.

"I don't think so," said Joe.

"Oh?"

"He's one of the players, and I want to talk to his ladies without him either around or interfering."

"Oh, again," said Natalie. "Only this time with a little more puzzlement and surprise."

"Percy was with Chuck last night, and his cell phone battery was dead today, so maybe he was busy all night. Maybe he …?"

"Okay. When you don't know who is, I guess everyone could be."

"Yes," said Joe.

They rode in silence until they arrived at the motel. Joe went first to the office, where Dexter was at the counter. He wasn't sure what to say, but fortunately Dexter recognized him, and Natalie as well.

"Hey, Doc. Lookin' for Percy? He ain't here."

"Yeah, I know," said Joe. "Got something for Maggie is all." He sounded casual, and that seemed to put Dexter at ease.

"Sure. Let me see if she's down there." She would be, Joe thought, particularly after what had happened earlier. He was right, and Maggie came down to get him. It occurred to him that she might have been checking to make sure it was really him. She seemed pleased to see Natalie as well, and took them both back to the rooms at the end of the motel.

There were half a dozen in the first room, eating pizza and watching TV. Several looked up, but the only one to acknowledge their arrival was Angie.

"Oh, hi," she said, looked back at the TV for a second and then at the pizza. She stood and asked, "How are you guys doin'? Ya want some pizza?"

"We're doin'," said Natalie, looking at the pizza and frowning.

"I wanted to talk to you a little," said Joe.

"Yeah, I guess," said Angie, looking at Maggie, who shrugged.

"Maybe where we won't disturb anyone," said Joe.

"Yeah, okay," said Angie again. "Our room's next door an' no one's in there."

"Yeah, that'd be fine." Joe smiled. They said some barely acknowledged words of departure and went next door. It was much like the room they had left; a TV on a dresser, with two single beds. The room was neater than the one next door, with no clothing lying on the floor, no unconsumed food lying about. Both beds were made; one very neatly, and one with the covers merely pulled up over it and smoothed out. Joe wondered briefly which lady had which bed.

"Have you heard about Harry?" he asked.

He didn't know why, but he somehow expected that they had heard; everybody had, and he wasn't surprised when Maggie said, "Yeah."

"What did you hear?" he asked.

Angie looked at Maggie, and Maggie just shrugged again. "That he was dead. Killed I guess, out in those old warehouses he hung around."

"That's what I heard," said Joe. "You knew about the warehouses then? You knew that Harry hides out there?"

"Everyone knew that."

Joe wanted to talk to them separately, but couldn't think of any way to do that without appearing to be interrogating them, and he didn't want to do that.

Natalie looked over at him and then at Maggie. "You got a call from Chuck? Which one of you did he call?"

"Oh, Angie," said Maggie. "She was real good friends with Katie, so I guess he must have had her number or something. Anyway, he called her."

Natalie looked toward Joe and he gave a slight nod toward Angie. "That must have been scary," he said to her.

She looked at her feet without answering. Natalie looked over at Maggie. "Were you in this room when he called? Were both of you here, or were you alone, Angie?"

Angie looked up sharply, almost challengingly. "Maggie was here with me."

"That's good," said Natalie, ignoring the challenge. She walked over to the window and opened the blind fully. "It's not a bad view," she said, sitting on the bed. "Is it, Maggie? Are those the casinos over there, or is that Fremont Street?"

Maggie walked over to look out the window and said, "That's the strip. Fremont Street isn't high-rise. It's too far away, too."

Natalie asked another question, which Joe couldn't hear, and Maggie sat on the bed beside her. Soon they were deep in conversation, and Joe turned to Angie. "Had you met Katie's father before, Angie?"

"No, just talked to him on the phone. I'd call 'im so Katie could talk to 'im."

"That's how he had your number, I guess," said Joe, walking over to the other bed and sitting. "I thought Percy said *he* called for Katie."

Angie came over and sat beside him, apparently no longer apprehensive about the questions. "Percy did too, but well … Katie was afraid someone would find her. She didn't want to use the same phone all the time." Angie shrugged and added, "Katie was really afraid she'd have to go back home."

"It was pretty bad, I guess," said Joe.

"Yeah. An' Katie was like, so paranoid. She thought everyone was trying to get her. You know, turn her in to the cops or steal her money. Like, she even thought Percy was stealing. Can you believe that?"

Joe didn't know what to believe about Percy, but did know he wanted to agree with Angie. "Percy wouldn't do that."

"Of course not. Lots a' pimps just use girls, but Percy's different. He cares about us. He'd do anything ta protect us." Angie was intense now, and Joe saw Natalie and Maggie turn to look at her. Angie did too, and continued more quietly, "Katie didn't trust no one. I guess it was bad for her back with her ma, an' that's why she was like that. That's how she ended up goin' with Harry."

"How's that?" asked Joe.

"She wanted ta get enough money to get outa Vegas," explained Angie. "She thought her ma was goin' ta find her an' take her back. Harry had a lot a' money that night."

"Where'd he get the money?"

"I don't know. People said he was goin' ta beat the slot machines or somethin.' I don't know, but Katie wanted the money. She didn't have ta go with 'im." Angie was almost crying now. "She was just afraid they'd make her go back."

"No," said Joe. "She didn't …" He let the sentence hang there, unfinished.

"She didn't have to worry 'bout that."

"Her mother wouldn't find her with you and Percy to protect her," Joe said in a comforting tone.

"Her ma couldn't have done nothin' if she did find 'er. Katie turned eighteen two months ago."

"What!?" said Joe.

"Yeah," Angie said. "That's just it. She was eighteen an' didn't have to go back, but she was just so scared, she …" Angie sobbed quietly.

Joe couldn't conceal his amazement as he reached over to place his arm around Angie. "Why did she …?"

"She was just so scared," said Angie. "She didn't believe she was ever safe."

"But she stayed here with Percy?" asked Joe.

"We was the only family she ever had."

"Yeah," said Joe. "Once it starts it never—"

"It's just not fair what they did to her." Angie began to sob quietly again, and Joe to wonder who "they" were. Katie's mother and her boyfriend, or Percy and the Vegas streets, or Harry? It was all part of the same *nightmare of unfairness* that surrounded them all.

Chapter 51

Maggie looked at them for a minute, but somehow decided it was all right to leave Joe and Angie as they were. She turned back toward the window and sighed. "Fremont's the best," she said to Natalie.

"Why's that?"

"Oh, it's exciting. Easy ta pick up the guys, too."

"Oh." Natalie smiled. "Do you still …?"

"No." Now Maggie smiled. "I don't do that anymore. Not since Percy got me a good job. But when I did, it was easy."

"The sex?" asked Natalie.

"Yeah. The guys just want … well, they knew what, and so did I. They were usually easy to please. With Percy around it wasn't nasty. Guys knew better."

"You didn't mind …?"

"No. Not really," replied Maggie. "It wasn't like I hadn't done it before, an' with guys I didn't like, either."

"Oh," said Natalie.

"Yeah. My mother was drunk most a' the time. The guys she brought home didn't care which one of us they screwed. I ran away, but had ta go back. My mother was really mad and I got beat for that. Then my sister moved in with her boyfriend an' I tried livin' with her, but the boyfriend … well, he didn't care who he screwed either." Maggie shrugged.

"Even I could see my sister was growing up to be like my mother, so I came out here. A friend of mine said it would be better, but she was wrong. Anyway, I ended up beat up here, too, and then Angie got me in with Percy."

"It's how you get the money," explained Maggie. "It's like any other job. It's just sex. Ya do it because ya have to. Same as when I sell phones. I don't really believe people need a new phone. You tell them they do because you have to sell them the new phone."

"Yes," said Natalie. "Sometimes you just do it because you have to."

"Were you …?"

Natalie smiled. "I never worked on the street, but I had relationships that were just about the same. Just about keeping the guy satisfied. No love, just sex." Natalie shook her head and sighed. "You have a fight so you have sex to make up to the guy."

"Or the guy has sex with me to get even with you," giggled Maggie. She paused for a few seconds, seeming to sense Natalie's discomfort. "It's not like it is when you love someone. Sex is different then."

"Yes," agreed Natalie. "When you love the guy, it's so different."

"Or the woman," said Maggie, turning to look at Angie sitting up and in control again. Angie cast a look at her, too, but turned away in embarrassment. It took a couple of seconds for it all to sink in for Natalie, but then it all made sense. Two beds in the room and one made up like it had never been used. It made sense now.

"We'd better be going, Joe," Natalie said.

"Yeah," said Joe, standing up. "So, Katie's father just called you and said he was sick, I guess?"

"No," said Angie. "He musta dialed the phone, but he didn't say nothin'. Just moaned."

"How did you know it was Katie's father and where he was?" asked Natalie.

"His name came up on her cell," said Maggie.

"He was only a block from here," said Angie, looking around nervously. "Maggie could hear the trucks pullin' in an' out a' the service station an' so we figured that's where he must be."

"That's a lie, Angie," scolded Maggie. "Ya can't lie to people. We followed Percy last night. He said he was going over to check on Chuck and we followed him there. We were going to go in, but we got scared. He left Chuck about seven and we just came back here."

"Scared?' asked Joe.

"We didn't want Percy ta be mad at us," said Angie.

"No, of course not," Joe said.

He and Natalie walked out and found a cab at the corner. Once inside the cab, they both began to speak at once. Natalie won, or maybe it was Joe who was more polite. "I do not want any of those women to be responsible for killing that bastard, Harry, and I'll not help prove that they might have done it. They have been through so much hell the world owes them a murder or two of the useless garbage in this town. Did you know they're lovers, Joe?"

"What? Maggie and Angie, you mean? No, I didn't, but … well, it makes sense. Is one of them protecting the other?"

"I'm not going to go there, Joe. If that's where you're going you're on your own. I don't think so, anyway. Maybe they're protecting Percy?"

"Could be. Everyone says he's a really nice pimp, but he's still a pimp, and even he says he's going to protect his own. No alibi, either."

"So what really happened this morning?" asked Natalie. "Chuck calls, and somehow those two figure out who he is and where he is and … how?"

"Probably just the way they said they did. His number is on Angie's phone, so she can ID the number easy enough. He's moaning and they figure he's in trouble, so like two little Good Samaritans they're off to the rescue. They'd followed Percy to the motel last night, so that's where they go to find him. Does that make sense?"

"Nothing makes sense," smirked Natalie. "Why did Chuck call Angie, anyway? Just because he couldn't reach Percy? There must have been someone else he could have called. Calling 9-1-1 would have been better."

"You're right. Nothing makes sense. He tried to kill himself, and then he called Angie to save him?" As Joe shook his head, Natalie's phone began to ring.

"It's Carolyn," said Natalie, looking at her caller ID.

She put the phone to her ear to answer and said, "So what are you up to, lover?"

"What?" said Carolyn.

"Just joking."

"And I'm just wondering, but that's for later. Are you too busy to come by the hospital and see a murderer?"

"Harry?" asked Natalie.

"That's one option, but there's another. Charles Noyes, a-k-a Katie's dad, Chuck, has officially been charged with the murder of the first murderer, if that's what Harry is."

"What?" said Natalie.

"And Lieutenant O'Conner seems pretty certain he has the right man. He came down to the ED to tell me personally … and to make sure I, and you, know we don't need to investigate any further. This is getting so very strange, Natalie."

"Yeah, stranger and stranger," said Natalie.

"Is Joe with you, by the way?"

"Yes, he is."

"Well, bring him along. He'll love this."

Joe didn't wait to be told what Carolyn had said. He heard enough to tap on the plastic between them and the cabbie, to tell him they would be going to the Medical Center instead of the hotel.

Chapter 52

They were quite close to the Medical Center in fact, arriving within minutes, and giving little time to think and less to talk. Joe paid while Natalie called Carolyn to find out where she was and where they should meet. "The lobby in less than five," was her response. It turned out to be less than five by three minutes.

"Well, things are interesting here," she said by way of greeting them. "What have you two been up to?"

"Some interesting things as well," replied Joe. "Not a competition, but I think we may have won the most interesting evening contest."

"Seven will get you twelve you're wrong," smiled Carolyn. "I have seen Harry, and he's definitely dead. Murdered most maliciously. Wanta see?" She pulled out her cell phone to show them. "Takes pretty good pictures for a rental. Jimmy let me see the body and distracted the cops for me to take a quick pic. Not bad."

Natalie and Joe looked, and what they saw was Harry, beaten, and gaping wounds at both groins. "Katie," said Joe.

He looked up from the picture to see inquisitive looks on his companion's faces. "That was exactly how Katie looked."

"That might be significant." Carolyn nodded.

"Vengeance," said Natalie. "And by someone who knew how Katie died."

"That's the way it looks," said Joe. "But you said Chuck had been charged?"

"Is there any serious money down on the Most Interesting Evening Competition, because this next part is going to close the betting. Lieutenant O'Conner came down to the ED to tell me personally that Chuck had killed Harry."

"That he had been charged," corrected Joe.

"Well, the lieutenant said he had been charged and was guilty," corrected Carolyn in her turn. "It seems that the lieutenant wasn't at all reluctant to tell me why he was so sure, if either of you are interested."

Joe smirked and nodded.

"Thought you would be," said Carolyn. "It seems that there was a knife used to kill Harry and there was a knife used to slash Chuck's wrists; and it seems that they were the same."

"What?" said Joe.

"Yup," said Carolyn. "Wounds apparently match, but more significantly in the eyes of Lieutenant O'Conner, there's Harry's blood as well as Chuck's found on the knife that was found in Chuck's motel room. He thought that just about closed the case. What do you think?"

"Sounds pretty solid to me," sighed Natalie.

"He told you all of this?" asked Joe. "He told you the whole thing just like that?"

"Pretty much," admitted Carolyn. "I think the message was: 'Okay it's over now. Thank you very much for your interest, but we no longer need your help on this one'."

"Yeah," said Joe absently.

"I have the feeling that the relief at having this all settled is less than complete," said Carolyn. "Am I right, Joe?"

"It's just that—" Joe began.

"You're never going to be happy," Carolyn interrupted. "With this particular situation, I mean. In other situations you're quite happy," she added, winking at Joe and then at Natalie.

Joe didn't notice. "Did Charles actually say that he killed Harry?"

"Lieutenant O'Conner didn't say," Carolyn admitted.

"That probably means Chuck didn't," said Natalie, "or the lieutenant would have said that, too, as anxious as he is to get us off this investigation."

"I wish I could talk to him myself," said Joe.

"Like that's possible," said Natalie. "Even this police force isn't going to allow that."

Carolyn frowned a little. "Maybe, maybe not. You know, Chuck is still a patient here, and O'Conner is so very anxious to have us stop nosing around ... let's go talk to him, shall we?" She waited not a second to hear any dissenting notion, but turned and headed toward the elevators.

Natalie hurried to catch up. "Do you know his room number, Carolyn?"

"I think so, but I know he's on the fourth floor for sure. Jimmy said that's where all the people in police custody are held."

Joe was close behind. "Do you think this is a good idea?" he asked, as they entered the elevator.

"No," said Carolyn. "Do you?"

"Well ..." began Joe.

"If I had a vote in this," said Natalie, "it would be that we can't lose by asking. These guys are so far from anything that even remotely resembles normal police procedure it just might work. Give it a shot."

Joe needed no other encouragement, and soon they were standing talking to Lieutenant O'Conner and a uniformed officer outside a hospital room. "It's good that this has been cleared up," Joe was saying.

"Yes," beamed the lieutenant. "It has been a brutal episode in the history of Las Vegas crime, but it's over now."

"Yes," agreed Joe. "I had to hear it from you myself to put my concerns to rest. I can't help feeling sorry for Katie's father. He must have been driven to it by the knowledge of what Harry had done to his little girl." Joe shook his head in sorrow, and looked truly sincere. Carolyn stifled an impulse to giggle, but Lieutenant O'Conner didn't seem to notice.

"Yes," he said. "The knife he used on Harry was the same one he used on himself. There was blood from both of them on it. The wounds look as if they were made with it on both of them as well. He had to have found Harry and killed him the same way Harry killed the girl. Only his fingerprints on the knife, just his."

The lieutenant shrugged as Joe said, "And you found it in his room?"

"Wrapped up in the bed sheets."

"Were you the one who found it, Lieutenant?"

Natalie drew a quick breath at this question, but Lieutenant O'Conner again seemed oblivious. "No, the forensics boys found it. Mitch and I hadn't even arrived yet."

Joe nodded. "It must have been there when Carolyn and Natalie were there, even though they didn't see it. Poor Chuck."

"Yes. It was wrapped up in the bed sheets. Mr. Noyes must have been driven crazy by the murder of his child, and then when he realized what he had done to Harry, driven even crazier by that. Nothing left to live for. He claims to have no recollection at all."

"The mind is sometimes kind that way," said Joe. "When the memory is too painful, we simply do not remember it."

The lieutenant nodded sagely at this.

"He did manage to call, though, and he probably saved his life with that call. Did you find his cell phone?"

"No. His bloody prints were on the motel phone, so we think he must have used that."

"Oh," said Joe. *Interesting,* he thought, but he wasn't yet ready to make his move. "Captain Mitchell was very upset as well. It's tough to be a police officer in a case like this."

Lieutenant O'Conner nodded his agreement. "The captain was very much involved in this case. Too much, I'm afraid. He's … well, he was hospitalized."

If Joe was as surprised as his companions, he showed none of this. "He was too involved, you're right. His hospitalization is for treatment of his bipolar disease, I hope, not any … well, self-injury."

"Oh no, no injury," said the lieutenant. "Although I was afraid he might have hurt himself, as upset as he was."

"Or someone else," said Joe, shaking his head.

"Yes," agreed the lieutenant quickly.

There was silence for a few seconds. "I have been over to talk to some of little Katie's friends. Do you suppose I could just speak to Chuck for a minute? To tell him what they said about Katie, I mean. It might give him a little peace."

Lieutenant O'Conner ran his hand across his bald dome and said, "Well, I'm not sure."

Natalie drew a sharp breath at this. Joe was so smooth. She knew he had won a few minutes with Chuck.

"I was wondering …" began Lieutenant O'Conner tentatively. "I mean, there's something you might do for me, if you would."

Joe was ready to do almost anything to get this man to give him those minutes. "What can I help you with?"

"It's … well, my hair."

The astonishment on all was evident; evident to everyone, it seemed, except Lieutenant O'Conner. "You gave some medication to Percy that seems to have helped him, and I was wondering if you could give that same medication to me?"

"Well," began Joe. "It's different, you see. Percy has a skin infection and you have … well, just normal male pattern baldness. I don't think it will help you."

"But it might," he replied. "Worth trying, I mean."

"I really don't think it will," said Joe.

"Well, not right away, but worth trying. Maybe you could write a prescription for me. Maybe some refills, too, in case you're right and it takes a while to work."

"I'm not sure …" began Joe again.

"Not sure, but worth trying. If you're not sure, I mean."

Joe's eyes rolled as Natalie and Carolyn stared.

"Yes, I guess so," said Joe finally. "No guarantees, but I'll write it for you."

"Excellent," said the lieutenant, rubbing the skin on his scalp again. "Why don't you talk to Charles first then?"

He stood aside and Joe entered the room. For a moment, Carolyn and Natalie stood dumbfounded, but this was so bizarre they just walked past the police and into the room themselves, with no interference, or even much notice at all.

"Mr. Noyes?" said Joe as the man in the bed looked up. "I wanted to talk to you about your daughter."

His words were greeted by a glassy stare, but no other response.

"She was a lovely young lady, and her friends thought very highly of her, particularly Angie. Very tragic," Joe said.

"Yes," Chuck finally said.

"You remember Angie?" asked Joe.

"Yes, I think so. One of Katie's friends. I'm sorry, who are you again?"

Joe sighed, "Joe Nelson. I'm a doctor, a pediatrician. I've been talking to Katie's friends to help them with all this."

"That's good," said Chuck absently.

"You called them?"

"I don't remember," Chuck said. "I don't remember any of it. I was too drunk, I guess. Blacked out. I don't remember calling anyone or cutting myself or … I don't know how I could have killed that guy."

"Harry?" asked Natalie.

"Is that his name? I don't remember any of it."

"The police think you killed him," said Joe.

"I must have," said Chuck. "I'm sorry. It won't change anything. My little girl is still dead. Maybe she's happy now. She's had a hell of a life; maybe she's happier now."

Chapter 53

They talked for a few minutes more, but nothing new was said. Joe wrote out a prescription for Lieutenant O'Conner on a piece of plain paper. "I'll call the pharmacy if they need that, or they can call me." He added his cell phone number to the sheet of paper.

They found a cab and began the half-hour drive to the hotel. It was late now, and this being Las Vegas, the traffic was densely packed along the strip. The silence lasted for only a few minutes.

"Do you think Chuck is a murderer?" asked Carolyn.

Natalie shook her head. "He seemed so out of it. Maybe he was in a blackout from the booze, but to not remember anything and still be able to function well enough to find Harry in an unfamiliar city and kill him? I don't know."

"He could have been faking it, do ya think?" asked Carolyn.

"If he was faking that, he's the best I've ever seen," replied Natalie.

Joe shook his head. "He didn't even remember Harry or Angie. We had to remind him who they were. He called Angie on his cell. She said she knew who it was because his ID came up on her cell when he called it."

"Why'd he call Angie and not Percy or 9-1-1, anyway?" Carolyn said.

"Percy's phone wasn't working, remember?" said Natalie. "As for 9-1-1, who knows? None of this is making sense."

"I wonder if Percy's phone *wasn't working* on purpose. Percy was very proud of how his ladies could reach him anytime they needed him, and then he lets his phone battery go dead? Does that make sense?" asked Joe.

"So it was Percy who killed Harry?" asked Carolyn.

"Let's not jump, here," cautioned Natalie. "I don't want it to be Percy any more than I want it to be Chuck or those poor little ladies. They didn't have to reach Percy last night anyway, so maybe Percy didn't bother with his cell phone." She didn't sound any more convinced than her listeners were.

"So, Captain Mitch? Would he have killed Harry?" Natalie asked.

"I think Lieutenant O'Conner thinks he might have. He's a strange one all right," responded Carolyn.

"Do you mean Baldy or Mitch?"

"They're both strange," said Carolyn. "And you're right about another thing, Natalie: none of this is making any sense."

"Maybe a long shot then. There's Tyla or Raul?" offered Natalie.

"Who's Tyla?" asked Carolyn.

"Oh," said Joe, coming back from his own thoughts. "She a blackjack dealer at the casino. Seems Harry was responsible for getting her daughter on drugs and she eventually overdosed and died. Tyla told me that she would kill Harry if she ever got a chance."

"Really?" said Carolyn.

"She has an alibi, anyway," said Natalie. "She spent the night with Robert Bevins, and I don't know why she didn't kill him."

"Maybe so he could give her an alibi?" suggested Carolyn.

"It wouldn't have been worth it to me," said Natalie.

The conversation vanished after that, and they were soon approaching the hotel in any event. Joe called Carl and he said he would meet them in the casino, among the slots. Was everything getting back to normal? Maybe Carl was.

They found him sitting at one of the slots, writing in his notebook, but apparently not playing. "Hello," he said. "Percy is around here somewhere looking for you."

"Percy?" asked Joe. "Why didn't he call us?"

"I'm not sure," said Carl, and returned to his notebook.

Joe opened his cell phone and looked at Carl. "Not playing, Carl? Does that mean you're out of money?"

"I'm compiling my data, Joseph," said an offended Carl as he looked up briefly. "I'm almost out of money. Only five dollars left. But I think I'm getting close."

Joe chuckled, and Carl ignored him. Joe dialed, and Percy picked up immediately. There was a brief conversation that ended with Joe saying, "Yeah, sure. The same café? It's still open I think."

He closed his phone and said to the rest, "He wants to meet us in the café."

Carl looked up and said, "Where we always seem to meet. I have some news for Percy."

He promptly got to his feet and began walking, followed by the others. Percy was already waiting at the café. He was still a Boston Red Sox fan and dressed like a pediatrician too. It looked like he might have been there for a while because there were several cups in front of him, but as they sat, they saw that they were all fresh. "Got you guys something to drink," he said. "Hot chocolate for me an' Joe, an' coffee for the rest. Regular okay, or should I 'a gotten decaf?"

"No," said Natalie. "Regular is fine."

"I was going to try hot chocolate tonight, Percy," said Carolyn.

"Oh, well ya can have mine then. I'll take da coffee," Percy said, reaching for the coffee cup.

"It was only a joke, Percy. Regular coffee is my drink."

"You is some kinda weird, Carolyn."

"*I'm* weird! Look who's talking, Percy Prince."

"Behave, children," said Natalie. "The hat looks good, Percy."

"Why thank you, Nat'lie," said Percy, taking off his baseball cap. "Where is Boston anyway?"

"France, I think," said Carolyn.

"Oh stop it, Carolyn," said Natalie. "You know as well as I do it's in Canada some place."

275

Both women were giggling now, as Percy was frowning. "Don't think I'll need it too much longer, anyways. My hair is growin' back, don't ya think?"

"It is not," said Carolyn. "It's way too soon to see any results yet."

"I think the skin looks better," said Natalie. "Don't you, Joe?"

"Well, maybe a little. What is it you wanted to talk to us about, Percy, and why didn't you call us?"

"Did, but it went straight ta voice mail."

"Oh, that's right," said Carolyn. "The hospital blocks cell phones because it interferes with the monitoring equipment."

"Yeah," said Percy. "Ya heard about Harry bein' killed by Chuck I guess."

"We heard he was charged," corrected Joe. "Do you think he did it?"

"He was pretty drunk when I saw him last night."

"Or acted pretty drunk," said Natalie. "When did you see him?"

"Watched a movie with the ladies. Some romance thing, an' then went over ta check on Chuck. Drunk, like I said. Left him about seven. Word is that's when someone started killin' Harry, right? So Chuck coulda, if he weren't too drunk." Percy looked up and smiled. "Or me, too, for that matter. I think Chuck was pretty drunk, but I don't know for sure."

Natalie smiled too. "And what about Percy? Just to keep the record all straight. Where was he after he left Chuck?"

"Yeah, Nat'lie. Percy got a alibi, an' I'll tell ya if needs be I do. That okay?"

"Okay," said Natalie. "We trust you, Percy. It's just that I think everyone wanted Harry dead for what he did to Katie, and you more than most. I don't think Chuck did it, but he's going to be hung out to dry if someone else isn't a suspect soon. Whoever killed Harry did it the same way Katie was killed. Vengeance is my guess, and that puts Chuck and you right up there. I don't want either one, but I don't have anyone else."

"It weren't me," said Percy, smiling. "You got a alibi, Nat'lie?"

"Yeah," said Joe. "We were all watching a movie last night, romantic something or other, maybe the same one you watched, and then some comedy adventure."

"Good," said Percy. "That takes care a' the' people at this table. Now let's find the bad guy. Ya know what bothered me about this whole thing: where'd Harry get the money, an' where's the money now? He had a lot a' money when 'e picked up Katie. That's what Angie says."

"He beat the slots," Carolyn said. "That's what everyone says, anyway."

"I, for one, do not think he was on the right track," said Carl.

"An, I was suspicious Harry didn't neither," said Percy. He nodded to Carl. "So's that's what I was doin' this evenin.'"

"And?" said Natalie. "Are you going to tell us or what?"

"I is," smiled Percy. "Ya see, folks is sayin' he musta' beat da slots 'cause he's been sayin' he was goin' to do it for so long an' now he's got money. Where else could a guy like Harry get a lot a' money?"

"The lottery?" shrugged Carolyn.

"Almost," said Percy. "His landlord, he's a friend a' mine, so I tracked 'im down. Good place to start, I figured. Seems Harry was behind as usual, but the very day he picks up Katie, he pays up the rent. My friend, he's astonished an' asks Harry what the hell is goin' on. Sorry 'bout da language, Nat'lie, but that's what he said." Percy winked at her. There was no sign of any residual offence remaining from her earlier implied accusation.

"I'll forgive you this once, Percy. What the hell did he say?"

"Harry said the government was payin' his way now."

"What?"

"That's just what my friend said, too, but it was the truth, an' my friend swears to it. Cursin' right now is more like it, since Harry's dead an' no one is payin' nothin' no more."

"Percy," said Carolyn. "Tell us what's going on before there's another murder."

"Okay, Carolyn. At least Nat'lie knows how to be polite. Seems Harry had this claim with the US Army. The VA, really. An' after years a' denyin' that Harry was disabled from his time servin' with Uncle Sam, they finally up an' pays 'im. Somethin' like twenty thou. They were goin' ta pick up da rent, too, my friend says. Harry even had some form he was supposed to fill out, but ... well, with Harry dead, there's no more rent comin' in. My friend's prob'ly the only guy in Vegas didn't want ta see Harry dead."

"The VA," said Natalie. "Holy shit. You were right, Carl. He didn't beat the slots."

"See, Carolyn?" Percy smiled. "Nat'lie knows how ta swear an' ta be polite, too."

"I doubted Harry had figured anything out the way he was going at it," sighed Carl.

"But everyone else is still sayin' he musta' beat da slots," added Percy.

"Yes," said Joe. "That's all anyone has suggested to us. But where is the money? He didn't owe that much rent, did he?"

"Don't think so," said Percy. "That's a puzzle all right. If Harry had that much, how come he was hidin' down in the warehouses? Why was he in Vegas at all after killin' Katie an' leavin' her body in his own house? Why didn't he run for it?"

"Maybe it was hidden somewhere he couldn't get to?" offered Carolyn.

"He had it that afternoon to pay his back rent, an' Maggie said she saw it," said Percy.

"Maybe it was hidden in his house?" said Carolyn.

"Police woulda found it," said Percy. "You know his house was a mess. I thought it was Harry bein' a bad housekeeper, but maybe someone ransacked the place an' found the money, ya think?"

"And ignored the body lying there?" said Natalie. "That would be pretty gutsy."

"If he hid it in his house, he would have taken it with him after killing Katie and he would be in Canada by now, or Mexico," said Joe. "And if he hid it someplace else, he would have gotten it and be somewhere far from Las Vegas as well. His landlord seems to have known he had money, but he had the best reason of all to keep Harry living where he was. Harry was his golden, egg-laying goose."

"That's what I's thinkin'," said Percy. "When Harry paid up to his landlord, he acts like was plannin' to stay right where he is. No movin' up in that plan at all. He even filled out da forms to get the gov'ment ta pay his rent there."

"True, but what are you thinking?" asked Natalie. "That Harry takes Katie back to his house, kills her, and leaves the money behind to hide in some warehouse? Then someone else breaks in, ignores the body, ransacks the house, finds the money and runs for it? Yeah, that works almost as well as the alternative. Maybe someone broke in before Harry came back with Katie, ransacked the place, and stole the money, but Harry ignored the mess and killed Katie anyway, and then hid in the warehouse. Am I the only one who thinks this is making no sense at all?"

Percy shook his head. "Don't got no answers, but I's goin' ta be checkin' on da ladies and den goin' home. I's expectin' Katie's mother ta be showin' up an' givin' me trouble any time now."

"I wouldn't worry on that account," said Carl. "I have taken care of Mrs. Noyes."

"Say what, Carl?" asked Percy.

"She's a disgusting woman," said Carl. "Do you know she even lied about her daughter's age? Or possibly she really didn't know that Katie had turned eighteen two months ago."

"What?" Percy said. "Katie was eighteen? Told me she was still … well, never mind. Hell of a pimp I is, what don't know how old the ladies workin' for me are."

"Yes," said Carl. "She was eighteen, and her mother told the state of Nebraska she was still seventeen. The records were easy enough to find. Anyway, she has been taken care of now, so you need not worry, Percy."

"Taken care of?" asked Joe. "What did you do, Carl?"

"I had her arrested, of course."

Chapter 54

Percy smiled and slapped Carl's back. "Thanks, chief!" he said. "Call ya tomorrow."

"Today, you mean," chuckled Carl. "It's after midnight."

"What?" Percy said.

"I'll explain it to you tomorrow," said Carolyn

Percy left, shaking his head, and they headed for the elevator. The casino was at full speed, but weariness had overtaken them all. Once in the elevator they were alone, and Natalie asked, "So, is Percy no longer a suspect?"

"He could have had an alibi by simply saying he was with Chuck," responded Joe.

"At least Chuck would have had an alibi," said Carolyn. "Chuck couldn't have told anyone who was with him last night, unless—"

"Unless Chuck is a better liar and a better actor than anyone I've ever seen," said Natalie. "As hard as it is to admit, I think Percy is just honest. He could have had an alibi and given an alibi, but he didn't. "

"Because he was with his lover, I'll bet," said Carolyn.

"What?" said Joe.

"Oh, come on, Joe. What else could it be? If he was sitting in some bar watching the Red Sox he would have just said so. If he were committing some crime he didn't want to admit, he wouldn't have offered to tell us at all. So what else? He was with a lover."

"Why wouldn't he tell us that?" asked Joe.

"You're so cute, Joe," replied Carolyn. "There are many different lovers in the world. Some whom you don't want to embarrass with scandal, some who will embarrass you, and … well, some people just feel uncomfortable openly discussing their sex lives, and practices, and preferences. Even people like Percy. You can understand that, can't you, Joe?"

The deep blush on Joe's face said that he did understand that.

"I don't think the Red Sox were playing last night," said Carl. When Carolyn and Natalie stared at him he added, "At least there was no betting on them in the Sport's Lounge."

Joe had recovered enough to ask, "Are we wrong to assume that Harry killed Katie, and someone copied it as an act of revenge? Maybe someone else killed both of them?"

"Killed them both the same way?" asked Natalie. "Who would that be, and why would they do that? Even if it were some serial killer, it doesn't make sense. The victims of serial killers are the same type of people. All young prostitutes, or all army vets or something like that. Not mix and match."

The door opened to let them out on the Sky Floor now and Carolyn asked, "Can we go to bed now?"

They could, and they did. A troubled sleep, but sleep nonetheless, until it was broken by a call from the administrative offices at eight the next morning. Could they all come down to those offices as soon as possible?

They could and they did, to be greeted by a very stern Robert Bevins in his outer reception area. Robert was frowning, and his administrative assistant was assiduously ignoring everything. The tension was almost palpable. When Joe asked if there was a problem, Robert merely pointed towards the heavy, solid door to his inner office, motioning them to go inside. He opened the door to show Raul standing to one side, and seated behind Robert's desk was Reginald Murphy, the owner of this hotel and much more, and the benefactor that had been allowing them to stay here in excessive luxury free of charge. He didn't appear at all happy right then as Robert followed them in and closed the door. Two additional chairs had been placed in the office.

"Sit, please," said Reginald. His obvious displeasure made obedience all the more imperative.

They did and Joe began to speak, but was silenced immediately by Reggie's raised hand. "Dr. Nelson," he said. "I have extended to you and your companions hospitality, at great expense I might add, and you have rewarded that hospitality, not with gratitude, but with meddlesome interference with the local law enforcement agencies to the embarrassment of me and my hotel. So much embarrassment that I have been forced to come here to address the concerns of my staff. I'm very disappointed." He looked much more than disappointed.

"Mr. Murphy—" began Joe.

"I do not wish to hear an explanation, Doctor. There's no satisfactory explanation for your behavior. You have no right, nor any reason to involve yourself in this crime. You have in fact been requested by the police and by my staff," he glanced at Robert Bevins for the first time, moving his stare from Joe, "and have ignored those requests, persistently and maliciously ignored those reasonable requests. I'm very disappointed."

They were dumbfounded. Silence pervaded the room, and Robert Bevins was the only one who seemed to be pleased at all right now.

Reggie cast a look at him, disapproval still etched into his face. "It's fortunate that Mr. Bevins drew my attention to this situation. I will not make this mistake again, I assure you. At least I will not make this mistake with any of *you* again. I expect that you will now desist from any further activity that might compromise me or this hotel.

"If you do persist, I'll be forced to take all necessary action to prevent you from pursuing that activity—all action, including all action necessary to discredit you in the eyes of the authorities, and any other institutions that might currently be considering an association with you. With *any* of you. Do you understand?"

No response seemed possible, and Reggie allowed little time during which one might be made in any event. "You, Dr. Prentiss, are applying for a position at the Medical Center, are you not?"

Carolyn could only nod; no words would come to her mouth.

"I'm on the board at that facility, and I hope nothing interferes with your appointment," said Reggie. "Now please leave. All of you."

Joe began again. "Mr. Murphy. If I may—"

"You may not, Doctor. Please leave. All of you."

As they stood, they saw Reggie staring at them, sternness upon his face. Raul behind him closed his eyes and shook his head. When he opened his eyes he looked first at Reggie, almost a look of pity it seemed, and then he transferred his gaze to Robert Bevins, and disgust replaced the pity. Robert was smiling very broadly as he opened the door, pointing them to the exit.

As they left the office they could hear Robert saying, "I bet you're glad I called you about this mess, huh, Reggie?" They didn't hear the reply.

Joe took a deep breath and began again to speak, but Carolyn cut him short this time. "I never really wanted to work at that damned Medical Center anyway."

Natalie frowned deeply. "Medical Center be damned if you like, Carolyn. I don't want to stay in this friggin' hotel another minute."

Joe shook his head. "I'm sorry for all of this."

"Don't be sorry. You did what was right. The police aren't even looking into this beyond pinning it on someone beside Captain Mitch, and I don't like it any better than you do," said Carolyn.

Only Carl seemed calm amid the rising anger in his companions. "I wonder exactly what Reginald was told about this. He's not usually so violent of temperament."

"Whatever Robert Bevins wanted him to know, I suspect," said Joe.

"I don't care right now," said Carolyn. "I don't want to be in this hotel another minute. It's early in the day, so let's go out for a walk and come back and pack later. I need to calm down or I'll trash the Sky Rooms just for spite."

"We can rent a car and drive out to Red Rock Canyon," suggested Natalie. "It's beautiful, I'm told, and the enormity of nature may put the minuscule Reggie in perspective."

"Yeah, yeah," said Carolyn. "Whatever. Anyplace but here. Let's go get our walking shoes."

"Fine," said Carl.

Joe looked truly embarrassed now. "I'm afraid I didn't buy any. These shoes—"

"Will not do," said Carolyn. "Oh, Joe. It will all work out. Go pick up a pair of cheap walking shoes and meet us at the exit, okay?"

"Okay," shrugged Joe.

They parted, and Joe walked to the boutique, or men's clothing store, whichever it was, where Janet worked. He picked out some shoes, and found her sorting clothing to put back on the racks. "Can you check me out?" he asked.

"Sure," she said. "You look depressed, Joe. Anything wrong?"

"Yeah, quite a lot, actually."

"Anything to do with your meeting with Reginald Murphy just now?"

Joe stared at her and she shrugged. "Big news on the rumor mill."

"Of course."

"Robert Bevins came by to tell me you had been summoned to the presence of the BOSS about meddling in the case of this young girl that got killed a few nights ago. He seemed pleased."

"I suspect he was," replied Joe. "He moves quickly."

"He's had it in for you from the beginning, I'm afraid. Maybe he resents that you have two such lovely women accompanying you, and the only way he can get laid is to force himself on the ladies."

"Is it all about sex with him?"

Paul Janson

"This is Vegas, Joe. It's never about the sex here. Sex is just another commodity that's bought and sold. It's way too available to fight over. In Vegas it's always about the money."

Joe shook his head. He didn't think Janet was right this time. He had expected to pay himself, but was distracted by her comments and handed her his room key.

She swiped it, and then swiped it again. "That's funny," she said. "It looks like you've already checked out, Joe. Some mistake?"

Joe smiled. "My mistake." He handed her cash for the shoes and said good-bye to her.

Chapter 55

He walked out into the casino and saw Tyla at her table, alone. He decided that he wanted to say good-bye to her as well, and since she was alone he could talk to her while he waited for his friends.

"How are you today?" he asked.

"I'm great." She frowned. "Better than you are."

Joe looked at her and she said, "Robert was just here telling me he had set you straight. Called the BOSS, he said."

"Yeah," replied Joe. "That he did. I wanted to talk to you, so I guess I have to play. Robert is probably watching, ya think?" He put a hundred dollars down, the last of his winnings from that first time he had met her.

"He's watching," said Tyla, nodding slightly, "but I'm quitting."

"Oh?" said Joe. "Not because of …"

"It's not your fault, Joe. Give your ego a rest. He's just a bastard. My eye is healing, and I'm not about to give him another chance."

"Oh," said Joe again, this time smiling. The chips were in front of him and he pushed them all into the play.

"Feeling lucky, Joe?" said Tyla as she dealt the cards. "Dealer has ten and Joe has eighteen." Joe waved over his cards, and Tyla turned hers.

"Seventeen, dealer loses," she said, pushing another hundred toward Joe. She looked around, but the pit boss was already behind her.

He nodded and she asked, "Betting it all?"

"Yeah," said Joe. "Let's get it over with."

Tyla looked back at the pit boss, who nodded to her again. She began to deal and said, "I'm quitting. Did you hear?"

"Yeah," the pit boss said. "Sorry to see ya go, but I can't blame ya, either." He looked over to where Robert Bevins stood and smiled at him.

"Robert told me a joke," said Tyla. "That last night he spent in my bed. Want ta hear it?"

"Sure," said Joe absently.

"Joe has only eleven and the dealer has ten showing." Tyla began to deal a card, but Joe waved his hand.

"You sure?" said the pit boss. Joe nodded, and Tyla turned her cards.

"Dealer has twelve." She dealt the card Joe would have gotten, another ten. "Player wins."

As she pushed another two hundred toward Joe she said, "So the joke is yours, too: for free. *What do you say to a woman with two black eyes?*"

Joe shook his head.

Tyla smiled and said, "*Nothing you haven't told her twice already*. I didn't laugh that much."

"Not laughin' either," said the pit boss.

"Again?" she asked, pointing to the four hundred in front of Joe. He nodded, and the cards were dealt.

"Joe has blackjack," she smiled. "You're up to a thousand now. Want ta keep going?"

Joe shook his head in disgust. "Let's get this over with, shall we?" He touched the chips lightly and withdrew his hand.

"A thousand?" said Tyla looking at her boss.

He just nodded. "You're doin' fine, Tyla." He looked over at Robert, still watching them, and waved. "Show the bastard some action."

Tyla dealt. "Joe has nineteen and the dealer has ten showing." As she went to deal, Joe tapped his cards.

"A hit?" she asked.

Joe tapped again, and after a whistle, she dealt him a card. "Shit," she said. "A two to make Joe twenty-one."

She turned her cards to show a jack to go with her eight.

"Shit." This time it was the pit boss.

"Let it ride," said Joe. There was a crowd behind him now.

Carolyn came up, followed by Natalie, who said, "We're locked out of the rooms, Joe."

Joe shook his head. "Not lucky today. My room key is canceled too."

"Lucky here," said a smiling Tyla. "You want to quit while you're ahead, Joe? You've got two thousand."

"Never does that," said Carolyn. "Not Joe."

Joe just nodded and Tyla dealt. "So the bastard called me at ten in the evening on his fancy cell phone to tell me he's coming over to fuck me. He shows up, tells me a joke, fucks me, and then gives me this," she pointed to her eye. "The bastard even took pictures, can you believe that? He always does that, the jerk. Pictures of his conquests. I'm going to quit while I'm ahead, even if Joe doesn't."

Joe looked up at her as she said, "Joe has fourteen. You want a hit?"

Joe waved over his cards and said, "He came over—"

He was cut short by the arrival of Maggie and Angie. "Have ya seen Percy, Dr. Nelson?" Angie asked.

"He said he was here," said Maggie.

"I gotta ask him what medicine ta take," said Angie. "It just for a cold, nothin' ta do with sex."

"But Percy is real strict about what we can take. No drugs or anything." Maggie nodded.

"I wanta know if I should take the red one or the purple one. That's all," said Angie. "It's nothin' to do with sex."

The pit boss looked sternly at them and laid a hand on Tyla's shoulder to stop her from dealing any more. "You two old enough to be here? Got an ID that says that?"

"Yeah," said Angie, reaching for her purse.

"Okay," said the pit boss, waving them away. "Go ahead and deal, Tyla. And be good. Okay?"

"Try my best. Joe has nine." She looked at a distracted Joe and asked, "You want a hit this time, Joe? You can take anything in the deck ya know."

Joe waved over his card and said, "At ten."

"What?" said Tyla. "Do you want a hit, Joe? That's the question you have to answer."

Joe shook his head and said, "What? No. No hit. It was at ten, you said?"

"No, Joe. You have nine." Tyla stood for a minute until the pit boss nudged her slightly. She turned her cards to show eight. She dealt herself a card while everyone watched intently; everyone except Joe, who was oblivious to it all.

"Thirteen," said Tyla, as she dealt herself another card, a queen. "Joe wins," she said, smiling, and began pushing the chips toward him.

"It was never about the sex," said Joe.

"No," said Angie. "It's just a cold.'

"It was never about the sex," Joe repeated, shaking his head.

Tyla stared at him and asked, "What are you talking about, Joe?"

He looked at her and said, "You were alone when Harry was killed, weren't you, Tyla?"

"Well, yeah, eight o'clock they say, right? I guess I was. What are you saying, Joe?"

"You were alone," Joe repeated, as he opened his phone.

"What is it, Joe?" asked Natalie, but Joe was talking into his phone now.

"Raul?"

There was something being said at the other end of the call, but Joe cut him off. "I know you're no longer working for me, but you're still working for Reginald Murphy, and he needs to be here in his casino right now!"

Something else was being said, but again Joe didn't allow him to finish. "Reggie needs to be here, so get him here now! At the blackjack tables, now, Raul!"

"What?" said Tyla.

"You were alone when Harry was killed, Tyla. There's no alibi, is there?"

Tyla began to speak, but Joe turned to face Robert Bevins across the casino. "I have a problem, Mr. Bevins. Can you come over here?"

"You're no longer a guest here, Doctor, and I don't think you're welcome here, either."

Joe was speaking loudly, and there were security personnel starting to move towards him. He looked around him and then at the pile of chips in front of him: four thousand dollars. He reached down, grabbing as many as he could hold in his hands, and threw them across the casino behind him.

There were shouts and a few curses as chips hit the backs and heads of unsuspecting players; that is, until it was realized that this was money that had hit them. People began scrambling across the floor after the chips, blocking the security officers who were trying to get to Joe.

Robert was moving too, through a path clear of players, since Joe had thrown the chips behind him, and Robert reached Joe first. "That's it, Doc. No friends in the high places anymore. You're out of here, and I'll make sure the police charge your ass for this."

Joe was calm now in the middle of the chaos. "I thought you were giving Tyla an alibi, Bevins, but it wasn't Tyla who needed an alibi. It was you. It was you all along."

"What are you—?" began Robert, only to be cut off by Joe.

"You killed Harry, and you killed Katie," he said.

There were gasps from all, but loudest from Angie and Maggie.

Robert turned bright red with rage and shouted, "Throw him out! Throw him out now, and call the fuckin' cops, do you hear me?" After a moment's hesitation the security officers began to move, but as soon as they did, a voice came from behind Joe.

"I am Reginald Murphy, and I own this hotel, and therefore you work for me. You all work for me. Leave Dr. Nelson as he is."

"He's correct," said the voice of James Monroe, standing next to Reggie. "We all work for him."

Everyone was looking at Reginald except Joe, who continued calmly as if he had expected this to happen. "It was you all along, Bevins. Harry was flashing the money around, and you thought he had finally figured out how to beat the slots. That was it, wasn't it? It's always about the money here in Vegas, isn't it?

"Harry wouldn't tell you how he beat the slots, because he hadn't beaten them. The money came from the VA, not the casino. You didn't know that though, so you followed him, and when he dropped off Katie after she did what he paid for, you picked her up and went back to Harry's place, but he was gone. Maybe you knew he would be, or were just lucky, but he was gone, and so you got Katie to go back in with you. Then you beat her and killed her by cutting the arteries in her legs. Isn't that right?"

When Robert said nothing, Joe continued. "You took some pictures, just like you did when you were with Tyla. Maybe you do that all the time, but you did it this time, and then you showed them to Harry. I saw you showing them to him, but I thought it was something to do with a line of credit, or money he owed you, but it was really the pictures of Katie, wasn't it?

"You thought that if you showed Harry what you had done to Katie, it would scare him into telling you how he beat those slots, was that it? You told him you would do the same to him. He wasn't able to run; you took the money from his house, didn't you, and he couldn't go to the cops because they thought he killed Katie. You sure made it look that way.

"So then you went and found him at the warehouse, and beat him and tortured him, trying to get him to tell you what you wanted to know, but he didn't. He couldn't, because he didn't know anything. He never did. Did he tell you the money came from the VA? Did you think he was lying, or did you realize it was the truth, and killed him just to cover it all up? You kept the knife, though. Maybe it was one from Harry's kitchen? I'll bet that's where you got the one you used to kill Katie."

Robert was silent as Joe continued. "You knew where Chuck was staying, probably followed Percy there. It was easy to follow that car of his. That might have been just lucky, too; but you went to Chuck's room, and he was passed out, or maybe you brought him some more booze to get him to pass out. It was vodka, not whiskey, like he had been drinking at the bar. He wouldn't have known who you were even if he could have remembered, as drunk as he was. The cops wouldn't have believed him anyway. Whatever it was, when he was unconscious, you cut his wrists with the knife you had used on Harry, put his finger prints on it, and rolled it up in the bed sheets so no one would find it and touch it, leaving their own fingerprints on it. No one's prints on it but Chuck's. You put his bloody fingerprints on the motel phone, too, to make it look as if he called after he cut himself.

"But you wanted to make sure Chuck was discovered soon, and by someone who would tie him in with Harry's murder, not some motel manager who was likely to destroy all the evidence you had left behind, especially that knife. So you called Angie, right? Maybe you called Percy first, or maybe you wanted Angie to go over there so the cops would arrest her, too. Whatever it was, you found her number on Chuck's cell phone and you called it. You didn't say anything. Angie might have realized it wasn't Chuck's voice, so you just moaned. Where's the phone now, Bevins? The police didn't find it in the room, but you wouldn't have called from the room, would you? They might get there before you could get away. Chuck had been bleeding for a while before you called. Did you throw the phone into a dumpster? Or is it in some bush outside Chuck's room? Maybe you thought that if Angie didn't go there, the cops could use the GPS in it to find Chuck. You didn't keep it, did you?"

Robert's face was pale now, but Joe was relentless.

"Perfect, you thought. No one would connect you with Chuck, and you had an alibi for Harry. You'd called Tyla after you killed him, and went over there, and then said you had been there all evening. I thought it was Tyla who needed the alibi, but it was you."

Robert finally found his voice. "You're full of it. You can't prove a thing. Tyla said I was with her."

"But you weren't," said Tyla.

"And I can prove it," declared Joe. "You called Tyla on your cell phone. I'll bet you called from the warehouse after you had killed Harry, so you had to use your cell. You couldn't leave until you knew where you were going to go. That's a fancy cell phone you've, got Mr. Bevins. The ladies are really impressed with it, aren't they? It has GPS in it, and that means that all your calls can be traced right back to where you were when you called. They can probably tell which end of the room you were in when you called, can't they, Maggie?"

Maggie looked surprised at the question, but recovered quickly. "Yeah, sure," she said. "They can do that. They do that all the time on those new phones."

"They have recordings of all the calls, too," Joe continued. "The police can voice print you. They can prove you were the one who called, what time it was when you called, and where you were when you called, within a couple of feet, probably. You were standing right next to Harry, weren't you? You didn't want to leave without knowing where you were going to go, did you?"

Robert glared for a second, and then started to run. Raul was blocking the exit, but Robert wasn't headed that way. He was headed for the back of the casino, to his office.

Chapter 56

Robert Bevins had a head start, since no one had expected that he would run to the back of the casino where there were no exits. Raul was the first to move after him, but Natalie was quick too, and being a little closer to Robert, they were running together now. Joe and Carolyn were running too, and Reggie and Carl as well, but with a little more dignity, and therefore a little slower. Joe had not noticed Percy standing in the crowd until they began to run. Percy spoke quickly to Maggie and Angie, and then all three started running too, easily overtaking Reggie and Carl. The security police were following at a distance, as surprised as they were at the events they had just witnessed.

Robert was in his office before anyone could catch up to him, and as they entered the outer office they heard the inner door close and lock. Beverly, the administrative assistant, stood horrified against the wall. Raul tried the handle to the inner office and said, "Locked."

Reggie had arrived, panting, but arrived. "Break it down," he said.

"Not with our shoulders," said Natalie. "It's too heavy. We need something to batter it down with."

Raul looked around him. "Desk's too big and chair's too small. What about the clock there?" he said, looking at the grandfather clock against the wall.

Beverly gasped. "That clock is worth fifty thousand dollars!"

"*My* clock," said Reggie calmly. "Break down the door."

The security officers had arrived, but were standing outside as if they were afraid to enter this office.

Carolyn moved first, reaching up to the top of the clock, saying, "Give me a hand, would you please?"

First Joe and then Raul, Natalie and Carl were pulling the clock to a horizontal position. "Heavy sucker," said Raul, as Reggie joined them to make three on each side.

"Oh, take the weights out, please," said Beverly.

"The door," was all Reggie had to say.

The first blow was tentative, as they were getting the feel of an awkward battering ram. Positions were shifted slightly, but as they went to strike the door again, a gunshot sounded from within.

"The door," said Reggie again, and this time the blow was strong and the hinges began to loosen.

"Oh my, oh my," said Beverly, as another blow almost knocked the door in. One more and it was open, leaning crookedly against the wall inside, and they surveyed the inner office.

What had been Robert Bevins lay back in his expensive chair. His head had been blown apart by the shot they had heard, and the gun that had been used lay on the floor beside the chair. Blood and tissue were splattered on the wall behind him, reminiscent of the scene that they had witnessed a few days ago in the Lexington, Kentucky airport. In front of Robert, on his desk, lay what looked like a loose leaf notebook; the kind high school students used to carry to class.

Reggie cleared his throat. "Someone should verify that he's dead," he said. "Would you, Dr. Nelson, please?"

Joe looked up with surprise, but then walked around the desk to place his fingers on Robert Bevin's neck. There was, of course, no pulse to be felt.

He looked down at the loose leaf notebook and saw what Robert had seen, just before he died. There were pictures inside slotted plastic holders; picture of Harry's mutilated body. Joe pulled his handkerchief form his pocket and began turning the pages to show what was on the others.

"You shouldn't be touching anything, Doctor," said Raul.

Joe looked up, but ignored him. He turned another page to see pictures of a bruised and naked Tyla. He opened the notebook with the handkerchief-covered hand and removed this page. He wondered briefly why Harry's were in front, but beneath Tyla's pictures were Katie's and he removed these as well. He folded them and slid them behind his back, putting them inside his pants and tucking his shirt in over them when he was done.

He closed the notebook and looked up at Raul. "Yes, of course. We should leave this room as it is until the police get here." With this he walked around the desk and out the door past Beverly, and then past the security officers still waiting outside the offices. He could hear Reggie ask Raul to look after *that woman*, meaning Beverly, he supposed, and to watch over the office until the police did arrive

There was a crowd gathering outside, but Joe pushed through it to walk back to the blackjack tables where Tyla still stood.

"Nicely done, Joe," she said. "Shall I color you out?" She pointed to the remaining chips lying scattered at the spot where he had been playing.

"No," he said. "That's the tip for the dealer."

"That's more than two thousand I'd say," said the pit boss. "You sure?'

"I'm sure," said Joe.

"Let me stack 'em up for ya, Tyla," he said, easing her aside. In a louder voice he added, "This table's closed, folks. Plenty of money to be won at the others, though."

That seemed to be all the encouragement that was needed as the crowd dispersed. Joe heard one elderly lady saying, "This is special money. Just lying on the floor. I know it'll be lucky money."

The pit boss was deftly making the neat stack of chips, paying only minimal attention to what he was doing, but each stack was exactly ten chips. Once staked, he exchanged them for the higher valued, more colorful ones, stacking these neatly as well.

Joe didn't notice him counting but when he had finished he said, "Not bad. Twenty-four forty, Tyla, honey. Biggest tip I've ever seen."

"Thanks," she said. "I'll buy ya a drink, okay?"

"I'll remember that promise," said the pit boss. "You still going to quit?"

"Maybe not."

"Good," he said, tapping her hand lightly. "That's good." He walked away, smiling, and leaving Joe and Tyla alone at the closed blackjack table.

"Here," said Joe, handing Tyla the pictures of her nakedness that he had taken from the loose leaf in Robert Bevin's office. He folded them and slid them across to her.

She looked at them and then at Joe and said, "Thanks."

Joe just shrugged. "I didn't want anyone, even the police, to see those. It won't make any—"

Tyla started to cry a little now, and Joe stopped talking. She smiled through the tears and said, "Thanks, Joe."

"You take care, okay?" said Joe.

"I will," said Tyla, looking after the retreating pit boss.

Joe turned away to see Carolyn and Natalie standing behind him.

"Pretty impressive, Joseph Nelson," said Carolyn. Natalie only nodded.

Percy and the two young ladies came over at that point. "You two okay?" Percy was asking.

"Yeah," said Angie.

"Did he really kill Katie and Harry?" asked Maggie.

"Yes," said Joe.

"Wow," said Maggie. "How'd you know, Dr. Nelson?"

"He's like that," said Carolyn.

"Wow," Angie echoed.

"Well, Maggie," said Natalie. "It was you that knew about Robert's phone and the GPS and voice recording and all that."

Maggie blushed and Joe smiled. "Can they really do that, Maggie?" he asked.

"I don't think so. Maybe they can, but … well, I figured you wanted me to say they could. You know, to get that guy Bevins to admit he killed 'em."

"And that's what I did want."

"You mean …" began Natalie.

"Joe can't even remember to charge his cell phone," said Carolyn. "He doesn't have the foggiest idea how they work."

"No shit," said Percy.

Joe just shrugged.

"I knew what he did, and I needed to convince him I could prove it. I didn't intend that he should kill himself," Joe apologized.

"Just a bonus," said Carolyn. She looked embarrassed as she glanced at the two young women standing next to her.

"Yeah," smiled Angie. "After what he did to Katie, that's what he deserved." There wasn't a hint of doubt in her voice.

Joe shrugged. "Take this, Percy, will you?" he said, handing him the pictures of Katie. He was careful not to let either Angie or Maggie see what it was he was handing him.

Percy looked quickly and said, "I'll take care a' this. Don't want no one ta see it. Thanks, Joe. Thanks for everything, man."

"How did you know?" asked Natalie

"It just never made sense. You kept saying that too, Natalie. I kept thinking: *Character is Destiny*. None of the suspects was the kind of person who would torture and kill someone. Harry was troubled, but he had never done anything like this before. Katie was the problem from the beginning. Who was her killer? Harry seemed like the only suspect, but he wasn't a killer. It always came back to that: *Character is Destiny*.

"Of all the people I've met in Las Vegas, Robert Bevins was the only one that fit. He was the one person that I could see doing this, but I couldn't see why and I couldn't see how. Then he made that big deal about spending the night with Tyla, but he hadn't been there until ten in the evening. When I realized that, I realized that he was the one who needed the alibi."

Percy nodded, "*Character is Destiny*. That's that Greek dude, Heraclitus, right, Joe? Way afore Socrates an' that hemlock party."

Joe just shook his head. "Yes, it is, and you're amazing, Percy."

Percy ignored him and turned toward Maggie and Angie. "Now you two pay attention, ya hear? Listen to Joe."

Neither Maggie nor Angie seemed surprised at Percy. *Maybe they had not understood what he had said?* thought Joe.

"Heraclitus," whispered Angie. "*Character Is Destiny*. Yeah, it is. What ya are is what makes ya do, what ya do. Heraclitus?"

Maggie just nodded her agreement. "Yeah. Like *her* clitoris."

They had understood, thought Joe. *Maybe Percy talked this way all the time?* That was a far more frightening thought.

"Kids these days," said Percy. "Smarter'n I ever was."

Maggie smiled, while Angie swelled with pride.

Carl and Reggie were walking slowly up now. Carl was looking at Reggie and saying, "I appreciate your sentiment, Mr. Murphy, but the apology is more deserved by Joe and Carolyn and Natalie, than I."

"Well," said Reggie, as he stood in front of them. "It wasn't that I didn't trust your judgment, exactly. I … well, I wanted to encourage you to solve this crime, and I thought the best way to do that was to free you from any association or obligation to this hotel, and therefore with Bevins. That's all I intended."

Joe's face showed surprise, while Natalie's could only have been called amazement. Only Carolyn seemed herself. "Bullshit," she said.

"What?" said a suddenly astonished Reggie, his face now matching the astonishment on the rest.

"Oh," said Carolyn. "There's a stain on the floor over there. You see it there? It looked like shit I thought. Bullshit, but it's probably just a stain." She smiled as sweet a smile as anyone had ever smiled, and looked at Reggie. "We see a lot of that back in Kentucky, you know. Bullshit, I mean. They raise cattle there, you know."

"Well I ..." began Reggie. "Of course you're correct, Dr. Prentiss. I owe you all an apology, and I find myself once again in your debt. You may of course stay here as long as you wish. About your appointment at the Medical Center, Dr. Prentiss. I'm on the board of directors there, and I'll see that the appointment is yours. I owe you that, and more."

Carl cleared his throat. "I'm not sure Carolyn would wish you to do that."

"Well ..." began Reggie.

Carl waved him away. "Carolyn. I'll do as you wish, but the Medical Center is ... well, I think there are other positions more suited to you."

"What?" asked Carolyn.

"The offices and lobby are well appointed, while the ED is marginally supplied and staffed. This," he said, indicating his surroundings, "is a hotel. They sell food and entertainment and luxury here. That's why people come here. The Medical Center sells health care. The clients are not stupid. They know the difference. They're not going to go to a hospital because the lobby is well decorated, or because the food is better." Carl frowned now as he prepared to finish his argument. "Mr. Jobs and Mr. Gates didn't rise to the top of the computer industry by serving coffee and pastries with their computers and software. Mr. Rockefeller shared his office with Flagler, his partner at Standard Oil. These people all sold a good product. That's how they succeeded. Some serious marketing too, of course, but behind it was a good product."

Joe smiled and nodded. Carl always seemed to say one sentence too many. Jobs' and Gate's marketing had nothing to do with his argument.

"Yes," sighed Carolyn. "You're right again, Carl. Thank you for your offer, Mr. Murphy, but I'll pass. And sorry about that bullshit stuff."

"Oh," said Reggie. "I'll make sure that stain is cleaned before morning. Thank you for pointing it out."

Joe stared at Reggie. Was it possible he was getting a sense of humor?

"It's Joe to whom you owe an apology," said Natalie.

"Yes, yes," said Reggie, "but my hospitality is all I can offer."

"Not so," Joe said. "The payback is considerable this time, Mr. Murphy."

Reggie looked at him with perhaps a slight hint of apprehension. "Yes?"

"This town sucks," said Joe. "All cities do, and so does this one. If not more, then certainly not less."

He waited just long enough for the shock of his words to settle before he continued. "There are runaways on every street here, exploited by everyone who cares to exploit them. I'm asking that you do something about that situation.

"Not alone," Joe continued. "The charities that try it alone often just add to the problem, but there are good people here too. Percy is one of them."

Reggie looked at Percy. His baseball cap was gone, replaced by a new, but equally outlandish wig. Also gone were Joe's loaned clothes, replaced in turn by sunglasses, a red baggy shirt and leather pants. It seemed very unlikely that Reggie would willingly work with such as Percy, but sometimes events surprised even Joe.

"I know you, don't I?" asked Reggie.

"Say what?" asked Percy, and Joe sincerely hoped that Percy had not once provided *services* to Reggie.

"At the Medical Center fundraiser, perhaps?" said Reggie.

"Well, yeah," said Percy warily. "Been there a few times."

"Yes, of course," said Reggie. "I distinctly remember your attitude."

Joe was again becoming nervous. He wasn't sure he wanted Reggie to remember Percy's *attitude,* either.

"You had made a contribution, a sizable one as I recall," said Reggie. "But you refused to allow them to give you any credit for it. Refused even to allow your name to be placed in the announcement that was to be published in the local newspaper. '*No friggin' way'* I think was what you said."

"Mighta been," said an embarrassed Percy, as Maggie and Angie started to giggle.

Soon the giggling spread until finally Reggie said, "I would be honored to work with you on such an endeavor, Mr. … Prince, is it? Yes, yes, Percival Prince; that's it. I remember distinctly."

Percy's embarrassment continued as the giggling resumed. "Well, maybe."

Carl cleared his throat. "Percy—that's how all his close acquaintances address him—is involved in fund management, particularly with those just initiating their careers. But he spends a great deal of his time and effort assisting with the problem of runaways and street people. Particularly the young women, as they're the most vulnerable."

Maggie or Angie didn't seem to realize, or at least took no offence of Carl's reference to them.

"We ought's ta talk, maybe, Mr. Murphy," said Percy.

"That's Reggie, I hope, and if you do not mind, may I address you as Percy?"

"Yeah, yeah, course."

"Come with me for a moment then, Percy," said Reggie, placing his arm over Percy's shoulder. "There's no better time than right now."

As they walked away, Reggie's arm slipped down to Percy's waist, and Percy made no attempt to remove it.

"Hmm," said Carl. "That's strange. I knew Reggie was gay, but I'm surprised at Percy."

"Oh, yeah," said Maggie, as Angie nodded. "Everyone knows that. That's what makes him such a good pimp."

Joe shook his head. That didn't make any sense at all, but by now he should be getting used to the lack of sense in everything around here.

Chapter 57

Maggie and Angie said their good-byes after Joe had assured them that either the red or purple would be okay. If it was really a cold, then purple might be better. He wondered if Angie would use either; she wanted so much to be perfect for Percy.

"So, Harry never did figure out the slots, did he?" asked Carolyn.

"He never would have, the way he was going about it," said Carl.

"But you have," said Natalie. "It was working a little when you showed me. Show Joe and Carolyn."

"Well ..." said Carl.

"This one right here," insisted Carolyn. "There's a winner right below the pay-line. Isn't that what you're looking for?"

"Well, that's what I'm tracking, but this machine ..."

"Oh, come on, everyone. Carl thinks this one is about to pay. Five-dollar machine, too. Pony up, everyone. Five bucks apiece to bet three coins it says and I'll spin. That's my system. Not the machine, but the spinner, and we're lucky as hell today," said Carolyn.

"But there's not going to be a payout when the tease-line has—" began Carl.

"You, Carl, are not listening to me," said Carolyn. "Five bucks right now. All of you."

They did, reluctantly all, and with protest on Carl's part. Carolyn hit the button to spin the wheels, and since this was in fact their second luckiest day, after the one in the Lexington airport, the lights and buzzer started to sound and everyone in the casino turned to look at them. A few even cheered and applauded.

"Holy shit," said Carolyn.

"Twenty-five thousand?" said Natalie.

"I don't believe it," said Joe.

"That wasn't supposed to happen," said Carl. "That throws off all of my theories."

The machines didn't pay that large an amount, of course, but the noise brought a hotel employee over immediately. She was followed closely by James Monroe.

"Congratulations," he said.

"Thanks," said Joe, still recovering.

"This is so great!" said Carolyn. "We split it four ways, right? And I know what Natalie and I are doing to celebrate tonight."

"What?" asked Natalie.

"There's a male stripper show here in Vegas, isn't there, James?"

"Two, actually," James smiled.

"Then we're going to both," said Carolyn. "What are you guys doing?"

Joe smiled. "Not the male strippers. I don't want to face that competition. Isn't there a Beatles show here?"

"Yes," said James. "I haven't seen it, but I hear it's quite good."

"Beetles?" said Carl. "I've always wanted to study a little entomology."

"What?" asked James.

"Entomology," repeated Carl. "The study of beetles, or insects in general, really."

Joe was going to explain, but as he looked up he saw a tall, beautiful lady walking towards him. She looked Scandinavian, with long blond hair swaying as she walked. He wasn't sure at first, but as she drew nearer it was clear that she was in fact coming to where they stood. When she reached them, she leaned over and placed a light kiss on James' check. "Did you win this, honey?" she asked, pointing to the slot machine.

James shook his head. "You know I'm not permitted to play in the casino where I work, Shelly."

"Then we'll have to go grocery shopping after all. Are you done for the day?"

"Yes," smiled James. "Let me introduce you to the people who did win this. This is Joseph and his wife Carolyn, and this is Natalie and her friend Carl. And this is my wife, Michelle," he said with glowing pride. "She was a dancer when I first met her."

"That was when I was younger and thinner and more beautiful, though," admitted Michelle Monroe.

For some reason, Joe thought right now that he was glad her first name wasn't Elizabeth, as had been the first name of the wife of the president, James Monroe. He also thought that Michelle Monroe had once been younger surely, and perhaps thinner, but he couldn't imagine that she could possibly have been more beautiful than she was right now.

"I'm glad to meet you," said Michelle. "James has been talking a great deal about you. Particularly you, Joseph."

"Something good, I hope," said Joe.

"Subject to interpretation," replied Michelle with a smile.

"No one ever says anything bad about Joe," said Carolyn. "We all feel so sorry for him."

"Yes," said Natalie. "Once in a while someone should cast an evil rumor about poor, boring Joe, even if no one would believe it."

Michelle smiled again, and Joe frowned. "There will be no grocery shopping tonight. You, Michelle, are going to see a show tonight, a spectacular show, with Carolyn and Natalie."

"Really?" said Michelle. "What show?"

"Carolyn and Natalie," replied Joe. "*They* are the show. You'll have to watch some male strippers, too, but these ladies are the show."

"Oh," said Michelle. "I think I still know a couple of the dancers there. We'll have to see if we can go backstage afterwards."

"Which show?" asked Carolyn. "James said there are two, and we want to go to the right one."

"Both, probably," said James. "I would have thought that the men would be getting old and ugly."

"You haven't," said Michelle, kissing his cheek again.

"And James will come with the old and ugly to begin a study of entomology," said Joe. "He will make Carl and me look bad, but there's nothing to be done about that."

"Entomology?" asked Michelle.

"*The Beatles*," corrected James. "I haven't seen it yet."

"Then it's settled," said Carolyn. "Shall we pick up condoms first, do you suppose?"

"Stop it, Carolyn," said Natalie. "Just stop it right now, or Michelle and I are going to leave you home."

"She's only joking," said Joe. "I think she is, anyway. With Carolyn, it's hard to tell."

About the Author

     Paul is an emergency medicine physician practicing at Lawrence General Hospital in Lawrence, Massachusetts. He lives in Georgetown, MA with his wife, Mary, of 40 years and two daughters. As he approaches retirement from medical practice he has become engaged in other pursuits, writing being among them. He has written a children's picture book about the adoption of his daughters titled: The Child In Our Hearts and his first novel: Mal Practice, a mystery of medicine and murder, has been given a Finalist Award by the IPNE (Independent Publishers of New England) in the 2014 Book Contest, Genre Fiction category for Map Practice. This is the sequel. He is now opening a family business, an ice cream shop. This novel is not based on his experience in the ice cream business. He continues to write so watch for another novel soon.

www.ingramcontent.com/pod-product-compliance
Lightning Source LLC
Chambersburg PA
CBHW061129200626
46817CB00016B/462